SWEET TEXAS KISS

"Sarah . . ."

Her gaze slipped beyond him, fastening with an ever-darkening fury. He swiveled to see what had her hackles up. Luisa was standing off to one side, also waiting to say her goodbyes to him.

"Sarah," he began, turning toward her. "Aren't you going to kiss me? For appearances."

"I don't want to kiss you."

"You're supposed to be my fiancée, remember?"

Those flirty dimples creased his cheeks engagingly, but she'd have none of his charm. "If I were your fiancée, I'd have saved a bullet for you last night. If you want a kiss, go grab one off her. I'll even give you the money to pay for it."

"I don't want Luisa's kiss. I want yours." He took a step closer, she one back.

"Well, you can't always have everything you want, Billy Cooper. And I'll be damned if I'm going to—"

But the second he pulled her up to him, Sarah was returning his kiss with a desperate passion. And there was no trace of the little girl, no trace of the tease as her arms came up to lock about the back of his neck.

Once she had him, she wasn't inclined to let go.

Sarah pressed her lips to his cheeks, to his neck, to the warm vee where his top shirt buttons were undone, his skin damp and salty from the morning heat.

Wild Texas
Bride

Dana Ransom

ZEBRA BOOKS
KENSINGTON PUBLISHING CORP.

ZEBRA BOOKS are published by

Kensington Publishing Corp.
850 Third Avenue
New York, NY 10022

Copyright © 1995 by Nancy Gideon

Zebra and the Z logo Reg. U.S. Pat. & TM Off. The Lovegram logo is a trademark of Kensington Publishing Corp.

First Printing: August, 1995

Printed in the United States of America

*For the English professor who once sneered,
"Is this what you're doing with your
college education?"*

*Thanks for making me mad enough to
complete that first book and
to become successful at what
I love to do!*

Chapter One

"Don't nobody move! This is a robbery!"

Those rough words woke Sarah Bass from her indifferent dozing. Disbelief was shaken from her when the train gave a hard lurch and shuddered to a stop on the tracks. Immediately, a wail of panic arose from a portion of the passengers who were sure they were about to die at the hands of desperadoes, a din taken up by the large Mexican woman seated opposite as she clutched her son and called upon the saints for mercy in a shrill Spanish tongue. The young man beside Sarah had gone rigid with shock. Beneath his derby hat, his face was as white as the scarce clouds in the West Texas sky above. He clutched his new travel case in his lap with trembling hands. Sarah also gripped her bag, comforted by the hard contour of the revolver she carried in it. She wasn't frightened, she was mad as hell. She wanted to get home in the worst way and had no patience for the interruption.

"Elevate your hands so's we can be about our business," came the easy voice from the back of the car. "Present your valuables when asked and nobody'll get hurt."

Sarah felt a sudden prickle of recognition. That voice! She knew it! Straightening in her seat, she craned her neck, trying to see back to where the train robber stood. She'd started to rise when the man across the aisle, who'd previously been sleeping under the tilt of his Stetson, rolled out from his place and clapped a hand upon her shoulder. In his other hand, he held a Colt Peacemaker.

"Nothing to see, ma'am. Plant your bustle and keep yer eyes front."

He shoved her back into her seat with a stay-put force, driving an indignant "Oof!" from her as she gave a hard bounce. He paid her no mind as he drew his neckerchief up over his nose and joined the looters.

"Cabron," she growled, then instantly regretted it when he stopped and gave her a reassessing glance.

"Now, that may be true, ma'am, but it don't sound nice coming outta a lady's mouth."

Chastised but no less furious, Sarah settled on the bench seat and stared sullenly ahead, her chin assuming an independent tilt that made the outlaw chuckle as he moved on.

"Miss Bass," the young easterner beside her whispered, "you shouldn't anger men such as these." He touched her arm with a soft, unblemished hand, his passivity sorely rankling her.

"What do you know of men such as these, Mr. Blankenship? I highly doubt that you've come into the acquaintance of any whilst selling your snake oil in the city."

Herbert Blankenship blushed and withdrew his hand as the deceivingly fragile Sarah continued her soft tirade.

"These men are cowards who hide behind masks and steal other folks' hard-earned dollars. My brother will hunt them down and grind them beneath his boot heel."

The smooth-faced salesman looked heartened. "Is your brother a sheriff, Miss Bass?"

"My brother's a Texas Ranger."

Sarah had the satisfaction of seeing the young man's eyes go round with awe. And she would have the further satisfaction of seeing these lawbreakers brought to justice. But first she would have to endure the humiliation of being robbed, and that sat ill with her. She clutched her bag. There were only two of them. A couple of well-placed shots . . .

Just then, there was a groan as the front door of the coach was thrown open and two more bandits entered. So much for heroics, Sarah thought grudgingly. She was impulsive, yes, but hardly suicidal. She wasn't carrying anything of value other than trinkets and gifts for her family. If they'd wanted money, they should have robbed her on the way *to* Austin, not coming home from there. None but a fool brought a fortune into the Big Bend of Texas.

The woman across from her was crying again, her sobbing prayers upsetting the child held to her breast. Sarah leaned forward to pat the mother's heaving shoulder, murmuring comforting words in Spanish. As she did so, one of the bandits strode by her toward the others at the front of the car. His long canvas duster was tucked behind an impressive brace of pistols. He was a tall man with a swaggering walk. A familiar walk. But she wasn't sure until he turned slightly and the coat swung away from long, long legs. She didn't have to see his face. As long as she lived, Sarah would never forget that expansive stretch of denim-hugged limb.

What in heaven's name was Billy Cooper doing robbing a train?

Surprise subdued her more efficiently than threat. Collapsing back against the seat, Sarah watched him as he spoke to the others. He, too, was masked behind a triangular bandana and wore his hat pulled low atop a head of unruly shoulder-length blond hair. But no amount of disguise could fool her. How could she mistake the man who'd given her the spectacular taste of her first kiss? How could she not know the young ranger who'd captured a thirteen-year-old's heart? She remembered every detail of that first meeting in her uncle's front yard. Seeing Billy Cooper seated on his horse in the company of his fellow Texas Rangers had started her pulse racing with an unknown excitement and she'd savored that sudden breathlessness. He'd been little more than a green kid then, a couple of years younger than her brother, Jack, who'd been a lean, hard twenty. She'd known the minute she looked up into those dark, daring eyes that this was the man she wanted to teach her all about kissing. At thirteen, she'd been dying to know what it was like. At seventeen, she was no less eager to learn other things. And she'd never given up hope that Billy Cooper would teach her all.

But that was before he'd gone from her brother's trusted second in command to a lowly train robber.

What would turn a man from an honorable life's mission to passing a hat to relieve folks of their valuables? Sarah wondered, frowning as Billy moved from seat to seat with the same charismatic cheerfulness as a tent evangelist, coaxing her fellow passengers to dig deep into their pockets. How could she have been so wrong about him? By the time he reached her seat, Sarah was seething with a confused outrage. Then his dark eyes touched upon hers and she held her breath, waiting for a shock of recognition. But he looked away without pause.

He didn't remember her!

"Your contributions, if you please," Billy drawled amiably. He gave his hat a shake, rattling the coins and jewelry he'd already collected.

"And if we don't please?"

As Sarah spoke up boldly, the young man beside her pinched her so hard she almost yelped.

The dark eyes gazing down at her crinkled up at the corners, and she could see the creases of his devilish dimples over the edge of the bandana. "Why, I'm sure a little lady as pretty as you would want to be obliging."

"Not when it comes to sniveling, underhanded, sneak thieves like you, sir."

Herbert Blankenship gasped and appeared close to swooning, but the bandit's good humor never faltered.

"I'm right sorry you feel that way, missy. Could it be you'd prefer if I was to search your delightful person myself?"

An unexpected tremor shook through her, Sarah refused to recognize it as anticipation. She'd liked his handling well enough at one time, but those were different circumstances. He hadn't been thinking of stealing anything but a kiss from her then. Her reply was tart. "That won't be necessary." She dug into her handbag to withdraw what few dollars she had left. Instead of putting them into the proffered hat, though, she dropped them to the aisle runner.

There was a low chuckle from behind Billy.

"That sweet thing giving you trouble, kid?"

Billy looked back at the man who'd spent most of the trip snoring across the aisle from Sarah. "Naw. I think she's flirting with me." He bent and scooped up the bills, never taking his eyes off Sarah's defiant features.

"Whatcha got in that there case, slick?" the second robber wanted to know. Herbert automatically hugged it to his chest.

"Just samples, sir. I'm a traveling medicine salesman," he stammered out in a thin voice.

"Then maybe you got the cure for what ails me."

"He doesn't have anything you want," Sarah spoke up tersely in defense of her pallid companion, who looked none too pleased with her protectiveness. He was expecting to be shot at any minute and was eager to appear very cooperative lest he rile the badmen.

"You two traveling together?" Billy drawled out softly with just enough implied menace to have Herbert quaking.

"Yes," Sarah snapped, wanting him to believe that.

"No!" Herbert yelped, praying he wouldn't be associated with the young woman's boldness.

Dark eyes darted back and forth between the unlikely couple, as if trying to understand why a tough Texas beauty would link up with a simpering salesman. The other bandit had no such curiosity.

"Empty yer pockets. Now!"

And with the six-shooter shoved under his nose, the young passenger fumbled to do as he was told, coming up with a shiny gold watch and a sterling money clip thick with folded greenbacks.

"I'm feeling better already," the robber confided. He relieved the man of his goods, then deliberately knocked the sample case to the floor. There was the unmistakable sound of shattering glass, then various-colored fluids seeped out onto the floor between the salesman's patent leathers.

"That was hardly necessary," Sarah said. She hated bullying almost as much as she hated lawlessness. A pair of chill blue eyes cut over to her. The man was no longer affable and she swallowed quickly. She recognized danger when she saw it, and this man was a rattler in the coil.

"A regular razorback, ain't you, miss? You think he'd be as quick to come to your rescue? I think not. You forgetting something?"

When a gloved hand reached for the locket she wore around her neck, Sarah covered it with her hand.

"It's not worth anything," she protested. "At least not to anybody but me."

Still, he caught her hand, compressing it until she gasped in pain and let go. With his other hand, he snatched up the pendant, breaking the slender chain with a jerk. Sarah sat back, panting in fierce frustration.

"Lemme see that." Billy took it from his criminal associate. He flipped the catch with his thumbnail opening the triple hinges, and regarded the small portraits inside. A man and woman, the woman an older likeness of the one before him. A pale-eyed handsome man. Two boys, both dark and similar. Another couple, the woman blond and delicate, the man swarthy with light eyes. She held a baby in her arms. He looked uncomfortable. There was no way Billy could not have recognized her family.

He closed the locket and let it drop indifferently onto her knees. "Junk," he proclaimed callously, then shouted to his companion, "Let's get a move on!"

Sarah scooped up the treasured locket. Junk? How dare he spit on her cherished memories! Or had he just saved them for her? She clutched the heirloom, wondering if she should be furious or grateful. Surely Texas etiquette didn't require thanking one's robber. She stared up into the unblinking dark eyes, trying to force some sort of reaction from him. He betrayed none. Then with an impersonal nod, he readied to walk away.

As the bully angled by to take up the collection, Sarah could stand it no longer. Grabbing the sleeve of Billy's coat to halt his progress, she hissed, "Why are you doing this?"

"Man's gotta eat, ma'am."

"That's not what I meant and you know it."

"I'm afraid I know nothing of the kind, ma'am. You must be mistaken—"

"I'm not!"

Then his fingertips touched her mouth, effectively stilling any further argument she thought to give. His fingers were rough and warm, the gesture gentle as they moved along the line of her lips as if to seal them shut. His dark eyes delved straight to her soul.

"You don't know anything," he corrected quietly. And before she could think of a retort, he was moving down the row of seats with his hat full of stolen treasures.

"Billy!" she called after him in an intense whisper. He paused for just an instant, then strode on without looking back, following his fellow outlaws out the rear door of the coach.

Within minutes, the train was wheezing and gathering steam again, the straining chugs evening out into the strong rhythm of the rails. The passengers began to chatter with a nervous exhilaration, grateful to be alive and grumbling about their losses and the boldness of the desperadoes. Sarah sat silent, fingering her locket.

He'd known who she was. Was he just too embarrassed to admit it? Too shamed that she would catch him at his nefarious work? Or had he truly forgotten a starry-eyed youngster who'd teased him for his kiss four years ago, having to be reminded of her by the picture she carried of her brother, the best friend that he was betraying by opposing the laws of Texas?

Beside her, young Blankenship was moaning over his case of ruined goods. Nearly all his sample bottles had been broken, yet he had a frail smile for her when she noticed.

"You were very brave, Miss Bass. That villain was right in what he said. I'd have never had the nerve to stand up to him the way you did." He didn't say he thought what she did was sensible, only that it impressed him. His eyes were warm pools of admiration. "You must have learned courage from having a brother in the rangers."

Sarah smiled. That was part of it, part of a long Texas tradition of heroes. But she didn't speak of it to Herbert Blankenship. Her father, Will Bass, had been a legendary ranger until he'd been crippled by a bushwhacker's bullet just before the Texas Frontier Battalion disbanded at the end of the War Between the States. Her uncle, Harmon, was equally well known as a part-Apache tracker who gained fame in a series of dime novel exploitations. Jack, her half-brother, had followed his stepfather's path in the rangers, joining up at sixteen when they were reformed and earning a lieutenancy in the Big Bend of Texas by the time he turned twenty. She'd grown up surrounded by examples of bravery. Even her mother and the two women who married into the Bass family were grit to the backbone. Sitting through a train robbery was next to nothing compared with the stories told around their kitchen table, tales of when the Texas frontier was truly wild and dangerous like the men who tamed it. Those were the feats she'd cut her teeth upon in her younger years, the reason she was more annoyed than terrified by the sight of a few masked men.

What had turned Billy Cooper to the wrong side of the law?

Sarah had thought nothing was more important than getting home, but the farther the train moved from the scene of the robbery, the more her thoughts lingered behind. What a fitting welcome back to the Big Bend of Texas! Her heart was pounding with a stir of emotion for the first time in a long while, making her aware of how tame her existence had become.

She'd spent the summer months in Austin, where her brother, Sidney, was going to school. Under the supervision of her father's sister, Sarah had gotten her first taste of city life. It had been exciting—the influx of people, the varied entertainments, the clothes . . . the men! Her aunt had scolded her regularly for being such an incorrigible flirt, but after only two weeks within society circles, she'd received no less than five proposals from city beaux. She'd been flattered, but she couldn't picture any of those proper dandies surviving more than a day without wilting in the scorch of the Bend where she'd grown up. Flirting was fine and fun, but for a life's mate, Sarah wasn't interested in a man who carried a top hat and white gloves and asked permission to kiss her cheek. She wanted the stuff of legends. She wanted to wed a hero.

What good was a man who had to ask if a woman wanted to be kissed?

Besides, after four years, her lips were still shaped to the fit of the first man who'd tasted them.

Homesickness had settled deep and desolate into her heart. She knew her mother was hoping she'd be taken with city life and choose to stay. Rebecca Bass was always harping on her daughter to better herself, but to Sarah, things didn't get much better than what she already had. She had a family who loved and pampered her shamelessly, and she had freedom. Out on the vast plains of West Texas, no one cared if she wore the proper shoes and pinned a silly little hat at just the right angle. She wanted to wear britches and a good Stetson and ride astraddle across the endless miles stretching from horizon to horizon. And she yearned for the company of folks who were a little shy of being completely civilized.

She missed her Aunt Amanda's cheerful prattle and her Uncle Harmon's stoic smile and endless patience as he taught her how to read signs off the hard-packed earth. She was hungry for the affection filling her brother Jack's house, like the warm, inviting scent of just-baked pies, and the noise of all her boisterous young relatives. Her hours were empty without the thrill of watching her younger brother break in a mustang or the lean and handsome rangers riding out to serve the sprawling state of Texas. She longed for the simplicity and security of home, and the thought of spending the approaching holidays without them was more pain than she could bear. And finally, her mother had agreed to let her return. She was on the first westbound train, her heart and mind filled with memories and faces, anxious to embrace them all.

Until Billy Cooper stole her cash and carried off her dreams with that long, lanky stride of his. She was frowning all over again just thinking about it.

Just wait until she told Jack . . .

Then what? He'd be forced to go after his best friend to see
justice done. And Texas justice was not a pretty thing to be-
hold or to wish upon those you knew . . . even if they had
betrayed a precious trust.

Sarah was troubled by her thoughts. No one else could
identify Billy as one of the outlaws, but when Jack questioned
her, could she tell less than the whole truth? What did she
owe the former ranger? Just because he'd kissed a giddy
thirteen-year-old and made her pulse race for four entire
years with hopes of more, what allegiance did she have to
keep his secret safe? If she said nothing, she was as good as
an accomplice in the crime. And that notion upset her
staunch sense of honor. She couldn't lie for him, not to her
own brother.

But if she didn't see Jack, he couldn't ask the questions and
she needn't choose to tell him any falsehoods. At least, until
she got her answers from Billy Cooper.

He owed her an explanation.

How dare he eat at her family's table, enjoy her brother's
trust and her uncle's rarely given respect, then do such a
thing! How could he kiss her and make her love him madly,
then compromise her moral well-being to cover up his mis-
deeds?

How could he forget her so easily?

The train slowed in a cloud of steam and cinders as it entered the next stop in Marathon. There, she was close to
beginning the southern rail loop home. But as the engine
hissed and snorted and the passengers were eagerly telling
their views of the robbery to the local law officers who got on
board, Sarah made her decision. She said a hasty goodbye
and good journey to Herbert Blankenship and got off the
Southern Pacific with only her travel case in hand. Purposefully, she walked away from the chaos of the station area and
made her way into town, where she found a merchant willing
to take her eastern finery in trade for a pair of sturdy boots
and a sensible split skirt. With a pang of regret, Sarah bar-

tered the gifts she'd bought for her family and purchased a good horse and saddle.

And then, without considering the consequences, she rode out of Marathon in search of Billy Cooper and the reasons for his defection.

Harmon Bass had taught her well.

No one shy of a full-blooded Apache could run a trail as well as Sarah's Uncle Harm and he had passed the rudiments along, first to Jack, then to her.

She backtracked along the rail until she crossed the outlaws's path. Seven horses ridden by heavy men. Easy to follow in the West Texas dust. She rode at a brisk pace, an eye upon ground that was sandy and flat. She didn't have to guess where they would lead. Once the Indian menace was curbed, the rugged Bend area had filled up with badmen seeking refuge. The Chisos Basin provided a hospitable home and a centralized base for raids on both sides of the border. And it was territory she knew well. Harm and his family lived on the western foothills at Blue Creek. Her own ranch was less than a half day farther out.

By nightfall, Sarah camped in the shelter of the mountains. She slept wrapped in her meager blankets, embraced by the endless heavens. It was cold but her anticipation held the chill at bay, along with the small fire she built. She cooked thick sections of rattlesnake for breakfast. She'd learned to like it while camping out with her uncle. He'd told her a smart man—or woman—would eat anything that didn't eat them first. Sarah took him at his word and enjoyed every bite. Then she was back in the saddle and on the trail again.

The going was slower in the hills. The ground was rocky, and she made several wrong turns and spent time retracing her steps. But she was patient and she was careful. She'd learned that from Harm, too. Unfortunately, she'd never absorbed his canny knack for self-preservation. He always knew when danger was near. It was like a sixth sense gleaned from his Apache relatives. Sarah's senses were dulled by pampered living and she missed the warnings of trouble to come.

Thus totally oblivious, she blundered right into the outlaw camp.

The scouts had been watching her approach for some time and the bandits were waiting. They converged upon her with guns drawn. Realizing her mistake too late, she simply let go of the reins and elevated her hands. When they saw what they had was a woman, her captors dropped their hostile attitude. What replaced it was hardly preferable, though.

They made no move to pull her from her horse, and Sarah rode right into the center of their hideout. It wasn't much; several ramshackle cabins huddling against the canyon wall, a cluster of crude tents hugging a narrow stream, a great store of weaponry and horses. And a number of border whores.

Her common sense was completely knocked askew when the first sight she beheld was that of Billy Cooper relaxing with a bottle and a lapful of harlot. Sarah was off her mount before her guards knew what she was about; they were too surprised to stop her as she marched across the camp.

Surprise was too mild a word to describe the expression on Billy's face. That look deepened into mortal shock when Sarah jerked out her pistol, directing it with steady purpose, not at him, but at the scantily clad tart reclining in sluttish abandon upon his chest.

With deadly calm, Sarah Bass growled, "Get up off my fiancé before I blow you straight to hell!"

Chapter Two

Under the persuasive bore of a Colt .45, the whore was motivated to move quick in her scramble off Billy Cooper's knees. Sarah wasted no more attention on her as she turned the gun on the ranger-cum-outlaw.

"You'd better talk fast and smooth, mister, and be giving me some darned good reasons why I shouldn't blow you outta your socks!"

"Friend a' yours, Billy?"

Sarah recognized the lazy drawl and just a second too late, realized the other robber from the train was right behind her. Neatly, he plucked the pistol from her hand and she spun on him, venting her well-rehearsed fury.

"Friend? I go off to Austin to pick out my wedding dress and he robs the train I'm riding back on! Then I find him holed up with some easy skirt, probably paying her with the money he took from me! I'd say that makes for a sorely strained friendship, wouldn't you?"

The outlaw grinned. "Yes, ma'am, I would."

She remembered the razor-sharp blue eyes, which combined with the rest of his harsh, angular features, made him a dangerous-looking package despite the amiable voice. Sarah supposed he was used to getting exactly what he wanted. That's all she needed—an arrogant, seemingly shrewdly intelligent bully as the man in charge. He was putting together the pieces all too quickly.

"The javelina from the train. I remember now. I wouldn't

have guessed the two of you knew each other." Then those astute blue eyes turned to Billy for an answer.

Sarah looked, too, and was momentarily alarmed. Billy didn't seem pleased to see her. In fact, his handsome face gave nothing away at all. And that was not a promising sign. For the first time, Sarah was forced to consider that she might have jumped into the fire in her pursuit of him. She was in the middle of a bandit camp at the mercy of whatever he would say next. Used to having the protection of strong men about her to cover her mistakes, she'd assumed Billy would take care of her in this nest of criminals. After all, he knew her and he was her brother's friend. Or at least, he had been.

But what if he'd truly gone bad? She'd left no word of where she was going, so she could expect no outside rescue. Even as she stood boldly waiting for Billy's reply, Sarah could feel the assessing stares of the other men. Not exactly the flattering assessment of the Austin city beaux. If Billy didn't back her story, she was in big trouble. Serious trouble. Sarah waited, playing out her bluff with an impatient scowl on her face.

"I was hoping she wouldn't recognize me," Billy answered at last.

The other man laughed at that. "Guess you was wrong. Which leads me to wondering how the little lady found us and who else she's told."

There was a sharp edge to those words, recalling Sarah to the peril of her circumstances. But she couldn't back down now. She gave her chin an imperious tilt. "I told no one. He can't very well support me if he's in prison, can he?"

"No, ma'am, he surely couldn't. That leaves how you found us. You been careless with your lips, Billy-boy?"

Sarah shot a nasty glare at the whore, who was still glowering at her from a safe distance. "Only in who he's been planting them on. I followed your trail. A blind man could have stumbled over it."

"Is that so?" He didn't sound particularly pleased with that notion, but he relaxed and even handed back her sidearm. She took it with the competence of one who knew how to use it, and that didn't escape him, either. "Billy, introduce me to your lady."

"Sarah Bass—ett, Ray Gant."

"Miss Bassett, my pleasure."

Ray Gant lifted her hand with a touch of southern gallantry but his eyes never left hers. This was a man who'd prove nobody's fool and Sarah would have to be careful. She noted Billy's adaptation of her last name. It wouldn't do to be connected with a Texas Ranger whilst smack in the middle of a passel of thieves. So that meant he was going to protect her after all. She was relieved enough to risk a flutter of lashes at Ray Gant.

"Mr. Gant, might I beg a cup of coffee from you? I've known little hospitality over the last two days."

"Why, certainly, ma'am."

Then her gaze cut to Billy. "And I'd like to talk to you. Someplace a bit more private."

He came up off the ground, his expression no more yielding than the hard-packed earth. She'd forgotten how tall he was, how his size dwarfed her and made her feel wonderfully intimidated. But it wasn't a calming experience this time, considering. She still couldn't tell what he was thinking. She couldn't remember him being so close with his emotions. But then she'd known a boy, not a man.

"Why don't we step on over there," he suggested with a gesture toward the stream. Its winding bank was overgrown with tough shrubbery that would provide a passable screen between them and the others. Sarah stalked toward the water with Billy close on her heels.

She walked fast and far, more out of nervousness than out of necessity. Finally, Billy gripped her arm and spun her about.

"This is fine." All pretense dropped from his voice. He was livid. "Are you crazy coming here?"

She slapped him. Even with the discrepancy in their sizes, the force of her hand knocked him back on his heels. "I'm not crazy, I'm mad!"

With a hand to the side of his face, he stared at her as if she were a madwoman. And that just made her angrier.

"How could you leave the rangers to become a train robber? Have you no shame or decency at all? Steal from folks who work for what they have, hiding behind a mask like a coward! You skunk, you snake, you—you—" Sarah could think of no other words awful enough to describe him. She was horrified to discover there were tears smarting behind her eyes. Oh, she couldn't cry! She couldn't. She was too mad. She had to make the attack less personal by shifting all her private disappointments onto Jack.

"How could you turn to such disreputable company after what my brother did for you? He took you in as his second in command! He gave you a chance to make something of yourself, to do something good for the state of Texas. And what do you do? Spit on everything that's honorable. How could you betray Jack's trust in you? It's going to break his heart to find out you've gone bad. How do you think he's going to feel hanging you, you miserable, selfish coyote? I ought to have shot you when I had the chance! I ought to have given you away on the train!"

"Why didn't you?"

His mild question shredded her outrage with a confused frenzy of emotion. Then she saw he was smiling, actually laughing at her. Her pride couldn't stand it.

"You wretched cur, I couldn't deprive myself of the pleasure of telling you exactly what I thought of you!"

"Or of the pleasure of this?"

His hand cupped behind the back of her head. Before she had an inkling of what he meant to do, so she could ready her defenses, he bent down. His mouth settled over hers with a devastating familiarity. Even as she uttered a squeak of surprise and protest, her hands were going up to grasp his face. She could feel his warm, rough cheeks become dimpled. Then he was leaning away, whispering, "Just as sweet as I remember."

He remembered!

Then she was reminded of her grievances, and her temper flared up again.

"Why, you—"

Sarah lifted a fist to swing at him, but he laughed and crushed her up easily against him. The moment she felt him, like a large, firm male wall, her body went traitorously lax, her lips parting for possession of his.

It was sweet. Sweet and wild and exciting, just like that day at her uncle's. Oh, the man knew how to kiss even then. He knew how to dissolve her will and flame her soul. She hated him knowing that, and at the same time she loved it just as fiercely. He kissed her deeply, passionately, until not an objection lingered in what was left of her mind. She seemed to have lost it somewhere after that first conquering thrust of his tongue.

After a long reacquainting minute, Billy straightened to look down into Sarah's dreamy expression. Her eyes were still closed, her cheeks flushed, her mouth moist and softly parted. God, she was gorgeous! He shook himself from the temptation to sample more, recalling his annoyance.

"Hope that'll shut you up long enough for you to listen. Sarah Bass, you're more trouble than a wildcat tied up in a burlap sack."

Her eyes flashed open, momentarily dazed and dewy, then sharpening like a black whetstone. Before she could begin another tirade, Billy clapped his hand over her mouth.

"Listen, okay? Then if you want to shoot me, I'll stand right here and let you. All right?"

Her dark eyes narrowed suspiciously, but she was curious enough to nod. He lifted his hand.

"Talk fast," she commanded.

"I'm not a train robber."

"Oh, excuse the mistake. What are you? A revivalist passing the donation plate?"

"Sarah, hush! I'm a ranger. And Jack knows exactly what I'm doing. In fact, he's the one who sent me."

Sarah opened her mouth once, then closed it with a snap.

Hasty words had already gotten her in trouble. It was time for some careful thought. "Go on. I'm listening."

"I used to cowboy with Ray Gant before I joined up with the Battalion. When we found out that he was piloting a gang of outlaws terrorizing the small ranchers in the Bend area, we thought there might be a good chance of me getting on the inside to find out who's bankrolling him. Ray's smart but he doesn't have the kind of influence to pull off the kind of things they've been getting away with. I've been riding with them for almost four months trying to gain their trust. And I was getting someplace—until today."

Sarah understood all in a dismal second. She was jeopardizing his mission and his very life. Now not only did he have to watch his own back but hers as well, within a nest of vipers that wouldn't think twice before striking.

But how could she just ride out and away from him with his kiss still sizzling on her lips?

"I don't see a problem as long as we stick to my story."

He looked plainly astonished. "You don't see—"

"What else are you going to tell them?"

He shut his sagging mouth. What, indeed?

"It's perfect, don't you see? I've got a reason to be here and I can back you up. I can help. With what I've learned from Uncle Harm and Jack, I'm more than capable with firearms and danger. No one's going to suspect me of anything and I can get information in places you can't."

"Like—?"

"From the other women." Sarah frowned in remembrance. "Not that you weren't doing fine on your own, but females do tend to talk more to their own kind than to a man they're hoping to take to bed."

And with her in the camp as his fiancée, there would be no danger of him doing any more bedding, she thought with some satisfaction.

Billy glared at her. Sarah could see the rapid calculations going on behind his dark eyes. He didn't like any of it. He didn't want her there. But he couldn't come up with any way around it.

"All right."

She smiled. "I promise I won't do anything to get in your way."

Why didn't he believe her?

Probably with good cause, because the instant they returned to where the others waited in thinly veiled amusement, Sarah strode over to the pouty whore and nearly pulled her hair out by its painted roots.

"You go anywhere near him and you'll wish I'd shot you! I don't like to share and I don't allow trespassing, you understand? What's mine I keep, and he is mine!"

With an angry screech and a flurry of Mexican curses, the harlot tried to wrestle away. When that didn't work, she threw herself into Sarah and they both fell to the ground. Hair and legs and nails all tangled together into one dangerous knot, and while the men laughed and bet on the outcome, none were brave enough to interfere. Until Billy had had enough and waded in the way he would between two spitting cats—gingerly.

"Sarah! Stop it! Let her up!"

He reached down, then jerked back his hand. One of the hellcats had bit him! That was when his patience ran out. He stomped over to a sudsy basin where one of the women had been washing her clothes, snatched it up, and heaved the dingy contents upon the two combatants. There was an immediate truce as both parties fell away, gasping and wiping the stinging soap from their faces and eyes.

"All right, enough," Billy announced with grim authority. Both females glared up at him with emasculating intentions. It wasn't something easy for a man to ignore, but he did his best. "Luisa, you'd be wise to stay outta her reach as long as she's here."

"What about her, the *puta?* Why do you not give her warnings? She started the trouble."

"I'll see to her." Billy made that sound ominous. "You stay outta her way." He flipped the whore a gold coin, which she deftly caught.

"For your inconvenience."

Luisa made a sullen face, but she pocketed the coin as she dragged herself up off the ground. Her contemptuous spittle landed just shy of Sarah's hand. As Sarah surged up, ready to go at it again, Billy looped his arm about her waist, cinching her tight until the breath was driven from her. But not the fight.

"Can I borrow your room for a second, Ray?"

"Sure, Billy. What's mine's yours."

Toting a squirming Sarah under his arm, Billy strode to one of the crude buildings. He slammed the door, pitching them into darkness, but didn't release her until he'd turned up a lamp. He dumped her unceremoniously to the dirt floor and stood over her, arms akimbo, expression thunderous.

"Don't you dare hit me!" Sarah railed up at him, all fiery rebellion. But there was just a trace of worry in her eyes that prevented any rash behavior.

"I'd like to turn you over my knee for a good thrashing, is what I'd like to do! No trouble! Is that your idea of no trouble?"

"Well, if I was your fiancée, don't you think I'd have taken exception to that—that creature draping herself all over you?"

Billy frowned at her for a moment because she sounded as if she really did object to it, and he had to wonder why that would be. It wasn't as if they had anything between them other than that kiss four years ago . . . a kiss between two kids that didn't mean anything at all. Why, since then and now, she must have kissed dozens more men—and suddenly, his frown deepened inexplicably, as if he took exception to that. Which was, of course, ridiculous. But just thinking it made him all the angrier. "In the future, try to act a little more like the kind of woman I'd choose to marry and not like some jealous little girl!"

Sarah recoiled from his summation, but she'd have rather died than let on how his words wounded. Instead, she flung his disagreeable mood right back in his face. "Well, then, I'll just have to start acting like some cheap bit of goods without a brain or a lick of common sense, since that's what seems to appeal to you."

Billy opened his mouth but no ready retort came to mind. Deciding he wasn't going to get down in the dirt and throw mud alongside her, he adopted a cool disapproving air, sounding like a parent to a child. "Sarah, what am I gonna do with you?"

From her ignominious position on the floor, Sarah regarded him with a saucy smile. "You could get me something dry to put on."

He threw up his hands. "I should have known better! I should have known kissing a baby girl was gonna be the ruination of me someday! Jack warned me, but would I listen—no! Serves me right, yes it does."

She was unimpressed by his fierce mutterings. "The clothes?"

"And just where am I going to come up with a wardrobe for you? I wasn't planning to entertain a fiancée."

She got all flinty-eyed. "I'm sure you could ask one of the ladies. It won't be the first time you've charmed them out of their skirts, I'll just bet."

Billy looked down at her and suddenly laughed, shaking his head. "I don't know why, but I surely do like you, Sarah Bass. Don't make me regret it."

She was grinning back, then gave a sudden shrill cry as if in pain. To his alarmed response, she supplied coolly, "We'd better give them what they're expecting to hear. You're supposed to be chastising me, aren't you?"

He banged his fist against the wall, making the warped boards tremble as if they'd received the impact of a hurled body. Sarah gave another yelp, then a groan and a whimper.

"That's enough," Billy cautioned. "There are some decent men out there who'd hang me if they thought I was enjoying abusing you."

"I shall consider myself chastised then."

"See that you act it." He began to unbutton his shirt and Sarah eyed him with an anxious wariness. "Put this on until I can get you something else. I'd rather you not go back out there in what you have on. No sense in riling them up. It don't take much to get them encouraged."

She glanced down and saw that a huge tear rent her blouse across the bosom, exposing the frail undergarments below. *Don't take much?* Sarah regarded her less than spectacular bosom. Did he mean that as an insult? She wasn't as blatantly curvaceous as his border tart, but she was female enough to coax many a male eye to linger. But apparently not his.

Piqued, she was quick to modestly cover the spot with her hands, but not so modest in her enjoyment as she watched the handsome ranger disrobe. He shrugged out of his shirt and tossed it to her. She caught it with a smile on her face, her gaze boldly detailing the width and musculature of his chest and shoulders. And liking what she saw very much. If he found fault with her, she couldn't say the same was true for him.

It wasn't as if she'd never seen a shirtless man before. She'd come from a house full of men. Working in the broil of West Texas had a lot to do with shucking off inhibitions. She was used to the sight of her uncle's bronzed sinews and her brother's darkly furred chest. Both of them were splendid specimens of the male form, but neither of them affected her the way the sight of Billy Cooper did. He made her heart gallop at a reckless pace. And her emotions race just as carelessly.

She reached out to him for a hand up off the floor, and when he supplied it, Sarah stood up with a fluid grace, melting right against him. Billy's gaze registered his surprise, the stiffening of his body showing he wasn't displeased by the feel of her slight proportions. Yet he was quick to step back to a judicious distance, making his tone gruff in warning.

"Sarah, it's my responsibility to protect you while you're here. See that you don't aggravate me into doing something foolish."

Did that mean he could be tempted? Her smile was pure hellion. "I won't."

He hesitated. She was already aggravating him beyond all reason. "No more hair pulling with the other ladies. No sassing me to the point where I have to do something about it."

No less meekly, "All right."

"Remember, you're supposed to be my woman."

And her lids eased down into a sultry half-mast, her dark eyes offering more promise than a man could tolerate with any kind of composure. "I'll do my best to be convincing."

That husky promise set off all kinds of alarms inside him.

"Just until I can figure out a way to get you outta here safely and back to your family. Jack's gonna kill me for sure if he finds out about this."

Sarah didn't mention that by now her suitcases had arrived at the station without her. She hadn't considered how her family would react to that. She hoped they wouldn't be too upset. After all, they were used to her impulsive behavior. But perhaps she should have left some message for them not to worry. Too late to think of that now. At the time, she'd been rather preoccupied. Even now, thoughts of her family were a distant second to the man before her.

"I'll tell him it's all my fault. He'll believe me."

Billy smiled wryly. "I'm sure he will, and for his sake, I'll be treating you just like you was my baby sister."

Her lips pursed up into a purely irresistible bow, mocking his good intentions. Time for him to get out of arm's reach—fast.

"Put on that shirt. I'll go tell the boys you'll be staying for a time. Remember what I told you now."

"I will."

"You stick close to me and I won't let any of them mistreat you."

Stick close. Yessiree.

Billy hesitated. She was looking him up and down with a provoking liberty. Not at all like a little sister. What had he gotten himself into? He should slap her down on the first fast horse and chase her fanny back home. But he couldn't do anything until tomorrow. Darkness would settle soon, and even if she was Harm Bass's niece, he wouldn't send any lone female out into the wilds of West Texas. Not with what he knew was out there roaming around. He'd just have to put up with her for a while longer. Then she'd be Jack's problem. And that was another problem all together.

Jack was going to kill him for sure.

"Change your shirt. I'll see if we can bunk down here. I'd as soon keep you outta sight as much as possible. There are them who wouldn't think twice about gutting me for a chance at you."

"Really?"

She didn't have to sound so damned pleased about it!

"Behave!" And with that dire warning, he stomped outside.

She was supposed to act like his woman. How difficult a chore could that be?

Alone in the stale little room, Sarah stripped out of her ruined blouse and slid into Billy's bulky shirt. She hugged it to her as if it still held his warmth. For the next couple of days, she was going to make all her dreams come to life. She was going to belong to the big blond ranger, and that notion pleased her to no end. He hadn't kissed her as if she were no more than a nuisance. A man didn't plant his lips on his kid sister as if he were hungry to plumb the depths of her soul.

She wasn't naive enough to ignore the danger they were in. Billy was knee-deep with some real hardcases, and if they found out he wasn't being square with them, they'd waste no remorse or lead. She'd have to do her best to see that that didn't happen.

Billy Cooper was the stuff of heroes—and Sarah knew all about them. She'd listened to her Aunt Amanda sighing over Harmon for years. They'd made three kids together and still acted like newlyweds. Jack had been ready to sacrifice his career, his honor, and even his life for Emily Marcus while she was yet married to another man. Her own mother and father plainly adored each other, and Will Bass wasn't a man to be free with his affection. Sarah was used to the women in her family winning and holding their men's devotion. And the men in her family were all heroes. That's what she wanted for herself.

She wanted to win and hold Billy Cooper forever.

Chapter Three

Sarah Bass. The girl was nothing but trouble!

Billy did his best to ignore the way the other fellows were grinning at him as he plopped down by the fire with his tin of harsh coffee. He could grumble to himself and even cuss, but there was no getting over the fact that he still remembered every detail of how she had looked standing there on Harm Bass's front porch, wearing a dress much too mature for her thirteen years and smiling up at him as if they shared some secret pleasure. Or were about to. He should have had enough sense right then to light out for the hills.

He'd never met a brassier female in all his days. She'd leveled him with a stare about as subtle as a 12-gauge, apprising him of her interest in no uncertain terms. Then she had chased him down for a kiss that was pure dynamite. He'd been ready to ruck up her skirts right then, thirteen or not! Of course he wouldn't have lived long enough to regret it. Still, he'd spent many a night under the stars thinking it might have been worth it. And he'd spent even more nights thinking of what a full-grown Sarah Bass would be like.

But the problem was, for all her boldness, Sarah wasn't a bad girl, and he made a rule not to fuss with any other kind. She wasn't the type a man could fool with and walk away from without obligation. She was the marrying kind and she had a whole passel of steely-eyed relatives who meant to see to it. The Basses weren't the kind of folk a man wanted to mess with—not if he meant to go on breathing. And he respected them as much as he did his own next breath.

If he were the type of man who was meant for marrying, she'd be the first he'd consider. But he'd made the rangers his life, and it was a life that had no place for a lady. Jack was the obvious exception, but his Emily was a superior female. Not that Sarah couldn't be, in time. Billy just had no faith in the wedded state, not with what he knew of women, . . . not when he could find plenty of conjugal pleasures outside the shackles of matrimony. There wasn't anything he needed from a wife that he couldn't get from his friends and the bad girls with whom he associated.

But he sure did like looking at Sarah Bass and thinking of how it might be.

And he was looking, thinking, as she crossed the camp wearing his loose-fitting shirt bunched at up at the elbows, lashed about a slender waist by a cord made from her tattered blouse. Swallowed up in the loose folds, Sarah seemed as fragile as a child.

She came up to him wearing a look so woeful and meek he felt an inexplicable guilt. After slinking up to him like a whipped pup, she sank down beside him at the fire and cast an apologetic eye. His heart dropped into his socks. With that soulful look, he would have forgiven her anything. Every warm instinct inside him said to gather her up close for comforting, but the knowledge that it was just an act to appear repentant before his cohorts curbed the desire. It irritated him to think she could manipulate his emotions so easily with falsehoods.

"My coffee's cold. Warm it up for me."

He was sitting as close to the pot as she was, but she didn't alert him to that fact. Sarah simply took his tin and leaned toward the fire to refill it. His gaze was drawn to the way her split skirt molded to her bottom. It was fine scenery and he wasn't the only one admiring it. Billy snapped his hand against one gentle curve and she jumped.

"Don't take all night."

She scooted back quickly and passed him the cup. From

under the docile sweep of her lashes, he could see the fire in her eyes. It took a lot of effort not to smile. He could act, too. In fact, he'd been living a charade for the past four months . . . living it so well, he'd begun to enjoy this rugged hit-and-run life. Too much.

Billy looked around the fire and an uncomfortable sense of belonging stirred within him. It was getting harder and harder to regard the rough and bearded faces and classify them as enemies. To the state of Texas, maybe, but not to him. He hadn't known many he could call friend in his life. There'd only been Ray Gant before the rangers. And now these men. Their unit was as tight and controlled as the one he'd enjoyed under Jack's command. And the camaraderie was just as fierce. The only difference was one group stood for justice and the other did its best to circumvent it. That difference was supposed to matter to him a helluva lot more than it did.

Before the sight of Sarah Bass sitting on that train, he'd been making excuses for the men with whom he rode. Tom Benton had a family of nine to provide for on played-out land. Jasper Collins had lost his wife and a child when a doctor in Marfa refused to treat them because they were Mexican. Pauly Thomas had been driven off his ranch by scheming neighbors eager for his water. Shad Randolph had had his ranch taken by the bank when the past years of drought cut into his chance for profit. And Ray was out for evens against a world that wronged him at every turn. He'd been nearly hanged for cattle rustling to cover up the foreman's thievery. He'd been forced to run from the law unfairly and figured Texas owed him for the inconvenience. Each man he'd gotten to know had a reason for doing wrong. That didn't make them bad men, but rather good men doing bad things because life had left them few alternatives.

Four months ago, Billy wouldn't have considered that logic. He hadn't realized how far his reasoning powers had turned off center until he saw Sarah sitting there with scorn and disappointment in her eyes. And he'd felt reduced by her summation. Because it wasn't far from the truth.

Seeing Sarah reminded him of who and what he was. He was a ranger out to betray these men with whom he rode. He was leading a dangerous double role, and he was not supposed to confuse the two in heart or mind. Maybe it was fate that had brought Sarah back into his life. He wasn't sure he believed in destiny but he sure was glad for the shock she had given him, waking him to his duty.

And she was giving him another shock as she leaned against his arm. He wasn't pleased to claim that sudden jolt of sensation for what he feared it was. Because she was Jack Bass's sister and under his protection. Because he didn't want to embroil himself with a woman like Sarah.

The hour got late, and talk was passed around the fire along with a bottle of rye. He drank deep and talked big, because he was trying to stave off the moment he was dreading, the moment he'd take Sarah over to that little shack to bed down for the night. She was clearly exhausted and had been nodding off at his side, but the increasing pressure of her slender form against him only increased his need to remain where he was—safe from temptation. Maybe if she fell asleep . . . Maybe if he drank just a little more . . .

Then Sarah settled it for him. She gave her head a rousing shake and stood. The eyes of every man within the circle of firelight followed her graceful ascent. His did, too. And he was mesmerized by the beauty of what he saw. Sarah Bass was deceiving. If one counted just appearances, she was small and petite, a delicate prairie flower. She came barely to his middle shirt buttons. Surrounding her was that same part-Indian ancestry: the lithe slightness of build, the deep sun-warmed skin, the dramatically sculpted facial bones, the expressive eyes and all that glossy black hair inherited from Rebecca Bass and her half-brother Harm. And from them, she had also acquired a firmly rooted toughness that enabled such a fragile bloom to survive in hostile surroundings. She might look vulnerable, but so did the lavender verbena carpeting the slopes of the Bend's jagged peaks. She may have adopted much of her Aunt Amanda's impetuous charm, but it was tempered with her uncle's determined steel. She was capable but not always cautious, and that was going to make his job of protecting her even more difficult. She was fresh, young, and lovely, and that was going to make matters worse—for the hard men who coveted such unspoiled beauty, and for him as well, because he had to pretend the part of lover without claiming any of the benefits.

"I'm going to bed," Sarah announced with a tone so meaningful, Billy could feel the tension inside every man present. Her hand reached out to stroke his cheek and cup his chin. "Are you coming?"

His good friend Jack had every right to kill him for what he was thinking at that moment.

Billy stood up, because he wouldn't get a moment's rest if he allowed her to go alone to that dark shack. If he didn't intend to enjoy her bed, plenty others would certainly welcome the opportunity to fill in for him, not caring two hoots that his was the legitimate claim. A man had to do more than stake his territory; he had to actively work it to establish possession. So Billy rose and followed the inviting sashay of Sarah's hips, more from anxiousness than from anticipation.

He'd left the lamp burning low inside the cabin and the wan light illuminated the stark interior. It wasn't much—just a roof over dirt without windows or comforts. There was a basin filled with dingy water on a chair and a grimy towel wadded next to it. Ray Gant's few personal belongings were held in a single bag in one corner, Billy's now occupying another. Then there was the bed. Billy tried to avoid looking at it, but he was acutely aware of the thin ticking suspended by sagging ropes, and of the unwashed sheets that probably smelled like sweat and whiskey but, knowing Ray, not like whore. Ray Gant had no liking for women, horizontal or otherwise. Billy thought it odd, but considering the choice of females in their camp, perhaps the outlaw leader was a bit more discriminating about whom he invited into his sheets.

And tonight, Sarah Bass was going to be in them.

She put her small travel case down on the bed, then sat beside it. The ropes gave a beckoning groan beneath her slight weight. Without sparing him any notice, she took out her brush and began stroking it through her long straight tresses until they sparked. Like dark silk afire, he thought, then quickly chased away that image. Sarah tied back her hair with a ribbon, then sat looking up at him. She wasn't being deliberately provocative, but that didn't stop his passions from growling to life. Feeling restless and claustrophobic, Billy grabbed his bedroll and jerked loose the strings.

"I'll just bed down here on the floor."

Sarah said nothing but a smile was working at the corners of her mouth. If she was chiding him for his gallantry, he was in no mood for it. He tossed his bedroll down at what he hoped would be a comfortable distance from the bed and levered out of his boots. He unbuckled his gunbelt and placed it on the floor within easy reach of his hand. Billy didn't remove anything else, and he was afraid to wait and see if Sarah was going to shuck off anymore garments.

"G'night."

He turned down the light, plunging the room into darkness. But that was no better. He could still hear her, and the combined sounds of the ropes creaking, the fabric rustling, and her breath sighing filled him with tantalizing mental pictures. Was she undressing? Best not to dwell on that, he thought, so he flung himself out full length on his blankets and prayed for instant unconsciousness. No such luck.

"Billy?"

"What?"

"Is Luisa your . . . lover?"

He didn't want to answer that. Truth was, she had spent a number of nights with him and probably would have been wrapped around him even now if Sarah hadn't arrived. Sarah wasn't stupid. She had to have guessed that, but there was a certain vulnerability to her question that made him want to spare her any details. He decided to be evasive by grumbling, "About as good a choice as that prissy tenderfoot you were coddling up to on the train."

He could almost swear he heard her smiling. "Herbert is a perfect gentleman, the kind a lady would be pleased to show off at home. Can you say the same of your dyed-haired harlot?"

"She'd fit in fine any place I chose to go."

Silence.

"So who's this Herbert?" Was that jealousy growling through his voice? No! Couldn't be!

"A delightful traveling companion who chose polite conversation instead of a Colt .45 to court a lady's attention. Was there some reason for your wanting to know about him?"

"None. Quit your chattering and go to sleep."

She was silent, and he wondered what she was mulling over in that clever and calculating little mind of hers. Was she attaching more to his questions than he intended? Did the notion of him with Luisa bother her? Why did he hope it did?

"It's too quiet," Sarah said at last.

Billy listened for a minute, hearing the muffled sound of camp activity. Everything was perfectly normal to his thinking.

"What I mean is, it's too quiet in here."

"What—" Then he shut his mouth, afraid he understood.

"If we're supposed to be engaged and reunited after long, celibate months, wouldn't we . . ."

"Sarah Bass, if you think I'm gonna climb up there . . ."

"No, of course not! But that's what *they're* supposed to think."

She was right. The others would expect to hear something going on after the lights went out besides snoring. It was all part of the deception but beyond the limits of the role he was supposed to play. A fiancée hadn't been part of his and Jack's plan. But here she was.

When he couldn't think of an appropriate response that didn't embarrass and incite the hell out of him, Sarah laughed softly and drawled like a seasoned harlot, "Well now, you jus' lay back, honey, and let me do all the work."

He wasn't even aware that he was holding his breath until it gushed out noisily.

She started by rocking the bed.

It didn't take much for the rickety frame to set up a racket of rhythmic creaks. Sarah's first soft moan filtered through the darkness, a gusty tone of female pleasure. She followed it with an escalating chorus of "oohs" and "aahs", until Billy's fingers were unconsciously clenching in his bedroll and his toes were cramping in his socks. If he hadn't known it was just the two of them in the room, he would have sworn someone was having one grand old time with Sarah Bass there beside him. His breathing quickened to match the urgent tempo of the bed frame, and by the time the head board was banging against the wall, he was ready to split a seam from wanting what those lusty sounds suggested.

When she gave a last, rapturous cry, he found he was wet with sweat and trembling with forbidden tension. What he wouldn't give right then to wring those satisfied groans from Sarah Bass.

And just where and with whom had she grown so familiar with the nuances of mating?

He panted raggedly in the ensuing silence, wondering.

"Good night, Billy," she cooed, and the covers rumpled as she snuggled into them.

Billy lay flat on his back, his eyes closed tight, trying to conjure up the image of Harmon Bass's scalping knife and the massive bore of Jack's single-shot Colt Dragoon. But not even those discouraging impressions could overcome the one he held of Sarah curled up in sleep an arm's length away.

Sarah awoke to a thin gray daylight and the unpleasant odor of stale bed linens and dirty clothes. It took her a moment to remember where she was, one glimpse at a sleeping Billy Cooper reminding her what she was doing there.

He was something to see when slumbering, and she braced her chin in her palms to enjoy a long minute of staring. Big and blond and browned by the sun. Even without his engaging grin and teasing dimples, he was enough to set her pulse fluttering. What would he do if she slinked in there next to him? The idea of fitting into his long, bold lines was intriguing. He'd probably pack her out of camp on a fast horse. Which he might be planning to do, anyway.

She frowned. It was no garden spot, but she was in no hurry to leave. Billy was walking a dangerous line and she wanted to be there to watch his back when there were those who might seek it out for target practice. He was doing a job for the rangers, and being a part of that appealed to Sarah's sense of adventure and duty. If she could be of assistance, she couldn't very well go off and leave him high and dry. That's not what her brother or uncle would do. They would stick close and be on guard. And that's what she would do. After all, if she hadn't been born a female, she'd probably be riding in her brother's company even now. She could ride, shoot, and track probably better than most of them.

And then there was the purely salacious idea of pretending to be Billy's lover.

But first she had to convince him that she was the best person to partner him, both on the job and, eventually, in his bed.

And she couldn't do so smelling like someone's month-old socks.

Quietly, Sarah slipped off the bed and crept out of the cabin, with her travel case and pistol in hand. Billy never stirred. The camp was equally still. There was no movement from the bedrolls arranged around the grayed ash fire and all the other shacks were closed up tight. A couple of slatternly women were busy grinding coffee beans and cutting off strips of bacon. They gave her cold, unfriendly glances. Probably allies of the ousted Luisa, who obviously had found another benefactor, for she was nowhere in sight.

Ignoring the women, Sarah strode down toward the creek. She followed it a ways until she felt fairly secure, then opened her bag to remove soap and fresh underthings. She had no other clothes with her, so Billy's shirt and her crumpled skirt would have to serve until—if she wasn't underestimating him—Billy could wrangle fresh garments from the other women in camp.

The water was cold and wonderfully refreshing. Sarah

waded out into it still wearing her cotton drawers and chemise. She'd wash both fabric and flesh and stay decently covered in the bargain. Nude bathing wasn't something she felt
safe in doing with a mess of outlaws underfoot. She lathered
up quickly, soaping her hair and her sleek limbs, then scrubbing the damp cling of cotton. Just as Sarah was readying to
dip under the surface for a rinse, she heard someone moving
about on shore.

She didn't panic. She'd come amply prepared for an intrusion. Calmly, Sarah plucked the pistol she'd tucked between
the crevice of her breasts, turning and leveling it with deadly
accuracy on a very surprised and angry Billy Cooper. He
stood there for a long minute doing nothing but taking his fill
of her hip deep in clear water, her figure accentuated by a
film of wet cotton and lace, ready to blow him to kingdom
come without blinking an eye. When he spoke, his voice was
low and hoarse.

"What the hell do you think you're doing?"

"Cleaning up. What does it look like?" She tossed him the
gun. "Hold this while I finish. I don't want to get the car-
tridges wet."

Sarah ducked beneath the surface, bobbing up to fling
back the slick black sheet of her hair and wipe her eyes. He
hadn't moved an inch.

"What's the matter?" she asked as she started toward shore.
"You look like you swallowed your boot down the wrong
way."

She saw his Adam's apple jerk up and down, then he was
all grim business.

"I woke up and you were gone. Then I find you out here
splashing around without a care in the world."

"I was hardly helpless. Besides, I needed a bath and I
wanted to get to it before it became a communal event—if
any of your *compadres* are familiar with soap and water, that
is."

"Maybe not, but they'd sure jump at the chance to watch
you enjoying it."

"Ah, yes, I remember you saying it didn't take much to excite them."

Apparently that was true for him as well, for the instant she cleared the water, Billy was having an awful time remembering how to draw his next breath. Did she know how her undergarments turned transparent when wet? There was virtually nothing left to his imagination and that was working overtime to fill in the rest. As soon as he could shake the paralysis from his body, Billy shrugged out of the duster he'd thrown on in his rush out of the cabin. He draped it about her slight shoulders to shroud the perfection of her slender form. She was completely oblivious to the way she rattled him. For that he was eternally grateful.

"Just what were you planning to do when you climbed out of the creek? Parade through the middle of camp like a drenched pup?"

Her look was amazingly haughty. She reminded him of her uncle.

"I've got dry things to put on. I was planning to change into them before you came snooping around in the bushes."

"Better me than someone else."

"If you say so."

Billy gripped her arm and he could tell from the way she winced that it was tighter than he'd intended. "This isn't a game, Sarah. These men aren't schoolboys or dumb ranch hands. You rile 'em up enough and they're liable to—"

Her brows lifted as she waited for him to finish. When he didn't, she concluded, "I wasn't worried, because you're here to protect me. And," she added, "I'd have blown a hole through anyone who even looked as if he was harboring a wicked thought. Now, be a gentleman and turn your back so I can get out of these wet things."

Billy did so, scanning the underbrush nervously for sign of anyone thinking to sneak a peek at her. He dearly wanted to, but before he could talk himself into risking a glance over his shoulder, Sarah came around in front of him fully clad and temptingly clean.

"I could sure go for some coffee. Unless you want me to

wait while you wash up." Her dark eyes ran a deliberate sur-
vey up his long legs, but before they got to anything interesting, he strode past her.

"I'll settle for coffee to wake me up." Lord knows, he was
already more wide awake than he could stand.

It got worse when they reached the camp. Sarah detoured
to the cabin to drop off her travel bag, then came to join him
at the fire, where a half dozen bleary-eyed men were hunched
over breakfast. She strode right up until they were toe to toe,
and while his brows soared in question, she wrapped her
arms around his neck and tugged him down for a mind-
spinning kiss. It was more than a kiss. Her hands were every-
where, threading through his hair, stroking his arms,
kneading his shoulders, clasping his pockets to tug his hips
tight against her. He should have straightened immediately
but he couldn't resist her lips. Finally, she stepped back and
looked up at him with a naughty smile.

"That was for last night."

A host of husky chuckles rumbled around the fire. Billy
didn't look amused.

"Fetch me some food," he growled.

"Sure, honey." Sarah managed one more rub of her palms
up his thighs. Even after her hands were gone, he could feel
the scald of her touch moving upward in his mind. And that
was a purely dangerous place for his thoughts to go.

He was beginning to think Sarah Bass was the more dangerous problem, though.

"Right friendly little gal."

Billy glanced toward Ray, noting the less than admiring
way the outlaw was following Sarah with his gaze. "She's a
lot of things."

"Which one of them things enables her to trail over solid
rock?"

It wasn't curiosity that prompted his question. It was the
shrewd demand of a man used to watching his back, a man
who lived long because he didn't trust coincidences. And he
didn't trust Sarah's sudden appearance in their camp on the
tail of the newest member of their gang. Former friendships

only went so far with a man like Gant, and he was waiting for Billy to convince him that he had no reason for worry.

"She's part Indian. Comes by it natural, I guess. Look, Ray, if you're nervous about her being here, I can send her home. It wasn't like I asked her to follow me. Seems I recall telling her to stay put until I came for her, but she's a right independent-thinking female."

"You marrying her?"

"That's what she says."

"You don't?"

"Well, you know how women are. She takes things more serious than I do."

Ray gave him a hard look. "Surprised you'd want to tangle up with a woman, Billy."

Those had been his feelings too, but suddenly Billy felt obliged to defend the role he played. Or was it the woman? "Sarah's not like most women."

The outlaw sneered at him. "That so? And what makes her so different from what we both know about the rest of female kind? Thought you'd learned your lesson. What makes you think she'll stick around any better than your mama or your sister?"

Billy hesitated, and Ray seemed pleased with the impassive glaze that settled over his features. " 'Cause I know better than to trust her, that's why. And I know better than to care one way or another if she comes and goes. If she's here, I aim to use her. If she's gone, I ain't gonna miss her."

"More than one good man's made a fool of himself over a pretty face and a twitching skirt."

"Not this man." It was said with a hard certainty, and Ray nodded.

"I don't want her causing any more trouble."

"I'll see she doesn't. Maybe it'd be better if I chased her off after breakfast."

Ray gave him a quick look. "You think someone might have followed her?"

"No. She only came after me 'cause I made her good an' mad by sticking her up on the train and pretending not to know her. Ain't but one man I know of who can follow a track better than her. I wouldn't worry about it, Ray."

"But I do worry, Billy. About every little thing. About her showing up without warning." He fell into a calculating silence, then announced, "I think we'd better just keep her here with us until we're ready to move our camp."

Keep her here? "No."

Gant gave him a questioning stare.

"I mean, I know she wouldn't show anyone the way back here."

"Better safe than sorry, I always say. Break it to the little lady that she'll be our guest for a time. Let her know we'll do our best to make her feel welcome."

And as he said that, Ray Gant was watching his young friend's expression. Was that the normal anxiety of a man feeling hemmed in by the presence of a possessive woman? Or was it something else?

His gauging eyes turned toward the fetching female spooning up a plate of beans. Billy Cooper may have said he was too smart to trust her, but just to be on the safe side, he meant to keep a right close eye on Sarah Bassett.

Chapter Four

In the days that followed, Sarah found a wonderful freedom. There was no one to tell her how she should act or what she should do. Even though she'd known more liberties than most young women her age, she'd been far more restrained than her brothers. Jack was a ranger, Sidney was off in Austin studying to be a lawyer, and Jeffrey was planning to work their family ranch alongside their father. Those were choices they got to make, following the dictates of their dreams. What kind of dreams did her parents allow her? Marriage to a man they approved of.

Not that Sarah had anything against marriage. She'd probably enjoy settling in with a man eventually and she truly loved children, but there was still a restlessness inside her that defied that predetermined role. What if she wanted to be a ranger? What if she wanted to run trail for them as her uncle had? She knew six strong-willed men who'd have plenty to say against it, and her mama would be leading the pack. Rebecca Bass had very set ideas about how her daughter was going to live her life, and Sarah chafed under the yoke of them. If Rebecca had her way, Sarah would be closeted away from any trouble until the responsibility for her was passed on in marriage.

But Sarah loved trouble. She'd listened to tales of adventure ever since the time she'd learned to walk. She didn't want to listen anymore—she wanted to experience. But that was kind of hard to do with family packed in tight around her. Oh, she loved her family, but there was a certain disadvantage in trying to tempt a boy into giving out kisses when he was quaking at the thought of her father, uncle, and brother's censure.

And then there was her mother's rule. Since she'd come close to being of age, it was unyielding. Sarah could have free rein of her home, along with the distance between it and her uncle's, but town was strictly forbidden, as was her brother's ranger camp, unless she was in the company of family. What kind of excitement was there in hanging out wash or watching over Amanda's youngsters? She longed for the distractions a girl her age desired: dances, courting, romance. She'd hoped to find those things on her trip to Austin but hadn't. At least not the romance part, which was by far the most important one.

Rebecca frowned on frivolity that could lead to trouble and she had a way of skewering prospective beaux with her gaze, as if she were tying them to a spiny cactus with green hide. It seemed the only men in whom she had any trust were those whose last name was Bass, and that killed any notions of romance right away. The closest thing to a walk in the moonlight she'd ever known was when Harm was teaching her to follow tracks. The biggest thrill she'd ever known was when the rangers, under the leadership of Jack's wife's first husband, had camped out at her uncle's overnight. And she'd gotten that kiss from Billy Cooper.

Sarah guessed her mother had good reason not to trust her. She was wild sometimes and she was absolutely fearless, which caused her mama to worry all the more. But there was something more behind her family's determined sheltering and no one would tell her what it was. And while there was a great deal of security in that circle of family, it also tended to smother. That's why her escape from the train had been such a liberation. That's why she didn't mind the edge of danger she was under living in the squalid bandit camp. She felt alive and vibrant and . . . and then there was Billy.

Sarah had watched the women of her family seduce their men often enough to know how to make Billy Cooper's life a squirming hell. She wasn't so naive as not to realize what she was provoking. He desired her and that was a powerful excitant. And because of the role they played and his vow to keep her safe, she could enjoy experimenting with passion without fear of consequence or condemnation. After all, it wasn't as if Billy was going to tell her family how shamelessly she was behaving. It was in his best interest that they know nothing at all about it.

She was supposed to be Billy's woman and she threw herself into acting the part. She fussed over him, taking care of his every need, doing his wash, bringing him food, ever at hand to respond to any request he growled at her. And in return she got to relish an intimate closeness with him that was, oh, so nice. She made him writhe beneath his oath to treat her like a little sister. But then, little sisters didn't find any excuse to offer a caress or claim a kiss the way she did. Knowing Billy couldn't object to them was a bittersweet satisfaction. On the one hand, he was forced to act the interested beau, but on the other, she couldn't be sure if he welcomed her overtures or merely tolerated them out of duty.

Maybe he preferred a seasoned touch, like that of the whore Luisa. He hadn't answered her question about whether she had taken the other woman's place in his arms, but Sarah had only to glance up and see the flashing black eyes upon her, so dark with hate and fury, to know she had. And knowing the woman would assume that spot again the minute she left made Sarah all the more willing to stay.

Aside from the freedom and Billy, it was a pretty grim existence in that Chisos Mountain canyon. They were like prisoners within the safety of the surrounding walls, always alert and suspicious of every sound, making for nervous companionship and short tempers. The women made no secret that they disliked her, perhaps because of her fight with Luisa or perhaps because she had the attention and protection of one man instead of enduring the whims of many. She was excluded from their circle of slovenly industry. If Sarah needed soap for washing clothes, Billy had to borrow it, and somehow, he did manage to secure an ample stack of clothes to outfit her, though the styles were a bit more revealing than she was used to. She might dress like them but she could never be like them, and that, too, set her apart.

Sarah watched the camp whores with curiosity. She'd never seen bad women before. While used to gestures of love and affection between the couples in her family, these women, though doing the same things, did so for a very different purpose. Their inviting smiles hid a trace of cold mockery and there was no hint of romance in their bold actions. And for all the supposed pleasure, there seemed to be no true enjoyment. It was a business arrangement of sexual benefit for shelter and protection, and it intrigued and saddened Sarah. Didn't these poor women know that such things were to be given out of love, not out of barter? But then, wasn't that what she was doing with Billy, too? He was forced to play her lover or risk exposure as a ranger. He wasn't returning her kisses because he wanted to—not that he had any aversion to them. But knowing he hadn't sought her out at her parents's ranch in all these years, that she'd snatched him out of the embrace of another woman, that he preferred sleeping on the floor to cozying in with her, were all demoralizing facts. She might play at being his woman, but once the charade was over, what would be left between them?

Sarah didn't want the answer to be nothing.

What could she do to make him care for her while he had no choice but to share her company? Did he still see her as that teasing thirteen-year-old girl whose flirtation was without fulfillment? Maybe it was time to change that impression while she had the chance. Maybe it was time to give him more than kisses.

Sarah had that quest in mind when she was changing her clothes before the evening meal. She selected a thin black skirt with colorful embroidery around the hem and a bright red blouse that tied at the cap of either shoulder. Because the straps of her chemise would show and spoil the effect of daring browned shoulders, she went without it and felt incredibly wanton with the rough cotton rubbing over bare skin. She knotted her dark hair back in what she hoped was a more so-

phisticated style and wished for a pair of the dangling earrings
the other women wore. Sarah would have gladly pierced her
ears on the spot if she could have those bangles dancing saucily against her neck. But she doubted that any of the ladies
would be generous enough to part with a pair. Earrings
would make her feel more adult. So would a touch of their
face paint, but she didn't dare experiment with that. Her
mother had very staunch ideas about such things and about
the kind of women who wore them. Apparently, she was
right. Only those seemed the kind of women Billy liked.

Since her sturdy boots seemed awkward beneath the flow
of her skirt, Sarah chose to go with feet bare like the border
women, finding the ground sun warm as she approached the
others. Billy was talking to Ray Gant, so she drew up and
hesitated. She remembered men like Gant from when she was
a little girl and a batch of badmen had given her family a
rough time. Gant had the same hard, soulless eyes and Sarah
wondered about Billy's relationship with him. The outlaw
leader watched her, not with the leering intensity of some of
the others, but with a cool suspicion, as if waiting for her to
make a mistake. His patience made her nervous. She sensed
his dislike of her, not for any personal reason, but because of
her tie to Billy. She guessed Ray didn't care for anyone who
tampered with his influence over his men, because the minute
he saw Billy's attention shift to her, his scowl grew deep and
dangerous.

With a parting word to Gant, Billy came to her. There was
no look of appreciation on his face for the expanse of shoulders she'd left bare. His expression was tense and Sarah felt
a stirring of alarm. She searched his gaze for some sign of explanation.

"Billy?"

His hands settled on the slope of her shoulders. Another
time, she would have delighted in the hot, rough texture of
his palms, but his wasn't an inciting touch. He was preparing
her for bad news.

"Sarah, we're riding out in the morning."

Her throat tightened up around her fear. Her question escaped in a tiny whisper. "We who?"

"Me and the boys. We won't be gone long."

She grew very still, considering the implications of what he was saying. "Where are you going?"

He looked down, seemingly mesmerized by the pattern of gay flosses on her hem. "I can't tell you."

"What do you mean you—"

"Lower your voice!"

Sarah glanced around angrily, glaring at those who looked their way, while her thoughts spun. He was riding out with the bandits. That could mean only one thing: Their mission was lawbreaking. They'd ride with guns drawn to steal from the undeserving. And the deep sense of justice that had been ingrained in her since childhood rebelled.

"You can't."

"Sarah—"

"You can't!"

"You'll be safe here."

But that wasn't her concern. She couldn't speak her mind in the midst of his pseudo companions, so she started to walk away, heading for the creek. Her agitation supplied a rapid pace, but with his long stride Billy had no trouble keeping up. After they'd gone a ways, he caught her wrist, turning her toward him.

"Sarah—"

"Who are you going to rob, Billy? Folks on a train? A bank? A stage? What if someone gets hurt, gets killed? Is that part of your job, too, living with that?"

"Sarah, no one's going to get hurt." His tone had lowered into a soothing cadence but she was too upset to notice. She flung off the hand he placed on her upper arm.

"How can you say that? How can you be so sure? Why don't you just ride away? Don't you have all the information you need to hang these men six times over?"

"It's not these men I'm after. Sarah, think."

"I don't want to think." Her arms were suddenly surrounding his middle, and her hot and shamefully damp cheek was pressed against his shirtfront. Her words were muffled and thick with emotion. "Don't go, Billy."

Recovering from his initial startlement, Billy let his hand drift over the spill of her hair. "I have to. It's what I've sworn to do."

"Ride with outlaws?"

"Uphold the law. And I can't do that until I know who's breaking it." He didn't tell her what Ray had told him and for very good reason. They were riding against a group of small ranchers. He knew her family was situated within their raiding perimeters and he couldn't leave her with the worry that they'd be harmed. He was going half crazy with worry himself, wondering what he'd do if Gant targeted one of the Bass spreads for their attack. If anyone in her family was hurt, there was no way he'd ever be able to justify his part in it.

It wasn't a conscious thing. His fingertips just sort of found their way along the soft skin bared by her bright blouse. And once he'd sampled that silky warmth, he couldn't draw away. He loved the feel of her.

"Sarah, you come from a ranging family. You know I can't pick and choose what I do. The work I'm doing here's important. If I was to back out now, it'd take months for someone else to get as far as I have . . . if they could. How many more innocent people would suffer in that time? I want this to be over, too, but this is the best way, the only way. Can you see that?"

She'd didn't move, so he had no way of knowing if he was getting through to her.

"Sarah, it'll be over soon and I'll be able to take you home."

That got a response. Her arms cinched up tight and he could feel her trembling. Was it worry over the situation or a reluctance to part from him? he had to wonder. And he had to know.

His big hand scooped under her chin, lifting to tilt her face up to him. Her dark eyes were glimmering like moonlight on midnight waters. He couldn't resist the invitation to plunge right in.

Her mouth parted eagerly beneath the crush of his, accepting the hard thrust of his tongue and all his hungry urgency. Like a fever, the wanting escalated. Like delirium, the higher it got, the harder it was to cling to sanity. He wanted Sarah Bass. He wanted what her kisses hinted at, a passion so deep, he could drown in it. After days of enduring her teasing, her provoking, he'd run out of patience and restraint. He wanted her now, right or wrong.

There was no guarantee he'd come back to her.

And he couldn't go off without knowing how it would be to have her and ride her to paradise.

His hands were at her blouse, rubbing, kneading the small, pliant mounds until they yielded up peaks that were hard and needy. There was nothing between them except the flame-colored cotton, and he was anxious to push aside that barrier. Billy was tugging at the ties, hurriedly, a little rough. He couldn't get the knots undone. He pulled himself back from her lips, panting raggedly.

"Sarah, help me out here."

Obediently, she began to work on the ties he'd inadvertently tightened in his clumsy haste. While he was waiting, he clasped her gently rounded hips and moved her lithe little body against his, letting her feel exactly what she was doing to him. That was when her mood changed. She started to struggle.

He didn't understand it. It seemed that up to this precarious point, she'd been willing enough. She'd made sweet little moaning sounds when he palmed her breasts. She'd almost sucked his tongue down her throat. She'd been ready to undress. Then, inexplicably, the willingness was gone on her part, but not the necessity on his.

"Sarah, what's wrong?" Billy demanded, trying to contain her within the circle of his arms. She was squirming, levering against his chest with her fists.

"Let me go." Her voice was strained, almost angry-sounding. And suddenly he was angry, too.

"You can't just stop and pretend nothing happened."

"What makes you think I wanted anything to happen? Stop your pawing and let me go!"

He released her so abruptly, she staggered. She was breathing hard, but not with the same need that directed his laboring efforts. For a second she looked wild, even a little scared, then her chin assumed a haughty angle.

"Pretty bold moves for a man who claims he thinks of me like a little sister."

Her taunting challenge was too much. His eyes narrowed dangerously. He should have known. What had he been thinking? "Always the tease, aren't you, Sarah? Grow up and leave the games to baby girls."

"I thought you liked games, Billy Cooper. Let me know when you're done playing and are ready to get serious."

She jerked up the ties to her blouse and whirled away from him, leaving Billy in a state so raw, his thinking capacity was practically nil. If she'd been anyone but Jack's sister, he'd have gone after her and demanded satisfaction for what she'd started. But he retained enough sense and pride to do no such thing.

Damn her for her tricks and damn him for his willingness to fall into them. After all his big words, he was letting her make a fool of him.

Soft feminine arms wrapped around him from behind, startling him from his fierce thoughts. Knowing hands rubbed over the swell in his jeans.

"What kind of woman walks away from such promise? I never would," Luisa cooed as her large breasts crushed to his back. Her fingers were plucking at his shirt buttons, pulling the hem from his denims without a trace of coquetry. And after his frustrations with Sarah, that direct approach to passion was just what he needed.

Billy turned and grabbed Luisa up, claiming her pouty mouth with a brutal kiss. No sweet moans or teasing wiggles. She was all business. Her hands tore open his shirt, yanking the rest of it free of his waistband. No emotional consequence, just a quick physical satisfaction. That's what he needed. He shouldn't have looked for any more than that.

It wasn't worth the pain.

54   *Dana Ransom*

* * *

Sarah stomped away from the creek, wiping at her eyes. Her hands were shaking the same way everything inside her was shaking.

What had happened? Everything had been so perfect—his kiss, his touch, the way desire had built between them. She'd wanted him so badly. She'd wanted to become a woman in his arms . . . his woman.

The feel of his hands upon her had been marvelous, awakening a wealth of scurrying sensations. She'd anticipated the friction of his palms upon bare skin. That had been good and she'd been so excited, she was willing to let passion lead her.

Then he'd pulled her up close and reality had hit the instant she felt his rock-hard arousal prodding into her. And she'd panicked. She hadn't expected him to be so . . . big. Her recall of the male member was sized proportionately to her preadolescent brothers, and this was nothing like that! The knowledge of what they were going to do collided with the seeming impossibility of it. Her mind was filled with all the wrong kinds of frantic alarms. This wasn't how she'd wanted her first time to be, not out of wedlock, not on dirty ground surrounded by outlaws, not without words of love. She'd wanted white sheets, a gold ring, and romantic murmurs, and the absence of those things warred with her desire to seize the opportunity that might never come again. She was seventeen, reason argued, and this man had made her no promises.

And after she'd coaxed Billy into thinking she was worldly in the ways of men and women, what would happen when he found out just how inexperienced she was? That while she was well acquainted with the sounds and preludes of lovemaking from living under her brother's and uncle's roofs, she was painfully ignorant of the actual mechanics?

All she could think to do was to pull away and cover for her confusion before he knew the truth and had a good laugh at her expense.

Sarah heard a heavy step behind her on the overgrown

path and turned, thinking it was Billy intent on having more disagreeable words. She was ready to let loose a string of disparaging phrases, when surprise left her wordless.

It wasn't Billy.

"Hey there, pretty thing. In a mighty big hurry. Shouldn't ought to be out here this close to dark all on your lonesome."

Sarah recognized the bearded face from camp but she had no recall of the man's name. He'd stayed to himself and his bottle mostly. She could smell the liquor on him now. It blurred his speech and his gaze. And assuming him drunk did little for her confidence. A drunken man was a mean customer, one who couldn't be reasoned with. Sarah assumed a fearless pose while her eyes anxiously scanned the path over the man's broad shoulder.

"I'm not alone. Billy's right behind me."

He laughed, a low, gritty sound. "Really? Funny, last I saw of him, he was right busy with Luisa down by the creek. Wouldn't imagine him coming after you any time soon, knowing Luisa like I do."

Luisa! How that hurt! She shouldn't have believed him, but somehow she did.

"So, I guess it's just you and me, and that's all we need, ain't it?"

He didn't waste any more words on sweet talk. Apparently, that wasn't his mode of persuasion.

He hit her.

The blow was so sudden and strong, it dropped her without a sound. From her dazed position on the sandy ground, Sarah saw him reach for his gunbelt and unbuckle it with an unhurried purpose. When it fell loose, he reached for his pants. The obscene bulge in front was all it took to goad Sarah into action.

She dove for the gunbelt, rolling, coming up on her knees with the pistol in hand, already cocked. The outlaw looked surprised and quite ridiculous, all round-eyed with his trousers halfway down to expose dingy long johns. But his startlement didn't last long.

"What do you think you're doing? Put that down, *puta*, before someone gets hurt."

Someone had already gotten hurt. Her face ached fiercely and Sarah vowed to suffer no more at his hands. "Jerk up your pants and get the hell outta here before I drop you on the spot."

He laughed with disbelief, and Sarah could see thoughts of a cruel retribution forming in his cloudy eyes as he snarled, "Who do you think you are fooling? You won't shoot me. Put it down or I'll have to punish you but good before we get on to the pleasuring."

She thought one would be very much like the other.

Sarah cast a quick, desperate glance in the direction she'd come, hoping to see some sign of Billy. But there was no one. She steadied her hand and glared up at her attacker.

"I will shoot so you'd better—"

He lunged for her. In the back of her mind, Sarah heard her uncle's calming voice. *Don't pull a gun unless you're willing to use it. Don't fire unless you mean to kill. There's no halfway in gunplay. Stop 'em and see they stay stopped. It's you or them, and happens I always think more of myself in such situations.*

So did Sarah.

She fired.

Hearing the shot brought Billy jerking back out of Luisa's embrace. Cursing, he had his own gun drawn and was racing in the direction Sarah had gone, envisioning all sorts of frantic scenarios. The one he came upon was bad enough to twist his conscience tight.

Sarah was crouched on the path, a smoking gun in hand. When she looked up at him, he could see the beginnings of a painful bruise on her face. He tore his gaze from her to the figure sprawled facedown at his feet. He recognized Joe Beals and he recognized death. Billy didn't have to ask what had happened. He strode toward Sarah.

"Give me the gun. Quick."

She passed it up to him without question. He placed his

own in Beals's outstretched hand just as the others from camp arrived. There was a lot of unsettled muttering as conclusions were drawn. Billy with a hot gun, his woman obviously abused, Beals caught in the act and cashed in for it.

"What the hell happened here?"

The men cleared a path for Ray Gant. He surveyed the scene with hard eyes, then glared at Billy, awaiting an answer. Billy put it simply.

"He was trying to force some fun on my woman. I stopped him. He drew and I stopped him permanently."

It was then Sarah noticed Luisa standing at Billy's back. Her clothes were in disarray and her red lips were swollen with kisses. His kisses. Kisses given while the whore was busy wrangling him out of his shirt, which even now hung loose and open. Kisses taken while she had been accosted on the trail without his protection.

Sarah looked up at him, conveying all those realized truths in one accusing stare. Then she climbed to her feet and made her way back to the bandit camp without a backward glance.

It didn't take him long to join her in the airless little shack. She was lying on her back on the soggy bed when the door opened, illuminating his large frame against the dimming twilight sky. He stepped in and the smell of the whore, Luisa, came in with him. How stupid she'd been to come running after him, and now there was no escape from that folly. If only there were some way she'd never have to face him again. Sarah clenched her teeth to stay her tears and to keep her teeth from chattering.

"Are you all right?"

She gave no verbal response to that soft-spoken question. In the shaft of pale light from the open door, her dark gaze said it all. *Where were you? You were supposed to be protecting me. Why weren't you?* And worse was the answer he saw there as well. He hadn't been there because he'd been with another woman, a cheap woman who meant nothing to him. He'd been enjoying her well-used charms while Sarah had nearly suffered the unthinkable. What could he say?

Billy crossed to the basin and soaked the washcloth in cool,

clean water, wringing it out before carrying it to the bedside.
He sat carefully on the frame and touched the cloth to Sarah's swollen cheek. She winced and gave her head an objecting toss.

"Don't!"

"The cold water will take the swelling down. Just hold it
there."

Sarah reached for the cloth, their hands brushing as he surrendered possession of it. She went rigid, denying her desire
to grab on to him while he was sitting there half undressed by
another woman's hands. The cool cloth did make the throb
in her face diminish, yet it did nothing for the ache in her
heart. She wanted to slap him, to wail "How could you?" but
pride held her silent. She knew the answer. Luisa was the
kind of woman who'd give him what he wanted when Sarah
refused.

Billy got up and went to pull the door closed. In the ensuing darkness, she could hear him removing his boots and
gunbelt.

"I'm gonna turn in. We're gonna light out early."

Maybe that was his reason. Or maybe he just didn't want
to leave her alone. What did it really matter what his motiva-
tion was? He was with her and Sarah was absurdly grateful.

The shock of all that had happened was beginning to dawn
on her. She'd killed a man. She'd never shot anyone before.
The glaze of mortality on that man's face would stay etched
in her horrified conscience forever. But still, better him than
her.

Billy may not have been there to protect her, but he'd
taken up her cause quick enough by claiming he was the one
who'd done the deed. The men in the camp would understand a fellow taking drastic measures in such a situation but
may have had different thoughts about a woman gunning
down one of their own. They wouldn't have cared two hoots
that she'd done it to protect her virtue. Billy's agile thinking
may have saved her much, but it wouldn't drive away the
look on her victim's face just before he crumpled in a lifeless
heap.

As Billy was spreading his bedroll on the ground, Sarah became aware of a cold so deep inside her, it was like a kind of dying. She was desperate to know warmth again.

"Billy?"

"What?"

"Would you sleep up here with me tonight?"

He didn't say anything. The rope webbing groaned as he reclined his weight beside her. Cautiously, he tucked one arm beneath her head, the scent of whore wafting from his shirt a potent reminder of his preference. Sarah rolled onto her side, putting her back to him, but she offered no objection when his other arm curled in an easy drape over the gentle dip of her waist. Instead, she hugged his sturdy forearm to her and burrowed back against him. Her shivering returned with a vengeance.

"Sarah, I—"

"Don't talk."

There was nothing he could say that she wanted to hear. All she needed was his comforting heat and strength, his physical presence not his apologetic purgings. Billy could give no acceptable excuse, but he could help her get through the night in the safety of his embrace. That was all she'd take from him until sleep finally came.

Chapter Five

Billy was tightening the double girth on his horse when he saw her emerge from the little shack they shared. Again, he was aware of the same gut-twisting response he'd felt when waking to find her in his arms. The intensity of that bittersweet pull had scared him into crawling out of bed in a hurry. And what frightened him more was his desire to linger there just looking at her, just feeling her curled close. Dangerous thoughts for a man to have when he wasn't meaning to get serious.

Sarah spooked him. He'd been lulled by the easy rapport they had between them, by the teasing and siblinglike sparring he so enjoyed. Then all of a sudden what he was feeling wasn't playful at all. It was sobering man-woman stuff—about the last thing in the world he wanted to experience at this point in his life. Especially for Jack Bass's sister.

Thinking that another man had almost hurt her had her kept him awake until the near-dawn hours. He'd cuddled her up tight against him and sworn he'd never let something like that happen again. What was he doing, making such a promise? Duty only went so far, and beyond that was a responsibility to Jack as his friend. But what he was reacting to as far as Sarah was concerned went deeper than either of those acceptable motives. It was more than guilt, and he didn't want to search out a name for it. Sarah was just a kid . . . a kid who was a tough realist and a mushy romanticist all at once. She'd taken a shine to him all those years ago and

he'd been foolish to let her polish up those feelings now. Yet
it had flattered the hell out of him that she'd come after him
just to see him back on the path of righteousness. She
wouldn't have done that if she didn't hold more than just little girl feelings for him.

She was dangerous to his well-being . . . and not the kind
of trouble he was interested in at all.

Then why was his heart jerking against his ribs when her
gaze met his over the back of his saddled horse?

Sarah stood waiting for him to come to her, rooted to the
spot as stubbornly as that delicate prairie verbena, looking
fresh and fragile amidst the harshness of the camp. All around
her there was a buzz of activity as the men readied to ride
out, but her attention was on him as if none of the others existed. And he didn't know what to make of her expression.

Was she still angry? Was she going to cry and make a fuss
about him leaving? He didn't know and it made his approach
cautious. As it was, either of those reactions would have been
preferable to the cool, dark stare that met his.

" 'Mornin'."

"Were you going to wake me or did you plan to just sneak
out with the others?"

Her tone set him back on the defensive. "I would have
come to say my goodbyes." Then his words softened. "Sarah,
I don't want you to worry—"

"Why would I worry? I'll be fine here. I'll keep to myself
and stay out of trouble, like I should have done from the first.
And if you think I'll be worrying about you . . . well, you're
mistaken."

"Sarah—"

Her gaze slipped beyond him and fastened with an ever-
darkening fury. He swiveled to see what had her hackles up.
Luisa was standing off to one side, also waiting to say her
goodbyes to him.

"Sarah," he began, turning toward her. Her expression was
like the wide bore of a Sharps buffalo gun. Suddenly, he
couldn't bear to ride off with that memory. "Aren't you
gonna kiss me? For appearances."

"I don't want to kiss you."

"You're supposed to be my fiancée, remember?" Those flirty dimples creased his cheeks engagingly but she'd have none of his charm.

"If I were your fiancée, I'd have saved a bullet for you last night. If you want a kiss, go grab one off her. I'll even give you the money to pay for it."

"I don't want Luisa's kiss. I want yours." He took a step closer and she one back.

"Well, you can't always have everything you want, Billy Cooper. And I'll be damned if I'm going to—"

But the second he pulled her up to him, Sarah was returning his kiss with a desperate passion. And there was no trace of the little girl, no trace of the tease, as her arms came up to lock about the back of his neck.

Once she had him, she wasn't inclined to let go. She pressed her lips to his cheeks, to his neck, to the warm vee where his top shirt buttons were undone and his skin was damp and salty from the morning heat.

"You be careful, Billy." She said the words the same way she'd heard Amanda say them when her aunt had sent Harmon off to meet danger, with a hard, possessive fervor. Billy seemed to like it, because he tipped her chin and took her mouth again with a purely scalding urgency.

"C'mon, Cooper," one of the men yelled. "You ain't got time to take her back to bed, so say goodbye and be done with it."

Sarah was looking up at him, her eyes dark and melting. Her fingers were curled tight in the fabric of his shirt.

"Billy . . ." She was going to say she loved him, but he cut her off just in time.

"I'll be back."

He took a step back and she followed, still clutching at him.

"Let me go, Sarah." There was a tenderness in his tone that she'd never heard before. A tone he'd never used before because he'd never felt quite the same way about anyone else. Then he grinned at her to ease their parting, his hand curving gently along the softness of her face. "You're one heck of an actress. I'm almost convinced that you care."

She smiled back, just as he'd intended, and challenged, "You're dreaming, Billy Cooper. It's all for appearances." Her fingers loosened their hold and she gave him a push, freeing him to leave. He didn't dare hesitate. Walking away from her was hard enough without drawing out the process. And he strode right past Luisa without even thinking to glance her way.

Somehow, Sarah managed to hold back her tears until Billy and the others were out of sight. Then she secreted herself in the hot little cabin and cried herself dry.

What he needed was a good hard stretch in the saddle to clear away the confusion from his mind. The sun was hot, the Texas ground was rocky, and there was no time for pondering on his emotions. He was a man of action and this was what he liked best: simple exertion with a dangerous purpose. He liked the way it made his heart pound, the way it cut through everything but the basics of survival. He enjoyed the way a common cause bound him to the men with whom he rode. It was what he'd always liked about the rangers. And it was what he liked about riding out with Ray Gant. Except the purposes were very different.

It didn't matter at first. It was good just to be on horseback covering miles by the minute. The feel of the sun beating down, the sharp scent of sage, the strong rhythm of the animal beneath him, the excitement churning inside, all made for a pleasure that stripped right to the soul of who he was. Out here, he didn't have to worry about keeping Sarah Bass out of trouble or fending off Luisa's or Ray's ready suspicions. Things were straight and sure. He had a good horse, a fast gun, a clear day, and pards to share it with. Billy thrived on the sense of peace.

Ray hadn't told them of their targets, only that there were some squatters sucking up water where they weren't wanted by men who could afford to wish them gone. He'd expressed his thoughts on it often around their nightly campfire, and for the most part, they were the gut feelings of every man of Lone Star persuasion. The land belonged to those with the strength to control it, and those men were the white Texans. Mexicans had no business sneaking across the Rio, plopping down on a good piece of Texas soil. They hadn't cleared the area of Indians just to lose it to another passel of invaders. Never mind that both the Mexicans and the Apache had been on the land long before they even knew it existed.

All Ray had told them was there was fifty dollars per man for every spread they raided, which was better than two months wages in any other job. And if they hit a dozen or more places, they'd be toting more wealth than they'd slave for during a year of honest labor. And what was dishonest about kicking a bunch of Meskins back across the border? When Ray Gant said it with all his proper indignation, it made a frightening amount of sense. By the time they crested the last rise and saw a neat little spread below, they were all riled enough and angry enough and territorial enough to do some serious damage.

Lassoing fence posts and jerking them out of the ground was as much fun as playing a kid's game. So was riding through a batch of wild-eyed cows, chasing them until this time next Thursday. Scattering chickens until the air was thick with feathers was a bit of humorous mischief, as was trampling down tidy rows of winter crops. It wasn't until a fat Mexican ran out onto the porch waving an ancient single-shot rifle, only to be met with a bullet square in the chest from Ray Gant's gun, that it ceased to be entertaining to Billy. Around that fallen figure gathered a wailing wife and four scared kids, and right then, Billy was looking out of hell. What had he been part of? When had he stopped seeing the situation for what it was: terrorizing, murdering, lawbreaking? These men weren't his friends and these people didn't deserve what they'd been dealt. By the time they rode out, leaving behind a chorus of desperate crying and bright flames dancing along the roof of house and barn, Billy was sick to his soul and wishing he could just ride off and far away from any culpability.

But he couldn't. Because as far as any of these men knew, he was one of them, just as bloodthirsty and conscience-weak

as the rest. And he couldn't afford for them to think differ-
ently, not only because his job and his life were on the line,
but because Sarah was back in their camp.

They stopped for a lunch of beans and bread, and Ray
broke out some bottles of *mezcal* to keep the morale high. Billy
drank because he didn't think he could get through the rest
of the day otherwise. The fiery liquor burned in the bottom
of his belly just as guilt flamed in the base of his heart.

They hit two more spreads that afternoon. The first was easy.
No one was home and they made sure there was nothing left to
come home to. By the time the outlaws rode on the second one,
they were caught up by a feverish violence and none blinked an
eye when Ray said softly, "No survivors in this one."

No one but Billy Cooper.

He'd promised Sarah. He'd sworn there'd be no killing.
What was he going to tell her when she asked? What was he
going to tell his own conscience when he tried to sleep? That
it was his duty? That it was for Texas? That it was for Jack
Bass? Somehow, none of those seemed reason enough when
the shooting began.

He was spared the sight of the woman and her young daughter being gunned down. He didn't know who pulled the trigger.
He didn't want to know. Smoke from the burning house and
outbuildings was intense. His eyes were tearing from the fumes
and from the horror of it all. His gun was out and he was firing
wherever he was certain he wouldn't hit anything. He just
wanted it to be over quick, so he could wash off the soot as he'd
wash off the shame . . . if only he could.

Then he was distracted by the sight of a young boy charg-
ing out of the blazing house. He couldn't have been more
than eight or nine and was dragging a rifle as long as he was.
When Shad Randolph leveled for a shot, something inside
Billy let go. No more. He couldn't stand any more. He kicked
up his horse and put himself between the bullet and the boy.

"Git outta the way, Cooper!"

"For God's sake, Shad, he's just a kid!"

And that's when the kid fired.

The force of the impact nearly knocked Billy from his sad-

dle. Woozy with pain and surprise, he was hanging on to the
horn, hanging on to consciousness. Then after seeing the boy
fall, shot dead, he purposefully let go of both.

He'd seen enough.

It was hunger and heat that finally drove Sarah out of the
shack at mid-afternoon. She was running with a sticky sweat,
too miserable with worry to care.

What if Billy didn't come back? What if he was killed? And
above the torture of those thoughts was another. What would
she do in a camp full of bandits without Billy's protection? It
wasn't likely that they'd just let her ride out, and the possibility of being passed from man to man like one of the camp
whores was too awful to imagine.

He had to come back!

If for no other reason than to continue what she'd run
from at the creek.

She couldn't stop thinking about the feelings he'd stirred
up with his hot kisses and urgent caresses. With so much anxiety crowding in around her, thinking of how it would be to
experience his lovemaking was all that kept her going. Suddenly, it didn't matter so much that no permanence would be
attached to the act itself. It didn't even matter that Billy
didn't love her. She'd come to love him enough for the two
of them. She wanted him to wake and woo the woman in her,
and to finally be the one to claim her. If only for one night.
Nothing else seemed important as she paced and fretted with
a loneliness she'd never felt before.

"You shouldn't fear for your man. They be back soon."

Sarah looked up in surprise at the young Mexican woman
who was still new enough at her profession to be pretty. It
was the first time one of them had spoken to her. "I know.
And I should be used to waiting, but it never gets any easier."

"You love your man."

Sarah considered the comment, then smiled faintly. What
harm would it do to speak the truth? "Yes, I do."

"Then you need to keep a careful watch on Luisa. She

does not love him but she wants him plenty. She like him because he treats her nice and he washes first. He is better than the others." She said it with a sad resignation, and Sarah felt a sudden empathy for the life these women led.

"I'm not sure I can keep him from going to her. He doesn't love me back."

"A man doesn't have to love to want. I think he wants you plenty."

"I need him to want me more." She brooded silently and found herself watching the delicate swing of the other woman's earrings. "What's your name?"

"Chonita."

"Where can I get some earrings like those you're wearing?"

"You can have these." She reached up and removed them from her ears.

"Oh, no. I didn't mean—"

"Please. I would like you to have them after the brave thing you did."

"What I did?"

"Joe Beals, he was a mean *hombre*. He liked to use his fists. I am glad he will not be coming back to me."

"But I didn't—"

"Luisa told us it was you who fired the gun. Do not worry. We will tell none of the men. It is our pleasure to keep the secret." She smiled hopefully and extended the earrings. Sarah took them, grateful for the sense of camaraderie with this woman. She examined the beaded wires admiringly when Chonita told her she'd made them herself.

"They are beautiful, but I'm afraid my ears aren't pierced."

"Oh, I can do that for you."

And by the time darkness seeped into the canyon, Sarah had a pair of heavy beaded earrings dangling from sore lobes, but she ignored the discomfort in her delight from the way they felt brushing her bare shoulders. She wore the red blouse and black skirt. She didn't have a lot to choose from, but this was what she wanted Billy to see her in when he came back. She wanted to give him a welcome he'd remember.

The wild whoops and hollars of their arrival echoed down

the steep canyon walls. The camp was in an immediate stir, the guards and women rushing out to greet the raiders. Sarah was amongst them, her gaze frantically searching the shadowed riders for Billy's familiar form. It wasn't easy to locate one when all were milling about in the near darkness. The mood was filled with excitement and success, but hers was sharp with anxiety until she finally found him. He was seated on his horse, weaving drunkenly in his saddle, finally toppling down—right into Luisa's anticipating arms.

Sarah didn't wait to see more than that. She'd waited too long, worried too much, to let the border tart steal away her welcome. Pushing her way through the revelers who were displaying stolen goods to the greedy delight of their whores, she stalked up to the embracing couple, ready to wade in with fists flying. Until she got a closer look. Luisa may have been all oozing invitation, but Billy didn't seem in the least impressed by it. There was a strained starkness to his expression that Sarah couldn't identify as he stood leaning on the woman rather than actively hugging her.

"What did you bring me, Cooper? Some pretty dresses like the others? Maybe some shoes like last time? Or petticoats? Some jewelry, maybe?"

But Billy had seen Sarah's approach and he was pushing away from the grasping arms and the grasping demands. And seeing that, Luisa was furious.

"I suppose you bring gifts for her now? Fine, you *cabron*. I can get my presents from the others."

As she stormed away, Billy took a quick step and swept Sarah up tight against him. There was an indescribable goodness in the feel of her pressed close, a sense of acceptance in the way her arms circled his middle and her cheek rested over his heart. He needed to lose himself in her sweetness, holding her fiercely as if she could chase the tormenting visions from his mind.

Sarah said nothing for a time, content to be close, thrilled just to have him back. Then she began to notice other things, like the smell of smoke that clung to him, the way tension shivered down the length of his strong arms and the way he seemed to depend upon her support. His was in a strange mood and she was growing frightened. What had happened? What had shaken him so severely?

"Billy?"

"Hush. Just let me hold you."

What was wrong? Something terrible. She could hear it in what he wasn't saying. She could feel it in the rapid pounding of his heartbeats. He was scaring her with his silent intensity but she tried to lighten it with teasing words.

"What? You bring me no presents? The other men have gifts for their women yet you come back empty-handed. I should be angry."

Billy didn't laugh. Instead, he clutched her tighter. His thoughts recoiled in horror at the idea of seeing her in one of the dead women's dresses. His voice was low and gruff. "I came back. Isn't that enough?"

Her dark head moved reassuringly against his chest. "It's enough."

"Hey, Coop," one of the men yelled, "yer lady know anything about doctoring? You should have her take a look at that bullet hole."

Sarah jerked back, her gaze flying up to his. "Bullet hole? You've been shot?"

"It's nothing, Sarah."

"Let me see."

"It's just a scratch. Really . . ."

"Let me see!"

He gave a sigh of resignation and shrugged out of his duster. Sarah gasped. His shirtsleeve was black with blood in the dim light.

"It's not that bad," he assured her. "Just cut some of the meat outta my arm, is all." His voice trailed off and his gaze took on that cloudy distance that worried her so.

Sarah touched his face with the spread of her fingers. "There's so much in your eyes that I can't read. What have they seen today? Billy, what happened?"

For a moment he was still, surprised by her sensitivity. But there was no way he could share the remorse swelling inside him. He blinked and looked away from her concerned stare. "Nothing I want to talk about. I—I'm going to go wash up."

He pushed past her and started for the creek with a slightly wobbly stride. Sarah was quick to fall in beside him, tucking up under his uninjured arm so that it draped along her shoulders. She didn't insult him by suggesting he lean on her, but he was grateful for her support. His sense of direction was none too sure.

"I'll bind that arm up for you," was all she said, and he nodded. The wound was in the upper well of his left arm, but since that was the one he favored, it was awkward for him to tend it. He wouldn't mind submitting to a tender touch.

At the stream he dropped down onto his knees and scooped up the clear water, rinsing the sweat and smoke stains from his face. He drank from the cup of his hand and a sudden roil from his taut belly made him fear he was going to be sick. Billy splashed more water on his face, breathing deep until the sensation subsided. He heard the sound of tearing cloth and looked around to see Sarah ripping long strips from her petticoat. With her skirts hiked up, a long, slender line of pale legs was exposed to his gaze. Nice legs. Great legs! A warming of lust felt wonderful after the grimness of his recent thoughts.

"Take off your shirt," she was saying with a crisp efficiency. When he stared at her rather blankly, she gave him an impatient frown. "It's not like this is the first time I've wrapped up a bullet wound."

Coming from her family, he supposed it wasn't. Nor would it be the last.

Billy managed to undo the crude bandage he'd made of his bandana and to unfasten his buttons with clumsy fingers, but peeling off the soiled shirt was beyond him. After a short struggle, weakness was threatening to steal his sensibilities away.

"Let me help you." Then her hands were gently easing off the sweat- and blood-soaked cotton. She drew a harsh breath at the sight of the nasty furrow gouged into his arm, but wasted no time in cleaning and rewrapping the injury. Billy endured it, then flexed his arm cautiously.

"Nice field dressing."

"Thanks. Comes in handier than knowing how to cook."

He smiled. "Yeah. Jack told me about your skill in the kitchen."

She scowled. "Did he? That skunk. Did he tell you my stew would poison you?"

"Something like that."

"Just wait until I see him again. He'll wish I had poisoned him. He'll be stew when I finish. Billy?"

His smile was gone and his dark eyes filled up with an anguish so overwhelming, it broke her heart to see it. He took a funny hitching sort of breath and Sarah was quick to let instinct take over. She cupped the back of his head and urged it down to her shoulder. Her arms enveloped him in wordless compassion, holding tight as he fought down whatever demons had been born in him that day. He wouldn't speak of them so she didn't ask. She settled for consoling him with her silence, with the gentle rocking of her body, with soft kisses to his thick smoke-scented hair.

After several minutes, he conquered the unevenness of his breath and the frailty of his spirit. He was aware of the way her palms shifted over the bare skin of his back and shoulders in soothing strokes that did anything but calm him. He hadn't expected such intuitive strength in someone as young as Sarah Bass, but maybe he should have. Hers was no sheltered life. She understood pain, perhaps better than he did. Jack was steeped in memories too dark to name. Harmon was spooky with the number of ghosts he carried. If anyone could understand him, Sarah could, but at the moment, talk was the furthest thing from his mind.

Sarah was surprised when he lifted up to claim her mouth with a bruising urgency. Her lips opened in response, welcoming him inside, greeting him with the eager mating of her tongue over and around his. His fingers clamped painfully upon the back of her neck, guiding her head roughly to match the angle of his. It wasn't a pleasurable kiss but there was a wildness to it that inflamed her, and Sarah found herself grabbing on to him with like intensity. Her aggressive pursuit literally bowled him over, and she rode him down until he was half reclined against a bit of gnarled tree root while she sprawled over him, continuing to pour kisses over his face and neck and chest.

Finally, he had to catch her head between his hands and wrestle her away. Their eyes met, their gazes mating as hotly as their tongues had seconds before.

"Sarah," he warned huskily. "Stop now if you're going to. Don't make this a game."

"It's not." Her voice was low, like a growl, and it woke an excitement in him that knew no equal. But then she stood and he held his breath in an agony of doubt. Would she run away as she had before?

She reached up under her skirts and then was stepping out of her drawers. Billy let go a gust of expectation when the significance hit him. She stepped one foot over him and came down astride his hips, leaning down to take his mouth again until he was groaning with impatience. There was nothing in her behavior, nothing in her practiced seduction, that would lead him to think she hadn't traveled this particular path of passion before, at some time. He gave no thought to caution, no heed to care, as his need for her rose to a throbbing pressure. With her lips still fastened on his, he reached down to undo his jeans. Billy burrowed his hands up under the layers of her clothing until he had her by the slender waist, lifting her slightly and bringing her down over him. The fit was so tight, he nearly lost himself the instant her hot flesh seized up around him.

"Oh, God, Sarah," he panted hoarsely. "Oh, baby . . ." His mind went blank after that, as pure sensation took over and he began to move her atop him. She made a faint noise; it could have been his name, he wasn't sure. The sound was muffled from where she had her face buried against his shoulder. Apparently, she was as overwhelmed as he was, and that knowledge acted upon him with a savage satisfaction as his thrusts grew harder and deeper with purpose.

Sarah was overwhelmed, but not with delight. The rending pain of his entry was a cruel shock to her senses. She would have twisted off him to escape the crowding discomfort if he hadn't had her fixed in such a firm hold. There was a second of relief, too quickly followed by another battering invasion that seemed to tunnel out space where none was available. She wanted to cry out for him to stop, that he was hurting her, but pride held her silent. She couldn't bear for him to know that this was her first time and that she was purely terrified by what she'd experienced thus far.

Determined to endure it until the pain turned to pleasure, she squeezed her eyes shut and hid her face, waiting for it to get better, praying it would get better. And just when she was so sore and raw and frightened she was ready to scream, he gave a raspy moan of fulfillment and went still inside her. She lay limp, rising and falling with his hurried breaths, too dazed to stir, too shaken to think straight.

His hand came up to stroke languidly along her hair and she rode out his great sigh of contentment.

"Oh, baby, that was nice."

Nice.

Nice? Not for her. Not in the least! Where was the splendid passion that wrung moans and groans and sighs from the women of her family and had them dragging their men off to bed at every opportunity? For this? She couldn't believe it. All her anticipation, all her hopeful expectations, destroyed by a few minutes of sweaty discomfort that would probably leave her bowlegged for days?

He lifted her up and her body knew a tremendous shivery relief as it was emptied. He continued to hug her close until aware of and alarmed by her lack of response.

"Sarah?"

She straightened at last. In the moonlit darkness, his face was cast in muted shadow, but there was no mistaking the lambent glow in his eyes or the beginnings of his smile.

"That's it?" she blurted out, blunt in her disappointment. She couldn't have wounded him more with a knee to the groin. "What do you mean?" he asked, afraid he knew. She'd been less than awed by his lovemaking. He tried to put his arms around her but she wiggled away until a shock of pain from his injury forced him to let go. Sarah staggered to her feet on unsteady legs, regarding him with a mixture of blame and disillusionment. Billy wasn't sure what was wrong, but it sure as hell wasn't his fault! He'd left too many sated smiles behind to believe that.

"What were you expecting?" he demanded of her. "Fireworks? A brass band?"

Her reply was a devastating blow to his male pride.

"I was expecting to like it."

"Well, excuse me. Give me a minute and I'll try harder to impress you." His tone was curt, his feelings were bruised, and his arm was aching like the very devil. And she was glaring down at him with the severity of a critic. What had she expected from him?

What had she enjoyed elsewhere that he hadn't provided?

"Just forget it!" Sarah snapped at him, bending down to snatch up her drawers before marching rather stiffly back toward camp, leaving him to his chafe of bewildered anger.

Billy let his head clunk back against the tree root and muttered a weary curse. Sarah Bass was turning him inside out and making him into the worst kind of fool. And the problem was, he couldn't seem to stop himself from letting her do it.

He should have known better than to think she'd be any different.

Finally, he was able to pull himself together, drag his soiled shirt and duster back on, and head back toward the fire, where he was hopeful of finding a boosting camaraderie.

He was wrong.

There was a strange current of tension in the camp and a wariness to the eyes that turned in his direction. A quiver of instinct told him to run like hell, but Billy forced himself to advance upon the oddly hostile group.

"Hey, what's going on?"

"Hey yourself, Billy-boy," Ray Gant drawled as he separated from the others and came to meet him.

Billy's eyes darted quickly around for Sarah but he didn't see her. A sweat of panic began to run as Ray came toe to toe with him. His words were soft with menace.

"We was all just wanting to know what a Texas Ranger was doing riding with us."

Chapter Six

Sarah could hardly see her way through the tears blurring her eyes. She didn't return to the camp. She hadn't the strength to maintain a stoic face around the others, and she couldn't bear the idea of being closed up in that little shack for another minute. Especially with Billy.

She'd get her horse and ride out. It was time to go home. Her family would be worried sick and she had no more reason to stay. Billy Cooper wasn't going to fall in love with her. He didn't treat her any better than he did the numerous whores who liked him because of his nice smile and clean smell. He didn't find her exciting nor their lovemaking memorable. At least not in the way she'd wanted it to be. He was probably bored with her silly passions and, now that he'd had her, wouldn't bother with her again. Why would he when he had the simmering Luisa eager to climb back aboard?

She wiped at her streaming eyes and turned off the path. There was just enough moonlight for her to see by but not enough to give her away, as long as she kept to good cover. And there was plenty all the way up to the makeshift horse corral. She wouldn't bother with a saddle. She'd bridle the first mount she could cut from the rest and be gone. She hadn't paid careful attention to the placement of sentries on her way in. It would be tricky business slipping through, but then they were concentrating on trouble sneaking in, not out. If she led the horse on foot until free of the canyon, she shouldn't have any problem getting home. She never got lost

by following Harmon's directions. Head toward the sunset
and don't fall in the Rio Grande.

"Sarah?"

The soft feminine whisper distracted her. She paused while
Chonita slipped out of the shadows. The young woman
looked anxious, even fearful.

"What is it, Chonita? What's wrong?"

"Did you know your man was a ranger?"

Sarah froze inside. If Chonita knew . . . "That's ridiculous."

"The others, they not think so. They mean to hang him,
but first I think they torture him plenty to see what he has
learned and told to others."

"Where is he?"

"They have him by the fire," she said with a dreadful
meaning.

Sarah refused to give way to the terror shaking through her
insides. Panic wouldn't help anyone. Billy needed her to be
clear-headed and thinking. She looked to the other woman
with a desperate calm. "Will you help me?"

Chonita drew back, shaking her head. "I have risked much
already. . . ."

"I know. I know. Please. I have to get a horse. You could
come with us. My family will see you are taken care of.
Please, Chonita. Say you will. Life doesn't have to be this
hard."

The woman thought for a moment, then she smiled sadly.
"You are very kind, and I thank you for what you offer. But
no. I cannot leave here. Better I distract the man who guards
the horses for a time, so you can get away."

"You would do that? But they'll know you helped us."

She shrugged eloquently. "What can they do to me? They
have already taken my dignity."

Sarah stepped forward to embrace her. "I won't forget you,
and I know we'll meet again."

Chonita smiled with a faint hope, then urged, "We must
hurry. Wait until we are gone for a few minutes."

Sarah didn't understand at first. Then she watched Chonita
sashay up to the guard, who was bored and restless at his post

and eager for the attentions of a soft woman. She could hear Chonita's husky laugh and watched her take the man's hand, leading him off into the underbrush. She waited for a minute, then darted to the corral, blessing the Mexican woman for her courage and praying their luck would hold out.

Billy Cooper wouldn't trade two cents for his luck. His gaze was riveted to the glowing tip of the stick in Ray Gant's hand. He could feel the smoldering heat and anticipated as impassively as possible the pain to come.

"How long you been with the rangers, Billy?"

"Ray, I sure as hell don't know what you're—"

The sudden smash of his fist sent agony exploding through his cheek. He staggered, but the men securing his arms held him up.

"C'mon, Billy. Don't be bothering us with lies. We know it's true."

Billy touched the inside of his cheek with his tongue, tasting blood. "Honest to God, Ray, I don't know who would have told you such a thing."

"No, of course you don't. That's how we happened to find it out. Now, then, why don't you tell us how much you've told them so's I can kill you quick."

"That'd be right nice of you, Ray," Billy drawled out with all the bravado he could muster. "You might as well hang me and spare yourself breaking a sweat, 'cause I'm not telling you anything."

"Dammit, kid, I liked you. Don't make me turn your pretty face into something that will have the ladies looking the other way. Not that you'll be looking back when I'm through."

The white-hot tip came so close Billy could swear his eyelashes were singed, but he didn't attempt to pull back. His voice was low and steady. "Do what you have to, Ray." He took a deep breath, preparing for hell. If he was going to die, he was determined to do it as well as he could.

Sarah.

The thought hit him so hard, he gasped. God, what would happen to her once they'd killed him?

But Sarah Bass had no intention of letting anyone kill Billy Cooper. Unless, of course, it was her.

When she stampeded close to fifty head of horses right through the middle of their camp, the outlaws were just as startled as she'd hoped they'd be. Torturing a ranger was the last thing on their minds, with all that horseflesh bearing down on top of them. There was a moment of confusion, then some men broke and ran while others attempted to wave off and recapture their mounts.

Sarah rode low, half off the side of her horse the way Harm had taught her when she was young and it was a game. But it wasn't a game to her now. She guided the animal with pressure from her knees, driving him straight toward Billy. She yelled his name above the hubbub of thundering hooves and shouting men, and she saw his head jerk toward her. When she put out her hand, Sarah knew a second of complete satisfaction when his palm clapped about her wrist and she was hauling him up behind her.

"Stay low," she hollered back at him, but she didn't need to tell him, for right about then, the outlaws got to noticing that someone was making off with their prisoner.

Shots whined past them as they rode hard, keeping well inside the body of racing horses that poured down through the canyon. They made a difficult target beneath the glow of the moon and the surge of the herd. And that's what Sarah had counted on.

But she hadn't counted on a lucky shot that just happened to find her in the dark.

It felt as though someone had smacked her in the side with a shovel. She pitched forward against the horse's neck, everything going numb and black at once. The fear of falling from the horse and under the hooves of those that ran alongside flashed through her.

"Billy—Billy, take the reins," she cried out as they dropped from her fingers. She felt his arms cinch up around her as he grabbed for them.

"Sarah?"

"Keep going. Keep going. I'm fine." And she kicked back her heels as hard as she could, driving the animal on with the thud of them against its hide. That was all she remembered.

"Sarah?" Panic leapt through him when she sagged back against him. It was too dark to see anything, but the feel of wetness on her side told him all he had to know. "Oh, God. No. Sarah, you hang on, you hear me! Hang on!"

He couldn't stop. She was right about that. They had to put a considerable distance between them and the outlaws, who'd be out for blood as soon as they rounded up their mounts. All he could do was keep her upright and keep the horse going full out until the darkness was so complete, it was more of a danger to push on than to wait out the dawn. Though he'd have preferred to ride all the way to Terlingua, it would have been foolish to continue blind. Their pursuers couldn't track them at night and he'd been careful to keep off the main trails. After a half hour of winding through a maze of arroyos and scrub thickets, Billy started looking for a place to pull up. He couldn't afford to go any farther until he'd checked Sarah's injury.

She was coming around as he reined in the lathered horse. Soft moans accompanied her every breath. He was quick about easing her down to the hard ground, then he efficiently saw to the care and protection of their horse. By the time he'd built a small fire, she was tossing in agitation, calling for him.

"Billy? Billy, where are we?"

He crouched down beside her and put on his best smile. "Still in the mountains. We'll have to wait it out until morning, but I think we've got a big enough lead on them. Hey, that was one helluva rescue."

Her smile was weak. "You think so?"

"Better than hanging."

Her expression suddenly sobered. He was about to ask if she was in terrible pain, when she demanded, "Are you all right?"

"Me?" He was astounded. "I—I'm fine. I'm the one who needs to be asking you that."

"It hurts," she confided with a panting brevity.

"Where does it hurt?"

"My ears."

"Your . . . ears?"

"The earrings . . . take them out."

"Okay. Hold still a second." It took some doing to ease the wires from her swollen earlobes and to untangle the beads from her hair.

"I want to keep them," she insisted. "They're important to me."

"All right. I'll put them right here in my pocket for safe-keeping."

Her fingers caught at his sleeve and his own were quick to cover them in a reassuring squeeze. Her knees were shaking and shifting restlessly, her breath coming in fast, shallow gasps.

"Billy, it hurts. It hurts something fierce every time I breath." She closed her eyes tight and wetness leaked from their corners, streaking down to mingle in her hair. "I'm sorry. I'm sorry. I don't mean to cry about it."

"That's all right." His big hand brushed the hair back from her brow in a soothing gesture. "I'm gonna have to take a look-see, all right? I'll be as careful as I can. I'll try not to hurt you."

She gave a jerky nod and her breathing quickened to a fluttery tempo.

Slowly, he drew the colorful blouse from the waistband of her skirt and unbuttoned it to lay bare the wound. To his surprise, when he opened the blouse, he was laying bare everything. He'd expected her to have something on under it, but there was nothing but Sarah, all smooth tawny skin, her breasts small, taut, and beautiful, just right for the cup of a man's hand. And his was itching to see how perfect that fit would be.

"Billy?"

"Ummm?"

"There's not that much to see."

Her soft chiding tone reminded him to exhale. He grinned at her. "Just pretend I'm your big brother."

"Billy?"

"What?"

"If Jack looked at me the way you are, I'd worry."

"Guess you're right about that. I'm gonna have to move you a bit, so hang on." She gave a short outcry, then clamped her lips together to hold any further sound while he examined her wound. She was able to breathe again when he laid her flat.

"How—how bad is it?"

"The bullet took a ricochet off your ribs. Think one or two of 'em might be broke, but probably saved your life. Bullet's still in there. It's not deep, but I don't have anything to dig it out with. For now, best I can do is bind you up real good to keep anything from shifting around in there 'til we can get you to the doc in Terlingua. Think I can charm you outta one of your petticoats to use as bandaging?"

"You already did once. Guess another time won't matter much."

She sounded too cynical for him to come back with any clever comment. He reached up under her shirt, trying to ignore the feel of sleek bared legs, and gently wrestled down one of the ruffled underskirts. The bottom of it was already ragged from the strips she'd torn to bind his arm. He finished the shredding, then, as carefully as he could, eased her upright so he could circle her damaged rib cage with a snug linen wrap. He struggled to shut out her soft, plaintive cries of discomfort, because they worked with a surprising fierceness upon the perimeters of his heart.

When he was done she was limp and silent, her head lolling, her eyes closed. Billy settled her back upon the ground and rebuttoned her blouse over the bulky dressing, resisting the temptation to sample the beckoning curves he covered. The wound wasn't life threatening but he still worried. She'd lost a lot of blood and they had a rough distance to travel. He was no doctor. He didn't know how badly her ribs were broken or whether there was the possibility of one puncturing a lung, but he knew better than to dwell on it. They couldn't stay where they were. The threat of Ray Gant was of a much more fatal nature. He could give her until dawn to rest up, then they'd have to be on their way again.

Sarah was tough. She'd make it. He couldn't allow himself to doubt that.

"Damn fool girl. Never should have come after me," he muttered angrily as he fed the fire with what he managed to scrounge from the selfish landscape. But if she hadn't come after him, he'd be screaming a tune for Ray Gant about now.

It was getting cold. He couldn't risk a bigger fire, but Sarah was shivering fitfully upon the rapidly cooling Texas ground. He shrugged out of his duster and draped it over her. It wasn't much but it was the best he could do with what they had, and what they had was damn little. No food or water, and not so much as a toothpick between them to wield in their defense. There hadn't exactly been time to pack for the trip. He paced the edge of brightness cast about their sad little camp, rubbing his shirtsleeves for warmth. His arm was aching, his stomach was growling, and he would have given just about anything for a set of good springs and a fat quilt. He was so tired and edgy, he was going in circles in both body and mind. Time to shut down for a few hours or he'd be good for nothing when he was called upon to count for something. But the notion of curling up beside Sarah kept him on his feet and restless in his wandering.

So many things he'd change if he could. He never would have let Sarah stay in the outlaw camp. Hell, he'd never have kissed her all those years ago! And he'd never have betrayed his best friend's trust by laying with his little sister. But he'd enjoyed the pretense, he'd enjoyed the kiss, and he'd loved the feel of her all hot and snug about him. And that was the hell of it.

Jack Bass was the most decent man he'd ever known—honest, loyal, dependable, and caring. If he could aspire to any kind of greatness, it would be to walk on that same path. Jack's faith in him when he was just a green kid gave him his

career boost in the rangers, and he'd sworn that his then sergeant and now lieutenant would never have cause to regret it.
He'd worked to be an exemplary ranger, using Jack as his
model. He wanted to make a stand for law and Texas, and he
wanted to make that stand beside Sarah's older brother.

How was he going to do that now when he hadn't been
able to keep her safe and out of harm's way? He'd suffered
from poor judgment and from a lack of self-control. He could
say it was Sarah, that she'd somehow derailed his thinking,
but that excuse wouldn't hold water when Jack was through
peppering it with buckshot. And if for some reason she didn't
make it back to her family safe and sound, he might as well
shoot himself right then and there and save the Basses the
trouble and the cost of the bullet.

Sarah's low moaning cry shook him from his brooding
thoughts. He went to her side and knelt down, discouraged
by the feel of fever scorching her brow. What was he going
to do if she took a turn for the worst? How could he ever forgive himself if anything happened to her? How could he go
on without the hope of her in his future?

For years, since that explosive kiss in Harm Bass's backyard, all he'd dreamed of was being half the ranger Jack Bass
was so he could marry Jack's sister.

Sarah gave a murmur of discomfort, and when he leaned
close to tuck his coat about her trembling form, she caught
onto his arm and hugged it tight, pulling him across her for
a blanketing warm. He felt her shivering and his resistance
gave without a whimper.

"Cold, huh? Me, to. Guess it couldn't hurt for me to
stretch on out beside you."

He did so, easing his sound arm beneath her head and
shoulders and curving the other carefully about her middle.
She burrowed in against his side without ever opening her
eyes. His will gave another reluctant notch. She felt good, a
neat fit along the longer contours of his frame. Without realizing it, he was stroking her hair, pressing soft kisses against
her warm brow until there was nothing left inside him to object to the swell of tender feeling.

"You're gonna be just fine, Sarah. Just fine. I won't let any-thing happen to you. You want to know why? I'll tell you. One of these days, years down the line, I might just up and decide to quit rangering, and if I do, I'm gonna want you there to be my wife. What do you think about that, huh? I might just get crazy enough in my settled old age to want a whole passel of kids."

He held her close and stared up at the stars, thinking of it, not believing it would ever happen but liking to imagine it. Sarah groaned quietly and shifted to a more comfortable curve against him.

"How many?" she mumbled.

Her groggy question startled him. He hadn't thought she was awake. "How many what?"

"How many kids do you want us to have?"

He picked a large number at random, thinking to scare her off. "Six."

"Okay." She sighed and nudged her cheek within the hol-low of his shoulder.

" 'Course, there ain't much chance of that happening, not once your Uncle Harmon makes a hatband outta my hide."

He felt her smile. "I won't let him."

"Good luck."

"Uncle Harmon's just a sweetheart once you get to know him well."

"I don't think he's gonna want to know me all that well."

"Are you scared of him?" She sounded surprised.

"Hell, anyone with half a brain is scared of him." But Billy was smiling, too, as he planted a kiss on the top of her head. "I hope you realize that if you mention any of this conversa-tion tomorrow, I'm gonna tell you that you imagined it all while delirious."

"Am I, or did you ask if I'd marry you?"

"You're plumb outta your head. I'm not the marrying kind."

"We could skip the marrying and just have the kids."

He laughed softly. "Now, there's a real sensible notion. How many kids do you think we could make between us outta wedlock before your uncle started carving off parts of me that I'm right fond of?"

She gave another sleepy sigh and murmured, "I love you, Billy, and I'd like to give you those kids."

He went completely still. He swore even his heart stopped.

Then Sarah chuckled and kissed his throat. " 'Course, you realize if you mention this in the morning, I'm gonna deny it and say I was delirious at the time."

That made his heart start up again but it was a cautious rhythm. He waited a long while but Sarah said nothing more. She was listless and burning up with fever. Maybe she'd been out of her head when she said it.

He hoped so.

He didn't dare believe it was true.

He must have fallen asleep at some time during the night, once Sarah was resting more quietly in his arms. He was aware of a pale brightness against his closed eyelids when wakefulness returned. Billy knew he should arise and get them going; but Sarah felt so good pressed against him, and he was so sore and tired.

And then thoughts of sleep scattered in an instant at the cold wedge of a rifle bore beneath his Adam's apple, followed by an even colder drawl.

"If you got any last words, you'd best be saying 'em now."

Chapter Seven

"She's been gone almost a week and I've been going out of my mind."

"Why didn't you say something sooner, Becky?" Harmon Bass asked as he watched his half sister pace the porch of her adobe ranch house.

He'd been waiting all evening for her to explain the reason for calling his family over for dinner. Not that he didn't appreciate a meal from other than his wife's kitchen. Amanda Bass was very lucky to have married a man who would eat dog, horse, or snake without complaint. Still, some of the things she served him gave Harmon a good long pause before he could raise a fork. No invitation for supper elsewhere was ever turned down. He was hoping his daughters would learn the difference between eating for the sake of survival and matrimonial harmony, and simply enjoying good cooking. He was hoping a little of his sister's or his nephew's wife's talent at the stove would rub off on his girls so he could approach his table without apprehension.

He hadn't been able to thoroughly appreciate this night's meal because he could feel something was preying on Rebecca's mind. She didn't come right out with it. She played the gracious hostess, saw everyone fed and sent from the table full, then hedged around it some more until finally he carried his cup of coffee outside and waited for her to join him. Which she did, almost at once. And now he understood her worry.

Rebecca sighed deeply and rubbed the faded calico sleeves of her gown. "Oh, Harmon, you know Sarah. Next to her, her brothers are souls of sensibility. She's—she's—"

"Like me," he supplied.

She gave him a slight smile. "She gets her independence from you. I've never seen a girl so sure and set on having things her way."

He smiled, too. "Have you looked at Leisha lately?"

Harm's nine-year-old daughter was as sober and self-sufficient as most of Texas's hard-packed men and twice as dangerous.

"But Leisha's got a level head. She'll never give you any cause for worry that I've been dealing with. Sarah . . . she's . . . I don't know . . . flighty."

"Musta' learned that from Amanda," Harm said fondly. "Sarah's like a mountain wind . . . all quick and playful and free. She makes the soul feel good."

"She's a tornado," Rebecca corrected without a trace of her brother's romanticizing. "Always whirling around in unpredictable directions."

"She's a fine girl, Becky. A good girl. What's got you so upset? The fact that she's late getting home, or the reason she might be staying away?"

Rebecca fell silent and he knew he'd hit on it. Slowly, he moved across the porch to ease his arms around her. The fact that she clutched at him was an alarming sign.

"What's wrong, *silah?*"

"I don't know what I'm going to do with her, Harmon. She takes nothing seriously. She takes foolish chances. She refuses to believe that there are things out there that can . . . hurt her. She's not careful."

"Perhaps you are being too careful. Perhaps there aren't as many things out there that can hurt her as you believe."

She turned out of his embrace, facing him with a dire expression. "But you and I both know better than that. Or have you forgotten?"

"No," he told her softly. "I forget nothing. I'll spend the rest of my life being careful and not taking chances. But I wish I could take things less seriously than I do. It'd make life more of a joy to live, don't you think? Not that I'm complaining about what I got. But if I was seventeen again and lived a life as good and clean as Sarah, I'd want to believe nothing could hurt me. Maybe you shouldn't tell her she's wrong."

"But she doesn't remember, Harmon. She's never seen how bad life can be."

"Does she have to know? Wouldn't you rather she trust in her heart and sleep nights with a peaceful mind? Or do you want her to be like us?" He let that hang there between them for a long moment, then said, "Let her be free, Becky. Don't saddle her with our ghosts."

"But how is she going to protect herself?"

"That's what she has us for. I'd never let anything happen to any of them, Becky. I love those kids like they were my own—Jack, Sidney, Jeffrey, Sarah . . . all of 'em. I'll gladly sleep with my nightmares so they won't have to suffer them."

Her arms stole about him, pulling him in tight. "I know you would and you have, haven't you?"

"You've been a good mama to those kids, Becky. Trust 'em to turn out fine. Let 'em take their own steps. They can't if you've got their ankles hobbled together. You keep 'em tethered down and they're going to bolt the first chance they get."

"Do you think that's what she's done?"

"Sarah?" He sounded surprised. "No, I don't. She might pull on the rope, but she's not ready to break loose yet. She's not the kind to run away."

"Then where is she, Harmon?"

That quiet question trembled with anxiety.

"I'll find out."

Rebecca went limp with relief at his answer. After a moment, she kissed his jaw and he was immediately squirming away. His Apache reserve made such displays uncomfortable for him to endure. She let him go. "I'd be grateful, Harmon. I was going to send Jack out after her, but he's leading his company over in Presidio and Emily wasn't sure when he'd be back. I don't want to wait any longer . . . not knowing."

"I'll go after her, Becky. Soon as I see my family home safe."

"Bring her back, Harmon. Jack has the state of Texas, Sidney has school, Jeffrey's Will's boy. Sarah was supposed to be mine. Maybe it's not too late to change that."

"It's never too late until you're starting to regret. I'll fetch her for you."

And when Harmon Bass gave his word, one could bet it was as good as done.

Rebecca stood out on the porch watching her brother and his family ride off toward his ranch at Blue Creek. For the first time in days, her mind was at peace. She heard the sound of her husband approaching, his crutches planting firm on the porchboards and the swish of his boots sliding through them. She waited until he came up beside her to speak.

"He's going to find Sarah."

Will Bass had no response. She didn't push the issue, knowing how it rankled him to be helpless in these situations. No man wanted to admit he couldn't keep his own daughter safe.

"Will, why wouldn't you let me tell him about the threats? He could help."

"Because it's not his business." The ex-ranger's voice was sharp with pride and frustration. "I can take care of things here. We don't have to run to Harm every time we have a problem. I don't want him involved. Harm tends to draw his own kind of trouble and I've had enough of him bringing it to my door."

"Will, how can you say such a thing?"

"Because it's true. If I could sit a horse, don't you think I'd be going after our girl?"

"I know you would."

"Well, I don't need Harm to hold my hand in my own house. I've dealt with this kind of intimidation enough to know how to handle it. Once we make it plain we're not going to be bullied, they'll leave us be. They prey on the weak, like coyotes. Bringing in Harm or Jack would just make it worse. They've both gone their own ways. If you don't trust me, Becca, you can just go on over and live with either of them."

"That's not what I want, Will, and you know it. My place is here with you. If you say there's nothing to worry about, I won't worry."

But as she stood nestled into his side, she was wishing she'd brought it up to her brother. Will Bass wasn't the kind of man anyone could push around, even on his crutches. But when it came to the kind of fight that involved her family, she'd prefer Harm's Apache stealth to her husband's bold bravado.

And as soon as Harm returned, she made up her mind to tell him everything.

It took Harm a day and a half to get to Marathon. It took half of the first day for the warmth of his wife's kiss to wear off, then he was able settle down into the basic thought patterns of what he was deep inside. He rode hard, partly because he had an Apache's disdain for the care of his horse and partly because of what he hadn't confided to his sister or his wife. He was worried about Sarah. It wasn't anything he knew for a fact. He knew she was kind of reckless but not wild. She was impulsive but not thoughtless. She would never give her family cause for alarm without reason. And that reason had his instincts quivering with an inner agitation.

Jack had always been his favorite of his sister's children. That was no secret, even though he'd always tried to love them equally with his time and attention. But Sarah had made a special place in his heart. She had Amanda's talent for reducing him to mush instead of brain. All it took was a baleful look in her big brown eyes, and he might as well give up any thoughts of holding to a rightful irritation.

Sarah was Amanda all over again, and thinking of Amanda at seventeen was enough to put him into a panic. Never had he met such a forward-acting, backward-thinking woman. If he hadn't fallen so crazily in love with her, he'd probably have left her out in the desert where only an occasional coyote would be annoyed by her ceaseless chatter. There was no arguing his wife's influence over the girl. Sarah had practically grown up at his house. Harm hadn't minded it, but he had wondered why the girl was more attached to Amanda and Emily than to her own mother. Of course he knew better than to try to figure out why a woman did anything. Sarah was more like Amanda's child than like Rebecca's. She had none of her mother's sober caution and all of her aunt's willful spirit. But they were different, too.

At seventeen, Amanda had had a solid grasp on how hard life could be. It wasn't the same rough existence he'd led, not in her fancy eastern cities, but it was emotionally tough. Her parents had died when she was seven, and she'd taken responsibility for her brother and her fortune amid a host of scheming relatives. They'd hurt her and there were times he wished the trip to New York weren't quite so far. He'd have liked to teach his wife's family a thing or two about manners.

For a woman with no common sense, she'd always impressed him with her moral maturity. She had a soul like the foothills of Texas: widespread and strong enough to support anything. And for over ten years, she'd supported him with a stability none would have guessed a silly rich New York schoolgirl could possess. Sarah was strong, too, but her strength was in knowledge, not in experience. She was savvy but not cynical, and that trusting innocence was going to get her into a trouble from which her talents might not be able to free her. And that's why he hurried. Because he wanted her to have what he and his sister had been denied: the chance to grow up safely.

He found out about the train robbery at the station in Marathon and about Sarah from a young salesman by the name of Herbert Blankenship, who was waiting for a new shipment of samples to arrive. His niece had made a definite impression on Blankenship. And listening to him tell of Sarah's response to the robbers had Harm alerted. Something was wrong with the way he was telling it. Sarah was full of vinegar, but she was too intelligent to sound off to a bunch of hard-edged criminals. Not for no reason. Again, that reason plagued him as he rode out of Marathon on a fresh horse. There'd been nothing but lather left of his.

Harm didn't need to look for sign. He knew where he was

going. To the Chisos. Back into the Bend after the outlaws. Where he had no doubt that Sarah had gone before him.

But why?

He knew why the minute he came upon a small camp still wreathed in the cool mists of dawn. And he wasn't pleased to discover his sister had worked herself into a frenzy and he'd fretted his nerves raw while little Sarah Bass had been cozied up in the blankets with some fresh-faced kid.

His greeting was a straightforward prod from the business end of his carbine, and the kid looked up with an expression so stark, Harm guessed he'd have rather found the devil and his denizens standing over him than one very tired and testy uncle, who was more than ready to let the hammer drop.

"H—howdy, Mr. Bass. This ain't what it looks."

"You trying to tell me I can't trust what I'm seeing with my own eyes? Is that my niece? Are them your britches she's got her hand tucked into?"

Billy glanced down in surprise to find that Sarah had indeed nudged her hand under the band of his denims, her palms resting against the flat of his abdomen for warmth. He gripped her wrist and removed her damning touch. Hell, the man might as well have come upon them naked! There was no reasoning with the cold circle of metal pressed into his throat or with the cold blue steel of Harm Bass's gaze as it pinned him to the ground.

"I'm William T. Cooper, sir. I ride with Jack and the rangers."

"I know who you are. What I want to know is what you're doing with my niece."

"Nothing."

He must have sounded unconvincing, because the hammer clicked back on Harm's carbine. "Try again."

That was it. Billy had had enough. One hell of a day behind him and a short future staring him in the eye. What did he have to lose? He'd probably feel a whole lot better if Harm Bass blew his fool head off!

"Less you're gonna shoot me right now, get that thing outta my face. I haven't had so much as a cup of coffee, and

I'm in no mood to argue with Sarah's relatives over what's none of their business."

Harm's eyes narrowed into flinty slits. "Come again?"

Cautiously, Billy pushed the rifle muzzle away. Harm took a step back to let him breathe easier. He wasn't going to kill him outright, but that didn't mean he'd refrain from gutting him out when he'd heard the whole story. Harm Bass made him plenty nervous. And at the moment, because he was hurting so bad and was so worried over Sarah, the stoic tracker made him plenty angry, too. Billy sat up, refusing to go to his Maker flat on his back and begging.

"You can shoot me now, or we can just wait around and let some of my friends finish the job they started."

Harm was looking at his bloodied sleeve. He gave it a poke with the end of his rifle barrel and Billy gritted his teeth. "What happened?"

About then, Sarah began to stir. She muttered Billy's name in a husky, sleep-warmed voice and kneaded his shirtfront with her fingers. Billy could anticipate Harm Bass's bullet ventilating his skull. The man had a face that could put caution into a grizzly bear.

"Talk fast," came his drawling growl.

"I'll fill you on all the details you'd ever want to know as soon as I see that she's all right."

Harm tensed up. "What's wrong with her?"

"A taste of lead poisoning."

The carbine dropped, forgotten, from Harm's hand. It was as if Billy Cooper had fallen off the face of the earth as he knelt down beside his niece. He put his palm to her flushed cheek, concerned by the scorch of her skin.

"Sarah? *Shijii?*"

Her eyes flickered open, glowing hot with fever, glimmering with a second of recognition. "Uncle Harmon."

"Shhhh. It's all right, little girl. I'm here to see to you."

"Billy?"

Defying Harm's severing glare, Billy took up her hand. "Right here. How you feeling?"

"Not too good. Don't shoot him, Uncle Harm. It's not his fault."

Billy gave a wry smile. So she'd been sincere about saving him from her uncle's wrath. But right now as Harm Bass's gaze lifted to demand an accounting from him, he wouldn't give his survival rate any kind of odds at all. Because it was spill all or have the man kill him on the spot, Billy spilled it. He told of his secret work with the rangers and of Sarah's misguided attempt to save him from a life of crime.

That made Harm smile. Billy didn't know he was thinking of another impetuous seventeen-year-old who'd done pretty much the same thing. Out of love. Harm's expression sobered quick as he looked between his niece and the handsome young ranger. And he didn't like the conclusion he drew.

Billy had gotten to the telling of Sarah's rescue, wisely leaving out the details of their rather unfortunate union at the creek. He'd no doubt Harm would kill him for that.

"She took a stray bullet in the side. Broke a rib or two, I think, and is fevered up. I was taking her to the doctor in Terlingua."

Harm was unbuttoning her blouse.

"Ummmm, Mr. Bass—Mr. Bass, she's not wearing any—"

Harm tossed back the edges of the gaudy shirt. His impassive gaze took in the wrapping and the smooth, bare skin above it, and his stare lifted to Billy with lethal consequence.

"Have you touched her?"

There was dying ugly in that cold question. Billy took a breath. What could he say that wasn't a lie that wouldn't get him killed?

Again, Sarah came to his rescue. "Oh, for heaven's sake, Uncle Harm," she moaned in a querulous tone. "He promised to treat me like he was my big brother." What she didn't say was how unsuccessful he'd been at it, but Harm was momentarily appeased. He shrugged out of his shirt, laying it in a modest drape across her shoulders and upper torso. Then he got out his knife and, with just a single smooth pull, peeled back the wrapping Billy had applied.

"Be brave, little girl."

He didn't give her much choice as he began to carefully check her wound. Sarah's fingers knotted up in his shirt and her eyes squeezed tight, but she didn't so much as whimper. When he was done, Harm's big hand stroked across her wet brow and her eyes opened.

"Sarah, I'm gonna take that bullet out. It'll be safer than traveling with it bouncing around in there. Okay?"

She looked up at him and nodded without hesitation, trusting his judgment, trusting him.

"Wait a minute," Billy put in tensely. "You can't just go chopping around. Leave it for a doctor. We got outlaws coming down behind us."

"Boy, them outlaws are busy packing up and moving on before you get to telling the rangers what you know. They probably figure they can track you down and kill you later. They're gonna be thinking about saving their own hides first. That's the nature of the animal. As for what I'm gonna do, who asked you?" And with that, he shoved the blade of his knife into the soft coals of their fire.

Billy looked from that wicked knife to Sarah's sweat-dappled face, and reason gave way before anxiety. "I'm not going to let you do this."

Harm blinked. "You're not going to *let* me?"

"Stop it, you two," Sarah snapped, then her soft moan distracted them both from their argument. "Billy?" She reached out her hand and he scooped it up in both of his. "Billy, you let Uncle Harm do what he has to. He's not going to hurt me. He's probably taken out more bullets than you've put in folks. Isn't that right, Uncle Harm?"

"That's right, little girl. I'll see it's done quick and clean." He glanced around. "I'll just get something for the pain if I can find what I need."

Billy watched him hunt amongst the scrubs for a certain plant. Then he ground it between two stones and mixed the powder with water from his canteen.

"Drink," he told her. She did. Then she closed her eyes, too sick with hurting to care about how strangely territorial both men were acting.

Billy was too riled to consider how strange it was. He
didn't weigh the fact that Sarah was Harm's family and that
her uncle had the right to do just about anything he pleased.
He only knew how much he suddenly resented the other man
stepping in and taking over the young woman's care. He
didn't like being pushed aside. He didn't like the total confidence that shone in the girl's dark eyes when regarding her
uncle. He hadn't been able to calm her like that.

But then, he wasn't a living legend, either.

"Cook us up some coffee while we're waiting. The makings
are on my saddle."

Harm never glanced at him when giving that brusque order.
It would have been foolish to disobey for pride's sake, so Billy
rose and saw to it. He needed coffee. He needed whiskey. He
needed whatever it was Harm had put in that water that made
Sarah's gaze grow so soft and dreamy. His own arm ached all
the way to the fingertips and worry was gnawing on his insides.
Worry over Sarah, over whether Ray Gant was breathing down
their necks hot for vengeance. Worry over what making love to
Sarah Bass was going to mean in the long run.

"Uncle Harmon, am I going to be all right?" Sarah's stoic
front was slipping. She'd never have let Billy know she was
afraid of anything, but she didn't mind her uncle seeing her
fright. And she didn't worry that he would sugarcoat the truth
just to ease her mind. He never lied.

"Why, sure. I'd never let anything happen to you. You
know that." He smiled, and the tenderness of that gesture
melted away her fears.

"Did Mama send you out after me?"

"She was . . . concerned when you didn't come home or
leave some word of where you were." His tone was too
smooth for her to tell if it contained censure, but she already
felt guilty. If her mother was scared enough to sic Harm on
her trail, she had plenty about which to feel ashamed.

"I'm sorry, Uncle Harm. I know it was a stupid thing to
do. I guess I didn't think."

"Shhh. Don't fret on it now." His knuckles rubbed down

the heated flush of her cheek. "You've got to stop listening to your Aunt Amanda."

She glanced over to where the blade of his knife was glowing in the embers. The sight blurred, doubled, redoubled, and she blinked to clear her vision. An odd sensation of weightlessness was seeping down her limbs, lifting her out of her twist of discomfort with an increasing disassociation.

"Uncle Harm, I feel real strange." Alarm edged her voice and he was quick to reassure her.

"That's all right. It's the peyote. The Mexicans and Apache use it to bring down fevers. You should be getting sleepy."

"I don't want to sleep."

"Just rest then. And trust me."

"I do."

"I ever tell you when your aunt decided she was in love with me?"

Sarah shook her head. She liked it when he talked about Amanda. It softened his features in a way nothing else could. He was a marvelous-looking man, and when she was younger, she'd been crazy about him. Before Amanda had come along and snatched up his heart, her childish fantasy had been to grow up and marry him herself. Of course, that dream faded with maturity, but she still liked admiring him with her eyes and listening to his drawling voice.

"Well, just after she'd hired me on to find her brother, we came across a bunch of cow thieves, and Amanda, being Amanda, wouldn't listen to what I told her and ended up getting her backside peppered with buckshot. Had to hold her on my lap and pick every one of them pellets out."

"No!" Sarah grinned, imagining it. She was beginning to feel decidedly light-headed. "She never told me that."

"It's not one of her favorite recollections. Guess she figured if she could trust me with her fanny, I was the right kind of fellow to fall in love with."

He didn't tell her the fanny involved wasn't Amanda's but rather his, and the way his wet Levi's had clung to it and the strong line of his legs. Amanda had taken one look and fallen madly in lust with him. Of course a man didn't want to tell anyone his wife had tipped head over heels because of the way his denims fit him. In fact, he mused with a small smile, Amanda still was partial to grabbing on to his back pockets for a squeeze.

"Here's your coffee."

Billy thrust the tin at Harm and sipped his own, chafing with restlessness and agitation. Instead of being grateful to pass off the responsibility, he envied the other man's composure and the fondness he saw in Sarah's eyes when she looked up at him. Why would she look at him that way? What had he done to deserve it? What had he given her besides a bunch of slick words and a broken vow to keep her safe? She'd taken a bullet to save him and now it was Harm she was looking to for help. He couldn't blame her.

Finishing his coffee, Harm set the cup aside and leaned down to palm the side of Sarah's face. "Hey there, little girl, how you doing?"

She gave him a silly smile. "Fine. I love you, Uncle Harmon. You know when I was little, I wanted to grow up and marry you."

"That so?" His smile was tolerant, his words gentle. "I'm right flattered to hear that, but seeing as how I'm twice your age and your mama's brother, and Ammy'd hunt me down and skin me out if I was to run off with another woman, especially a young, pretty one like you, you'd best be looking for someone else to pin your fancy to."

"Already found him," she murmured groggily as her eyes slipped shut.

Billy held his breath.

Then she smiled again and muttered, "But I was outta my head at the time." Then she was still.

Harm reached for his knife. "Let's get this done and get her home." He looked up at Billy. "You grab on to her, hold her down, and hold her tight. It's still going to hurt her plenty and I don't want her jumping around."

Finishing the rest of his coffee in a single gulp, Billy knelt at Sarah's head, scooting his knees up on either side of and bracing his forearms above her breasts. She stirred languidly, touching his arms, rubbing them leisurely in her daze of dreams.

"Go ahead," Billy said grimly. "I got her. She's about out of it."

The instant Harm went after the bullet, Sarah's fingers clamped down on Billy's arm, bruising flesh and muscle. While she didn't open her eyes, her breath labored in quick, jerky pants.

"Don't let her move," Harm warned, never looking up from what he was doing. Billy didn't want to watch him.

Instead, Billy bent down low over her until his lips brushed her hot brow. Her head stopped tossing and she seemed to listen as he whispered, "Still want those six kids?"

"Not right now," she whimpered, fingers biting deeper into the meat of his arms.

"Which do you want first, boy or girl?"

"Boys first, then the girls to pick up after 'em . . . oh, Billy!"

"Hang on, baby. Hang on. I know it hurts but you can't go moving around. Hold on to me. That's it. Hold tight. Just think, now you'll have as pretty a set of scars as any of the rest of your family."

Sarah started to smile, as if pleased by the thought. Then abruptly she gasped, stiffening up as he fought to contain her movements. Finally, she went totally limp.

"Sarah?" Panic slammed through him like a freight train as he looked down upon her pale face.

"Got it," Harm announced softly. "Wish I knew who put this in her. I'd be making him regret it real bad."

Once he was assured her unconsciousness was natural, not permanent, Billy straightened, his heart chugging in a hurtful rhythm. He glanced at Harm and found the hard-eyed part-Apache staring at him through eyes as unforgiving as the bullet nestled in his palm.

He froze up solid as Harm concluded, "The same way I'd deal with anyone who brought her pain."

And he slowly, with all the deadly meaning in the world, he wiped his blade upon one taut pant leg.

Chapter Eight

Sarah rode back to Terlingua bundled in front of Harm on his saddle. She never once stirred back to consciousness from within the cradle of her uncle's arms as her head bobbed gently against his shoulder. Whether it was the peyote or the pain that kept her under, she managed to make the trip a lot easier than did Billy Cooper.

He trailed behind in disgrace. Harm never said as much to him, but he figured the man held him in a one-rung-up-from-a-dog contempt. And if that was what Harm thought, how would Jack take the news of what had happened to his little sister? That was worrying Billy more than reporting his falling out with Gant and his men.

The ranger barracks under Jack Bass's command were situated about three miles outside the dusty West Texas town of Terlingua. It wasn't much to look at, just a line of tents and simple cabins leading up to the Basses' front door. Jack, his wife, and children lived in a squat adobe building that Emily had made into a home, filling it with loving touches—her own son, Kenitay, and Carson, a son made between her and Jack. And it was obvious as she came out onto the shaded porch, one hand propped upon the swell of her belly, the other raised to block out the sun, that another was on the way.

"Harmon, Billy. Is that Sarah you've got there?" Concern edged out her smile of welcome. "What's happened? Bring her inside."

Billy swung down quickly and went to reach up for Harm's burden. Cold blue eyes met his for a long second before Harm would surrender her. Then with Sarah held carefully to his chest, Billy strode inside behind Emily.

"Hey, Kenny, how you doing, son? Get your little brother outta the way." He brushed past the two curious boys, carrying his lax armful into Jack and Emily's bedroom.

"Put her down here," Emily ordered as she tossed back the top sheet. No hysteria, no wasted time voicing shock or unnecessary questions. Just right to the point. Emily Bass was a practiced Texas realist. "What are we looking at here, Billy?"

"Bullet wound and broken ribs."

"Kenitay, ride over to Terlingua and fetch Doc Himes fast as you can."

As gently as he could, Billy settled Sarah onto the mattress. Against the stark white linens, she looked so small and fragile. The sight had his heart pounding like crazy. He couldn't force himself to straighten until he'd sampled the soft curve of her cheek with his fingertips. At that light caress, her eyelids flickered open.

"Billy?"

"Right here, baby," he answered soothingly.

"Where's here?" She sounded anxious and disoriented. Her gaze flashed about with no recognition.

"At Jack's. The doctor's on his way, so you just rest easy. Everything's gonna be just fine."

"Don't go!" Her hands groped the air wildly until they caught his and clasped them tight.

"I'll be right here for as long as you need me." He sat on the edge of the bed, aware at once that Harm had come into the room and was filleting him with his razor-sharp stare. "Your Uncle Harm's here. Would you rather he sat with you?" Then he felt absurdly gratified when she shook her head.

"You stay, Billy." Her fingers were kneading his in restless little spasms. "Uncle Harmon?"

He came up behind Billy with his silent glide. The young

ranger felt the hair on the nape of his neck prickle. "What do you need, *shijii*?"

"Would you go tell Mama I'm all right?"

"I'll bring her—"

"No! No, don't bring her here. I—I'm fine. She has enough to do at home without running here to fuss over me. I'm not a baby."

It sounded like a reasonable explanation but Harm didn't believe it for a second. Still, he smiled blandly and said, "No, you're no baby." He looked to Emily. "Where's Jack?"

"He'll be back tonight. I can see to her, Harmon. Tell Rebecca we'll put her up and fuss over her until she's fit to travel."

"I'd be obliged, Emily."

She put her hand on Harm's shoulder and pressed gently. "We'll take good care of her. You go on home. You look worn through. I can feed you first if you want to wait until I get Sarah settled in."

"No, thanks. I'll grab something at Becky's." He nudged by Billy to bend down over Sarah, brushing a light kiss across her hot brow. "You make me proud, little girl. Now, don't make me worry."

The girl smiled up at him weakly. "Thank you, Uncle Harmon. I'm sorry to put you to so much bother."

"No bother," he declared, as if that were really true. Then he straightened and fixed Billy with a look that echoed threat right down to the toes of his boots. Billy didn't back down and Harm begrudgingly respected him for that.

The young ranger had no intention of giving Harm Bass any cause for worry, either. Now that they were under the Basses' roof, he planned to relinquish his responsibility for Sarah as soon as possible and then stay far away. He'd seen the deceivingly slight tracker go after a man with murder in his eye, and he never wanted to be in that precarious position. And more dangerous than that was the way his own emotions were melting down to a dangerously caring consistency as Sarah clutched at his hand. Better get far, far away and fast. Even if he did like the thought of sharing six kids with Sarah Bass.

After Harm had gone, Sarah fell into a fitful state, mumbling in incoherent snatches while gasping for hurtful breaths. The pressure of her fingers never lessened on Billy's hand so he stayed where he was, patient and wrought up tight with a panic that somehow she wasn't going to be all right and it would be his fault and he'd never have those kids for whom he'd begun thinking of names.

When the doctor arrived, he should have seen it as an opportunity to escape from his duty, to slip from the hold she had upon him. That would have been the expected and the smart thing to do, but he couldn't. Because he had to know that she'd be all right. If she called for him, if she needed him, he wanted to be there.

So he waited anxiously in Jack and Emily's front room, absently eating what Emily put in front of him, while all his attention was focused behind that closed door. He'd almost managed to calm himself down, when a small cry of hurt sent him nearly bolting from his chair. It was the gentle restraint of Emily's hands upon his shoulders that kept Billy from pushing himself in where he didn't belong. He sank back down with a reluctant trembling.

"She'll be all right, Billy," Emily assured him. Her palms began a nice firm massage of his tense muscles. But he couldn't relax, he couldn't let go. Everything inside him wanted to be there holding Sarah's hand. Knowing he didn't have the right to demand it made no difference. Wondering why he should feel so desperate was only a vague whisper against the fervor of his agitation.

"Billy, she's going to be fine."

He glanced up then, into the smiling face of his lieutenant's wife. Billy had a mountain of respect for Emily Bass. She was a good, solid-souled woman from a less than perfect past. Which was probably why she always seemed to understand him so well. He'd never had a home of his own or a strong female figure to guide him, but if he had, he'd have wanted what his friend Jack had: a place to live and love in, a wife to adore and attend him, without question, without regret. He didn't envy Jack's possession of her, because his friend had gone through hell to have her and deserved every second of happiness she gave him. But being in this house made him aware of an emptiness he'd never had filled inside him. It was just a small hollow, one he usually overlooked or easily ignored. It couldn't be eased by drink or cards or ranging or even by wicked women. Billy was suddenly very afraid he knew what it would take. And she was in the other room.

What in God's name had he gotten himself into? He didn't need a woman to complicate his life. He didn't need the heartache. He didn't believe for a second that he could ever have what Jack had or Harm had, because they deserved it and he never would. No matter what he did. Even if Sarah had agreed to have his children.

The door to the bedroom opened and Billy shot up from the chair to confront the doctor.

"How is she?"

"Nice piece of work, whoever took that bullet out. Nothing left for me to do but take a few stitches and bind up her ribs. Clean, closed fracture there. Knit up in no time as long as she doesn't do any heavy lifting or the like. Bed rest for a couple of days, then moderate activity when she feels up to it. She won't need to see me again unless she starts running a fever. Then I'll want to take another look."

Billy didn't listen to the rest as he pushed by to get to Sarah's bedside. She was tucked in beneath that pure white sheet and her face was as pale as sun-warmed skin could get. Her lashes made dark crescents upon chiseled cheekbones. Signs of what they'd been through were evident in lines of exhaustion and in her dirty disarray, but she looked beautiful to him as he sat carefully on the edge of the mattress.

"Son, I'd best take a look at that arm."

Billy shrugged out of his shirt without comment, without taking his eyes off Sarah's serene features. And he never so much as flinched while his wound was poked and purged.

"Should take some stitches if it's gonna heal up nice. Want to step on into the other room?"

"Go ahead and do it here," Billy said distractedly. He sat, watching Sarah as the doctor ran his neat seam.

And from the doorway, Emily Bass watched him.

Emily waited until the doctor had gone to come up behind her husband's youthful second in command. He gave a slight start when she touched his dusty hair.

"Billy, why don't you help yourself to a cup of coffee while I clean her up some?"

He looked up through eyes dark with reluctance and deeper sentiments, which warmed through Emily's heart. When he spoke, it was with obvious difficulty. "I should be going anyway. You don't need me here taking up space."

Emily smiled because he was so transparent. She had to think of his pride, however, and couldn't wound him with her knowledge of the truth. Her touch skimmed down a strong stubbled jaw to rest beneath his chin.

"You aren't in the way, William. Have some coffee. Jack will want to see you when he gets back, so you might as well make yourself at home. Sarah'd probably be flattered by your attention . . . once I make her more presentable, that is. A lady doesn't want a man seeing her at less than her best. Go on and get."

Billy could argue that Sarah looked just fine to him, but he muttered, "Yes, ma'am," then shuffled wearily into the next room.

Emily smiled after him, then looked down upon her sister-in-law. "Well now, Sarah, it looks like you caught yourself a Texas Ranger."

Cup of coffee in hand, Billy sank into one of the front room chairs and stretched long legs out before him. He ached all over and was itching for a bath and a set of clean clothes. But he couldn't leave just yet. He told himself it was because he needed to talk to Jack, but his heart knew it was Sarah who held him there. What was he going to do about that? What could he afford to do? If she woke up and he was there, how much harder would it be for him to walk away without ties? Without her expecting things that could never be?

"Hey, Ranger Bill, you and Miss Sarah been fighting outlaws?"

He smiled over at Emily's son Kenitay and let the swell of fondness overcome his glum mood. "Hey there, Kenny. Nothing so glamorous as all that. More like we was running for our very lives."

The boy nodded as if he understood, and the ache around Billy's heart got tighter. He loved kids. They were God's gift of joy to an all-too-unpleasant world. And he'd always had a warm spot for Jack's adopted son. Kenitay was about eight and full of his Apache father's haughty pride as he looked at life through eyes too wise for such a young age; green eyes, like his mama's. Jack had opened his arms and his heart to the little half-breed boy after nearly giving his own life to reunite mother and son. There were some who frowned on that, on the acceptance of his tainted blood, but Billy wasn't one of them. When he looked at Kenitay, he saw a child, and children needed loving, not blame for something beyond their control. When he looked at Kenitay, he saw his sister's oldest boy. And when he stared up at him now, he saw that squatter's kid with the big rifle lying dead on his family's front porch.

"Hey, Kenny, you mind if I was to hug on you for a minute?"

When he opened his sound arm wide, the boy stepped in without question and allowed himself to be crushed up close. Billy clung to the slight figure while all the harsh and horrible memories haunted him, feelings from which he was too weak to hide. They battered him like the cruelest of blows, until he was reeling and confused and hurting so bad he wanted to wail in misery.

"Billy? What are you doing here?"

Kenitay pulled out of his embrace with a gladsome cry of "Ranger Jack!" and from the younger Carson came a gleeful "Daddy!"

Watching Jack kneel down to scoop up his boys twisted

through Billy like Harm's big blade. Damn, Jack was lucky, and he knew it, too. He was a man who would never take the love of his family or their importance for granted, and that was one of the things Billy admired most around him. Family first, then the business at hand.

"Where's your mama?"

"Tending Aunt Sarah," Kenitay volunteered.

"Sarah? What's Sarah doing here?"

"She and Ranger Bill were shot by outlaws!"

Jack looked over the two boys. "You mind explaining that to me, Billy?"

Over a pot of coffee, Billy laid it out plain, making no excuses and keeping to a simple storyline, which was unusual for him. He liked to tell a colorful tale, but not in this case. With Jack's temper, not to mention his treasured friendship in the balance, he wanted the details as downplayed and glossed over as possible.

While Billy was talking, Emily came up behind Jack's chair. She didn't interrupt the two men as they discussed ranger business. Instead, she touched her husband's shoulder. Without shifting his attention from his corporal, Jack took up her hand for a tight squeeze and placed a kiss upon her palm. Then she walked into the kitchen. No grand gestures were made but the exchange was unmistakably intimate. He was home. She was glad. And that would last them for the moment.

Billy concluded his report and waited anxiously for Jack's pronouncement. His superior officer gave a heavy sigh and rubbed his palms over his face. His expression was one of disappointment, but not blame.

"Well, it was worth a try. It was a long shot to begin with. I'm just sorry you had to pay for it the way you did. You did your best and I'll not complain."

Billy stared at him, agog.

"You did do your best, didn't you?"

"Yes . . ."

"Then go wash up and get some rest. Maybe I can figure out some other way to go after them."

That was it? Billy sat, stunned. No chewing out, no angry words? Watching Jack slump in his chair, his expression spiritless and weary, Billy almost wished he would lash out at him for failing to make their plan succeed. But Jack would never chastise anyone who'd done all he could do. That's all he ever asked of those in his command. And that's why, to a man, they'd follow him right into hell.

"Jack, about Sarah—"

Jack held up his hand. "You don't need to tell me about my sister. I know she put you on the spot and you did what you could to work around her being there. I appreciate your seeing to her, Billy. She got herself into it, she can talk her way out of it. I'm grateful you didn't shoot her yourself for being such a distraction."

Distraction? Oh, Sarah had been more than distracting. She'd proven an irresistible temptation. But he could hardly tell that to her brother. Instead, he owned, "She was a nuisance, but truth be told, she saved my life by being there, Jack. They'd have killed me for sure when they found out. . . . How did they find out?"

Jack's features grew grim. "Something else I'm gonna have to work on. If we've got someone on the inside working against us, they'll have us in a stranglehold there's not much chance escaping."

Billy thought on that a minute, then he looked up at Jack. "Maybe not."

Jack wasn't thrilled by his idea. He summed it up with two phrases: "It's too dangerous" and "You're crazy." Billy didn't argue that, but he did think it might work. He talked about it while Jack ate what Emily served him, but his lieutenant didn't like it any better on a full stomach.

What Billy didn't like was having to leave the Basses house without a chance to look in on Sarah. There didn't seem to be any right way to request it without tacking on a bunch of awkward explanations. He wasn't supposed to be all that concerned about his friend's pesty little sister. But he was, and it was harder than hell to just walk out and pretend she didn't matter to him.

He shared one of the barracks cabins with three other rangers, who were lounging idly in their bunks when Billy stomped in.

"Heya, Billy. Where the hell have you been?"

Normally, Billy always had a friendly word for Pete Meyers. The older ranger had been responsible for signing him up years ago and had been his friend even longer than Jack. This time, however, he didn't spare a look and growled, "Out savin' West Texas. That's what I get paid for, ain't it?"

He tossed off his bloodied shirt and was aware that he had every man's attention. Bullet wounds were always a good source of conversation.

"Whoa there, what happened to you?" Clayton Wainright wanted to know.

"Looks like fresh stitching," Pete echoed.

"Don't you boys have anything better to do?" Billy snapped, then began the difficult task of washing up without popping any of those new stitches.

"Awful touchy, Billy. What's eatin' you?" That was from Matt Cobb. He was a new recruit, just a kid with a chip of arrogance the size of a telegraph pole on his shoulder. He wasn't gabby like Pete or harmlessly affable like Clayton, and Billy was never quite sure how to take him. But he remembered how it was to be on the cocky side of twenty, so he usually cut the boy some latitude, but not this time.

"What's eating me is my business unless I say otherwise." Billy eased into a fresh shirt and buttoned it clumsily. "If anyone wants to know any more of my business, I'm going into town to tip over a bottle and a whore."

"Jack's not gonna like that," Clayton mused, rather mystified by his pard's behavior.

"Well, maybe I don't give a tinker's damn what Gentleman Jack likes. If he's got a problem with me being gone, he can ride on over and shoot me for desertion. If not, I'll be back in the morning."

And with his three *compadres* gaping at his back, Billy Cooper headed for Terlingua.

* * *

"Billy?"

Sarah licked dry lips and dragged her eyelids up. She was stretched out on a big comfortable bed dressed in a soft nightgown that wasn't hers. And for a moment, she was totally confused—by the room, by the darkness, by the tight wrapping about her aching middle, but mostly, by Billy's absence.

Where was she?

Then she saw the short roundabout jacket hanging from a peg on the wall and recognized it as her brother's. She remembered then. She'd been shot. Billy and Harmon had brought her to Jack's.

But where was everyone?

She tried to sit up, but a shock of pain and the sheer bulk of the wrappings around her rib cage prevented it. Billy had said he'd stay, yet there was no sign of him. Had he been in that great a hurry to be rid of her?

Then she heard voices murmuring outside her closed door—Jack's, Emily's.

"Tired?"

"Beat to the socks. Mmmm, that's nice."

"Too tired?"

"Never that tired. Em, I'm all dirty."

"I like you dirty. That way I know where you've been and what it took for you to get back here to me. I like you any way I can get you."

"I missed you, Em."

They were kissing.

Sarah lay back in the lonely darkness, unable to help overhearing. That seemed less intrusive than calling out and interrupting their tender moment together.

"Since you went and gave away our bed to my little sister, where we gonna put down for the night?"

"There's the floor in front of the fireplace and your bedroll. I remember a time when you didn't mind stretching out on it with me."

"That's before I got to be an old married man and used to my own bed."

"Well, if you want your bed, you can bunk in there with your sister. Or . . ." Emily let that play out seductively, "if you like, you can get out of some of those dusty clothes and stretch out on me."

Sarah heard the sound of Jack's gunbelt hitting the floor, followed by the clatter of his buttons as he shucked out of his shirt. There was silence and she assumed they were kissing again. It lasted a long time, until she heard Emily's breathless laugh.

"Oh, I guess you did miss me. Let's put this to use, Jack Bass, before you forget how."

"No danger of that, wife. C'mon. I'll show you how much I remember."

Sarah lay awake for a long while pondering over Emily's urgency and the anticipation in her brother's voice, comparing them to what she'd had with Billy Cooper. It didn't add up and she didn't know which of the figures wasn't right.

She should have liked it when they'd made love, and Sarah wondered why she hadn't.

Chapter Nine

Smelling coffee and hearing voices made Sarah decide it was time to get out of bed and face her brother. Emily had peeked in on her earlier but she was still half asleep when her sister-in-law had draped a woolen robe over the end of the bed. Now she was wide awake, and though her ribs hurt as if a horse had kicked them, she wasn't the type to wait for things to come to her.

Sarah took it one step at a time, easing up, feet on the floor, pushing off the bed, straightening . . .

"Oh, God! Oh!"

Pride and panic were the only things that kept her going from there. She inched her way across the floor, clutching her side and trying not to take in more than a thimbleful of air at a snatch. By the time she reached the door, she remembered the robe on the bed but there was no way she was going back for it. No retreat from this point on, she told herself.

Jack and Clayton Wainright were talking by the front door and they didn't sound happy. Sarah edged down the hall and paused in the shadows, not wishing to interrupt her brother when he was talking business. And then she heard what, or rather whom, they were discussing.

". . . lit outta here surlier than a bear. Sheriff Lowe sent over a message this morning that he's got him locked up in his jail. Seems he got into a fight over some painted woman at the Midas and busted up the place pretty good. Even threw the bartender through the front window 'fore they wrestled him down. Ain't never known Billy to lose himself to liquor thataway. Musta been one helluva lady."

Suddenly, the pain in her side was nothing compared with the hole those words shot through Sarah's heart. How foolish of her to think he'd prefer waiting at her bedside, when he couldn't wait to get rid of her!

"Thanks, Clay," Jack was saying heavily. "I'll go on over and throw his bail." Then the ranger strode off and Jack was turning, leaving Sarah no chance to escape his notice. "Hey, what are you doing outta that bed?"

"Can't you even say hello?"

Jack gave her a narrow look. "Hello, little sister. Give me a reason why I shouldn't kick your butt."

"I can't," she said in a tiny voice. "I can't give you a reason."

"What?" He'd prepared for bluster and fire, not this timid squeak. Frowning, Jack crossed to her, expecting Sarah to launch into some wide-eyed sympathy-grabbing act to melt his anger. "Don't you try to make me feel sorry for you, because I don't. You went where you had no business going and you've only yourself to blame if you're hurting from it now."

Oh, how right he was. She swallowed hard, unable to deny it.

"Sarah, I ought to tan your hide, but I guess Mama'll be wanting to do that herself. Do you have any idea how much trouble you could have caused by jumping blind? What were you thinking, girl?"

She lifted her gaze, and her eyes were large and wet, her tone wavering pitifully. "I don't know. Oh, Jack, I made such a mess of things. I was so stupid. I did everything wrong."

To his surprise, he realized she was sincere. One blink liquefied the glossy sheen in her eyes into a steady stream of tears. And he couldn't very well shout at her if she was crying. The role of big brother was too much a part of him to ignore her distress.

"Hey, now. Don't do that. C'mere."

He enfolded her in a gentle embrace and she clutched at him, dissolving into gusty wails of guilt and shame. The circle of his arms was reassuring. The feel and scent of starched shirt linen was familiar and she was wilting it with her watering. She felt all of Kenitay's age tucked into his protective care. It was a good feeling, one she wanted to cling to for a while as everything else in her world teetered on disaster. Jack was a constant in her life, just as Harm was, always there, always dependable, unfailingly kind, unfalteringly strong. And she mourned the fact that she would have only brother and uncle from whom to draw that security. After what she'd just learned, it was obvious Billy had pulled out of her life in a hurry. Making love to her wasn't something that was going to bring him back with urgent whispers of "I missed you".

Pride was what finally braced her. She'd rather die than have Jack guess what had really brought on her deluge of tears. Dashing away the last of them with the back of her hand, Sarah lifted off her brother's chest and smiled weakly up at him. He was a good-looking Texas man, all tall and whipcord tough, with an amazing capacity for tenderness considering he rode with a Ranger star pinned to his coat. He was all that was brave and true, and he'd never done an impulsive thing in his life—except when he ran off with his best friend's wife and made Emily Marcus into Emily Bass. Sarah had always been closer to Jack than to her other siblings. It didn't matter that he wasn't her full brother as were Sidney and Jeffrey. She didn't know who Jack's father had been, but she guessed the man who lent his pale blue eyes and auburn hair to Rebecca's son was the reason for much of her mother's cautious attitude toward men.

"Better now?" Jack asked, smoothing her hair back with the glide of his broad palm.

Sarah nodded.

"Okay, then you get yourself back into that bed or I'll tie you down. You've got some serious mending to do. We'll talk when you're better rested. No arguments."

Again, she nodded. She hurt too much to protest. It was a numbing pain that ached all the way to the soul, not the kind that would mend with rest. It was the fracturing agony of heartbreak.

She let Jack guide her back into his bedroom and bundle her up beneath his sheets the way he would one of his kids. Sarah felt like a child just then, a lost, frightened child from whom all hope had been torn. But obediently, she closed her eyes when Jack bent down to buss a kiss against her brow, and to her surprise, sleep was waiting within seconds to rock her into a thankful oblivion

"He's in here, Jack. But be warned: It's not a pretty sight." Calvin Lowe led him back into the cell block of the jail. He'd known Cal forever. The man had ridden with Will as a ranger before taking on the sheriff spot in Terlingua. He was Harm's best friend outside of family. And he'd gotten Jack into the rangers when he was a green sixteen. Nowadays, he sported a thick mustache to compensate for thinning hair and carried thirty extra pounds over his belt, but he was the fairest and finest lawman Jack had ever met. The rangers had a good working relationship with him and his town. Except on occasion when one of them got rowdy. Then Cal would take no such stuff, ranger or not, and would throw him in a cell.

The sound of rattling keys woke Billy from his face-down position on the single cot. It was an inordinately loud noise and he groaned in protest.

"C'mon, Cooper," Cal called boisterously. "Get on outta there and go work for a living."

"How much for damages, Calvin?" Jack was asking.

"Oh, probably enough to dock his pay for better'n a year, but ole Jed down at the Midas is willing to be right reasonable seeing as how his man was outta line, too. Go drag him out, Jack, and I don't want to see his face back in there any time soon. Got real lawbreakers to house."

"C'mon, Billy. Haul on up."

Billy shoved the helping hands aside with a rusty growl of "I can do it myself, damn you." Then to prove it, he staggered off the cot and abruptly went into a wobbly spin. Jack caught his arm and towed him from the cell. Cal grinned at him in passing, recognizing in the fiery whites of his eyes the misery that was to come.

"Nice having you, Cooper."

"Yeah, well, your accommodations stink, Sheriff."

"Take it up with the taxpayers, son. My best to Emily, Jack."

"See ya, Calvin, and thanks for lookin' out for him."

"Yeah," snarled a truculent Billy over his shoulder. "Thanks for nothin'."

During the silent ride back to the ranger's camp, Billy never opened his eyes. His head was pounding from too much drink, his arm from too much action. He hadn't meant to knock that fellow through the window, but things had gotten out of hand fast. He wanted nothing more than his familiar bed beneath him and a cool darkness around him, but he knew that wasn't meant to be.

His arrival in camp, bringing up Jack's rear in disgrace, brought an immediate notice. He didn't want to meet any man's eye as he crawled down out of the saddle. He clung to it for a long moment, trying to get his bearings. Wouldn't do to walk into a post or fall into a trough. Then he felt Jack's hand cup his elbow.

"C'mon, Billy. Dunk your head and get ready to ride out on patrol. Your sorry state's your own fault and I got men waiting on you."

"Well, let 'em wait," Billy roared, then was immediately sorry as the echo of his voice vibrated through his head. He lunged away from Jack's grasp with a harsh "Lemme go, you self-righteous sumbitch. Hell, just 'cause you don't know nothin' about having a good time don't mean you can sneer down on them that do."

"Yeah, looks like you had yourself a real good time. Can't say I wish I was there. Get a move on, Corporal."

"I'll move when I'm damn well ready." He planted his heels and took a belligerent stance in the center of the street. If the other rangers didn't know they were best of friends, they'd suspect they were about to see gunplay.

"You got about five seconds to get ready or I'm gonna be motivating you with my boot."

"Big talk, Gentleman Jack. Can you back it with anything but hot air?"

"I can back it with something better than whiskey. Now back down. You're looking like a fool in front of everybody."

"Better my own fool than yours."

The volume of their talk had escalated and those not already on the street were drawn toward the din, including Emily, her children, and a tottering Sarah. They gathered on the porch to watch the hostilities mount between two men who'd been friends too long to entertain such foolishness. But Billy was still under the effects of the liquor and Jack was angry, and their audience was tense and troubled.

"I'm telling you one last time, Corporal, get yourself cleaned up and get on your horse. I'm sending you out after some fence cutters over Packsaddle Mountain way."

"I ain't going after no fence cutters. Hell, them squatters deserve what they get."

"That's your opinion," Jack drawled coolly. "You don't get paid to voice it."

"I don't get paid enough to ride against what I know is right. And I don't get paid enough to take your high and mighty tone."

"And the rangers don't pay you to consort with whores and rye whiskey. We got rules—"

"Rules? Since when you so set on rules, Jack? Am I supposed to stand here and listen to a cheatin', lyin' wife-stealer like he was the Almighty?"

There was a collective gasp from those who heard the vicious words, but Jack was still clinging to his temper. "Move now and I'll forget you said that to me."

"I don't want you to forget it. It's true. Everybody here knows it. You go 'round preaching on virtue and right, then turn right around and snatch a good man's wife and set her up in your bed before he's even cold."

Jack hit him. Had Billy been sober, the blow probably

would have shattered his jaw, but the whiskey helped him absorb the brunt of it as he stumbled back.

"Jack, no!" Emily cried out. She was off the porch before Sarah could catch her, running with an ungainly speed toward the men as they squared off for more.

Billy plucked the ranger star off his coat and flung it to the dust at Jack's feet.

"Pick it up or pick your pay!"

"To hell with you and to hell with your measly twenty-five a month. I can make better'n that—"

"Then do it and good riddance."

Billy didn't back down as the others hoped he would. Instead, his swelling jaw squared. "Yeah, well who needs you? I've had a belly full of your rules, them rules only you can break."

Jack swung on him again, but Billy dodged back with more luck than agility and managed to land a fairly solid hit on Jack's chin. Before he could get off another one, he felt a restraining tug on his arm and he struck back blindly with a snarl of "Get your hands off me." There was a smack of sound impact and a short feminine cry. Billy turned in time to see Emily Bass fall to the street.

"Mama!" Both kids ran to their mother, with Sarah following at a hitching pace. Emily tried to sit up too fast and fell back with a moan, clutching at her abdomen.

"Em?" Jack was down on his knees, his arms around her in support and restraint. "Don't move."

"Jack," she panted wildly, her hands clinging to him as she fought the spasms wrenching through her belly.

"Stay still, Em. Stay still. Somebody get Doc Himes!"

"Emily." Sarah sank down beside them awkwardly. Her eyes were glistening with fear when she lifted them to a stunned Billy Cooper.

"Oh, God, Jack. I'm sorry," he blurted out in horror. "I didn't see her. Honest to God, I didn't see her there."

Jack looked up at him through eyes like hot ice. His voice was low and emotionless. "You get your gear and you get the hell outta this camp. I see you again and you'll be sorry for it. And if anything happens to my wife, I'll be looking for you to blow you to hell!"

"Jack—"

"You sonuvabitch, get outta here!"

Billy took an unsteady step back, then another, then with one last look at Sarah's anguished expression, he whirled and headed for his cabin.

"Billy!"

Sarah started up but her brother's hand clamped down hard on her arm, staying her.

"Let him go."

"But Jack, he didn't mean—"

"I said let him go!"

So she sank back down in a helpless agony of confusion and let him stalk away.

Billy was stuffing all his meager belongings into a bag.

"Where you headed, kid?"

Billy dashed the back of his hand across his eyes before answering Pete Myers's question. "I don't know. Does it matter? Anywhere but here."

"Give it some time, Billy. Jack'll cool down."

"It's too late. I don't belong here, Pete. I thank you for what you did for me. I tried to make a go of it but it just didn't work out."

"You're not thinking straight, boy. You had a good thing here. You were making a decent future for yourself."

"Well, that's done and gone now."

"So that's it?"

"Pretty much."

"You just gonna fall back into what you was doing?"

"Well, I was a fair hand at it, anyway, and the money was better."

"You forgetting that I caught you? The next time, there'll be a rope instead of a chance."

Billy closed the bag and took one last look around him. "Guess I was just born to hang."

And he would have, too, if it had been other than Pete Meyers who'd nabbed him red-handed rustling cows at seventeen. He'd been an angry, desperate kid who was man enough to stretch hemp for what he was doing. But Pete had given him a chance to turn it around. He'd told him that he could earn an honest keep with the rangers, protecting the expanding frontiers of Texas for twenty-five dollars a month and feed. Billy had had nothing to lose then but he'd lost it all now.

He put out his hand. "Glad to have ridden with you and called you friend, Pete."

Meyers gripped his hand hard. "You take care, Billy. Keep your neck outta the noose."

"I'll do my best." Then he smiled with more bravado than he was feeling. "I'm heading into town. I'll put up there till something comes along. I'd appreciate it if you could . . . get word to me about Miz Emily."

"Sure thing, Billy." Pete caught a hold of the bag he was carrying. "Why don't I just hang on to this for a while? It'd make coming back easier."

"I don't think so, Pete."

But Meyers tugged hard and Billy relented, letting him take all his belongings and toss them back by his bunk. "Give it some time, Billy. Jack'll come round. If he doesn't and you want to head out, you come back for this and a goodbye."

"Thanks, Pete. See you around." And Billy walked away from all his worldly goods and rode out on the last five years of his life.

Emily was resting easy, the boys were asleep, and Jack sat at the table staring at Billy's star. He looked worn down to the boot heels by the scare he'd been given, and Sarah was cautious as she approached him. He gave a soft sigh as her arms eased around his shoulders and she pressed her smooth cheek against his.

"How you holding up, big brother?"

"'Bout as well as a mud hill in a rainstorm. How 'bout you?"

"The same, I think." She pushed a stray lock of auburn hair and kissed his temple. "She's going to be fine, Jack. Just fine. Doc Himes wouldn't have said so if it wasn't true." Her embrace tightened as a tremor raced through him.

"I'm glad you were here, Sarah. You were good with the boys. I'm afraid I wasn't much help."

"You were worried about Emily. But that's over now. She and the baby are strong and healthy. Now you'd better see to yourself. Go to bed. I'll bunk down out here tonight."

He nodded wearily but didn't move. He was looking at that circular symbol of Texas. Sarah decided to risk it.

"It wasn't his fault, Jack."

"I don't want to talk about this, Sarah."

"You know he would never, ever hurt Emily."

"Well, he did, didn't he?"

"Jack, Billy's your best friend. You can't just turn your back on him."

He shrugged out of her embrace, sounding angry, looking worried. "Well, that was his choice, wasn't it? He made a mess of things all on his own. He was careless and he almost got you killed."

"That wasn't his doing."

"Drop it, Sarah. Just drop it."

"No, I won't. Billy Cooper's a good ranger, and he's been a good friend to you and our family. You can't just throw all that away because of some crazy things he said while he was drunk. If you won't do it, I'm going into Terlingua to talk some sense into him."

Jack gripped her by the shoulders. The intensity of his command startled her.

"You'll do no such thing. You stay out of it, Sarah. Do you hear me? You stay away from him."

"Someone's got to do something, Jack."

"If something needs doing, I'll do it. And you . . . it's time you went home to Mama."

She stared at him, aghast. "No!"

"You're fit enough for the ride. I'll have a couple of the boys escort you over in a buggy—"

"No, Jack. I won't go!"

"Yes, you will! Haven't you made enough trouble? You go home where you belong, where Mama can look after you."

"You mean where she can smother me! Jack, please, don't make me go. You might as well be sending me off to prison. I'm not a child—"

"Well, then you shouldn't have acted like one. Running after Billy like you did, getting everybody all stirred up with worry, getting yourself shot, and now talking about meddling where you don't belong. Enough, Sarah. You're not old enough to handle your own decisions. I've got enough on my mind without having to fret about what you're going to do next. You're going home. Maybe a few more years'll settle you down, but for now you need safekeeping, and Mama'll supply it."

Panic was settling in and she reacted to it with a self-righteous fury. "It's not like you've never made any mistakes, Jack Bass, but I have to pay for mine!"

Her brother smiled sadly and shook his head. "Oh, Sarah, I've paid and paid dearly for my bad judgment. I don't want you to have to do that."

"It's my life!"

"And someday you'll be mature enough to make your own calls. But until then, you'll do what you're told. Now, you'd best be thinking about turning in—"

"Just who do you think you are—"

"I'm your brother and I love you, and I'm not gonna let you do something you'll regret for the rest of your life."

"Too late," she cried out with a thin little laugh. "I've got plenty of regrets already. And one of them is counting on you!"

The door slammed behind her as she stormed out onto the porch. Jack let her go, figuring she needed time to blow off her frustration before common sense could sink in. He'd learned long ago that there was no use trying to push reason on his sister until she was ready to recognize it. Then she'd see he was right in what he was doing. It was for her own good that he was sending her home.

And for his peace of mind.

Slowly, Jack reached out and let his fingers close over the discarded star. He brought his fist up to his mouth and whispered against it, "Be careful, Billy."

Sarah stalked the waning twilight hours in restless anger. She was furious with Jack for being so callous to her situation. He couldn't ship her off to their mama like a naughty child. He just couldn't!

But he would. First thing in the morning, she'd be bundled up and gone, and nothing she could say would talk him out of it. He'd drum her out of his ranger camp in dishonor and she couldn't bear the thought of it.

Sarah thought of going home, and protest welled up with a sting of tears. She imagined what those weeks and months ahead would hold for her and wanted to wail in objection. Her mama's cautious watchdogging, the endless lectures on responsible behavior, the suffocating boredom. All because she'd made some wrong decisions: She'd trusted in Billy Cooper, then she'd depended on Jack to take her side. Both of them had let her down, and she couldn't think of what else to do. Sarah continued to walk, drowning in desperation until a solution came to her.

There was one person who had never failed her.

She went to the ranger corral and gave her most becoming smile to the nighthawk watching over the horses.

"Would you mind saddling me up one for me, Mr. Baines?"

"Miss Sarah, does the lieutenant know you're out here?"

"It was his idea, private. He knows I like to ride when I'm sorting out my problems."

The man grinned affably. "Now, just what kind of problems could a pretty young thing like you have?"

"You'd be surprised. I want that one there." She pointed to a large buckskin with a chest made for speed and endurance.

"Now, missy, that's a man's horse."

"Then I guess I'll just have to make do with him as best I can." She flashed an engaging smile and he chuckled.

"You go fallin' off him and you gots to promise you won't let Jack hang me."

"I promise."

He rounded up the huge animal and slapped down a good saddle. Because she couldn't lift her foot without paining her ribs something fierce, Sarah let him lift her up. She gathered up the reins in capable hands.

"If Jack asks, where'll I tell him you're going?"

"Tell him I decided not to wait until morning. Tell him I'm going home."

"But, Miss Sarah, it's almost dark and—"

She kicked back her heels, refusing to hear more. If she didn't care to take orders from family, she certainly didn't need to listen to strangers.

"Dammit, Jack's gonna cash me out!"

"Sorry!" she called back over her shoulder, then looked straight ahead over the flat barren land that led to Harmon Bass's door.

Chapter Ten

Sarah sorely underestimated the difficulty of the trip.

She'd been riding since childhood. She was conditioned for long overland hauls on horseback through sleet and hot summer sun, through moonless nights, but she'd never made the ride with a newly stitched bullet wound and broken ribs.

After a while even the animal's easiest gait was sheer torture. There was a full moon overhead to light the way, so she pushed on through the night, afraid if she stopped she wouldn't be able to climb back onto the horse. She passed by the turn-off to her parents's ranch with a steely determination, and by the time she hurt bad enough to regret it, it was too late to go back. All she could do was go on.

Sarah breathed a sigh of relief when she came to the meandering edge of Blue Creek shortly after daybreak. She followed the fast, clear waters until she could see the two-story frame house her aunt had had shipped from the East. It looked incongruous out there in the middle of nowhere, but no sight had ever been more welcomed to the weary traveler. As she reined up in the yard, she could hear a girlish shout.

"Mama! Mama! Sarah's here."

Amanda Bass came out of the big house, her smile of greeting fading fast when she took a look at her niece. She started running to catch her as she began to slide.

"Harmon, come quick!"

By the time Amanda reached up, Harm was there beside her to carefully lift Sarah down.

" 'Morning," the girl muttered faintly. "Thought I'd stop in and visit a spell . . ." And she swooned dead away in Harm's embrace.

"The girl's crazy." Sarah could hear Harm's grumbling as she swam back in leisurely waves toward consciousness. "She gets that from you, you know."

"Harmon, Sarah and I are not blood relations."

"Coulda fooled me. Not a lick of sense difference between you and her when you were her age. No brains whatsoever. A man shouldn't have to suffer through this twice in his lifetime."

"Stop ranting, Harmon. You have to admit I matured quite nicely."

"Well . . . yes."

"And so will Sarah, so quit being so prickly and let me talk to her."

"Talk? Spare me. I'm going out for a walk. I'll be back in about three months. You should be done talking by then."

"Harmon, I am not amused. Oh, look who's awake. Sarah, how are you feeling?"

"Probably like she rode from Terlingua with a bullet hole the size of Santa Elena Canyon in her side."

"Harm, you aren't helping!"

Duly chastised, he paced the spare bedroom while Amanda smiled down at their unexpected guest. "Ignore him, Sarah. He's just grouchy because he was hoping we'd be using this room for another baby by now."

Harm was stopped dead by shock. "Amanda!"

"Well, it's not like I can complain that you haven't been trying your darnedest." And she smiled with a purely salacious satisfaction while the tough part-Apache tracker went crimson all the way back to his ears.

That was enough humiliation for Harm. With a gruff rumble of "I'm going," he stalked to the doorway, to be halted by his wife's soft call.

"Harmon?"

"What?"

"Don't go far."

He made a noncommittal snorting sound of annoyance and disappeared.

Amanda turned back to Sarah and patted her hand. "There. I knew that would get rid of him for a while. Nothing more bashful than an Apache man. Now we can talk without him hanging over our shoulders."

Sarah stared at her, truly amazed by her manipulation of her stoic uncle. She'd never seen anyone make Harmon Bass jump through hoops on cue, but he jumped for his pretty eastern wife. And he didn't mind it. That was what astounded Sarah.

"Now, then, would you like to tell me what brings you here when your parents' ranch was a half day closer? I know it's not for my cooking."

Sarah tried to think of a plausible answer, but an achy un-happiness was welling up inside and she ended up blabbing everything . . . well, almost everything, to her sympathetic aunt. It didn't take three months, but a good three hours passed before Amanda rejoined her surly husband in the front parlor.

"Well, you finished discussing our love life with a sev-enteen-year-old?" Harm drawled with an acidic drip to each word.

Amanda paid his mood no mind. She walked straight up to him, grabbed his face between her hands, pulled him down, and planted a hard kiss on his frowning lips. He tried to resist . . . for all of two seconds. When she was content with the de-gree of his response, Amanda leaned back to smile up at him.

"Harmon, the details of our love life were not meant for the ears of a seventeen-year-old. They'd shock her insensible. Not that I wouldn't mind bragging a bit."

"I'm sure you wouldn't mind at all and that's what has me worried. I'm surprised *you* haven't written a book about it."

Amanda looked impossibly smug. "There are parts of the Harmon Bass legend I prefer to keep to myself." Her arms went around him so her palms could rub immodestly over his

back pockets. He didn't blush, but he did try to distract her
before he forgot what he'd meant to say.

"Why's Sarah here?"

Amanda nudged her nose against her husband's shoulder.
It was an affectionate gesture, but its purpose was to shield
the clever turnings of her mind from his probing gaze. She
didn't want to lie to him exactly, but she wouldn't betray Sarah's confidence, either.

Amanda could relate to the way a young girl's obsession for
the wrong man could push beyond the point of sensibility.
Harmon Bass had been that man for her. And she knew Billy
Cooper was that man for Sarah just by listening to the way
she spoke of him. Infatuation was all over the young woman's
intonation. But Harm wouldn't understand that. Men never
understood things of the heart unless their heart was the one
breaking. So she would approach the problem another way.

"Jack threatened to ship her home in disgrace so she's
asked us to put her up for a while until she's ready."

"Ready? Ready to what? Go home where she belongs?"

"Harmon, Sarah and your sister haven't been getting along
very well lately—"

"And since when is that my business?"

"Since Sarah's in our upstairs room."

"I'm not getting involved in this."

"She's already here."

"Well, I'll take her back on over to Becky's right after
lunch."

"You'll do no such thing!"

"Ammy, this is between Sarah and Becky. They have to
work it out for themselves. I'm not going to let her hide over
here under my roof—"

"You let Jack when he and Will weren't getting along. Or
had you forgotten?"

"Well—well, that was different."

Amanda leveled a steady stare at him. "Different, how?"

"Sarah's a—a girl."

"And how, might I ask, does that make this situation any
different?"

"A man's got a right to get out on his own. A girl belongs home with her mama."

Amanda shoved away from him with an indignant cry. "Don't you give me any of that big-talking Tex-Apache man nonsense, Harmon Bass. I don't want to hear it. Sarah's situation is no different from Jack's. We invited him to stay—"

"I said no."

Harm watched her pace and silently fume, bracing himself for the explosion to come, not liking it one bit. He hated the thought of his usual tranquility being disrupted. And he hated to go counter to Amanda's wishes, but on this one thing, he knew he was right and she wouldn't argue him into changing his mind with temper tantrums or pouting. But she did neither, and he should have been suspicious right away.

"All right, Harmon," Amanda said with a resigned sigh. "I don't want to fight with you. If you say no, it's no." She came up to hug him, nestling in as sweet as could be, and he was so grateful for it, her next words struck like an axe handle between the eyes. "You go up and tell her."

"What?"

"I said, you go up and tell Sarah that you're refusing to let her stay. You tell her that we're closing our doors and our hearts to her problems, that she can just work them out on her own. You go up and look that scared, upset, injured girl, who trusts you more than anyone in the entire world, right in the eye and tell her you're tossing her out on her ear because you don't want to involve yourself. After all, it's your house, your decision."

Harm swallowed hard. It felt as if his moccasin were wedged halfway down. Amanda took a step back and looked up at him patiently. She had him cold. She knew the Apache in him believed the house was a woman's domain and under her complete rule. Yet the arrogant Texas part was still putting up an admirable fight.

"Well, Harmon, go tell her."

"What's this got to do with that kid Cooper?"

He turned the tables so slick and sly, Amanda was almost caught unprepared. "You mean Billy Cooper, the ranger?"

"Do you know another one?"

"The problems between Sarah and Becky have nothing to do with Billy."

He squinted at her, obviously doubting it. That sign of his distrust wounded and Amanda drew back from him even farther. She was done trying to work him to her will. She'd put it plain and let him chew on it until it got too tough to choke down.

"She came to us for our help, Harmon. I want to give it to her. But she's your family. It's your choice."

He held to that impassive face for a long minute, studying his wife, weighing her words. Finally, she drew a shallow breath of defeat.

"All right, Harm. I'll go get her ready to travel."

She was halfway to the stairs when he called to her.

"Ammy, come here to me."

She paused, considering the nature of his request. It wasn't an order. He never commanded her to do anything. He didn't waste his breath. Because he asked, she was inclined to obey.

His expression didn't alter as she approached, but as soon as Amanda was within arm's length, he grabbed her, crushing her to his chest. For a moment he didn't say anything, just held her. When he did speak, it was from the soul.

"Sarah is your family, too. You are my wife, Amanda. Our spirits are one in the same. There is no part of me that is separate from you. Don't play upon my heart's weakness where you're concerned. I don't like it. There is nothing I'd deny you if you want it and you ask me for it, straight out. You know that. You are my world, Ammy. Tell Sarah she can stay."

Amanda didn't respond at first. Her breathing gave a telltale hitch as she rubbed her face against his shirtfront. She looked up at him through misty eyes. "I love you, Harmon. You are my world, too."

"Let me go, little girl. I'm going out."

"Out where?" She was stroking his sleeves in a provoking manner.

"Out to bang my head against the barn. There must be something loose in there if I'm gonna put up with the both of you a-yakking away."

She smiled. "Don't damage the barn."

"I'm going to grab up the kids and head out for a while. Give you and Sarah some time for your woman talk. I'll be back by dark. Think you can have it worked outta your systems by then?"

"We'll try." She touched his face and he leaned into her palm, his eyes half closing. "Thank you," she whispered.

"Thank me later."

An overcast sky made for a cool afternoon. Sarah had slept away a better part of the day and now was enjoying the chill of approaching December from the porch swing. She was bundled under one of her mama's hand-tied quilts. She recognized the fabric squares as being from her mother's and her dresses and from her brother's shirts. It was warm and it felt like being wrapped up in family.

"Join me in a cup of tea?" Amanda asked from the doorway.

"Sounds good."

Her aunt carried out two cups. "Harmon says it tastes like dog spit to him, so I don't get to share it with someone very often. I miss having tea in the afternoons. It's one of the few things I miss about the civilized East."

Sarah took a cup and savored the heat of it between her palms. It was comforting, as was sharing the swing with Amanda. Ten years separated their ages, the same span as between Harm and Jack. It made them seem more like contemporaries than aunt and niece. Amanda had always refused that title and Sarah liked her for that. She'd always wanted a sister, and Amanda filled that space in her lonely West Texas world.

"Amanda, did you know you were going to marry Uncle Harm the first time you saw him?"

Her aunt laughed. "The first time I saw him, I thought he

was dead." She could see Sarah didn't understand. "I'd hired this famous tracking legend from out of the dime novels I loved to read. I came all the way to West Texas to have him find my missing brother. I had a very definite idea of what *the* Harmon Bass would look like. He'd be tall and sophisticated and armed to the teeth with shiny hardware. I'd picked him out in the saloon, only to have him shot dead in a card game. Turned out, my handsome hero was just a card cheat. And *the* Harmon Bass turned out to be a short, unarmed, insignificant-looking cowboy who hardly looked any older than I was. I was so disappointed I could have cried."

"Until Blue Creek," Sarah added with a grin.

"What do you know about Blue Creek?"

"Uncle Harm said you had an interesting pattern of buckshot and that you fell in love with him after he took the shot out of your—"

"Rump," Amanda supplied wryly. "How nice of him to share that story. It wasn't his doctoring that impressed me."

"Oh? Just what was it?"

"When I looked at him at Blue Creek, for the first time, I saw the man he was. Not the legend, not the image, but the man. And oh, Sarah, my heart was gone."

Sarah sighed. Oh, yes, she knew the feeling. She sipped her tea and worked up her courage. "Amanda?"

"Yes?"

"What—what was it like the first time you and Harmon were together?"

"Well, we met in the hotel bar I was just telling you about, and . . . but that's not what you're asking, is it?"

Sarah blushed hotly and shook her head. She stared down into her teacup, then finally canted a glance up at her aunt. Amanda didn't look shocked in the least. Nothing shocked Amanda. Sarah was heartened. "Was it nice?"

"Nice?" Amanda leaned back against the back of the swing and smiled. "As I recall, I was planning to kill him if he ever so much as touched me again."

Sarah blinked in surprise.

"It was awful," the pretty blonde confided. "Nothing like

I'd expected. I had all these grand illusions from reading books and listening to a schoolmate talk. I thought it was going to be beautiful and romantic. Was I ever wrong! He made me cry. I made him mad. Neither of us had the slightest idea what we were doing. It was a total disaster. I liked kissing him. I liked looking at him. And I loved him, so I didn't give up. I'm glad I stuck with it."

Sarah couldn't claim ignorance was Billy's problem. She knew he'd been with plenty of women. The fault must have been hers. She sank down in the quilt, feeling guilty and miserable. "But it got better?"

"Oh, more than better! The very next time. It was beautiful and romantic, and Harmon was—was everything I'd dreamed of. More, because I'd had no idea how it could be."

"So, just because you don't like it the first time doesn't mean you never will?"

Amanda gave her a sudden shrewd look. "Sarah, are you asking just to be asking, or is there a reason? A tall, blond, good-looking reason?"

Sarah couldn't meet her eyes. "Just asking," she murmured. And of course, Amanda didn't believe it for a minute.

"Hasn't Rebecca ever talked to you about this?"

"No. Mama gets mad and upset when I talk about . . . well, about men."

"Oh." Of course, she would. Considering. She draped her arm about Sarah's shoulders and hugged gently. "The first time for we women is scary and it hurts and you don't want to ever have anything to do with it again. Men take to it like spitting and swearing. It's not fair but they do. We have to learn to like it, and if a man loves you, if he's the right man for you, he'll want to make you like it with him. He'll want to make you believe it couldn't be that good with anyone else."

"And would he be right?"

Amanda smiled. "Harmon was. After ten years, the new still hasn't worn off. I've been known to track him and take him down where I find him, I want him so bad. He, of course, puts up a modest struggle, but I think he likes giving in to me. It keeps his Apache pride intact. He's a graceful loser. There are times when I start thinking about him, about the feel of him, and it's all I can do to wait . . ." She broke off and finally looked embarrassed. "Well, you get the idea. Goodness, I forgot I was talking about your uncle. I should be ashamed of myself carrying on in such a fashion." Then she grinned mischievously to show she wasn't ashamed at all.

And Sarah smiled back, encouraged.

"What do you do to get a man to love you? What did you do with Uncle Harm?"

"I—I'm not really sure. He just said it one day and I believed him. I never asked why."

"Was it because you made love with him?"

Abruptly, Amanda read between the lines. She looked at the young woman who was blushing with a contemplative eagerness and she saw herself ten years ago. And she remembered how she'd considered using a physical intimacy to trap herself a wild and reluctant Texas husband. "Sarah, are you and Billy—"

"Hey, haven't the two of you run outta things to talk about yet?"

Both women looked up, alarmed to find Harmon standing on the bottom porch step. Neither had heard him. Amanda was quick to recover.

"We were talking about sex."

Harm recoiled as if she'd shot him. He opened his mouth, then snapped it shut in a hurry.

"Was there something you wanted to say on the subject?" his wife asked sweetly.

"Ammy, I swear, you make me blush right down to my socks. This is not something I want to get into." He climbed the steps and made for the door, looking mortified.

"I bet you won't be of that same mind later on."

"Excuse me," he muttered. "I'm gonna go dig a hole and pull it in over me." The door banged behind him and Amanda was grinning wide.

"You'd think he'd never heard the word before!" she shouted after him. "Let alone enjoyed the practice."

There was no time for further talk as the three Bass children converged upon the porch looking for supper. Afterwards, while dishes were carried to the kitchen, Sarah was too weary and sore to do more than drag herself upstairs and crawl into bed. Though she'd wanted time to mull over all she had learned from her aunt, she drifted off almost at once.

Later, in the room next door, Amanda slipped under the covers to snuggle up to her husband. He gave an objecting snort and rolled away.

"If you're looking to find a topic of conversation with Sarah tomorrow, you can look elsewhere."

She gave a soft chuckle and contrarily fit herself tight along the hard line of his legs and flanks. But Harmon stayed as stiff as a fence post, even when she started peppering little kisses along one brown shoulder and rubbed his back, her palms gliding over the scars of his past. Amanda reached her fingers up to thread through his sleek black hair, then nibbled determinedly on the back of his neck. He moaned softly deep within his throat; it sounded suspiciously like a purr.

"Harmon?"

"Ummm?"

"Why did you marry me?"

"I wanted to go to bed with you."

Her tone grew prickly. "You didn't have to marry me for that."

"I didn't want anyone else but me to ever go to bed with you."

"Harmon, I'm serious."

"So was I!"

"Harmon?"

"What?"

"Why did you fall in love with me?"

"It sure as hell wasn't my fondness for your conversation."

"Or my cooking."

Wisely, he left that alone. "Why you asking after ten years?" He rolled onto his back to look up at her. She touched his face, adoring the angles and hollows with light strokes of her fingertips.

"You never told me."

"You never asked me."

"I'm asking now. What made you fall in love with an annoying, gabby, stubborn schoolgirl?"

"And those were your good points."

"Remember what it was like? The first time I kissed you, you didn't like it."

"I liked it. You scared me, is all. You had a way of shaking me to the soul, little girl."

She smiled. "Do I scare you now?"

"All the time. You scare me when you do crazy things like throwing yourself between me and a bunch of Apaches with nothing more than my knife and a bellyful of my child. You scare me when you look up from my arms and ask me to give you forever and I know I can't. You scare me when I think of what my life would have been without you. And it scares me when I realize how much I love you."

"Why? What made you love me?"

"Because no matter how bad things got, how dangerous they were, how crazy I was, you were there to stand by me. Always. Always. You never doubted me even when I doubted myself. You never backed off for a second. You never hurt me. And you never let me down, not once. You made me believe it was safe to trust you with my heart. Does that answer your question?"

She stretched up to kiss him, fully, slowly, until his hands rose to cap her shoulders and he used his weight to lever her onto her back. Harmon moved against her, hard man over yielding woman, and he enjoyed watching passion build in her dark eyes, as it did every time he touched her.

"You wanting me to give you something to talk about tomorrow?"

"I want you, Harmon. Make love to me like it was our first time."

He laughed. "You don't want that, little girl. I didn't know anything then. We've learned a lot since that dirty little hotel room. Think of how much you've taught me."

"You are a good student, Harmon." She caressed his shoulders and upper arms, thrilling to the feel of him, so lean and tough, like Texas. "Show me what that first time could have been like if you'd known then what we both know now."

"You mean like this?" He lowered his mouth, then paused above hers as she opened wide to receive him. Just the tip of his tongue traced the shape of her lips and she moaned wildly in anticipation.

"Yes."

"And maybe this?" He sketched the fullness of her breasts with his fingertips until she was trembling.

"Yes! Oh, Harmon . . . don't make me wait. I want you now!"

"Woman, after ten years, you'd think you'd learn a little patience."

"To hell with that!" And she seized his face to suck up his kiss voraciously.

On the other side of the wall, Sarah lay with her eyes closed, imagining what the sounds suggested. She'd woken to the murmur of their quiet conversation, held spellbound by its content. She considered Harm's answers and wondered if the same applied to Billy. Make it safe for him to trust her with his heart. Was that all it would take? She pondered that as the sounds of pleasure escalated in the adjoining room. Amanda wasn't quiet or subtle.

Never doubt, never back off, never hurt, never let down. And he would love her for it.

How could she prove those things from a distance? She'd already let him down when she let him walk away. What kind of faith had she shown in him? What kind of trust?

As the headboard bumped vigorously against the other side of the wall and Amanda's cries became a tumultuous keening, Sarah knew she'd given up too soon. If what Harm and Amanda had was what lay beyond that miserable first time, she wanted it for herself.

And she wanted it with Billy Cooper.

Chapter Eleven

"I'm heading out after breakfast," Sarah announced as Amanda poured their coffee.

"Heading out where?" Harm was alerted by the evasive nature of her gaze. He stared across the table, blue eyes direct and demanding.

"I need to talk to Jack, then I'll be going home." Her gaze canted down toward her plate.

To avert her husband's suspicions, Amanda asked, "Are you sure you're healed up enough for the ride?"

"It's been a week, and I haven't done anything but eat and sleep. If I don't move around soon, you're gonna have to cut a wider door for me."

"What do you need to see Jack about?" Harm was a tracker. It was hard to throw him off a trail once he caught the scent.

"We've got some things to settle between us."

"What kinda things?"

"Personal things," Sarah concluded, and that should have been it, but Harm refused to let go until he'd followed all the way to the end.

"Something to do with that Cooper kid?"

"Harmon, that really isn't any of your business, is it?" Amanda filled his cup and sweetened it with a warning smile. He ignored it.

"Could be I'll just ride along with you, just to make sure you get there and back to Becky's safe and sound."

While he took a drink of his coffee, Sarah shot her aunt a desperate look. How could she ever accomplish anything with her Uncle Harmon hanging over her shoulder? It wasn't as if he was going to agree with anything she meant to do!

Understanding the signal, Amanda sidled in close to Harm, her arms gliding about his neck so her palms could push up and down his shirtfront in a distracting movement. When he glanced up, wary of her intentions, she leaned down to buss a wet kiss upon his ear.

"Harmon, why don't I pack up the kids and we'll all go. I'm expecting some packages from New York, and it'd be nice to visit with Jack and Emily and the Lowes."

Harm's expression darkened with displeasure. "More gifts from the Duncans trying to buy their way into your fortune?" He noticed the way his children's attention perked up and that made him all the angrier. "Send 'em back, Ammy. I don't want any part of their bribes."

"Harmon, you know Leisha, Becca, and Rand are their family. There's nothing sinister about them wanting to remind the children that they have relations up north."

"And they send such pretty things," Becca piped up. "Things you can't get around here."

Harm softened slightly and reached out to touch his seven-year-old's cheek. He knew she didn't understand the connotations of those pretty gifts, and he couldn't blame her for her eagerness to have them. That's when Leisha cut in fiercely.

"They send nothing we need, Becca. What we have is good enough, Daddy. We don't need their charity."

"Leisha," Amanda corrected gently. "It's not charity, not when it's from family."

"No. Not when your mama could buy and sell them six times over."

"Harmon, there's nothing wrong with them trying to keep up ties."

"When were they ever family to you, Amanda? Answer me that? We're your family, here in Texas. We're the ones who love you and care about you. Not them. All they want is your money. Well, you can just write and warn them that if anything happens to you, I'm gonna bury every last penny with you. They're never gonna see a cent of it."

"Harmon! Since when is my money so important to you?"

"It's not. It never has been. I'd have taken you happily with what you had on your back. But, Ammy, I can't abide buzzards circling."

"Can we go to New York and meet your relatives, Mama?" Randall wanted to know. He was only four and the nuances of the conversation went right over his head.

"Not while I'm still breathing, son.'

"Harmon, that's enough." Amanda's tone was unexpectedly stern and they all looked at her with varying degrees of surprise. "I won't have you teaching our children to be ashamed of who I am."

He blinked. "That's not what I'm doing."

"Isn't it? You're telling them that what I am and where I'm from is nothing to be proud of, that they should despise and distrust the members of my family just because of the way I was treated in the past. That was past, Harmon. That was a long time ago. I've forgiven them for what they did."

"Well, don't expect me to, not after they hurt you. Take their gifts, go visit them if you want, tell our children what marvelous, upstanding citizens they are, but to me they'll never be anything but greedy bloodsuckers, and I will never ever trust or forgive them."

Amanda said nothing for a time, then she placed her hand atop his head, stroking back through the short black hair. "You carry a tolerable grudge, Mr. Bass."

"No one abuses what's mine. Not and lives to tell about it." Then his gaze shifted to Sarah, who knew nothing of Amanda's family's neglect of her and her brother after their parents' death, but everything about her uncle's devotion. "You might want to make mention of that to your ranger friend." He pushed back from the table with a gruff "If we're going, let's get going."

They left an hour later, Amanda handling the reins of the buggy carrying Sarah and the younger children, while Harm and Leisha rode on horseback. Sarah gave her aunt a hug of appreciation, knowing that Amanda's presence would keep Harm under control and out of her affairs. At least, that's what she was hoping.

Their welcome at Jack's was noisy and warm. Harm stepped off his horse, welcoming Jack's firm embrace and the news "Hey, Uncle Harm, just in time to sit down to supper."

"You got a place to put all of us?"

"Always got room. I'll just tell Em to knock out a wall. Hey, Amanda, those girls are getting prettier every day. Lucky they take after their mama." And then a more reserved, "Sarah, surprised to see you."

Sarah allowed a wan smile as her spirits plummeted. Her brother was going to make it difficult. He came to the side of the buggy and put up his hands to her. She let him grab on carefully, and as he swung her down, her arms stole about his neck for a hard squeeze and a fervent "Please don't be mad."

He gave a heavy sigh and she felt his smile against her brow. "I'm not, you little hellion. How you feeling?"

She settled to the ground with a glorious grin. "Much better now."

"Well, c'mon inside and cut the dust. How long you staying?"

"Long enough for you to be sick of us," Harm predicted. He bent to lift Carson onto his shoulders and murmured a fond Apache greeting to Kenitay that made the boy beam. Leisha Bass glowered.

After a meal that filled the men up to a contented lethargy, sending them out onto the porch to sigh and loosen their belts, Emily, Sarah, and Amanda gathered in the women's domain of the kitchen. The two older women were discussing childbirth and Emily's condition, while Sarah was trying to think of a way to broach what was on her mind. Then Emily caught her glum look and smiled in empathy.

"I haven't seen him, Sarah."

Her expression crumpled. "You mean Jack wouldn't take him back?"

"I don't think he's come asking. They've steered clear of one another. Jack won't speak of it, not even to me."

"Where is he, do you know?"

"Still in Terlingua, I guess."

"Oh, Emily, he never meant to hurt you!"

"I know that, Sarah. Billy's a sweet boy and that's what I don't understand. He and Jack were so close."

"It's my fault, Emily. Jack blames him for me getting shot. It's so unfair of him, but the men in my family are the most hardheaded things."

Emily smiled. "That they are."

"Will you talk to him?" Sarah pleaded.

"To Jack? About what?"

"About letting Billy back into the Rangers."

"Oh, Sarah, I can't do that. I don't interfere in Jack's business."

"But it's not just business to me!"

Emily gave her a long look and nodded. "I know. And I'll do what I can." When Sarah's features brightened, she warned, "Just don't expect any miracles. You know your brother. Now, if you feel up to it, why don't you round up the kids. It's time for them to bed down for the night."

After Sarah had gone, Amanda asked, "What's going on?"

"What do you mean?"

"I can see it in your face. You're worried about something."

"I wish I knew what it was. Maybe it's just the baby coming. I always get overly sensitive to every little thing. But then again, I think I'll talk to Jack, just in case it's not a pregnant woman's worries. Think you could sidetrack Harmon for a minute?"

"No problem." And Amanda went out onto the porch to see to it. She had her own purpose in mind.

Jack and Harm were slouched back on a bench, talking companionably, when Amanda gave her husband a brief look, then walked down the porch steps to the dusty yard, going far enough out to allow for private conversation. She waited a few seconds, then smiled as Harmon's arms slipped about her waist and he tucked up close behind her. He nudged her cheek with his own and murmured, "What is it, *shijú?*"

Amanda said nothing at first, too absorbed in the feel of him, knowing his mellow mood would last only until she spoke up. She put her hands on his forearms and rubbed the hard cording of muscle. His strength never failed to arouse a possessive passion in her.

"Harmon?"

"Ummm?"

"Would you do something for me?"

"Anything."

She took a breath. "Would you ride into Terlingua and see what you can find out about Billy Cooper?"

She felt him tense up, sinew by sinew.

"Why would I want to do that?"

Amanda turned slightly so she could look him in the eye. "Because I'm asking you to."

He studied her for a second, then said, "I suppose I could go tempt Calvin with a cold beer." His eyelids lowered slightly. "And then, to show your appreciation, you can tempt me with other things."

"Suppose you'll like my kisses any better than you did over in the hotel ten years ago?"

"I just might." And he leaned forward to find out. Amanda stopped him with the touch of her fingertips against his mouth.

"Close your eyes, Mr. Bass. That's how it's done."

Contrarily, he left them open until the last possible instant, then they slid shut of their own accord. After a long, tempting minute, he pulled back and, with a shaky breath, started walking toward Terlingua.

"Harmon, you're forgetting your horse."

He turned. His smile was a gleam of white against the darkness. "I'll run. I need the distraction." And with several quick strides, he vanished into the night.

As Amanda climbed back onto the porch, Jack asked, "Where's Harmon off to?"

"He found himself needing something cold to drink in Terlingua."

Jack started to lift up. "Maybe I'll just—"

"Emily was wanting to talk to you, Jack. She's in the kitchen."

He looked in the direction his uncle had disappeared, then back at his house. He rose the rest of the way and went inside, knowing that even on horseback, he'd never catch up to Harmon once he had a head start. Jack found Emily putting away the last of the plates. She smiled at him as he stroked her rounding belly.

"Need some help in here?"

"All done. I could use a kiss."

He was happy to supply it. "What's on your mind? Amanda said you wanted to talk." Her hesitance piqued his curiosity. "Em?"

"Jack, why haven't you gone to make amends with Billy?" She felt his immediate freeze and plunged on. "You would have done it with any of your other men. You would have crawled through a cactus patch on your belly to bring them back if they strayed. Why are you letting Billy go?"

"Emily, I don't want to discuss this with you."

His expression was inflexible. Ordinarily, Emily would have backed down from her questions. But she'd promised Sarah. And she wanted to know.

"Jack, what's going on? Billy is your best friend. I can't believe you'd be ready to cut him loose because he drank a little too much and displayed some bad judgment."

"He hurt you."

"Oh, Jack, that was an accident and you know it. If you hadn't been so set on brawling in the street, it never would have happened. Again, I'm asking you, what's going on?"

He looked anxious and evasive, the way he did too often of late for her peace of mind. "Em—"

Her palms framed his lean face so he couldn't turn away. "Jack, tell me."

His hands covered the backs of hers and gently drew them down. "You're gonna have to trust me on this, Em. I know what I'm doing. Leave it alone. Billy made his choice and I have to stand by it as best I can. Don't make this harder for me. Please."

She looked up at him, reading so much more than he was saying in the intensity of his gaze. And she knew she was right to worry.

"Emily, promise me you'll let it go."

His words were so desperately sincere, she could only say, "All right, Jack."

He scooped her up in a tight embrace and she could feel his heartbeats hurrying like crazy. Then he kissed her, and that tasted of agitation, too. By then, she was close to panic.

What on earth were he and Billy involved in?

When Harm stepped into the saloon, Billy was involved in hot and heavy play with a gathering of hard cases. Harm spotted him immediately and recognized the signs of reckless self-abuse. The boy was sloppy drunk and looked as though he'd been that way for some time.

"Two," Calvin Lowe told the bartender as he made room for his small friend at the scarred bartop beside him. "Good to see you again, Harm. How's your family?"

"Good. And Elena?"

He patted his burgeoning belly with a contented sigh. "Can't complain." Then he thumped Harm's lean girth. "Amanda's cooking no better, I see."

"I've survived on worse." Then he grinned, unexpectedly. "Can't remember when, though."

Calvin laughed. "Damn, you look fine, son." Only Cal would call him son as if he were still that tough, haunted-eyed kid who'd rescued Calvin's bride-to-be from the Apache some twenty years ago. The bond of their friendship had been unbreakable since then. They sipped through the foam of their beers companionably, and then the sheriff gave him a scrutinizing look. "Watcha need, Harm?"

"Answer me something."

"Name it."

"That kid, Cooper, what do you know about him?"

Calvin followed his harsh stare. "He's a good kid, Harm. Good ranger. Leastwise, he was until he and Jack parted ways. Afore that, he'd come in with the other boys, roughhouse a bit, fool with the upstairs girls, but never get into trouble. Lately, he's gotten to be a handful." He shook his head sadly. "Bad company."

"You know any of those fellers?"

"Calloway and Hogan are local toughs. The others are Benton and Collins. They ride with a bad one name a' Gant. Understand that Cooper used to do some rustling with Gant when he was younger."

"Rustling." Harm didn't like the sound of that news. Not in the least. Old habits being hard to break and all. "Stupid kid."

"I seen it a hundred times, Harm. Kid with no family, taking up with bad sorts and ending up in a noose with no one to cry over him."

Only problem was, Harm knew there'd be someone there crying a whole river. And that was what he wanted to avoid.

"Harm?" Calvin cleared his throat and looked uncomfortable.

"What is it, Cal?"

The lawman fidgeted and glanced away. He was chewing on something unpleasant. "Something I think you need to know."

"Calvin?"

"You ain't gonna like it, Harm."

And he didn't. Not at all.

Amanda woke with a start. Even before her eyes opened, she was reaching out beside her for her husband. The space was empty. Alarmed, she slid out of the warm covers and into her robe before leaving the room, knowing where she'd find him.

The night was clear and cold. Panicked breaths plumed the air in rapid streams where Harm stood at the edge of the porch, his arms wrapped tight about himself, his eyes squeezed shut above wet cheeks. He'd pulled on his denims since their rather savage lovemaking earlier that evening and the skin of his bared back gleamed golden in the pale light.

"Harmon?"

A wildly unsteady hand swiped at his face before he turned to her. His voice was hoarse. "I'm sorry, Ammy. I didn't mean to wake you."

"It's all right. Are you all right?"

"Fine. Just a bad dream."

Not just a bad dream. *The* dream; the one he woke from in a cold sweat, unable to breathe, teetering on the edge of frantic madness. Amanda wondered what had brought it back.

"Can I stay out here with you for a while?"

"If you want."

He flinched when her palm pressed to his back but he didn't shy away. She ran her hand gently over the scarred ridges that formed a road map of the abuse he'd suffered as a child. Such awful reminders, but they weren't half as bad as those that marred the inside of his soul.

"What's wrong? What's happened?"

"Sometimes I wake up and the remembering's so clear, it's like being there again. . . . There was so much pain, I didn't think I could stand it. It was dark and I could smell the earth, that rich, wet scent you get to when you dig down deep. I tried to move but something was pressing down on my back, and I couldn't seem to draw in any air. I couldn't see anything but I could feel the shape of my mama underneath me, and she was so cold and so still and so stiff. And—and I tried to scream but I couldn't. That's when I realized that they'd buried me in that box with her. I tried to get out, and the weight of all that dirt was on top of the lid and I couldn't breathe and I couldn't cry. Oh, God, Ammy, I don't want to go back to being crazy again."

Amanda curled her arm about the back of his head, drawing it down to the hollow of her shoulder. She held him fiercely and pressed a hard kiss to his temple. "You're fine,

Harmon. You're just fine. I won't let you go back. I won't let anything hurt you, not ever!"

He gave a shaky laugh. "You're one tough lady, Amanda Bass."

"No one abuses what's mine. I love you, Harmon. I won't let you go. I won't let the past have you back."

She felt him relax slowly within the possessive circle of her embrace. His shivering shifted from horror to the chill of the night.

"It's cold out here, Harmon. Come back to bed."

He did draw away then, and when he glanced at the dark interior of the house, the fear in his eyes was like looking into the shadows of hell.

"I can't go back in there, Ammy."

"Harmon—"

He shook his head. "I can't. Not tonight."

Amanda stroked his bare arms, nodding before going inside herself. She returned a few minutes later carrying an armload of quilts. As she spread one upon the porch boards, Harm regarded her in question.

"I'm tired," she explained. "Lie down with me."

He understood when she stretched out on the quilt and pulled another over her. She patted the space beside her and gave him a beckoning look.

"Ammy, it's too cold out here for you."

"Then come down and keep me warm."

Wrapped up in the quilt with limbs entwined, there was plenty of shared heat. Harm drew a deep breath of fresh night air and expelled it on a sigh.

"I love you, little girl."

He kissed the top of her head and within minutes was asleep.

Only then did Amanda realize that he'd never told her what was wrong.

"Lemme pour you another, Coop. You can still see straight. You need another drink."

Tom Benton tipped the bottle and Billy nudged the glass over to catch the whiskey as it spilled out on the tabletop.

"What I need is some money," he corrected with a good-natured slur. "Hell, my pockets are so empty there's an echo when I reach into 'em. Nice a' you boys to let me share your room. Been spending most a' my nights on the street or in jail. Can't even afford to bunk in with a cheap woman."

Benton and Collins exchanged a look.

"We thought you had yourself a job, Billy," Jasper Collins drawled out.

"Oh, yeah. Scratching for twenty-five a month by turning on your friends. Helluva job. Couldn't do it no more."

"You given up ranging, Coop?"

"Never was my idea for a line a' work. Got nabbed running stolen cows. Was either put on a star or take a short drop off a tall horse. Which one would you boys pick if you had the choice?"

They both laughed and passed another look between them.

Billy stared glumly into his glass. "Thought I had some pards there but I was wrong. A man's friends don't turn their backs on him jus' 'cause he gets tangled up with the wrong woman and makes a few mistakes."

"We're your friends, Billy."

He looked up, his smile crooked and grateful. "Yeah, you are. I 'preciate it. I best get some shut-eye. Gots to head out early. I owe a bunch a' folks here a heap a' money and I want to be a county away afore they realize they ain't gonna get it. Just as soon keep my hide where it is, if you know what I mean. Leastwise until I can earn me a few dollars."

"Coop, me and Collins was talking and we was thinkin' maybe you should ride on back with us."

Billy gave a gusty laugh. "Why? So's Ray can kill me? Now, that would be a right quick solution to my money trouble. I don't think so. He ain't all too forgiving and he gots no use for me."

"Hey, what if we was to clear it with him? You know, get you another chance to prove yourself. Hell, you're a good man to ride with. All of us thought so."

"Yeah? You'd do that for me?"

"Sure, Billy. Why not? Can't stand to see a man down on his luck, and you look to be dragging yours."

"That's so. That truly is. I tell you, boys, you're the best kinda friends . . ." He broke off, his blurry eyes tearing up. He wiped them on his sleeve and bolted back the last of his whiskey. The momentum carried him down flat on his back on the faded bedspread. His eyes closed and didn't reopen. The other two watched him for a long, silent minute.

"Well, what do you think? You think he's being straight with us?"

"Can't tell. Guess we'll leave that up to Gant. Them two was pretty thick in the old days, from what I hear. I'll head on out tonight and ask him. You bring Billy on up to Presidio with you day after tomorrow, and if Ray don't like the idea, we can kill him there and toss him in the Rio Grande."

Billy muttered to himself and rolled onto his belly. He risked a tight smile against the nap of the spread and let his consciousness go.

And then he enjoyed a series of wicked dreams in which he was rolling around with Sarah Bass under a warm West Texas sky.

Chapter Twelve

Harm reined their buggy up in front of the mercantile. The dusty emporium served as the area's postal center as well. While he was giving his kids a gruff account of how much they'd be allowed to spend inside, Sarah started to climb down to the boardwalk. Her skirt caught on the wheel and in wrenching it free, she twisted her body in such a way that agony streaked through her ribs. She gave a soft cry of distress as her balance gave way. As she teetered precariously, strong hands clasped about her waist.

"I gotcha."

Sarah turned, ignoring the sharp stab of pain it caused to wounds both physical and emotional, to stare into Billy Cooper's dark eyes. For a long moment, both were lost in the looking. Just when she thought she saw an answering desire flame in the depths of his gaze, he blinked and adopted a cocky smirk. He then swung about easily to settle her on the boardwalk, but he didn't move his hands.

"Well, howdy there, Miz Bass. Can't keep yourself outta trouble, I see."

He sounded funny, all blurry around the edges, and he looked strange, too—unkept, unwashed, and totally unsavory. Not like anybody she should be ogling with her stare, but Sarah couldn't help it. Her heart was hungry for the sight. Her nose wrinkled up when she finally identified the scent permeating his clothes. "You're already drunk and it's not even noon."

"Still drunk, thanks to you." He glanced up at Harm and

waved a negligent hand. "No need to get that squinty look about you, Mr. Bass. I got no intention of messing with her. Once was enough to ruin my life." He tipped his hat to Amanda and spared a halfway genuine smile at the kids. " 'Scuse me, all. Nice to see you."

As he rejoined his equally rumpled friend on the walk, Sarah took a quick step toward him.

"Billy, I want to talk to you."

"Baby, we got nothing to say to each other. Your brother done said it all with the back of his hand. Now, get the hell outta my way and outta my life."

She put herself more determinedly in his path. "Billy, please. You're making a terrible mistake."

"Oh, you know all about other people's mistakes, don't you? When you make 'em, you got a whole passel of relatives ready to make things right for you. It ain't like that for everybody, so maybe you should think about that next time you let your little girl imagination run away with you and you go throwing yourself at a man who don't want you."

Sarah drew a short breath and stared up at him, her expression so stricken, Billy almost backed down on the spot. But he couldn't afford to.

"Now, then, baby girl, you go on home to big brother and your hero daddy and your . . . uncle and let me be. I ain't gonna pick up after your recklessness. Now, move or I'll knock you outta the way."

"You like knocking around women, do you, Cooper?" Harm had swung down from the buggy and stood braced in front of Sarah. "Try shoving me outta the way."

"Uncle Harmon, don't." Sarah grabbed on to his wrists to keep him from reaching for anything lethal. He didn't wear a sidearm. He didn't need one. He could impale a man on his big blade before most could clear holster leather.

"I ain't afraid of you, Mr. Bass."

"I'm not asking you to be afraid. I'm expecting you to be smart. You move outta our way. Now."

At that last deadly growl, Billy sidestepped, making a dramatic gesture with his hat to offer them the boardwalk. Harm started forward but Sarah balked, her eyes still on Billy. Harm pushed her to get her going, then was half dragging her.

"He's not worth it, little girl. He's a yipping coyote. Walk away from him and don't look back."

By then, Amanda and the children were out of the buggy. As Harm towed her, Sarah continued to gaze over her shoulder, reluctant to move on with her family until the man with Billy—she recognized him from the outlaw camp but couldn't remember his name—said something to the big ex-ranger and she heard Billy's reply plain.

"She ain't half as pretty as Gracie or Cammy and don't know nothing about pleasing a man."

That snapped her spine up straight. Her head swiveled forward and she marched stiffly beside her uncle with her chin at a haughty angle.

Billy watched her retreat, struggling to keep his emotions from registering on his face. *Dammit, Sarah, why can't you just let it go? Why do you make me hurt you?* he wondered in a frustration of longing. All he'd wanted to do was seize her anguished face between his palms and kiss the lines of pain away. But of course he couldn't do that. Not now.

"Holy cripes, Billy! Was that *the* Harmon Bass?"

"The original," Billy affirmed, unimpressed. Tom Benton gaped at the group as they disappeared into the store.

"Then your little lady—I mean, the little lady—is a Bass, too?"

"Daughter of Will, sister of Jack, niece of Harm. That Bass enough for you? Sums up why a man don't stack up to nothing in their eyes, don't it? C'mon, Tom. I want get myself a bath and some grub and something nice to wear to go courting a woman who knows what to do with a man's passions."

Tom was still staring over his shoulder in a glaze of awe. "*The* Harmon Bass. I'll be danged! And you ain't scared a' him a-tall?"

"He's just a little guy with a big mouth." And a bigger knife. Billy was shaken right down to his boots by the confrontation. Harm Bass wasn't someone you messed with. That didn't make him a coward. It made him smart.

* * *

Harm stood back stoically as his family tore into their gifts from the East on Cal Lowe's front porch. Becca squealed in delight at a life-sized baby doll with big china blue eyes and golden hair, and was modeling her starchy petticoat over her plain calico skirt. Rand was fascinated by a gilded carousel with horses that moved up and down as it turned and played a tinkly tune. Harmon received nothing. Amanda had clued her relatives early on that the effort wasn't appreciated. But she was breathless over her present as she removed the intricately carved game pieces from their shipping paper one by one.

"What are those, Mama? Soldiers?"

"They're game pieces in the uniforms of the Confederacy and Union," Amanda explained while examining the Jeff Davis king. "Oh, Harmon, aren't they beautiful!"

"For checkers?" Harm asked with an indifferent glance, refusing to be appreciative.

"Chess," his wife amended. "I used to love to play with my cousin Roger."

"The one who liked kissing you?"

Amanda flushed slightly and said, "Yes. That one. Will knows how to play, too. Maybe I can talk him into a game over the holidays."

"You never said you liked playing chess."

"I never had any—any of the pieces or the board." She was going to say anyone to play with, but wisely caught herself. Harm didn't like having his nose rubbed in his lack of refinement, and that's what seemed to happen every time the parcels came from New York.

"Is it like checkers?" He was gauging her enthusiasm, thawing in his stance. If it meant that much to her . . .

"A little. I could teach you to play. It's a game of stealth. The Apache in you would love it." She smiled and he was momentarily appeased. Until she drew out the next package and gave a soft cry of delight. "My picture book! Oh, children, look. There's your grandmother and grandfather Duncan. And my brother, Randy." Her eyes misted up as they always did when she thought of him. Harm had met him once. They hadn't had much to say to one another. Randolph Duncan had been dead for some time.

"And here's your cousin Roger and my aunt Millicent and aunt Gwendolyn. And this is my cousin Stanley and his sister Bertie."

Harm looked away, feeling uncomfortable and wary. Then he caught sight of Leisha opening one of her boxes. She lifted out a beautiful dress, all white lace and silk ribbons. By contrast, her hands looked very dark. She beheld it with a look of sheer wonder for the longest time, then when she noticed her father watching, she crumpled it up and stuffed it back in the box, unhappy that he'd caught her admiring it. Harm saw what he was doing to his children through the anguished eyes of his daughter.

He pulled the dress back out of the box, smoothed it, and held it up in front of Leisha. "Oh, *shijii*, you will look like an angel in this."

She warmed slightly to his praise but still grumbled, "Where would I wear such a silly thing?"

"We'll make an occasion. Your mama used to make my heart stop when she'd get all gussied up in her eastern clothes. She always makes me feel like the most important man alive. Now I'll have all the more reason to feel that way. Don't you like the dress?"

"Y—yes, but . . . it's from them."

"It's a gift, and a gift should always be received in the spirit of gratitude. To do otherwise is a sin of pride and vanity. Something I've been guilty of and didn't know it until now."

He felt Amanda's arms encircle his middle. Her lips moved over his ear as she whispered, "I love you."

Watching the two of them together, Sarah experienced a misery inside that was the depths of loneliness. She couldn't bear it. She left the porch without a sound, walking around the back of the Lowes' little house to the small garden Elena had scratched from the reddish dirt. She tried to hold the dwelling agony at bay by studying the neat rows of different winter vegetables, but the lines wavered and fogged until finally a soft sob escaped her. It was then she was encompassed in a caring embrace.

"Not for him, *shijü*. Not for a man who will not return what you long to give."

"Oh, Uncle Harmon, I love him!"

She felt him recoil at that, but his hold on her never slackened. "No, little girl, it's not love. Love is something shared, not stolen, not selfish or one-sided. You will understand when you feel it for the first time."

She didn't argue with him. What was the point? He wouldn't believe her. Instead, she pressed her cheek against his shoulder and quietly wept for all her folly.

"He's not the man for you, Sarah. You don't want someone who can forget you in a haze of drink with a saloon whore. Calvin said he spends all his nights at the Boots and Saddle bar in town. His is not a good soul. He will only hurt you." Harm's hand soothed through her hair and he kissed the top of her head. "Elena has supper ready. Come with me. Enjoy your family and friends. We'll stay here tonight, then tomorrow we'll say goodbye to Jack and we'll drop you off at home."

Nothing had ever sounded more like a death sentence to a young girl whose heart was breaking. She managed to nod and to smile for him. And she ate the hearty meal Elena Lowe prepared, pretending to take part in the table talk and the laughter. But in her heart and mind, all she could see was the look in Billy's eyes when he lifted her from that buggy.

He wasn't as indifferent as he pretended. But if she didn't do something fast, she'd never be able to find out just what he was.

The boy sweeping up behind the bar gave a start as a whisper hissed out of the shadows.

"Do you know who Billy Cooper is?"

The boy nodded.

"What room is he in?"

There was an unmistakable glint of gold as a coin spun on the floorboards. He was quick to put his boot over it. "Top of the stairs. Second door." As he heard the figure retreat, he called, "But he's not alone."

He was alone when Sarah pushed open the door without

knocking, but she could see in an instant that he didn't plan to be for long. He was propped up in a big brass bed, a sheet covering him to his middle. Everything above it was bare except for the bandage on his left arm. On the night table next to his elbow was a bottle of whiskey and two glasses. He didn't move, probably because she had the business end of a Peacemaker trained on what the sheet covered. But he was understandably angry as she stepped in from the hall.

"Sarah, what the hell are you doing here?"

Before she could answer, there was a shush of stockings and taffeta as one of the working girls swept in. Her gaze was canted down as she struggled with the back of her dress.

"Billy, honey, could you undo this for me?" Then she stiffened at the sound of a .45's hammer thumbing back.

"I'm afraid Mr. Cooper is otherwise occupied for this evening. I'm sure he'd be happy to pay you for the inconvenience."

The whore cast an anxious look at Billy, but he nodded to let her know everything was all right.

"Another time, Gracie," he told her with a flash of his dimples.

"Any time, Billy." Then she backed out nervously and Sarah slammed the door shut.

Billy crossed his arms over his bare chest and regarded Sarah with elevated brows. "Well?"

"Like I said, I want to talk to you."

"Well, hell, looks like I got nothing else planned for this evening, thank you very much." All his patience with her was gone. "You gonna force-feed me with lead, or can I put my pants on?"

Sarah's gaze did a quick once-over of the sheet and she swallowed hard as she lowered the revolver. But as he reached for the edge of the covers, she blurted out, "You just stay put." Grinning wryly, he leaned back and she concluded with a growly "What I want to say won't take long, then I can send your little companion back up to you—if she thought you were worth the wait."

"Which you obviously didn't."

Her jaw squared off at his crude reminder. "I didn't come up here to talk to you about . . . that."

"No?"

"No." She could feel the blush on her face and cursed it. The last thing she wanted him to know was what was really on her mind. And it had everything to do with . . . that. "I wanted to talk to you about going back with the rangers."

"What?"

"It's my fault you and Jack got into that fight. Emily's going to talk him into taking you back if you'd just make the first move."

"Sarah, wait—"

"All you have to do is talk to him. Jack's not one for grudges. I'm sure he'd listen."

"Sarah, would you—"

"If I talked to him and told him how it was, that none of it was your fault, everything could go back the way it was."

"What have you told him already? About us, I mean."

Her face was positively flaming. "Nothing. What's to tell?" And her gaze dipped to the floorboards. She cleared her throat of its need to waver and continued. "Billy, you can't just throw your whole career away over such a stupid misunderstanding. Uncle Harmon told me you'd been in here drinking every night, and I know that man you were with this morning was from the camp. Billy, please don't get all turned around over something you could settle with just a couple of words. You can't just walk away because of me and what I did. You have to go to Jack and—"

"Sarah, hush a minute. What's between Jack and me's got nothing to do with you. Nothing at all."

She opened her mouth, then shut it with a snap. Nothing? And here she was making such a prize fool of herself?

"Sarah, I told Jack nothing happened between us and he believed me. Me leaving the rangers isn't your fault, so you just go on home now and forgot about making up for something that doesn't concern you. Go home!"

She stood there, huge tears glimmering on the tips of her lashes as she struggled for something to say that wouldn't come out as foolish as what she'd managed so far. The hurt and humiliation was crushing. She should have known it had nothing to do with her. Why would Jack have suspected someone like Billy of wanting to mess with his little sister? Not when he could have a woman like Luisa or Gracie, who was indeed prettier and more endowed than she'd ever be. Her pride demanded she say something before making an awkward retreat.

"I should have known. If Jack suspected you were the first man I'd been with, he'd have done more than kick you out of the rangers. He'd have killed you. My mistake for not thinking it out a little more clearly."

Then it was crystal clear to Billy Cooper. Realization exploded through him like a stick of dynamite. "Wait a minute, Sarah. Are you saying that what happened at the creek . . . that it wasn't just *our* first time but *yours* with anyone?"

"What if I am?" Her voice quavered and she tried to offset it with a belligerent stance.

"Then you were a—"

"Fool," she concluded harshly. "Yes, that's exactly what I was."

She was standing there with that same look of pain and panic on her face that she'd had then. Only then, he'd been too preoccupied with his own passion to see it. Or to understand what it meant: that Sarah Bass had been a virgin when he'd taken her, and his rough and rather hurried possession was the only one she'd known.

That knowledge delighted him.

And made him feel guilty as hell.

No wonder she'd been so upset and skittish. It wasn't because she was playing some teasing game with him, it was because she'd been scared to death! And what had he done? He'd taken her like an experienced whore, expecting her to know what to do and what to feel, instead of showing her. He'd done worse than betray Jack's trust; he'd torn away her innocence with a hurtful indifference. And that wasn't how it should have been. That wasn't how he'd wanted it to be.

"Why didn't you tell me?"

"Tell you what?"

"That I was your first?"

Sarah wiped at her eyes angrily. "Why? And make you more conceited than you already are? What difference would it have made?"

"A lot." He patted the edge of the bed coaxingly. "Sarah, c'mere."

Her heels dug in at the door.

"Sarah, come on over here. You aren't scared of me, are you?"

"Scared of you? Don't be silly!" And with that prodding of pride, she marched over to the bedside to prove him wrong, just as he'd intended.

"If I'd known, I'd have made it nice for you."

"Oh?" Her knees were knocking nervously and her heart was banging a frantic rhythm as she stared at him straight on with all the bravado she could muster. And she had to ask, "What would you have done?"

He caught at her skirt and began reeling her in toward him an inch at a time, until she had no option but to sit on the bed or be dragged across him. Her gaze darted anxiously to the outline of him beneath the sheet, but with the way his knees were tented up, she couldn't make out any threatening contours.

"I'd have done this for starters."

His hand opened behind the back of her head and compelled her forward. After a token rebellion, she surrendered to his kiss sweetly enough. He made it into a gentle foray, testing her opposition and finding no great resistance. But the moment he slackened his grip, she was pulling away, her head down, her breathing shallow with panic. Billy found her sudden timidity as devastating to his heart as her aggression had been in its assault on his desire.

"I'm not going to hurt you, Sarah. I want to make it nice. I promise I'll make you like it if you let me."

Her gaze lifted to fix upon his. So many things flickered in the shiny darkness of her eyes, things she couldn't hold inside. Then one fact surfaced and wouldn't be ignored.

He'd been lying here naked in this bed waiting for another woman to please him.

Sarah reared back with a fierce narrowing of her eyes. "What a noble gesture on your part, Billy Cooper, not to mention that you'd be saving yourself the fee you'd planned to spend for the same satisfaction."

He gave a sudden laugh. "You're just spoiling for a fight, aren't you?"

She surged up, but Billy caught her by the forearms and gave her a toss down upon the bed. He rolled himself up over in an easy move, pinning her in the wrap of the sheet. Her struggle of protest was quickly curtailed by a shock of pain through her side. At her soft cry, Billy lifted off her but kept her trapped within the straddle of his arms and legs.

"You're hurting me!" Sarah cried as discomfort spread with every agitated breath.

"No, I'm not. Settle down. It's not the same with you as with the others. Sarah, stop it."

He finally put a stop to it by lowering himself on her soft mouth. Immediately, she surrendered and accepted his kiss with the gracious parting of her lips. When he came up for air, Sarah was docile and dewy-eyed.

"What do you mean, it's not the same with me?"

Had he said that? He surely hadn't meant to. That was a surprise, almost as much a surprise as realizing it was true. It wasn't the same with Sarah. It never would be.

To his thinking, women deserved no more than a cordial tip of his hat. He never bedded down with any who expected more than cold coin for his pleasure. He liked it honest. If they enjoyed it, too . . . well, that was fine, but he'd never gone out of his way to see to it. How was a man supposed to tell? A man couldn't pretend such things, but he knew women were as good at acting as they were at lying. Some of them thought a little extra enthusiasm would earn them more, so he'd developed a cynical attitude. Payment up front, and whatever they wanted to give him was just fine by him. Straight and quick or long and sweaty, it didn't matter and it didn't mean anything.

He hadn't known it could matter or mean anything until he'd observed Jack and Emily together.

And then there was Sarah. When she'd claimed she hadn't liked it with him, he'd been next to mortally wounded. He'd never stopped to wonder why. He'd never cared before. Maybe it was because he felt he'd cheated her by giving back nothing in return for his enjoyment. But he was afraid it was more than that. He was afraid it meant he needed to know he was giving back as good as he was getting. He wanted to hear her make those sultry little moans and know he was the cause. Maybe that was too much to ask. Maybe it was sheer craziness to want sincerity from a female. But damn, he wanted her to respond to him, to what he was doing to her, for her.

But he couldn't tell Sarah Bass any of those things, so he kept it simple.

"I've known you since you were a little girl. Your brother's been the best kind of friend to me."

"Oh." Her tone sounded deflated.

He smiled, allowing his dimples a brief dance. "When a man waits a long time for something he wants, it means something special to him. I've wanted you since you were thirteen years old."

"Really?"

She said that so hopefully, sounding so amazed, it did wonderful things to his male pride. That, coupled with the fact that his was the only trespass upon this virgin territory, goaded him to further candor.

"Oh, yeah. I wanted you bad."

"You forget where I lived?" She snapped that so saucily, he had to grin.

"No. And I didn't forget how much I liked that kiss. Probably why I stayed away."

"Oh." That was sighed out softly.

He stroked his fingertips along the fine cut of her cheekbones. "Sarah, if you want to go now, I'll let you. If you want to stay, I'll make sure you don't regret it."

She stared up at him for a long tense moment, then said, without the slightest doubt, "I want to stay."

Chapter Thirteen

"Are you sure?"

"Billy, are you gonna talk or are you gonna kiss me?"

"I reckon I'll kiss you."

And he did, very slowly, very wetly, very thoroughly. Her hands came up to make tentative circles over his shoulders and back, moving lower with each revolution until they reached the edge of the sheet, then nudging lower still to cup the firm contour of his bare buttocks. She chuckled against the pressure of his mouth.

"What?"

With her hands still engaged in a provocative kneading, she smiled up at him with a wicked appreciation and murmured, "To think it was always your long legs I admired. Silly me."

He grinned, obviously flattered. "You're a naughty girl, Sarah Bass."

"Then I ought to suit you just fine, seeing as how they're the type you like."

Still grinning, he began to work his way leisurely down the buttons to her dress. When he pushed the fabric aside, he was reminded of how fragile she was by the bulky tape around her rib cage. Billy hesitated, then recalled how perfectly shaped her breasts were and how badly he'd wanted to touch them. Not nearly as bad then as he did now. He started down the buttons of her chemise, noticing how quick and shallow Sarah's breathing had become. He glanced up to see she had her eyes tightly closed, and a great tenderness unwound inside him.

"Sarah, I'm not rushing you, am I?"

She peeped at him cautiously. Her voice was tiny. "No."

"You're not afraid of me, are you?"

Again the little "No." But as soon as he started to peel back the last layer of cotton covering her, she was gasping, "Billy?"

"What?"

"Could we do this with the lights off?"

"Sure. If you want to."

Her heart was thrumming like a baby rabbit's beneath the spread of his fingers.

"Is that how you usually do it? In the dark?"

He smiled. "Depends on whether or not I like the looks of who I'm with."

There was a pause, then her insistent, "Well?"

"I'd prefer we left the lights on."

Her dark eyes smoldered. "Okay." As his hand slipped in next to her bare skin she sucked in a ragged breath, letting it out in a shuddering sigh as he gently kneaded in much the same way that she had over his taut seat.

He kissed her again, dipping his tongue inside her mouth, once with a teasing flicker, again with a possessive plunge. Then his head moved downward, and before she had any idea what he meant to do, she felt the hot dampness of his mouth upon one tightly budded nipple. A shock of sensation rocketed through her and Sarah buried her fingers in his hair, clutching tight, anchoring him there as he continued to taunt and tantalize her to a near frenzy.

After several minutes of having her wild and writhing beneath him, Billy lifted up to suck at her neck, her jaw, and finally her lips. She went after his kiss with an urgent appeal that was hell from which to break away.

"Sarah . . . Sarah, baby, stop a minute."

She lay back panting, her fever-bright gaze hungrily detailing his face.

"Sarah." He kept his tone pitched low, full of husky vibration. Like a purr. "Baby, you want to climb on outta all those clothes and slip under these covers with me?"

A shadow of fright and embarrassment flickered through her big eyes, then she answered swiftly, "All right."

He lay back so she could shinny across him, then he scooted over and waited. Her hands were visibly trembling as they drew down the sleeves of her gown, but she didn't hesitate in stripping to the skin. She didn't give him much of a chance to look before ducking under the sheet, but what he did glimpse inflamed him plenty. Then she was easing up to him, quivering shyly, so exquisitely soft and warm, he had to fight not to snatch her up tight. When she fit flush against his side, her palm slid gingerly across the flat plane of his belly, coming to a modest stop when encountering the crisp furring that trickled suggestively downward.

"If there's anything else you're curious about, help yourself," he coaxed. He could hear her frantic swallowing.

"N—no. That's all right." Then, with an impertinent little smile, she encouraged, "If there's anything you're curious about, you feel free, too."

"Thanks for the invite." His hand settled big and familiar over her navel. She shook beneath his touch like an unbroken mare under the first feel of a saddle blanket. He took his time, letting her get used to the weight and presence of his hand before beginning a seductive stroking, rubbing, gliding, which got her shifting restlessly for more. As he came to the downy nest of black hair, Billy felt her stiffen and he wondered if she'd fight him with a maiden's alarm. Instead, her thighs parted trustingly as she breathed his name.

And surprisingly enough, he was curious. He'd never done much intimate touching, usually in too great a hurry to get right to the point of things. But Sarah's sweet response to him made him long to linger, gauging the gusty quality of her sighs as he explored the slippery heat of her, experiencing a twist of exciting tenderness as she turned her face into his shoulder and banded her arms about his neck. Her breathing was now impossibly fast, stroking along his throat with the intensity of a steam engine working its way uphill. When he sank his fingers inside to check her readiness, he never expected her inner body to grab onto him with a sudden clutching spasm.

Sarah jerked and quivered violently against him as she cried out in surprise and wonder, "Oh, Billy! Oh, my!" He didn't dare move until her tension melted down into a liquid contentment. She nuzzled his neck and murmured, "Oh, Billy, why didn't you tell me?"

Hell, he'd have been glad to if he'd had the slightest idea it could be done that way!

She tipped back her head and her eyes were aglow with lambent pleasure. Billy grinned wide with the pride of accomplishment, as if he'd had every intention of guiding her to that particular paradise. But when he tried to stroke her again, she muttered in complaint and shifted her thighs together to lock him out. At that point, he was throbbing so hard, his head was aching. Billy pushed back her tangled hair with a gentle hand. He whispered in his most persuasive voice, "Baby, there's more. That's not all there is."

"Mmmm . . . it's enough for me," she sighed languorously.

It was a struggle to keep his frustration in check. He rocked against her, prodding her insistently with his rock-hard erection. "Sarah, don't you want to give back to me what I gave to you?"

She looked up at him, genuinely perplexed, then her mouth formed an O of understanding. Somewhat reluctantly, she said, "Yes, of course."

He was up and over her before she had a chance to change her mind, probing with a rigid urgency against the tight seal of her thighs. And her fear was back as her closed fists braced against his shoulders.

"Sarah, you'll like this, too. I know you will." Did they? he wondered subconsciously. Did women like it? He knew they claimed to, but being women, he couldn't take their word for it. It was suddenly vitally important that Sarah enjoy what they were about to do together. "Don't you want to love me?" he crooned sweetly, and there was a slight drop in her

cautious pose. "How we gonna make those six kids?" He nibbled a line of kisses along her elegant jaw, tasting the tension.

She took a panicked gulp. "What if it hurts like last time?
What if we don't . . . fit?"

His laugh was shaky. "Baby, if I had a pair of boots that fit
me as good as you do, I'd wear 'em until the day I died!" He
was getting desperate, torn between the want to gentle her
slowly and the need to be inside her quick. "It's not gonna
hurt this time."

"That's what Amanda told me."

"Aman—what did you tell her?"

Her smile was small. "Nothing, or my uncle would be
wearing your pretty blond hair on his belt."

"Great!"

"I thought you weren't afraid of him," she taunted.

"Just being smart. I thought you said you weren't afraid of
me."

"I—I'm not." And slowly, she parted her legs and let him
sink into the valley between them. "Please . . ." She bit back
the rest because it came out a whimper.

"I'm gonna make it nice, just like I promised."

"Billy, I want to go now."

He groaned at the very thought and clutched her shoulders
tight. "You'll see. You'll like it." And he pressed against
her.

"Billy, I don't want to—"

"Yes, you do. Yes, you do. Sarah, just let it happen, baby.
Let me make it good." He knew he could, if she'd just relax.
If she'd just trust him. If he could just—if he could just manage to get inside without tearing her apart. He thrust hard in
his impatience and Sarah's slender body reacted beneath him.
He kissed her hard, scared senseless that he'd hurt her after
all his assurances. Her legs thrashed along the outside of his
as he settled in deep. Then she went alarmingly still and in
his shame, he withdrew.

"I'm sorry, baby," he began. Then he got a good look at
her face. Her magnificent dark eyes were wide open, and

there wasn't a trace of fear or discomfort in them. She looked dazed. She looked like a sensual invitation.

Her palms moved over his taut features, fluttering slightly, stroking boldly. "Oh, please don't tell me that was all there is."

His grin broke wide in relief. "No, ma'am. Far from it."

"I'm waiting, Billy Cooper. Impress the hell out of me."

"My pleasure."

And it was obvious the minute he was snug up inside her, that it was her pleasure, too.

The fit was tight, and that made for a heated friction when he moved within her. Fissions of sensation shivered out from that searing contact, warming along her limbs and shaking right down to the arches of her feet. She tried to move with him but the effort was too much for her splintered side. When she moaned softly and flinched in complaint, Billy slowed his tempo and murmured hoarsely, "It's all right, Sarah. You lay still. Let me do it, baby."

So she lay back and let him surge above her, within her. He was being careful, carrying his weight so he wouldn't burden her with it, thrusting deep and sure with more consideration than she guessed he showed to most of his women, because his features were taut with concentration. She would have liked to have seen into his eyes but he kept them tightly closed, focusing on something unseen when she'd rather his attention be on her. Eager for his notice, she clasped his face between her hands and hauled him down for a soul-snatching kiss.

With a sudden urgency, his mouth opened over hers, sucking up her breath and breathing it back in hard, forceful pants. She felt his muscles tense and quake, and her legs wound around the long length of his, pulling him up as far as he could reach inside her as his passions spilled. She was thinking about those six children as he sagged along the length of her, trembling fitfully, swallowing down great gulps of air. When his eyes finally opened, they were shiny with amazement.

"Oh, Sarah" was all he could say before emotion choked

up in his throat. He kissed her softly parted lips and her brow, but he couldn't meet her gaze again. For glowing in her eyes was every evidence of a woman in love, and he didn't want to recognize it. Instead, he eased from her and cradled her close to his racing heart, trying to control his breathing and trying to calm the panicked notion raging inside that said he was in love with her, too.

Sarah had no idea how much time had passed. It was either very late or very early. Billy was sleeping beside her, stretched out on his side. She could hear his sonorous breathing and the sound was strangely soothing. He'd made love to her and he was right. She had liked it. Very much. She was slightly sore from that fit he'd boasted about, but it was a proudly borne discomfort. Just like bearing his children would be.

Restless with him so near, Sarah snuggled up behind him, skimming his ribs and flank with her palm and nuzzling her face against the unruly waves of his hair. In a few hours he'd be gone. What, then, would she do without him?

Her hand curved over his hard thigh. Living out of the saddle made for muscles like iron. Boldly, she slid lower, touching where she hadn't quite dared touch before. And as she stroked him gently, she had the thrill of feeling him awaken within her palm.

"Sarah, what are you doing?"

"If you have to ask, I must not be doing it right."

"You—you're doing just fine." His breathing deepened and his passion increased threefold. She marveled at him and found herself wanting him quite ferociously.

"Billy . . ." Her kisses rained upon his bare shoulder, then she licked up the hot, salty taste of him.

Abruptly, he snatched her hand away from its determined pleasuring and he rolled to face her. His expression was somber. "Sarah, we've got to talk about what tonight means."

She was very calm. "I assume it doesn't mean anything beyond what it is: some very nice lovemaking."

"It can't, Sarah. Not now."

"I understand."

Her complaisance disturbed him. It should have made him grateful. He'd expected a clinging, teary display, yet she was cooler about the whole thing than he was.

"Do you? I gotta leave in the morning."

"So do I."

"W—where are you going?"

"Home. You know where that is, just in case you want to ride out there someday for another kiss."

"I got no place for you right now. I got things I got to do. I couldn't come close to supporting a wife and—"

"Wife? Billy, I didn't say I was going to marry you. At least not for a long time to come."

That stopped him cold. "What?"

"I'm seventeen years old. I'm not ready to sit around the house waiting for my man to come home. There's more I want to do than darn socks and learn to cook."

"Like what?" His voice was gritty.

"Lots of things," she told him boldly, letting her imagination stretch out because he had that same smothering look in his eyes that her mother got. Although she liked the idea of them sharing a future, Sarah didn't like the thought of him snapping any chains around her ankles ... not yet. "Like maybe do some traveling. California, maybe even east. Amanda wants to take me to New York City."

"New York City?" Panic was edging in over his attempt to remain calm.

"And I want to meet people—"

"What kinda people?"

"What?"

He'd come up to his elbows fast and grabbed hold of her upper arms. "What kinda people?"

"Billy, you're hurting me! Let go! People people."

"Men people?"

"What if they are? Are you going to the monastery tomorrow?"

"But that's—"

"Different? No, it is not. You come around every four years or so, whenever it suits you, and you expect me to wait?"

There was such indignation in her fine dark eyes, such fiery challenge. The sheet had slid down from her shoulders to pool at her trim waist, where the bandages added a slight thickening. From there upward, she was gloriously bare to his view. To his and how many others once he rode away? Thinking of it, worrying about it, put a fire in his brain that reason couldn't extinguish.

"Yes," he told her with a low, savage certainty. "I expect you to wait."

"Well, you can just forget about that, Billy Coop—"

His kiss effectively cut off the rest of her objection. While she made some rather angry sounds muffled against the forceful pressure of his mouth, he took her down on her back on the rumpled covers, crushing her breasts against the wall of his chest, yet mindful of her injury. When he'd kissed the fight from her, he opened her mouth with his own and let passion become its own persuasion. She moaned and met the thrusting of his tongue with her own, matching his ardor, surpassing it even. Her hands came up to mesh in his hair, holding his head so she could kiss him back with a mind-spinning fervor.

"Wait for me, Sarah."

"Make love to me, Billy."

"Wait for me."

"I want you now."

He groaned because she wasn't telling him what he wanted to hear. "Dammit, Sarah, say you'll wait!"

Her eyes opened, so deep, as they delved into his with a fierce intensity. "I love you, Billy."

And those words shook him to the soul. Because he wanted to believe her and he'd sworn never to heed that vow. He knew better than to listen, but his heart had already heard and was pounding a vigorous response. His jaw clamped tight to contain the answer building up to a chest-clogging pressure. He would never say those words. Never. He wouldn't speak them and give a woman that kind of power over him, the kind of control that could reduce and destroy him.

But as Sarah drew his head down and met his lips with the sweetness of her own, he realized he didn't have to say it to make it true. Sarah Bass had him whether he admitted it or not. There was nothing his head could say to lessen her stranglehold on his foolish heart.

"Love me, Billy," she was murmuring against his mouth, as sweet as an angel with a devilish intent. Her bare toes were stroking the calf of his leg. Her hips were pushing up against the desperate achiness of his, asking, pleading for fulfillment.

Sarah cried out and clutched him tight as he claimed her. When he moved in a strong pleasure-building rhythm, the sounds she made weren't those lusty rapturous moans and groans, but rather fragile feminine whispers sighing in harmony with his sure strokes. There was something so gratifying in those breathy little cries.

He could feel her legs begin to shiver alongside his. He felt the tension bunch tight within her belly as she seemed to stop breathing.

"Oh, Billy!" She expelled his name as a convulsive ripple of delight swept through her. He rode it out, then with one last thrust let ecstasy claim him explosively with a double-barreled force. It was some time before he was aware of her fingers combing through his hair or of her warm little kisses sprinkling over his face and neck and shoulders. He'd just begun to sink into a splendid lethargy when he heard her say "I love you," and then all traces of restfulness were gone. Billy held her in his arms until she was limp with sleep, then he lay for a long while staring up at the ceiling. Troubled. Terrified.

"Hey, Cooper. C'mon. Get a move on."

Sarah woke with a start and grabbed the sheet up to her chin. Beside her, Billy gave a long, limbering stretch and rolled out of the covers without so much as a word to her.

"We got time for coffee?" he asked the man sitting on the foot of the bed as he pulled up his jeans.

"Only if you can drink it in the saddle."

"I've managed before." He reached for his gunbelt and buckled it on. He'd yet to look at the wide-eyed figure bundled in his bed.

"Billy?"

"I gotta go," he told her brusquely, stepping into his boots. Boots that didn't fit him half as well as she did. But those sultry comparisons seemed miles and years away in the light of morning.

"Hey, Cooper, ain't that—"

"Sarah, Tom."

"That's the Bass girl!"

"She came calling last night and kinda ended up staying." Billy grinned and Benton took his meaning. He fixed his hat and looked at her finally. "Be seeing you, baby."

Her expression crumpled. "Billy, you can't just . . . leave!"

He frowned impatiently. "We been through this. I told you I was riding out in the morning."

"Riding where?"

"Out."

"With whom?"

"Tom here, if it's any of your business."

Her gaze searched his face and came up with unwanted answers. "You're going back to Gant, aren't you?" When he didn't answer, she had her answer. "Billy, you can't! He'll kill you!"

"Better him than your family, when they get to wondering where you got to last night." He put one knee up on the bed and bent down. His kiss was all too quick and impersonal. With a soft cry, Sarah surged up to catch him around the waist, hugging tight, pinning the sheet between them.

"Billy—"

"I gotta go."

"Take me with you!"

"I can't. Not where I'm going."

Her head tipped back and she looked up through eyes glazed and wild.

"Thanks for last night, baby. It was real nice."

She sucked in a wounded breath and expelled it in a fury. "You bastard! You're going back to that whore Luisa!"

"Now, Sarah—"

"Don't you now Sarah me, you son of a bitch! Well, don't go back empty handed!" She shoved away from him and reached over the edge of the bed. He took a step back as she flung her petticoat at him, momentarily buried in white linen as it slapped around his face. Billy peeled it off to reveal a dimpled smile.

"Why, that's right generous of you, Sarah." He bunched the flounces up and stuffed them into his saddlebag.

Sarah sat staring up at him, her face as white as the sheet she wrapped across her bosom. Dampness welled in her eyes. "When are you coming back?" she asked in a small voice.

"When you see me."

Her trembling chin squared. "Well, I'm not gonna wait for you."

"Yes, you are."

He bent to kiss her, proving it to both of them as her arms wrapped in a frantic clutch about his head. Her mouth was hot and hungry in its demands, and it was all Billy could do to straighten.

"Goodbye, baby."

She snatched a deep, strangling breath, and it was let him go or lose the sheet. Her arms opened and Billy stepped out of them. He strode to the door with Tom Benton, never looking back. As it closed behind them, she shouted, "I'm not waiting, Billy Cooper! Do you hear me?"

Silence.

He was gone.

Sarah dropped back onto the mattress with a tiny moan of distress. She cried until the pain in her side was almost as fierce as the ache in her heart. Then she lay panting weakly, staring up at the cracked ceiling.

What was she going to do? Let him go? Let him ride back to Ray Gant and back into trouble?

Regardless of what he claimed, she felt responsible for him leaving the rangers. If he returned to the fold, she'd know where he was. There'd be a chance to see him off and on. But if he rode out with Gant, he was going to die, if not by Gant's hand, then by someone else's. Maybe even Jack's. How could it have gone so far? An argument between friends had become the pivotal point of a man's life. If he went back to Gant, she'd lose him. Not necessarily to Luisa, but to that deceivingly easy lifestyle, to his old friend's slick smile and clever manipulation. Right and wrong in West Texas was sometimes just a matter of where one was standing, and she couldn't bear the thought of Billy standing in the wrong place when the right time came.

But what was she going to do about it?

Just then the door to the room pushed open and she sat up with his name on her lips in hopeful gladness.

"Billy!"

But it wasn't Billy Cooper, and Sarah sank down in the covers with a squeak of dismay.

"Uncle Harmon!"

Chapter Fourteen

One quick look told Harm everything. His niece, un-dressed, in a bed that slept two. Sarah shrank beneath the conclusion gathering in his blue eyes.

"I'm not saying a word," he bit out. "Get your clothes on, girl. I'm taking you home."

"Uncle Harmon—"

He put up his hand. "I don't want to hear it. Save it for your mama."

Her uncle turned his back and Sarah scrambled to get dressed. She was buttoning her last button when he glanced at her.

"Wash you face."

She did so, scrubbing off the tears and the feel of Billy's kisses. And with the application of that cold cloth came a cold reasoning.

"I'm not going home, Uncle Harm."

"Yes, you are."

"No, I'm not. I'm going after him."

"You're going home if I have to tie you over the back of my saddle! You've been running loose too long, and look where it's got you. Seventeen and holed up in some ratty ho-tel with a kid you don't know nothing about!"

"Just like you and Amanda."

He drew a slow, seething breath. "I'm not talking about me and Amanda."

"Don't you preach to me, Uncle Harm. I remember finding you and Amanda in bed together before you were married."

"Enough! Like I said, this ain't about Amanda. She was alone. She didn't have any family to protect her. All she had was me. And she still has me. What's your excuse, little girl? What's your excuse for breaking your mama's heart? That boy? You think he cares about you? You think he's coming back for you? If he cared, he wouldn't have left you here like this."

Sarah's chin quivered and she stilled it with difficulty. "I have to go after him, Uncle Harmon. He's riding into trouble and I've got to stop him."

"Let him go. Good riddance. You're crazy if you think I'd let you light outta here alone."

"You could go with me."

Harm's jaw dropped. "What?"

"You could ride with me. That way, Mama wouldn't worry and—"

"And nothing! If I go after that kid, it's not going to be to save him from trouble. I'm gonna be his trouble! And he's gonna wish to God that he'd kept his hands and his . . . whatever to himself!"

She gripped his hard forearms. "I'm not going to let you hurt him!"

"Then you go home and you stay away from him."

"I can't! I can't go home in disgrace. I have to go after him, Uncle Harm. I might be carrying his child."

She could see the profound effect her words had on him. A deep, cold shock glazed his eyes and he drew in a hissing breath. He cursed softly—in Apache, in Spanish, and finally in English. Then he turned away from her. Nothing he could have done could have hurt her more or forced a greater shame upon her. She stood, adrift, in the center of the hotel room, tears pooling in her eyes.

"Uncle Harmon?"

He didn't move.

It was her last chance, her last hope of saving Billy and, perhaps, of preserving her own future. She swallowed down

her conscience and did what she had to do. In her most fragile tone, she begged, "Don't hate me."

Harm's shoulders slumped and he came around to draw
her into his embrace. "I don't hate you, little girl. You are of
my heart. Don't cry."

"I have to see him. I have to talk to him. He's riding off
to meet with Ray Gant, and if he joins up with those outlaws,
he's going to get killed. Uncle Harm, he said he loved me. He
said he wanted to marry me!"

She squeezed her eyes shut as he took in those lies. Then
she felt his hand move very gently upon her hair.

"I'll take care of everything for you, *shijü.*"

Sarah sagged against him in relief.

Harm left a note at the hotel desk with a coin and instruc-
tions to see it delivered to Calvin Lowe. In it, he'd scrawled
a brief message to his wife. He and Sarah were seeing to
some business. Don't worry. Back soon.

After asking a few quick questions, Harm learned which
way Billy and Tom had headed out of town. He fetched two
horses from the livery in the time it took Sarah to purchase
and change into a split skirt for riding, and they were off in
pursuit.

It was a hard a silent ride, with Harm studying the trail
and studiously avoiding conversation. Sarah said nothing.
What could she say? She couldn't read behind his closed
Apache facade. She didn't know if her behavior had gravely
offended him. There was a good chance it had. He was of extremely high moral character, regardless of what had happened in the past between him and Amanda. Sarah felt bad
about throwing that up in his face. She felt worse about dis-
guising her situation with Billy. She was placing a treasured
relationship on very shaky ground, but what choice did she
have? Harm was the most capable man she knew. If anyone
could get her safely to Billy and perhaps get him to see reason, her uncle was that man. If Harm didn't kill him first.
There was always that possibility, too. Harm Bass wasn't easy
to second-guess. It was hard to figure what moved in his

thoughts. He was dependable but he was dangerous, too. Another risk she'd have to take.

By the time the reined in for the night, Sarah was hurting so bad, she didn't care what her uncle thought or if she ever saw Billy Cooper again. Her side was on fire. Breathing hurt. Movement made her groan. She curled up in the bedroll Harm spread for her and wished the world would go away. She managed to mumble a good night to her uncle, then let sheer exhaustion suck her down until daylight came again.

The next day was even harder on her but she didn't complain, afraid Harm would insist they stop and rest. Time was vital if she was to get to Billy before Ray Gant worked his way on his mind.

"Looks like they're heading into Presidio. Now, there's a thieves' paradise for you."

Sarah had no reply. Her teeth were gritted up to the ears to hold in her want to whine and moan in pain. And when the rough and tumble border town of Presidio appeared, it looked like a paradise to her, too. A place where she could wash up and stretch out and pass out cold. As soon as she found Billy.

Harm came around to ease her out of the saddle. She slumped in his arms.

"Having a pretty hard time of it, little girl?" he asked gently.

Sarah nodded. Why bother lying? He could see she was going on sheer Bass determination alone.

"I'm gonna get us a room in this here hotel, and I want you to lie down and close your eyes for a spell."

"Uncle Harmon—"

"Whilst I find your boy for you."

She nodded against his shoulder and murmured, "Don't hurt him, Uncle Harmon."

"Now, why would I want to do such a thing to a fine feller like him?"

"I want your word, Uncle Harm!"

"I won't hurt him . . . until you give me leave to, that is."

Sarah smiled groggily and awareness started to seep away.

She felt him lift her up in his arms and the cool of the shade inside, then there was the delicious weightlessness of a bed beneath her.

"Rest easy, *shijii.* I'll be back soon."

"Don't hurt him," she whispered.

"I gave you my word."

And she was gone before he was.

Something wonderfully cool was brushing across her hot brow. Sarah's eyes fluttered to see darkness and her uncle's smile.

"How you feeling, little girl?" He was sponging a damp cloth upon her face. Immediately, she tried to sit up but fell back, groaning miserably. "Stay still. Take it real slow."

"Did you find him?" she demanded urgently.

"I found him. I'm taking care of things."

"Where is he?"

"Take it slow. I'll give you a hand."

She couldn't have sat up without his help. Sarah clutched at his arm, sucking tiny breaths of air that never satisfied. "Where is he?" she asked again.

"I'll bring him here to you. All right?"

She nodded anxiously.

"Now, then, think you can get yourself washed up? Look what I got you?"

She took the parcel from his hand, smiling wistfully. "I remember when you used to bring me yellow hair ribbons. Do you remember?"

"Those are the things my heart holds dear. Open it."

He was being so sweet, so kind, Sarah was close to weeping. "Oh, Uncle Harm!" She lifted out a delicate white lace shawl. He took it from her and draped it over her hair the way the Mexican women wore them. His expression was oddly intense as his palm cupped her cheek.

"So beautiful. Like your mama. Like my mama." He kissed her brow and stood. "I'll be back in a bit. You get prettied up."

She looked up at him through a haze of emotion. "I love you, Uncle Harmon."

He didn't smile.

"Well, well, well. Lookee who's here. The return of the prodigal son. Howdy there, Billy-boy."

Billy took the chair Ray Gant gestured toward, sinking into it as if he were sinking into his own grave. Could be he was. Ray was smiling as if genuinely pleased to see him, but that didn't mean anything. He'd seen Ray smile as he popped a cap on a man, shooting him dead. Smiling was an all-purpose expression to him.

"Ray. You want to kill me now, or can I order up a drink first?"

Gant laughed. "Have a drink, by all means." He motioned to one of the girls. "A glass for my friend here."

Ray poured and Billy reached for the shot glass. His hand was shaking noticeably. He didn't make an effort to control it as he bolted down his drink. Gant filled the glass a second time. The two of them were alone at the table in a room full of saloon patrons. Not a one of them could step in in time to keep Ray from killing him dead if that's what he had in mind. Nor would they make it any of their business.

"Something got you nervous, Billy?"

"Plenty." He smiled slightly, not apologizing.

"It took a lot of guts for you to come here."

"I didn't have any place else to go. Tom and Jasper thought— Oh, hell, they was wrong. I'll just head outside and you can shoot me down at your leisure." He started to stand.

"Sit down, Billy. Finish your drink. I ain't gonna kill you. Yet."

"If I'm not gonna die just yet, mind if I order up a steak?"

"Help yourself."

"Can I borrow some money?"

Gant laughed out loud. "Boy, you sure got your share of cheek! Sure, help yourself to anything you need."

"I need a meal."

"And?"

"I need a job."

"Got fed up with rangering, did you?" he drawled silkily.

Billy's smile was wry. "Something like that."

"You asking me to take you back in?"

"No. Why would you ever trust me again?"

"Why would I? In fact, why come to me at all?"

"You've always been square with me, Ray. I could always count on you for a meal and a room and a piece of advice. That's all I'm asking now. I don't deserve any more than that."

"Seems to me like that's plenty. Considering."

Billy nodded, his head downcast, his gaze riveted to his glass. He waited, wondering what Gant had heard, wondering what his chance of walking out of the saloon was. He was so absorbed in his concerns, he completely failed to be alert to another danger. One even closer and more deadly, as a voice drawled out sharp as the knife point edging under his ribs.

"Don't be making any sudden moves if you want to keep your liver."

"Oh, God," Billy groaned, his eyes closing tight.

Across from him, Ray Gant went rigid, his eyes on the unimpressive newcomer standing behind Billy's chair. Nobody to give a second look. Or so he thought at first. "Trouble, Billy?"

"Ray Gant, Harmon Bass."

"Bass? Heard of you. Not quite what I expected."

Harm smiled blandly. "Looks can be deceiving. Take this one here." He nudged with his blade and Billy twitched. "Who'd have thought he was stupid enough to make my little niece cry."

Ray frowned, then enlightenment shone. "Bassett. Bass."

"Is Sarah here?" Billy wanted to know, and he didn't sound too happy in the asking.

"Expecting you. I'd be obliged if you wouldn't keep her waiting."

"Now, just a minute, Mr. Bass—"

"Don't you raise your voice to me, boy. I'm not in the mood to teach you manners. You'll walk with me and you'll do what I tell you, or I'll vent you like the back of a good coat."

"Where we headed?"

"Over to the hotel. Got some business to attend. Shouldn't keep you more than a couple of minutes if your friend don't mind waiting."

"And if I do?" Gant asked.

"Well, that's just too damned bad. Get up, Cooper, or I'll be standing in your blood."

"Billy?" Ray questioned softly.

"It's all right, Ray. Let me see what they want." He stood cautiously, hands spread, heart in his throat. He was thinking perhaps Sarah wasn't anywhere nearby, and that Harm was going to take him outside and gut him like a deer.

"I don't like this, Billy."

"I can handle it."

Harm gave another mild smile, but his eyes were hot and glittery. No one could mistake him for anything but dangerous now. "Your friend can come along if he likes. I could use another witness for what I've got in mind."

Ray stood up just as carefully.

"Walk ahead of me. Don't do nothing funny with your hands, or I'll chop through the boy's backbone like he was a jackrabbit. And believe me, I wouldn't mind doing it at all."

Billy believed him. So did Ray. And they walked.

Sarah heard the commotion outside her door and was moving toward it at an awkward pace when it pushed inward. The first thing she saw was Billy. Relief turned her knees to water. Then she saw Ray Gant and terror leapt within her breast. And when her uncle followed bringing in a stranger with him, she was confused.

"Uncle Harm?"

"Like I said, I took care of everything. You"—he gave a

curt nod to Billy—"stand over there with her. And don't you touch her."

Sarah watched his approach through wide, uncertain eyes. This wasn't what she'd expected. It wasn't what she'd planned at all. Not a roomful of people. Not Billy looking so grim and fierce. She couldn't think of what to do. Her mind was feverish from the strain through which she'd put her unmended body. But under all the bewilderment was the wild satisfaction of seeing Billy again, of seeing him whole and well, if not too pleased to be there.

"Let's get on with it," Harm growled.

And that's when Sarah saw what the fourth man, the stranger, was holding. It was the Holy Bible.

"Uncle Harmon, what's going on?"

"I'm seeing the two of you married."

"What?" That incredulous cry tore from both Sarah and Billy.

"Uncle Harm, you can't do this! I don't want to marry him. This isn't what I wanted. I won't—"

"If you think I'm gonna stand here and be bullied into—"

"Shut up, the both of you! Boy, you gonna stand there and tell me you didn't lie with her?"

Billy's jaw clenched tight. He didn't say anything.

"Sarah, you gonna tell me that he's not the one responsible for you being in a possible family way?"

Sarah paled dramatically. She didn't say anything, either.

And watching the goings-on, Ray Gant was highly entertained.

"Marry 'em," Harm ordered the border town preacher.

It was a short ceremony between two emotionally paralyzed people. Sarah was swaying slightly, so dizzy, so stunned, she barely heard the words. Beside her, Billy was rigid, his expression giving nothing away. And after the vows were exchanged, hers whispered, his gritted out, and the preacher sanctified them, Sarah looked up at the man who was now her husband and a trembling of disbelief overcame her.

Her husband!

She was vaguely aware of signing the legal papers and of

Billy's signature penned in cramped letters next to hers. Then Harm was dismissing the preacher and squaring off with Billy.

"Now, you get the hell outta here!"

Billy stared at him. "But she's—"

"Nothing to you but a name. There'll be no more in my family running around without a proper one. You can come by in a month. If she's hasn't conceived, we'll cut you loose and you can go to hell, if that's what you want. If she has, she's got the protection of a legal name. Either way, it don't concern you."

"Don't concern me? I just married her!"

"You just saved your skin. Don't put a finer point on it than that. You'd be dead now if she'd have let me have my way. And if I ever see you around my family again, I'll cut you up into so many pieces, the coyotes won't be able to make a meal outta you."

"C'mon, Billy." Ray was tugging on his arm. But Billy hesitated. His gaze was on Sarah. She looked so fragile beneath that billowing white veil of lace, so innocent. But that was a lie. His lovely bride that duty and Harm Bass was denying him. What other lies were there? Was there any truth at all in the lift of her big dark eyes? Had it been her intention from the first to force him into this trap? Or had she meant it when she said she didn't want to marry him? Either way, their holy union was as false as the role he was playing. Sarah Bass didn't want to be his wife. She just wanted his name.

Fine. Let her have it.

He spun on his heel and stomped from the makeshift chapel, leaving his silent bride and her vengeful uncle.

And when it was just the two of them, Sarah stared aghast at her solemn uncle and wailed, "How could you do this to me!"

"*Shijii*, I wasn't the one who did something to you. Let's go home."

* * *

By the time Billy got his steak, he had no appetite for it. Ray sat across from him, watching him mutilate the piece of beef with his knife and fork.

"You got something against that cut, or you just pretending that there's Harm Bass?"

Billy cast aside his tableware and slumped back in his chair. "That interfering sonuvabitch. Who the hell does he think he is?"

"He's a Bass. That pretty much says it all. Your little bride comes from a pretty intense family line."

"Arrogant, pushy, and holier than thou, the lot of them!"

"Then how'd you get tangled up with one of theirs?"

Billy crooked a smile at him. "She's mighty fetching, don' you think?" Gant shrugged and Billy signed in resignation. "I don't know, Ray. She was young and pretty, and I was stupid and my heart just got in front of my head. Hell, you don't want to hear this."

"Don't need to. I've seen it before. Pretty little gals working their smiles on a man to get what they want."

Billy was about to say that that wasn't true with Sarah. But it was. When he thought about it, it was true. She'd had him in knots since her first bold smile and she knew it. She hadn't let up, she hadn't let him breathe, she hadn't let him alone. And now she had him. Damn her, and she didn't even want him!

Ray Gant was staring at the tabletop, his eyes taking on a faraway gleam. "I remember this little gal. I musta been maybe fifteen and riding for her husband. Well, she called me in one day to do some chores around the house, and pretty soon them chores got redirected to her bed. Next thing I knew, I was mooning around like a fool. Couldn't see nothing wrong with the idea when she asked it. Said if her husband was to suffer some kinda accident out on the range, the two of us could be together. Well, that poor feller turned up dead, and do you think that pretty thing would give me the time a' day? Tole me if I didn't make fast tracks, she'd set the law on me. And all I got for my trouble was a quick roll with her, and that wasn't even that good." He laughed. It was a hard sound. "I know all about smart-thinking women, boy. Ain't a one of 'em you can trust like you can a good horse and an oiled gun. Or a good friend."

Billy looked up at him slowly. And he nodded. "That's true."

"If you're not doing anything, why don't you ride on out with me?"

"Out where?"

"Yonder. Luisa's been asking after you."

Billy snorted. "Got enough woman trouble."

Ray Gant stood up. "You coming?"

"If you're asking."

"C'mon, then."

Billy rode out of Presidio feeling much better. He was riding toward his work and away from the woman who'd wronged him. And he had no regrets.

Harm had plenty of regrets.

If his wife was the talkiest woman, his niece sure was the weepiest.

She'd cried for two solid days, until he was so edgy and aggravated, he was tempted to give her something to wail about. He didn't understand the problem. What had he done that was so bad? He'd seen to a legitimate name for any issue her bad judgment might arrive at and he'd chased off that poor cur of a husband. What more could she have possibly wanted from him? She'd asked him not to kill him and he hadn't. He thought he'd shown admirable restraint, yet he couldn't look her way without her letting go with a whole new stream of tears. Harm stopped looking at her. And he was thoroughly grateful when they rode into Terlingua.

Sarah went from horse to buggy without a word. When Amanda looked to him for explanation, he gave her a double-bored stare that would have quailed a lesser soul. But not Amanda. Still, she wouldn't make a big deal out of it in front of the kids. She'd save it for when she got him alone. Some-

thing to look forward to, he thought glumly as they pulled ou
of the ranger camp and headed toward the Chisos.

Sarah made the rest of the ride in complete silence. He
eyes were nearly swollen shut and she looked ready to swoo
at the slightest provocation. Harm was glad to drop her off a
his sister's door. Sarah climbed down without protest and ra
right into Rebecca's arms. Then she glanced around fearfull
as her uncle came up to the porch. He could see the ruin o
her entire future pooling in her dark eyes.

"Becky, I brung her home. It's up to you from here on out
Little girl, you take care." He could hear Sarah's startled gas
as he walked away. Then she was calling after him. He
turned and she was immediately burrowed up against him.

"I'm sorry, Uncle Harmon," she sniffed miserably. "Aren't—
aren't you going to tell her what happened?"

"Figured you'd tell her what you wanted her to know.
None of my business." He felt her tremble with relief when
she realized he wasn't going to give her away.

"I love you, Uncle Harmon."

"Just trying to do what I thought best for you."

But Amanda wasn't of the same thinking when he finally
had to tell her everything.

"You did what!"

Her shout echoed in his head for a good minute as they got
ready for bed. Patiently, he explained the situation and her
mood got no better as the details filled in.

"Harmon, how could you?"

He was mighty tired of that question. His mood was none
too good, either. "Well, what was I supposed to do? The bastard owed her something! I don't know what all the yelling's
about. The man laid with her and now he's paid for the priv-
ilege."

"Oh, Harmon, you are so dense! Sarah is in love with him
and now you've made things impossible for her."

"Why? By making them take the consequences of what
they did? You think I should have let him walk off?"

"I think you should have asked Sarah what she wanted."

"I think she got what she wanted when she went to bed with him."

"Harmon!"

"In love with him." He made an uncharitable sound. "She wanted him and she's so spoiled by all of us, she's used to getting exactly what she wants. If he was any kind of man, he wouldn't have taken advantage of a little seventeen-year-old girl all full of dreams."

"And what kind of man does that make you, then, for doing the exact same thing ten years ago?"

He squinted at her and she glared right back at him.

"And what kind of man does that make Jack for laying with another man's wife?" she continued. "You didn't have any problems with the two of them lying together right under this roof! You have a very convenient moral code, Harmon. You were wrong in what you did. Who made you in charge of her happiness? Who made you their conscience? You've ruined her life."

"Only if he doesn't love her." And with that conclusion, Harmon levered out of his boots, stripped to the skin, and dropped down on his bed. "Good night."

Amanda didn't answer him. After a while, she turned down the lamp and slid in beside him. Not touching him. He lay there, wide awake, waiting for her to give up and come to him. She didn't. From the far side of the bed, he heard her quietly breathing in her sleep.

Harm awoke with the scent of wet earth in his nose and the metallic taste of terror in his mouth. He lay there in the darkness, shivering with remembered horror, and the first thought he had was to seek security.

"Ammy?"

He rolled toward her but her back was to him, a reminder of their earlier words, and Harm was reluctant to intrude upon her slumber. Panting in restless dread, he got out of bed and paced to the bank of windows that overlooked the mountains. He opened one and leaned out to catch the cold night air on his face, letting it dry the sweat of fear and the trail of a boy's tears.

When Amanda's arms encircled him, he grabbed up her hands gratefully and pressed hard kisses to them. Somehow, she'd known he needed her and here she was, asking no questions, calming him just by being there. He felt her lips move against the back of his neck, along his tense shoulders.

"I love you, Harmon." That's all she said. And it meant everything to him.

"Ammy, Calvin told me McAllister's out on parole."

She took a quick breath and her embrace tightened. "Is he back in West Texas?"

"I don't know. Calvin hadn't heard. I should have killed the bastard, Ammy. You should have let me kill him."

"Harmon, the man's your father."

"No! He's the man who laid with my mother on a bed of lies to beget me, but he's not a father to me. He saw to it that my mama died a horrible death and would have wished the same on me and Becky. He tried his damnedest to see us all buried. He had your brother killed. And now he's free. To do it all over again. Ammy, where's the justice in that?"

"I don't know, Harmon. I don't know."

He could feel her tears, wet and hot, against his bare skin.

"If he comes near me or any of my family, I'll finish him, law or no law. I won't let him hurt me. I won't ever let him hurt me again."

Amanda hugged him tight, deciding right then that she'd pay a visit to Jack and ask him to use his ranger resources to keep an eye on Russell McAllister. If the wealthy rancher decided to step foot in her backyard, she'd blow him to hell herself before she allowed him to be a threat to her happiness.

And Harm was her happiness.

Chapter Fifteen

Had there ever been such a wretched existence?

Sarah wondered as she moped through her days. Billy was lost to her even as she held to his name. Held to it until the end of the month, that is. Then, as soon as he discovered she wasn't to bear his child, he'd be gone. And she'd be alone with the sorrow and shame she'd brought upon herself with her foolish thoughts of love.

Wait for me. Oh, how silly of her to have read anything into his lies. She could wait and she could grow old, but he'd never come back to give her those promised children or those cherished dreams. She brooded and she wanted to damn her uncle for his high-handed actions, but she couldn't. He, alone, had acted in her best interest. He was protecting her the only way he could, shielding her from disgrace and any child she might carry from scorn. And he'd kept her secret from her family. Oh, he'd probably told Amanda, but her aunt would never betray a trust. All she had to do was wait out the month in silence, and it would be as if Billy Cooper had never lain with her or stood beside her before a preacher. She could get on with her life as if untouched by the events of the past weeks. If only her heart and mind would allow it.

A dozen times she came close to confiding in her mother. But it was too late to wish for a closeness that had never been there. Rebecca loved her and cared for her, true, but there had never been an intimacy in their relationship. The only one her mother was close to was Will. And Harmon.

And there was something else going on within their household. She'd almost been too wrapped up in her own troubles to notice, but slowly, Sarah became aware of how her father and brother's terse conversations would break off when she came into the room. And there was always a loaded rifle by the door. She started to pay more attention and learned that all the small ranchers in their area were under pressure to sell out or be driven out. Several of their neighbors had already succumbed to ready cash or intimidation. Sarah sensed both fear and stubbornness from her mother when Rebecca talked about having lost one home and refusing to part with another. Will and Rebecca had more than one heated discussion over whether to involve Harm, and good-natured Jeffrey was hard pressed to find anything to smile about as he performed his chores with a Colt strapped to his hip. It was definitely not a time for her to be crying over lost love, so Sarah held to her tears and waited out the days.

She worried about Billy. She knew she shouldn't, not after the way he'd upped and left her and refused to heed any of her advice. She worried because he was with Ray Gant and she knew what they were doing. Unlawful things. Things that would run cross-grained to Jack and his fellow rangers. Sarah should have been furious with him for having a character weakness that would allow him to turn his back on what was right. But she wasn't. She was remembering his kiss and the touch of his hands and the power of him inside her where no man had ever been. Or would ever go again. She remembered those pleasures he'd awakened within her on long, isolated nights when sleep was hours away and her body was restless with recall. Shamefully, she admitted to herself that if he were to show up at the front door, she would give herself to him all over again, regardless of the consequences. That was her character weakness.

But now he was her husband, and no one could fault her for doing it.

Her husband. The idea both thrilled and angered her. Sarah hadn't been prepared for marriage. For years, instead of learning the things she'd need to know to run a successful household, she'd been pestering Harm to teach her about tracking and survival. Instead of watching bread rise, she'd been off watching the sunrise from the high Chisos peaks while a wonderful sensation of freedom overcame her. Instead of making preserves and other winter stores, she'd been practicing her marksmanship, as if there weren't already four men who were crack shots in her family. But Jack and Sidney were gone, and she'd liked the idea of protecting her home. She just didn't like the idea of cleaning it. Some Texas wife she was going to make! She wanted to run with the men, not pick up after them.

Marriage. The thought kept tantalizing. Billy Cooper at her table, in her bed. Children, loving, home, security; she liked those things just fine. But she had no home of her own, no husband to share her sheets. Where was this man who was supposed to supply them? Off robbing and stealing? Off running with his renegade companions? Off with Luisa and those of her profession? Was he still expecting her to be waiting, or had he forgotten all about her?

She spent her days alternately wishing Billy Cooper would fall off the face of the earth forever and longing to be with him wherever that might be.

Then Harm arrived at their door. His presence stirred relief in Rebecca, resentment in Will, and uneasiness in Sarah. Will made it a point not to let his wife have a moment alone in conversation with her brother, and Harm was distracted or he would have noticed her desperate glances. Sarah was the one he'd come to see.

After dinner, he walked with her down to the windmill he and Jack had built one hot summer long ago. Harm was reluctant to speak at first and Sarah realized he was embarrassed.

"How are you feeling?"

"Fine. My ribs knit back together and I've got a scar to the envy of all the Basses."

He smiled at that but still avoided her gaze. "Anything you want to tell me?"

"No."

"No, meaning no, you don't, or no, you don't want to?"

"I don't. I don't know if I'm pregnant."

He flushed hot and kept walking. "Shouldn't you know by now?"

"Yes, but I'm not sure. I—I guess I could be."

Harm's tone sobered. "And how would you feel about it if you were?"

She gave him a taut smile, grateful to be able to speak of it to someone at last. "Scared. I love kids. I plan on having lots of them, but Uncle Harm, I'm only seventeen. I'm about as far from ready to be a wife and mother as a woman can get. Half the time I think I'm not weaned from my own mama yet."

"Amanda wasn't much older when she had Leisha," he reminded gently.

"But Amanda had you. And I don't have anyone."

"Oh, little girl, you're wrong." His arm slipped about her shoulders, hugging firmly. "You got family that loves you and would love any baby you bring into this world."

"Even a baby with a stupid mother and a father who doesn't care enough to come see for himself if he's a daddy?" She was blinking hard, trying not to cry. Tears wouldn't solve anything and she desperately needed some solution. Harm had helped her out of tighter spots—though she couldn't remember just when.

"The hows and whys don't matter, Sarah. They didn't matter to my mama when she had me and they didn't matter to your mama when she had Jack. And they won't matter to you."

"What am I going to tell everyone, Uncle Harmon? That you got me a name at knife point so I could hold my head up?"

"You got nothing to be ashamed of, Sarah. And nothing to be afraid of."

"Mama and Daddy are gonna hate me."

"No. They'll understand." When she looked unconvinced, he smiled reassuringly. "But if they don't and if things get bad for you here, you got a place with me and Amanda. Any time you want. You remember that."

She stopped and leaned against him, so overwhelmed by his care that she wanted to bawl like a baby. But she didn't. He'd seen more than enough of her tears.

"Thank you, Uncle Harmon."

"Now then," he began as his forefinger hooked under her chin, lifting it so he could command her gaze, "what do you want me to tell him?"

Sarah sucked a shaky breath. "I don't know. What if he doesn't come by to see?"

"I could go looking for him if you want me to."

"No. I don't."

"Do you want me to cut him loose? I can't see what good he's gonna be to you, anyway."

Sarah thought a minute but she couldn't find clear reasoning through the sudden panic that she might never see Billy again. "I want to talk to him first, Uncle Harm."

"You don't have to, Sarah. I can take care of all of it for you."

She was kneading his arm in agitation. "No. I want to handle it myself. It's my mess, after all, and I should be the one to get myself out of it." It was time she started working on her own answers. She'd made adult choices and now was the time to own up to the consequences in proper Bass fashion. And that meant not running from them. Sarah made her decision. "Will you take me into Terlingua?"

He gave her a gauging look, then nodded. She thought she saw approval in his pale inscrutable gaze. "If that's what you want. And I'll be right there for you."

"I'd appreciate that, Uncle Harm."

"We'll head out first thing in the morning then. You pack up and I'll talk to Becky."

"What are you going to tell her?"

He smiled. "I'll think of something."

* * *

Heading to Terlingua under the pretense of helping Harm purchase his Christmas gifts for the family, Sarah reached two important decisions. True, her husband had to be threatened with bodily harm to wed her, but if she was carrying his child, she would do her best to make Billy a good wife. She knew there was goodness in him hidden beneath all the anger and confusion, and she was certain she could turn him from his wrongful path. It might not have been the perfect time, but she did want to be Mrs. William T. Cooper more than anything and it wouldn't do to start off married life by having her brother hang her husband.

And that meant telling Jack everything.

But she couldn't afford to harbor any illusions. If there was no child, there was little chance that Billy would allow the marriage to continue. He didn't love her. If he had, he wouldn't have let her uncle chase him away before a wedded kiss was exchanged between them. If he showed up at all, it would be to see if they'd made a child between them, not because of any fondness he felt for her. And if he didn't come . . . She'd concern herself with that when it happened.

Emily and her boys provided a warm welcome. With the baby due around March, Emily was getting heavy and cumbersome and was more than happy to have Sarah around to help with the kids for a few days. When Emily greeted Harm she kissed him with unrestrained affection, causing him to blush and sidle away.

The afternoon seemed to drag by until Sarah heard her brother's step on the porch and the thump of him beating the dust off his hat. By the time he came in, grinning with pleasure at seeing them, she couldn't stand the anxiety of suspense.

"Jack, I need to talk to you."

"Oh? What about, little sister?"

She took a breath, glanced at Harm to see his prompting nod, then jumped right in. "I need you to take Billy back into the rangers."

He gave her a cautious look and a half smile. "That's a

pretty tall order, seeing as how it was his idea to walk away from my command."

"But if you don't take him back, he's going to get himself killed, and—and seeing as how he's my husband, I thought you might make a few exceptions."

Jack stared at her, flabbergasted. "What?" He looked to Emily. "Did you know about this?" When she shook her head, he turned to Harm.

"I arranged it," Harm said flatly.

"I gotta sit down," Jack mumbled, and he dropped into the nearest chair, shocked beyond comprehension. "All right now, someone want to tell me what the *hell* is going on? Sarah, you sit yourself down and come clean with it all."

Sarah eased into a seat with unusual timidity.

"Maybe I should take a walk or something," Harm began, but Sarah reached out to latch on to his shirt with a desperate entreaty.

"No. Stay. Some of this is your fault, after all." Her eyes fired at that last statement and Harm regarded her with an impossibly haughty look that denied it totally. But he stayed . . . and close to where she was sitting . . . and for that she was grateful. He wouldn't let Jack strangle her.

Softly, with eyes lowered and fingers clenched together, Sarah told her brother everything, sparing no details but glossing over several of the more objectionable ones. By the time she'd finished, Jack was sitting with his face buried in his hands.

"Oh, Sarah, you have no idea—*no idea!*—what you've done!" he moaned.

Sarah sank into a terrible wretchedness. Guilt weighted down upon her heart. She didn't even think to remind him that he'd done worse himself.

"How could you? Harmon, how could you have allowed it?" He straightened at last, his features drawn and slightly stunned by what she'd told him. He wasn't in the least bit moved by the shimmering moisture clinging to the end of his sister's lashes. But Emily was, and she came to place placating hands upon her husband's shoulders.

"Jack, don't be too hard on her. You remember what it wa
like to love unwisely."

"Love?" he roared. "This doesn't have anything to do wit
love! My God! I can't believe things could go so wrong.
warned him they would, but he wouldn't listen to me."

Sarah sat up, her mood more attentive. "Jack, what ar
you talking about?"

"Billy, and how he's risking his life to find out who in ou
company is giving information to the likes of Gant."

Beside her, Harm made a stricken sound in his throat.

"I don't understand," Sarah murmured, upset and needin
to know everything. Afraid that if Jack wasn't all that con
cerned abut her and Billy Cooper being in bed together . .
how much worse could this be?

"Billy never left the rangers, Sarah. That fight we had, hi
leaving . . . that was all staged to fool whoever was workin
here on the inside so he could try to get back in with Gant
He was sure he could make them believe the falling out wa
real if he wallowed around low enough."

She'd believed him. So much so that she'd conned her uncle into tracking him down and dragging him to the altar,
purportedly to save him from something he was in no danger
from in the first place!

"Then he was never going to ride with them?" Sarah asked
in a shaky voice.

"No. It was just part of his plan to get back on the inside
for us. And now you've gone and jumped right into the middle of it and probably ruined everything! You could have gotten him killed!"

"No," Harm put in quietly. "If anything, she made them
believe him. Dammit, I believed him."

"You were supposed to. Everyone was supposed to."

"Well, how was I to know that all this was some stupid
scheme cooked up between the two of you? You should have
told me, Jack. If I'd known . . ." If she'd known, she wouldn't
have gone chasing after Billy so desperately, thinking she was
saving his life. Instead, she'd place it in terrible jeopardy.

"Well, now you know. And now we got to figure out what

WILD TEXAS BRIDE 199

o do about it. We'll get you an annulment. No need for your
heroics now, and Billy's got work to do."

An annulment. Sarah's head swam. No, she didn't want
out of her marriage. But she didn't have a marriage, did she?
Just a sham as false as the game Billy was playing with Ray
Gant.

"I don't know where he is," she told her brother in a small,
raw voice.

"No problem. He'll be here tomorrow morning."

Sarah couldn't sleep. All night long, she pictured her confrontation with Billy, mulling it over and over, but it was
never the way she wanted it to be. He wasn't going to come
into her brother's house, sweep her up in his arms for a hot
kiss and a husky "I missed you." How on earth was she going
to face him after the foolish way she'd behaved? He and Jack
had been in the middle of a dangerous scheme and she'd
blundered in, dragging her uncle behind her, thinking to play
the rescuer. No wonder he'd been furious with her.

He wasn't a criminal.

He was a hero!

Why had he married her? Why hadn't he just told her? Of
course, that would have been kind of hard to do, with Harm
all bristled up and ready to gut him, and Ray Gant there to
serve as witness to the happy event.

Billy would be here in the morning.

Then what was she going to do? How could she stand it if
he didn't want to keep her? Anxiety built to a roiling turmoil.
By the time daylight arrived, Sarah felt sick and weak. When
Emily knocked to ask if she wanted breakfast, there was no
stopping the indelicate surge of nausea. Emily took charge of
her with a firm, gentle hand, insisting she return to bed to
rest. Sarah lay there in misery while the room spun and her
stomach rolled, and she clutched Emily's hand, moaning,
"He's going to leave me, Emily. He's going to leave me."

But Emily supplied a reassuring pat and soothed, "I don't
think so, Sarah."

* * *

Having to sneak into a camp full of his friends sat bad wit Billy. What sat worse was knowing one of them wasn't h friend at all. And it was frustrating not to know which one

He tapped lightly on the kitchen door, careful to keep h face shaded beneath a broad-brimmed Mexican hat. Whe the door opened, he slipped in quickly and doffed his ha ready to start making excuses and apologies.

"Howdy, Miz Emily. I—"

"Oh, Billy. I'm so glad you're all right!"

Her tight embrace was enough to stun him into speechless ness. It felt so good, he was returning it before he realize how dirty he was. Entering Jack's house always brought wit it that feel of coming home. He didn't know why. It wasn't a if he'd experienced that feeling before. There was somethin so right about it: the fragrant scent of the kitchen, an armfu of child-plumped woman who was happy to see him, the sen sation of a soul-hugging warmth and welcome. Billy coul have stood there all day just soaking it up, but he was re minded of his purpose and his position, and he levered back

"I'm sorry, ma'am. I'm getting you and your floor al dirty."

"Both will wash, William."

Her palm touched to his stubbled cheek and he melted in side like butter. He let his gaze drop to the floor, suddenly embarrassed by the strength of his emotions and by his desire to hug her once more. Billy thought again how lucky Jack was to have such a home, such a woman.

"Jack's in the front room. I'll put on some more coffee and bring it in after the two of you have had a chance to talk for a bit."

"Thank you, ma'am."

"You're always welcome, Billy."

Blushing with pleasure, he strode down the hall to meet with his lieutenant.

"Hey, Jack."

And Jack greeted him with a jaw-numbing punch.

From where he sprawled back across the sofa, holding the side of his face, Billy looked up blankly at the raging features of his friend. And then he understood. Personal first, then business.

"What do you mean putting your hands on my sister! You think I wouldn't mind you treating her like one of your cheap saloon pieces that you can play around with and drop when you're done? Think again! I told you—*I told you!*—to stay away from her."

Billy could have mentioned right then that Sarah had made that impossible, but he wisely kept silent. Jack wasn't in the mood for explanations. He had a mountaintop of brotherly outrage to blow off, so there was no point in interrupting until he wore down to hot steam.

"I trusted you to take care of her! She's seventeen years old, Billy. What were you thinking? Were you thinking? Obviously not. And then to top it all off, you go and marry her!"

He couldn't keep quiet about that. "Well, now, Jack, your uncle didn't give me much choice there. He wasn't in the frame of mind to listen to any objections."

"He should have killed you! You ungrateful, immoral—"

"Jack, we both know my good points. You want to shoot me, shoot me."

"I want to tear you apart with my bare hands! How could you do such a thing?"

"It's done."

"Well, it can be undone." Jack took a deep, calming breath and let his murderous intent ebb. "She thought she was saving you from a life of crime and Uncle Harm thought he was saving her from a life of shame. I wish someone had at some time thought to talk to me first! I mean to see about an annulment. It's what Sarah wants now that she knows the truth of it."

Billy sat motionless for a long moment. That meant there was no baby. He should have been wild with rejoicing. Jack was handing him back his freedom.

Why wasn't he jumping to take it?

She didn't want him.

For weeks he'd thought of nothing but Sarah, of what it would mean having her for his wife. She was young and impetuous and she couldn't cook worth a damn, but damn, he wanted her. He wanted to know what it would be like to have her wrapped around him in welcome in their kitchen. He wanted to bend down and scoop up his own kids. He wanted to take her to bed and love her all night long, every night. He wanted to believe those things would happen. He wanted desperately to believe her when she said she loved him.

He should have know better.

She'd told him, hadn't she? She'd said she didn't want to marry him, that she wasn't ready to be a wife.

He refused to admit he found that news devastating.

It was for the best. He had a dangerous job to finish for the rangers and he couldn't let her distract him from it. He had no time to settle in with her properly. There wasn't time to chase after vague dreams of happiness, and now that there was no child for him to own up to, he had no excuse to hang on. Especially when she didn't want him.

"Well, if that's what she wants," Billy said with an indifference he was far from feeling, "I'll ride on out to your folks—"

"Sarah's here. Uncle Harm brought her over."

Good old Uncle Harm. It wasn't enough that the man had forced him up to the altar, now he was anxious to snatch back the offer before Billy got a chance to savor it.

Sarah was here. Now. An uncontrollable anticipation got a hold of his foolish heart, until he reminded himself that she'd come, not to see him, but to escape him. She'd only married him out of a misguided notion that she was saving his life. Now, there was no reason to carry on the pretense.

"I'll talk to her, Jack, and we can get things settled before I head out."

"Good."

"Yeah, right."

Jack gave Billy a long, hard look and the impossible occurred to him. Could it be that Billy Cooper was really in love with his sister? He didn't like the idea. As much as Billy meant to him, as a friend, as his second in command, he could never think of him as good husband material. Not for Sarah. Sarah was rebellious and young, like a colt that would need a firm, patient hand to tame. Billy was little more than a kid himself, too young, too wild, too reckless to be responsible for his little sister. He was too set on furthering his career in the rangers to put down roots and family. Besides, the timing couldn't be worse. They were very close to cracking down on the ring of terror threatening the Bend area, and Billy was an integral part by his own choosing. His odds of survival were discouragingly low.

Even if there was love in the balance, better the two of them be apart until they both matured some.

And that's when Emily came in carrying the coffee service. She smiled at Billy and beckoned Jack to join her in the doorway. Emily whispered to him and Billy heard his friend's enraged bellow.

"She's what?"

Emily clutched his arm and did some more hurried talking, but Jack's expression was grim as he approached Billy.

"What's wrong?"

Jack leveled him a chill stare. "Looks like you're gonna be my brother-in-law whether we like it or not. Emily thinks Sarah's pregnant."

Billy stared, saying nothing.

"Tell me there's a chance that she's wrong."

"I can't." And Billy couldn't honestly say that he'd want to. Sarah was pregnant with his child.

There could be no annulment now.

Chapter Sixteen

"Sarah?"

The soft call of her name was followed by a tap on the door, and Sarah experienced a brief panicking desire to crawl under the bed to hide until he was gone. But knowing that wouldn't solve things, she took a steadying breath and smoothed down her gown before telling him to enter.

When she saw him standing there, hat in hand, looking as uneasy as she felt, Sarah's initial impulse was to run to him and throw herself into his arms. But a cautious pride held her back. She couldn't afford to forget that her condition trapped him into a situation he didn't like. He hadn't wed her by choice and he wasn't here, even now, by choice. Her first words reflected that grim fact.

"I'm sorry."

A tense spasm jumped along his lean jaw. "Well, now, it's a little late for regrets. We should have thought of such things . . . before."

"Yes, indeed, we should have," was her strained reply. But at the time, she'd been too busy pursuing the moment to consider the consequences.

"How are you feeling?" How politely that was asked. Sarah almost cringed.

"Terrible. How do you think I'd feel?"

She could see his teeth grinding. How he must hate this, she thought miserably. He was staring at her flat middle, and self-consciously, she placed her hands over it.

"Emily might be wrong," she said hopefully because she figured that's what he'd be hoping.

"Do you think she is?" No clues from that flat tone.

"No."

"I just want you to know that I'll stand by you and see you're cared for. We'll make things work out . . . somehow."

Sarah's chin quivered. Not one tender word, not one fond gesture. Nothing about how he was feeling. He was probably blaming her for everything, for forcing him into this intolerable position. Of course, the fact that he'd had a hand—and other things—in it, too, would have escaped him. Suddenly, she didn't want his reluctant charity.

"No need for such sacrifice, Billy Cooper. You don't want to be tied to this marriage any more than I do. I'd rather raise this child alone than weigh a man down with responsibility he doesn't want. I won't hold you to vows made at knife point, and you needn't fear my brother or uncle will make trouble. I'll see they don't interfere."

Billy was at first astounded by her angry statement, then furious. His reply was cold and certain. "That's my baby and you're married to me. The fact that we don't like it much can't be helped."

"Yes, it can."

She said that so soft and determined, an awful fear leapt in his heart. In two long strides he was across the room, grabbing her by the forearms.

"What do you mean by that, Sarah? Don't you dare try to do anything foolish to get rid of that baby. If I find out about it . . ."

She pulled back, alarmed and angry. "I mean to do no such thing! How could you even think I'd consider it?"

Billy ran an unsteady hand through his hair and looked away. "I don't know. I'm not saying any of this right."

She stared up at him, then coaxed, "Why don't you start over, then?" And she waited, hoping for those right words to come.

"I know neither of us wanted this, but we got it and we got to make the best of it."

Sarah frowned slightly. "If you're only saying this because of Uncle Harm . . ."

"Your family doesn't have a damned thing to do with it! I'm not scared of them. They weren't there when it happened and I don't want them involved in it now. This is just between you and me, Sarah, and that little baby-to-be is right in the middle. I know I said I wasn't ready to start a family, but I got no choice now. And I mean to do the right thing. I swear to you, I'll be a good father to our baby. Don't you ever, ever concern yourself with that. I mean to see it's raised right, with everything I can provide. It ain't gonna be much. I wasn't exactly prepared to set up house, but we'll make do. No kid of mine is gonna feel unloved or unwanted. I don't care what I have to do. I aim to be the best father I know how to be."

But what about being a good husband? Sarah noticed he made no mention of that. The responsibility he felt was to their child, not to her. She'd lain with him, and now it was too late to wish she'd first earned his love. She was going to have to make do, too. For the sake of the child they shared, she was going to have to settle for a man who resented her intrusion into his life.

"Well, now that we got that settled, I've got some business to take care of with Jack."

How that brusque dismissal hurt! "Don't let me get in the way of it."

He could have said something cutting and painfully true, but he saw a vulnerable sheen in her eyes so he kept silent. "I'll talk to you again before I go."

"Go? Are you leaving right away?" She reached out instinctively to catch his sleeve and his hand slid over hers. The contact surprised them both with the sensations of warmth and want it evoked.

"I have to. I've got a job to finish up and I—"

She held up her other hand. "You don't have to explain to me. I know all about the work you do."

Of course she did, growing up in the family she had. That

was one good thing about Sarah Bass. Sarah Cooper, he amended to himself.

Another good thing about her was the way desire heated unashamedly in her uplifted gaze. She might not want to be married to him, but that look said she wanted him plenty. It was a mutual attraction.

His hand curved around her delicate jaw and she was rising up to meet him even as he was bending down. Their kiss was slow, searing, yet unsatisfying, suggestive of what they couldn't pursue. Or could they? They were man and wife. He had every right to take her down on the bed and make love to her. The only thing restraining him was the fact that they were under Jack's roof, and somehow, loving her there didn't feel right.

Billy straightened, and the sight of her still stretched up to him, her eyelashes fluttering with a fragile passion, her mouth damp with a not-so-innocent desire, struck harder than her brother's slam to his jaw. When he placed another quick kiss upon her brow, she shook from her daze to regard him solemnly. He had no idea what she was thinking and that scared him more than any of the uncertainties that lay ahead.

Was she congratulating herself on neatly corralling his support, or was she cursing the circumstances that bound them together?

Harmon Bass was sitting in the front room with Jack when Billy returned. He stopped and regarded the tough little tracker through less than fond eyes.

"Howdy, Mr. Bass."

"Cooper. You see to things with Sarah like you should?"

"I don't need you to tell me how to do the right thing."

"You should have listened to somebody a couple of months back and we wouldn't be talking about it now."

"Uncle Harm, Billy, stop it."

Billy turned to his friend, ready to display a show of thanks, when he saw how Jack was staring at him. The look was none too amiable. He realized unhappily that Sarah was standing between them, too. Jack was less than thrilled to have him in the family. So that left only business.

"I can't stay long so I'll make it quick. I'm in, but I don't know how much Gant trusts me. I'm watched, but I can come and go as I please. Had to slip the fellow following me to get here. There's some big money behind all this, but I still can't get a name."

"McAllister," Harm said softly. "It sounds like the kind of thing he does best."

"Ain't never heard a' him before, but I'll keep my ears open. Ray's planning on hitting a couple of places hard, then heading across the Rio Grande to lay low until after the first of the year."

"What places?" Jack wanted to know.

"He don't trust me enough to say."

"Then we're no better off than before. Any idea who's slipping them information from outta our camp?"

Billy shook his head. "No. But all of them knew about the argument we had for their benefit. Dammit, Jack, it makes my skin crawl wondering who it might be."

"Yeah, I know what you mean. How hot's it getting to be for you in there?"

"I'm holding my own."

"If you think they're starting to suspect, you get outta there, understand?"

"I won't take any chances." He couldn't afford to, could he? Not with a new wife and a baby on the way. He had to be careful for their sakes.

"C'mon back as soon as you think it's safe," Jack concluded, then came Harm's quiet drawl.

"I'd hate to have to come out and hunt you down."

The insinuation was clear. Billy glared at him. "I'm not running off, so you needn't worry about it. If I don't come back, it's not because I'm trying to shirk my duty to Sarah. I'll be dead. And if that's not a good enough reason for you, Mr. Bass, you're more than welcome to try to revive me."

No reaction. His stare was flat and flinty. "She'll go home with me. We'll see to her."

"*I'll* see to her. She's *my* wife." It suddenly became very important for him to establish that before these two men. Sarah was his, perhaps not by choice, but certainly in fact. *His.* That notion lingered, enticing strange and strong feelings of possessiveness.

"Jus' because she's carrying the name Cooper don't make her any less a Bass." Harm stated with a territorial growl. "We take care of our own."

"Harmon," Jack interrupted, but before Billy could feel relieved by his friend's support, Jack followed with a firm, "she can stay here with me and Emily." His gaze leveled on his second in command with an unknown degree of gauging wariness, making the young ranger purely furious.

"It's up to me to decide where she goes," he claimed. His commanding tone wrought an instant stiffening from both Bass men. "She's going—"

"She's going home," Sarah cut in with a crisp annoyance, and that ended it. "Uncle Harm, can you take me? I need to talk to my folks and I'll stay there until Billy can come for me." That last she said with a limp resignation, as if she didn't really think it was going to happen. And if it did, that she wasn't exactly looking forward to it.

Faced with so much doubt in his abilities, Billy figured it was time to leave, before he was tempted to grab his wife up and tow her out with him against all his better judgment. She was, he knew, safer here with them, and they could provide for her in a way he couldn't. But he wasn't happy about it.

"I gotta go." He nodded toward the two Bass men, then gave Sarah a brief intense look. He wanted to hold her tight and kiss her senseless, but not with Harm and Jack boring holes in his back. "Sarah, see me out."

She went along with him without a word. They paused by the kitchen door. She didn't want him to go. She was afraid of where he was riding and of the work that kept him away, but she'd been in a ranging family too long to voice those fears. Instead, she spoke around her worries.

"I'm going to try my best to be a good wife to you, Billy."

His penetrating look never altered. He bent and kissed her

once, firmly, fiercely on the lips. As he straightened, he told her, "You be a good mama. That's all I ask of you."

Not exactly the most reassuring thing an uncertain young bride wanted to hear.

The minute he rode back into camp, Billy knew something was wrong. The first face he saw was that of Ferguson, the fellow Ray had sent to follow him. Then, as he was swinging down off his horse, Ray Gant approached and he knew he was either dead or in with the outlaws.

"Where you been, Billy-boy?"

"Had a private matter to tend to. Hope you didn't wait dinner."

"Fergus, see to Billy's horse whilst we make some talk. C'mon over here with me, Billy. Pull up a stump and get cozy."

Ray lead him just far enough away from the others so they wouldn't be overheard. Billy settled down and waited for the other man to begin.

"Where were you?"

He gave a heavy sigh, deciding to stick as close to the truth as possible. "I went to see my woman. I had to know if she was carrying my baby."

"And?"

A faint smile. "She is."

"Well, that's mighty good news. Calls for a drink, wouldn't you say?" He rummaged for a bottle of mezcal and handed it to Billy, who drew deeply and gasped for the return of his breath. "So," Ray drawled, "how's her family?"

"Fine," he answered glumly.

"Something you want to share, kid?"

And suddenly he did. He wanted to talk to someone and Jack was no longer a suitable confidant, not since he'd gone from friend to shirttail family. "It's them, the Basses. They make it mighty hard for a man to hold to any pride. She's my wife, and they're looking to deny me the chance to keep her and the baby. They figure she'd be better off with them. Hell,

I'm nothing to their way of thinking. I got no place to keep her. I didn't ask to have her pushed off on me, but now that I got her—"

"Now that you got her, what?"

"I want her." He looked up, his expression stark and serious. "I want her, Ray. I know it's crazy. I know about women and what it takes to keep 'em. Loving 'em is just opening up for a whole heartful of hurt. But I don't want my baby raised to think its name is Bass. It's Cooper. It's my kid. And she's my wife."

"Then go get her."

"What?"

"Go take her. She belongs to you, not them."

"I don't think she'd come with me, Ray."

"You'd give her a choice? Hell, kid, I don't belive what I'm hearing. You whine about not having her, then won't do what's gotta be done to get her."

"I don't want her living on the run with me. That's no kinda life. She's expecting a baby. I couldn't go off and leave her here, worrying about somebody like Beals having at her whilst I was gone. If I had the money, I'd buy a little place to keep her, even if I had to carry her shoes off in my saddle-bag every time I rode out, so she couldn't leave me. I want to be able to give her things, Ray, things for her and the baby like I never had. You know what I mean."

"Yeah, I do." Ray Gant did know. He was the one person who would understand exactly how important these things were to him. He knew Billy's past, he knew Billy's family. And he said, "I'll see to it."

"What do you mean?"

He put his hand on Billy's shoulder and pressed hard. "I'll see to it for you. What are friends for? Haven't I always looked out for you? You need money, let's get you some. You need a place to keep her, let's find you one. How's that sound?"

"Damn good." Billy smiled, thinking how wonderful it would be to provide for Sarah and their child, to make them Coopers, not Basses. Not once did he think of what the cost would be. He was looking from the hurtful past, not from the present, and he was remembering how Ray Gant had stood by him through the thick of it, how he'd always helped him get by through the toughest of times. How Ray had never once looked at him as less than an equal, the way Jack Bass had done just an hour ago. "Thanks, Ray. I won't forget this."

Ray Gant grinned and said, "I know you won't, kid."

For the next week, Billy lost himself in being one of Ray Gant's gang of countryside terrorists. He rode hard, he drank harder, and he lay awake nights trying not to think about Sarah. And somewhere in all the liquor and exhaustion and edgy excitement, the line between who he was and what he was doing began to blur.

Billy listened to Tom Benton talk about how hard it had been to provide for his big family. The love and determination in the outlaw's voice struck a chord in him and started him thinking. How would he take care of Sarah on twenty-five dollars a month? How was he going to raise a child when he was gone most of the time? How was he going to establish his family, set up a home, and still give heart and soul to the state of Texas and Jack Bass? Jack, the man he'd have lain down and died for, who hadn't even welcomed him into the family with a handshake or a smile. He guessed it was one thing to share rations and saddle, and quite another for him to part with a sister. Damn Jack, anyway. Jack should have known he'd do everything possible to see to Sarah. Jack should have known he was a good man inside. But that hard look of doubt was tough to accept.

He though of Harm's smug claim to see to Sarah's welfare. As if he'd give his family over to someone else! No way was he going to let them live off another's charity! No way was he going to have his wife look at him with dull, disappointed eyes before she started looking elsewhere. He'd make good for Sarah, and it was that push of desperation that drove him through the lawless days riding with Ray Gant. He'd stopped thinking about the state of Texas. He was calculating how many raids it would take to set aside enough to take Sarah away from the Basses.

And then Ray came up to him, smiling, patting his shoulder to confide, "C'mon, Billy-boy, this is what you've been waiting for. Ride with me. I got us a little job to do and it's gonna pay off big for the both of us. You in?"

"Yeah, I'm in."

He'd asked no questions as he rode with Ray into Lajitas.

They waited in a small upstairs room over a squalid saloon. Ray was relaxed and was generous with the bottle of whiskey he'd brought up with them. All he'd say is they were there to meet with someone, and Billy was to be sharp and be ready. Then Ray got to talking about the old times they'd shared, when he'd gotten Billy a job cowboying when he was just shy of fourteen by vouching for a green kid with his own position. And later, when Ray had been caught in the middle of some shifty doings and blamed for the disappearance of range cattle, he'd skipped the noose with Billy's help and the two of them had ridden into the hills and some dark, wild times. That was before Pete Meyers caught Billy with stolen beef and saved his neck from a rope. Ray purposefully kept his young companion's rememberings from going that far. He dwelt on their adventures, their friendship, and by the time the bottle was empty, Billy was convinced that Ray Gant was the best friend he'd ever had.

The man they were to meet was late, and Billy was restless and edgy with anxiety. The fellow was a big Mexican, who seemed to know Ray well enough to smile and offer his hand. They talked for a while and Billy couldn't follow much of what they said, his Spanish comprehension dulled by drink. He understood that they were talking about taking stolen stock across the border. And then the Mexican produced a fat satchelful of greenbacks, and Ray looked to him and said, calm as you please, "Billy, kill him."

Taken by surprise, he sat for a moment, too stunned to react. But the Mexican got off a few choice curses and grabbed quickly for his sidearm. Billy drew faster and shot him dead.

He sat in his chair, his heart beating furiously up in his throat, staring down at the man he'd killed, his mind pulling together no kind of objection at all.

It was him or the Mexican. If he hadn't shot him, Ray would have. And somehow, that was all the justification he needed.

Then Ray took the satchel and upended it in Billy's lap.

"There you go, Billy-boy."

He stared stupidly at all the cash. "What's this for?"

"For standing by me when I needed you. I told you I'd take care of you, didn't I? That's yours, for you and your little lady. Now, let's get out of here before someone comes asking questions."

So Billy scooped up the scattered bank notes and stepped over the dead man, following Ray Gant into hell.

Sarah stared at the note delivered by a dusty courier to her parents' front porch. It had her name scribbled on the outside, *Sarah Cooper,* and on the inside, one line: *I'll be at the Majestic in Terlingua tonight.* Clutching the note to her bosom, she hesitated all of five seconds. Then she was in the house, changing into riding clothes.

"Where are you going?"

She never even turned toward her mother. "Into Terlingua. Emily's not feeling well and she wants me to stop in." The lie came so easily, it scared her.

"Sarah?"

She turned and was swept up in Rebecca's embrace. For a moment, the truth trembled on her lips. *Oh, Mama, I love him. Please understand! I have to go.* But she said nothing.

Since hearing the news of her marriage, the tension under their roof had tripled. Rebecca was shocked and worried. Will was furious. He blamed Harm for forcing the situation without consulting him first. They had strong words and Harm rode out angry. Her father wouldn't speak to her and could hardly look her way. Rebecca held her tight but she didn't have much to say, either. Sarah guessed they were disppointed in her and she couldn't blame them. The fact that her new husband hadn't come with her didn't help matters, nor did the determined morning sickness that confirmed her pregnancy. She was thinking seriously of either moving to ack's or to her uncle's. At least, they'd supported her and hadn't made her feel like a criminal.

First she had to talk to Billy.

But Billy wasn't too interested in talk.

The moment she entered the tiny hotel room, he grabbed her up for a hard, hungry kiss. He tasted of whiskey and a picy meal, probably more of the former than of the latter. He broke away from her mouth long enough to mutter huskily, "Oh, baby, I missed you," before dragging her straight to the bed.

Those were the words she'd longed to hear, but the meaning was all wrong. So was the fact that he never said another word to her, not hello, not how are you, not thanks for making the long ride. He tugged down her split skirt and drawers, then dropped her onto the bed beneath his eager weight. Before she had a chance to say yes or no, he'd thrust up hard inside her and was driving toward a quick, shattering climax. His. Only then did he try to kiss her again. And she wouldn't let him.

"Get off me!"

Surprised by her gruff, angry tone, Billy complied, dropping onto his back beside her as he struggled to recover his breath.

"Don't you ever do that again."

He stared at her, amazed and growing angry himself. "You're my wife."

"That's right. I'm your wife, not your whore. Don't go mistaking the two."

He was bewildered and affronted, and all he could think to do was adopt an arrogant defense. "I suppose you didn't like it?"

"What was to like? I might as well not have been here."

"You didn't have to be, you know. I could have found someone else." That was true enough. Luisa had been all

over him when he and Ray had returned to the camp. She'
had him flat on his back, with her tongue down his throa
and her hand in his pants before he thought to protest. He'
pushed her away. He was plenty aroused, but it wasn't th
camp whore he wanted. It was Sarah. And now she had th
gall to make him regret coming to her! "I won't bother nex
time."

She gave him a look that was so stark with hurt, he woulc
have given anything to take back the words. He reached fo
her and she pulled away.

"Sarah . . ."

He grabbed faster and caught her before she could leave
the bed. Then he pulled her tightly against his chest, over
whelming her fight, suffering for her tears.

"Sarah, I'm sorry. I didn't mean that, not a word of it. I
ain't gonna go to nobody else, not ever. It's just you, baby. I
just wanted you so much. I'm sorry. I am."

She quieted against him. Her palms stilled in their pushing
and began a sensuous massage of his shoulders. Just that subtle response made the hot pleasure he'd taken from her chill
in comparison. He was startled to discover that this kind of
touching was just as satisfying as the act of taking her. But the
night was young, and he had every intention of making up for
her disappointment in his greeting.

"Hey, look what I brought you."

She was smiling wryly. "Not someone else's petticoats, I
hope."

Billy grinned, his heart lightening for the first time in
weeks. "Naw, something better." He brought the satchel up
onto the bed and spilled out the contents. He waited, watching her expression with an anxious anticipation. Sarah stared
at all the money, not touching it.

"What is this?"

"It's for us, to get us started. I want you to take it and find
us a nice little place."

"Where did you get this?"

His smile stiffened. "What does that matter?"

"It matters to me, Billy."

"I earned it, all right? It's mine—ours."

She looked at it, then she looked at him. Her expression was impassive. "I don't want it."

"You don't . . . What? Why not?"

"How did you get this? Honestly?"

"Yes."

"I don't believe you." Something in the hard set of his face told her not to. She was scared, frightened by this huge amount of cash and by his insistence that she take it.

"Fine," he growled out at last. His features flushed and he was frowning as he stuffed the bills back into the bag. "Don't take the money. Don't buy us someplace nice. But I'm not moving in with your family. You understand that, Sarah. I want you with me, not them. You're coming with me."

"Where? Back to Gant's camp? No."

"With me. I want you with me." His dark eyes filled up with a sudden deep possessiveness and she balked without knowing why. Hadn't she been waiting for Billy to ask her to go with him? But intuition overruled the invitation.

"Not there. I won't go with you there. When you're done with that job and you're back with the rangers, you come get me and I'll go anywhere in the world with you."

He searched her expression for a sign of capitulation and found none. Very softly, he asked, "What if I don't go back to the rangers?"

Sarah drew a short breath. "What are you saying, Billy?"

"I'm asking you a question. What if I don't go back to the rangers?"

"Are you saying you want to stay with Gant and his outlaws? Is that what you're telling me, Billy?"

"Baby, the money's good and—"

"I don't care about the money!"

"You have to think about it. When we have our kid, I've got to have the means to take care of it."

"Not on blood money, Billy. You won't raise my child on blood money."

"*My* child? It's *my* child, *too!* And you'll do whatever I decide! You're my wife, Sarah."

She said nothing. Her very silence defied him. A long, taut impasse settled between them, then Sarah asked, "Billy, what's happened to you? I can't believe you're even thinking like this. This isn't another one of your and Jack's schemes, is it? Because if it is, I don't think it's very funny."

"Sarah, I'm serious."

"So am I."

"I guess there's not much more to say, then, is there? Sorry to make you ride all this way for nothing." He jerked his denims back together and rolled from the bed.

He was leaving.

"Billy!"

Sarah was wound around him so tight, he couldn't tell where he ended and she began.

"Don't leave . . . yet."

She was pulling his head down to feast upon his mouth, hers so urgent and bold he was instantly ready to have her again. But this time, he vowed he'd go slow and he'd make it nice. And when he did, she liked it plenty.

When she awoke to a gray dawn, Billy and the money were gone.

Chapter Seventeen

"Well?"

Billy gave Ray Gant a surly look as he swung off his lathered horse. "She ain't coming."

"Wasn't it enough?"

"They money was fine, Ray. It's the woman that fell short on me."

Ray gave an understanding nod as his young friend stalked toward the fire and a plate of simmering beans. He snagged up a bottle and went to hunker down beside him. "Wash it down with this, Billy-boy."

Billy took a big gulp and shuddered as the liquor burnt all the way to his belly. It was a hot sear, as hot as the frustration scorching his heart. Damn her. Why wouldn't she give an inch? Just like Jack, so damn proud and self-righteous. Just like all the Basses. He took another swallow and his eyes teared up. Just the whiskey, he told himself as he rubbed his sleeve across his face.

Would Sarah run right to her brother and spill everything he'd told her? Probably. If so, there was no longer a choice for him to make. He was back on the outside, just as always. Where Jack had pushed him with that hard punch to the jaw and that scornful glare. Why hadn't his friend accepted him? Everything would have been so different then. He would have worked so hard to fit in and make them proud to have him. He'd have faithfully performed his duty to the rangers and to the Basses. But they'd all made it painfully clear, hadn't they?

He wasn't one of them. To Jack, he was nothing more than a twenty-five-dollar-a-month ranger under his command, not a trusted friend and equal. To Sarah, he was a disappointing dream, not the man she wanted to provide for her as a husband. To Harm Bass, he was in the way, because once a Bass, always a Bass. And there wasn't a damned thing he could do to change any of their minds.

So why try?

"Hey, Billy-boy, you all right?"

He glanced up and gave a tight-edged smile. "Yeah, sure, right as rain."

"Ready to do some more riding?"

"Whenever you are."

"Sure you're ready to let go of where you came from?" It was a quiet question, one that had many shades of meaning. And Billy understood them all.

"You know where I come from, Ray. That ain't never gonna change. I got nothing to go back to."

That truth sank deeper and deeper into his mind as the night wore on. The feeling of camaraderie around the camp fire embraced his drink-sodden soul with a numbing comfort. This was the only family he needed, one that would accept him and appreciate him as he was. He didn't need more than that. He'd never had more than that and it was foolish to believe anything was out there for him. Born to hang. His daddy had told him that and he remembered how hard he'd struggled against that fact. His daddy hadn't been right about many things, but it seemed he'd been right about that.

Through glazed eyes, he saw the pretty whore, Chonita, skirting the fire. Well, not so pretty now. Ray had scarred up her face and knocked out a few teeth when he'd heard she'd aided in his and Sarah's escape. But she'd stayed on. Because she knew what she was and where she belonged, and that no one else would take her in. Just like he did.

Billy stood up, fighting for balance and a bolstering courage to do what needed to be done. When he grabbed a hold of Chonita by the front of her blouse, she looked surprised, even protesting. But she came with him into the shadows doc-

ilely enough. When they were away from the others and
Luisa's hard, jealous look, she began to unbutton her bodice
with no great enthusiasm. He put his hand on hers to still
them.

"That's not what I want."

"What do you want, *Senor* Cooper?"

"I want you to take a message to my . . . wife."

"You not want to give it to her yourself?"

"No. It'll be better this way. Give her this"—he passed her
the satchel—"and you tell her to take it. It's for the baby. It's
worth more than I'd be as its father. Tell her I'm sorry. And
tell that I love . . ." He broke off, then continued thickly. "No.
Here's what I want you to tell her."

Chonita listened, hearing so much between the lines, seeing
so much in the young man's face that would never be relayed
to Sarah Cooper.

"Think you can remember that and remember where I
told you to go?"

"*Sí,* I do it for you."

"And Chonita, there's no reason for you not to take some
of that money for yourself so you don't have to come back
here."

She smiled at him sadly. "Where would I go, *Senor?* I give
her your message."

"Thanks."

After she'd gone, Billy stood out in that lonely darkness,
telling himself it was the right thing, the only thing to do. For
Sarah and for himself. And for the little baby she carried that
would always be a Bass rather than a Cooper.

Sarah's joy in seeing Chonita was overshadowed by the
horror of her cruel disfigurement. The young Mexican girl
would say nothing, but Sarah knew it had been her punish-
ment for the help she'd given. But her guilt was forgotten
when Chonita told the reason for her visit.

"What message, Chonita?"

Chonita hesitated at the sound of the other woman's obvious excitement. Then she held out the satchel. From Sarah's change of expression, she guessed she knew what was in it.

"What did Billy say?"

She relayed the words, watching the young bride's features tighten a notch with every syllable. The concluding phrase brought a shimmer of anguish to the dark eyes. "He said not to wait any more."

Sarah took in the dismissing words with a quiver of devastation, but pride gave her the strength to reply, "You give him a message for me. You tell him that this baby will always be a Cooper."

"Anything else?"

"No, just that." What more could she say? If the promises exchanged and the vows they'd spoken before God weren't enough, if the fact that the life she carried wouldn't make him believe in her love, what more was there she could do?

After Chonita rode out, wild things ran through her mind. She wanted to mount a fast horse and race in pursuit. She wanted to call on her brother and uncle to go fetch Billy and drag him back to her. But what good would that do if he didn't want to stay, if he didn't want to work on their unconventional marriage? What good would it do if he didn't love her?

The time had come for her to stand firm and let him make the decision. Right or wrong, she'd have to stand by it. She'd interfered in his life and forced situations for which neither of them had been ready. She'd told him how things were for her. She wouldn't live with an outlaw. She couldn't put herself or her child through that kind of pain. It was time to let go and trust him. If he didn't come back, he wasn't worth having.

But that would never stop her from wanting him.

Billy rode in with the rest of the gang, covered with the same soot and sweat and the stubble of a beard he hadn't bothered to shave off. He was looking forward to the fiery liquor and companionable laughter that followed a hard day's work. But he found himself confronting a somber-faced Chonita. His determined gaiety fled.

"Did she take the money?"

"*Sí.*"

His gut dropped. Why had he been hoping Sarah would fling it back at him? Why had he been secretly expecting her to come barging into the camp to claim him as she'd done before? He had to face the fact that those things weren't going to happen now. The ties were severed between him and Sarah Bass. And it was for the best.

"Did she say anything?" he asked glumly, wanting to know even if it made no difference.

"She said she would raise your child to be a Cooper. And she said it in a voice of love."

A sudden impulse struck him with a stunning force. Go to her, it goaded. Go to her and hang on tight. Burrow deep into her loving arms until all the wickedness of the past weeks was purged from his soul.

But it was much too late for such naive hopes, calmer reason told him. By now, Jack already knew of his defection and he'd be treated no different than any of Ray Gant's gang if he showed up on the ranger's doorstep. There was no chance that the Bass family was going to let their little Sarah anywhere near him now. He'd crossed the line and could never go back to what was decent or admirable or acceptable. He was exactly what he appeared to be, a tough-edged, cold-hearted killer on the run, a product of his past growing into the only future open to men like him.

"Hey, Billy-boy, how come you ain't smiling?" Ray draped an arm about his shoulders as Chonita quickly faded away and he gave Billy a shake. "Want me to call Luisa on over here? She's been aching for an excuse to make you smile."

"Naw, I don't want any of that, Ray."

"Missing your woman?"

He shook his head. "That's done with."

"Sorry to hear that, kid. I truly am." But he didn't look or sound it. "Tell you what, I got some news that'll cheer you up some."

Billy gave him a dull look. "Yeah? What?"

"There ain't a man here who's proved himself the way you have. I'm proud to take you on as my right hand." And he extended that hand with a warm smile.

That gesture reached past all the reluctance, past all the remaining reservations, to the isolated soul of him. With a grateful smile, Billy shook his hand. "Thanks, Ray."

"Now, I want you to do something for me. I'm trusting you, Billy, so don't let me down."

"I won't." He'd let everyone else down, and he wasn't about to lose his last chance to fit in with the feel of family around him. His fall into darkness was complete as he walked with Ray Gant toward the fire.

The town of Terlingua was quiet. The dusty streets were almost empty in the cool early morning hour. Billy and two others waited patiently for Bob Westerly to make his way down the boardwalk to his mercantile store. Then they nudged their horses forward to follow at a leisurely pace before tying up in front. Even before the sign in the window was flipped from Closed to Open, they were in the door and spread out as they made their way to the back office.

"I'm not open yet," came a call from the rear. "If you can wait about ten minutes, I'd be happy to get you—"

Westerly turned and found himself confronted by a trio of firepower. He swallowed nervously and edged his hands upward.

"Take what you want, just don't shoot me."

"That's right neighborly of you," Billy drawled behind his bandana mask. "Empty out your strong box."

With trembling hands, Westerly complied. About three hundred dollars spilled onto the counter. "That's all I got. Take it and go."

"That's not all we want."

"I got nothing else!"

"Oh, now think on it a minute. Happens we know you've been right generous to the nesters hereabout, extending 'em credit and all. Well, we're here to relieve you of the burden of carrying 'em. Fetch us the notes and be quick about it."

"But I can't—"

Billy shoved his pistol under the man's nose. "Sure you can."

In a matter of seconds, a stack of unpaid credits was piled next to the cash.

"Now, I need you to write out a little note saying you give to the bearer the right to collect on money owed." Billy quoted what Ray had told him and waited. "C'mon now, ain't got all day!"

"Bobby, your door was open. Are you back there?"

The feminine voice distracted the outlaws, and Westerly made the fatal mistake of grabbing for the shotgun beneath his counter. He was dead before his fingers closed on the grip.

"I said no killing!" Billy snarled at the quick-triggered bandit.

"Bobby?"

The woman ran into view, pulling up short when she saw there had been foul play. Billy's heart sank. It was Elena Lowe, the sheriff's wife. Before she could retreat, one of the others seized her and clamped a hand over her mouth. When she struggled wildly, her captor thumped the butt of his pistol against the side of her head. She went down without a sound.

"There was no call for that!" Billy cried as he went to kneel beside the woman's crumpled form. There was a lot of blood from the gash opened at her temple. He put an anxious hand to the side of her throat, feeling for a pulse and gratified to find one.

"C'mon, Billy, let's get the hell outta here," urged the bandit, who was scooping up the cash and papers.

Billy hesitated, his gaze riveted to the pale features of the woman on the floor. The pool of blood just kept widening. He jerked off his bandana and bound it gently about her wounded brow.

"Billy, we gots no time for this. Leave her before that shot rouses the whole town!"

He yanked away from the hand pulling on his arm, suddenly wildly angry that they'd have no remorse about leaving an innocent woman to die.

"She needs doctoring in a bad way."

"And you'll be needing an undertaker if you don't c'mon." But when their leader didn't move, the pair exchanged a nervous look and unanimously opted for flight and freedom. They ran, leaving him to tend their victim.

Elena Lowe was moaning as Billy gathered her up in his arms. He spoke softly, soothingly to her, not sure she could hear him.

"It's all right, ma'am. I'm not gonna hurt you. I'm gonna get you on over to Doc Himes, and he'll see you fit and fine again in no time. I'm right sorry this had to happen. Wasn't supposed to go down this way. Honest to God, I never meant for anybody to get hurt."

Billy rose to his feet with the limp burden cradled to his chest. Just as he'd begun to turn, the cold bore of a .45 jammed into his right ear.

"Don't you move, son, or I'll kill you where you stand."

Billy recognized Calvin Lowe's voice. And he knew from its gritty quality he was as good as hung.

Loud voices escalated in the outer room. Billy recognized Jack's and Cal Lowe's, and he didn't have to guess what they were arguing about. He couldn't hear their actual words and they didn't much concern him. He had little interest in his fate. All he knew was it would come to an abrupt end soon.

The door dividing the cell block from the sheriff's office opened and Jack Bass strode in.

"C'mon, Billy. I got supper waiting."

Billy stared at his former lieutenant, too stunned by the suggestion to move. Even when Cal Lowe fit the keys in the cell door and swung it open, he couldn't believe his eyes.

"Well, you gonna move, or do you like it in there?"

He grabbed his hat off the bunk and exited the cell. As he passed Lowe, he asked, "How's your wife, Sheriff?"

Lowe squinted a shrewd look at him. "She's got one

helluva headache. But she says you were trying to help her, so I guess I should say thanks. 'Course, Bobby Westerly ain't feeling nothing at all."

Billy swallowed hard and had no comment.

Two horses were tied out front. Jack stepped up on one and looked down at him impatiently from the saddle.

"Well? You got a case of the slows today? C'mon."

Billy mounted up, totally mystified. Maybe Jack was taking him back to the camp for ranger justice. He'd rather hang in Cal Lowe's town than submit to that.

He followed Jack, seeing no point in trying to run for it. Jack was armed, he wasn't. Not that he'd shoot Jack in any case. Any more than he could have left Elena Lowe. He didn't speak. He wouldn't argue his decisions with a man who'd never understand the choices he'd made. He'd made them and now he'd stand by them, even knowing they were wrong. As he rode, the emotional distance between him and his former commander widened and the hard shell of defensive toughness around Billy Cooper cemented in solid. He could have been any one of Ray Gant's gang riding toward a quick, violent end.

Jack Bass had nothing much to say on the ride to the ranger camp. He sat his horse easy, his mind frantic in its turnings.

What the hell had happened?

He wasn't stupid. He could feel something was very wrong with Billy Cooper. He just didn't know what or how to handle it. He'd shrugged off suspicions that perhaps Billy was more working outlaw than undercover ranger, but seeing him sitting in that jail cell all negligently scruffy and hollow-eyed, he began to wonder. Jack knew the look of a cornered animal when he saw one, and that look was all over his friend. Maybe it was from riding in the thick of it for too long. Maybe the hard-edged habits had rubbed in a little too deep while playing the dangerous game. He didn't know. All he was sure of was that he wasn't about to let Billy go—not as his second in command, not as his friend. It was time to bring

him back in before he got so far out, retrieval would be im
possible.

They dismounted at Jack's doorstep and again Billy hesitated, hanging back with that spooky shadowed glaze to his
eyes, as if he'd forgotten he was always welcome within.

"C'mon, Billy. Coffee's hot, and you look like you could
stand a bath and a meal."

Jack put his hand to the back of his young friend's arm and
there was no mistaking the way the muscles bunched in objection. He pretended not to notice, but inside the uneasiness
kept building. Finally, Billy gave in and went up the steps as
if he were marching to the gallows.

"Sit on down. I'll have Emily set an extra plate."

Again, his offer was met with a chill silence. He waited until Billy was settled in a chair, then left the room with reluctance. Jack was surprised at his own reaction: He was
uncomfortable leaving Billy there alone. He wasn't sure why,
but it had all the feel of turning his back on someone he
couldn't quite trust not to rear up and stick a knife between
his shoulder blades. This was Billy Cooper! He had to keep
reminding himself of that. Billy, his friend, his corporal. The
kid who'd always been there so willing and ready to ride into
hell with him. But Billy had the look of someone in a whole
other kind of hell, and that scared Jack plenty.

He stepped into the warm, fragrant heat of the kitchen and
his wife's smile was a balm to his worry. He moved up close
and caught her to his chest with the curl of one arm behind
her back. When his mouth clamped down on hers with an
unexpected urgency, her floury hands flew up, fluttering
briefly in indecision before clasping the sides of his face with
an answering passion. When he finally drew back, she smiled
and murmured, "My, so much fuss over my *mancha manteles*."

He smiled back. "Billy's here. You got enough to feed
him?"

She used the corner of her apron to clean the powdery
handprints off his cheeks. "Sure." Then she paused, studying
her husband's expression. "What's wrong, Jack?"

"Can't say that I rightly know. Something's not right with Billy. Take a look at him and see what you think."

Emily frowned in concern as she squeezed Jack's forearms. It wasn't like him to intuit a situation the wrong way, which meant Billy was in some kind of trouble. She untied her apron and went to see for herself.

"Hello, William."

He came up out of the chair with a tense energy. "Ma'am."

"You're more than welcome to stay for supper, but unless you plan to overpower my cooking, I'm encouraging you to take a dip in our washtub. I've got hot water on already but you stand to need it more than Jack. You can use his razor. I'll find you a clean shirt but you'll have to beat the dust out of your denims. None of Jack's are long enough for you."

His mouth worked silently, as if he were trying to latch on to some excuse to say no. She stepped in to neatly circumvent his protest.

"No arguments. You look to be wearing two week's worth of hard work on you and it's not attractive in the house. Scrub, then supper. C'mon."

Billy looked as though he might balk, but he finally gave way to meekly trailing behind her. The tub in the back room was already half filled, and when she emptied a steaming kettle into it, the temperature rose to a pleasant degree. She pointed into it with the insistent manner of a mother to a reluctant child.

When Emily rejoined Jack in the kitchen, his gaze was questioning.

"Oh, Jack, there's somebody else inside that boy's skin, somebody I don't know at all."

A freshly laundered and unusually withdrawn Billy Cooper sat to the Basses' table. Jack and Emily watched him worriedly as he ate with his gaze fixed to his plate, responding only to the determined friendliness of their two boys.

By the time Emily cleared away the emptied plates, Jack was in an uncertain panic. He didn't know what to make of his friend's wary and woeful manner. He recognized the shifty evasion in the younger man's eyes. He'd seen the same look on a hundred outlaws and he didn't like seeing it on Billy.

Jack set Billy's ranger star on the tabletop. Dark eyes assessed it for a long moment without a flicker of expression then rose to meet his.

"What's this for?"

"Pin it on."

Billy made no move to pick up the badge. He shook his head slightly. "I don't understand. What about—"

"I'm calling you in. Calvin could have killed you this morning. It's gotten way too dangerous and I don't want to lose you. It's time to take another track."

Billy stared impassively at his star. Unpleasant and haunted shadows moved behind his downcast gaze. He wanted to demand an accounting of Billy's deeds. He wanted to ask on what side he stood. But he didn't, because he feared the answer. As long as he didn't know for sure, he could give his friend the benefit of his belief. But it was a strained belief at best. Gut instinct told him Billy Cooper had gone over the edge, and a deeper anxiousness whispered there'd be no bringing him back.

"What were you dong at Westerly's?" Jack broached casually, observing how his friend received the question. Billy took his time answering, easing up on it, then speaking a silky response.

"Trying to keep what happened from happening."

"Well, if you hadn't been there, Elena Lowe would probably be dead."

"I couldn't walk away and let it go down like that." That was said with a taut defensiveness, as if he thought Jack might think he could have.

"Who were you with and what were they after?"

Again, the dark gaze canted down with a sweep of secrets. "A couple of nobodies after cash."

Liar! Why are you lying to me? Jack held on to his temper with difficulty. If he was going to coax Billy back into the fold, he knew he had to court him with care.

"You've done a fine job, Billy, more than I could have asked of most men. Time for you to get back to rangering work. I need you here with me."

He was met with a noncommittal stare through soulless, flat black eyes.

"You can bunk here for the night, then go on back to the barracks tomorrow after I have a talk with the boys to explain where you been and what you been doing."

"What did Sarah tell you?"

Jack was taken aback by the unexpected question. "When? I haven't seen Sarah since the last time the both of you were here. What was she supposed to tell me?"

Billy's jaw gripped tight. "Nothin'. Never mind. I'm gonna get some air. Tell your wife thanks for the dinner."

Emily came up behind her husband. He was covertly watching through the window, where his corporal sat on the front steps of their house. He clutched at her hands when they banded around him.

"He's gonna run, Emily. I know it. I just don't know what I'm gonna do about it when he does."

Chapter Eighteen

"Nice night."

Billy glanced up at Emily Bass and managed a weak smile. "Yes, ma'am, that it is."

"Mind if I join you in enjoying it?"

Though he preferred the silent company of his own brooding, Billy shrugged. He put up a hand to steady her by the elbow as she eased down on the step beside him.

"I'm afraid I'm not as graceful as I used to be."

"That's understandable, ma'am." His gaze lingered on the swell of her belly, then realizing he was staring, he quickly looked away.

"Thinking about Sarah and the start of your own family, William?"

"Some." Always.

"Kinda scary business, isn't it?"

"Ma'am?" He wouldn't have believed that coming from her.

"Oh, don't look surprised. I've borne children under some pretty strenuous circumstances. Cathy, my first, was born on a ramshackle farm in Galveston. Neil always resented the fact that we had to delay our departure west until she was old enough to travel. A few months either way might have made all the difference in how things turned out for me. Cathy might still be alive and I might still be married to Neil instead of Jack."

She looked unhappy and moody, and Billy grew uncomfortable. He didn't want to pry into painful business, and those months of tense challenge between Neil Marcus and Jack Bass over Emily's love were full of unpleasantness. Losing a child and a husband and then almost a lover couldn't have been a fond memory. "You don't need to be telling me this, ma'am."

"It's all right. It was a long time ago. If things hadn't happened the way they did, I wouldn't have Kenitay or Jack or Carson or this little one." She put protective hands over the protuberance. Her smile was serene. "Sometimes, even the worst things happen for the best."

"Yes, ma'am." He didn't sound as if he believed it for a minute.

"I'm glad you're back with the unit, William. Jack was pacing the floor daily worrying about you."

His gaze flickered to her. She saw surprise there and wondered why. Had he thought Jack wouldn't?

"It'll be easier on Sarah, too. You'll be wanting to bring her here and set up a place of your own."

He didn't argue, but he didn't answer, either.

"It'll be nice having another woman close by. We can help each other through the colic and those sleepless nights when you and Jack are out on patrol. I never let on to him, but I fret something terrible every time he's gone. Sarah will be better about it than me. She comes from a ranging family."

And she doesn't love me the way you love Jack, Billy thought to himself. But he didn't say that out loud.

"I've never heard you talk about your family, Billy. Are they here in Texas?"

Billy gave a start, then an agitated smile. "It wasn't much of a family to brag about. I've got a sister in Fort Stockton."

"That's not that far away. Don't you get over to see her?"

"She's a working girl, ma'am. Can't say I enjoy visiting with her all that much. She's got a couple a' kids. Jessie, she's nine by now, and Jed's eight. They're great kids." His smile grew bittersweet when he spoke of them and Emily could see the affection tearing at his heart.

"What about their father?" Emily asked gently.

"Julie don't know who their daddy is. Probably not even the same man. I send 'em money when I can. Wish there was a way I could know it was going for food and not for her whiskey. But I guess it ain't my business how she chooses to run her life."

He looked off at the distant stars, his profile taut with the concern to which he refused to own up.

"What about your folks?"

"Dead." He said that firmly, as if it buried their memories along with them.

"I'm sorry."

"Don't be, Miz Emily. They weren't much. My mama, she run off when I was little, and my daddy sorta fell into a bottle after that. He forgot about us unless he was knocking us around. Got himself shot and killed in a bar brawl. Took two days for somebody to come out and tell us so. And here Julie'd been trying to keep his supper warm." His smile took on a wry twist and Emily's emotions turned just as wrenchingly. Such a hard, cruel life for one so young. She put her hand on Billy's arm. He stiffened at that soothing contact but he didn't jerk away as she feared he might.

"You've got family now, Billy."

"If you say so, ma'am."

"They took me in, and it was the first time I ever felt like I had someplace to belong. I know how lonely life can get. I don't feel that way anymore."

"Nobody's invited me in, Miz Emily."

"You're Sarah's husband, William."

"And none of 'em are too happy about it." Including Sarah.

"Give it a chance. Give them a chance. Put down some roots and let them grow. You'll be glad you did."

There was a childish screech and a wail from inside the house. Distracted, Emily looked behind her. "I'd better go see to that. Jack's too much of a softy when it comes to the kids. I'm the real disciplinarian." She grinned and winked, as if they should keep that secret between them. Billy smiled back, a small but genuine gesture, his first since his arrival. "Give me a hand up, William. Once I'm down, I'm like a turtle on its back."

He stood and cupped her elbows in his hands, drawing her carefully to her feet. She tottered for a moment and was forced to cling to him for support. One of his hands brushed across the mound of her abdomen and he let it pause there, fingers wide spread while his expression puckered poignantly.

"That's one heckuva kick!"

"What do you expect from a Bass? Stubborn and ornery already."

Another ripple of movement stirred beneath his palm and the look of awe intensified on his face. Suddenly, Billy blushed and began to pull his hand back with a stammer of "I'm sorry. I don't know what got into me."

"It's all right," Emily soothed. She caught his hand and returned it to the taut convex of her stomach. "Come spring, you'll be feeling yours moving around just like this."

He made a sudden thick sound in his throat and pulled away, backing down the steps. A wild look glazed his eyes. *He's going to run!* Emily thought in a panic, and she knew she couldn't let him go. She reached out impulsively to grab him, cupping one hand behind his head and drawing it down to her shoulder, despite his weak resistance.

"What's wrong, Billy? What is it?"

He leaned into her, unable to fight her insistent mothering. He was too desperate for that tender sympathy, for the caring embrace he'd never known in his own childhood.

"It's all right," she murmured softly. "You can talk to me."

"It's nothing really," he mumbled hoarsely, choked up by memories too awful to admit."

"It must be something. What?"

"It's just that—that I was reminded of how I used to put my hand on my mama's belly to feel the baby moving. 'Course, she didn't like it none and she'd push me away. And then—then she went and got rid of it."

Emily froze, her hand poised on the top of his head. "What do you mean? She got rid of the baby?"

"I don't know what she did. I wasn't very old at the time.

I just remember her bleeding something fierce and Daddy yelling because she'd done something to keep it from being born. Her saying she didn't want any more of his good-for-nothing kids. She came real close to dying. And then as soon as she was fit enough, she took off and left us without so much as a word. I was really looking forward to her having that little baby, you know. I thought maybe it'd make us more a family. What'd I know?"

Emily hugged him tight. "Oh, Billy, I'm sorry. It's not going to be like that with Sarah. It's not. She's going to be such a good mother. I know it. She loves children. You'll never have to worry about a thing."

"But what if she doesn't want it because it's mine?" he asked in a fragile tone.

Emily lifted his face in the valley of her palm so she could smile at him reassuringly. "She'll want it all the more because it is."

He looked so hopeful, her heart broke for him. Then he pulled back and rubbed his hand over his features, erasing away the signs of vulnerability as if they were something about which to be ashamed. "I didn't mean to go on like that."

"I'm glad you felt you could trust me with it." She touched his cheek. He looked down but didn't withdraw. The balance was so tenuous, she scarcely dared to draw a breath. "I'm going to settle the boys in for the night. I'll leave a bedroll in the front room for you. Turn in whenever you feel like it, and I'll have a big breakfast ready in the morning. All right?"

After a long moment, he nodded. She didn't want to leave him there on the porch. Darkness made an invisible haven all around them, and if Billy chose to step off into it, they'd never find him. But if he didn't feel they trusted him, he'd be gone that much quicker.

Emily went inside and almost at once an idea came to her. They were going to have to make it as difficult as possible for Billy Cooper to walk away.

* * *

"Hey there, Ranger Bill."

Billy turned to smile at Emily's half-Apache son. "Hey, Kenny."

"You left this on the table." In his extended palm lay Billy's Texas Ranger star. What could he do but take it? It wasn't as if he could explain how things were to an eight-year-old. Not when he couldn't figure them out himself. The piece of metal felt familiar in his hand, as comfortable as his gun grip, his bridle reins, and Sarah's soft skin. Unexpected emotion wadded up in his throat as he thought about the things the badge represented and what it had meant to him when he proudly wore it: a symbol of decency and acceptance, the chance to rise above his past, to be somebody, to be like Jack. He'd failed in those treasured expectations. He'd failed Jack and his fellow rangers. He'd failed Sarah and his unborn child. And all he had left as a reminder was this circle of cold tin, warming even now within his palm. He closed his fingers over it.

"Thanks, Kenny."

"Aren't you gonna pin it on?"

"Don't want to stick myself."

"I'll do it for you."

And the boy was pulling it out of his hand, affixing it ceremoniously on the breast front of his jacket. Over his treacherous heart. Kenitay stepped back and observed his work with a pleased smile. "There you go, Ranger Bill. Looks good."

But looks could be deceiving. Wasn't that what Harm Bass had said?

"It's getting cold out here. You coming in soon?"

"Pretty soon. I got me some thinking to do."

Kenitay nodded like a wise little soul, then pressed an unexpected hug on him. The feel of that hearty squeeze woke all sorts of hellish feelings in Billy's jaded spirit.

"G'night, kid."

" 'Night, Ranger Bill. See ya in the morning. You'll be here, won't you? Ranger Jack said you would be."

"Ranger Jack doesn't lie, so must be I'll be here."

Kenitay grinned and went inside with a slam of the door.

It was cold. It was cold outside and within him as Billy stood on the step and tried to make sense of the spot he was in. He should hightail it out fast and not look over his shoulder. He should guard his heart and soul and get the hell away from those who would hurt him. Or care about him. He didn't know which it was. He'd thought he did, but thinking on it now, perhaps that was the whiskey talking. And Ray Gant's subtle influence.

Sarah hadn't told Jack anything.

Could it be as easy as stepping back into his ranger role? Could he turn away from the things he'd done and been ready to do without consequence? Without anyone ever knowing? Jack would never learn how he'd betrayed his friendship and his trust. The rangers would never find out he'd ridden the outlaw trail for his own benefit instead of theirs. Only Sarah would know the truth.

Would she keep his secret?

Even if she did, even if no one ever knew, he would know it in his heart and soul. How could he live amongst the virtuous and the good of his ranger company knowing he was every bit as bad as the lawbreakers they hunted?

This was his third chance. How many men got even one? He knew he didn't deserve it. Not one damn bit. But he'd be crazy not to take it. Or at least enjoy it for a while. What was the alternative? Jail? Hanging? Following Ray until he met one or both ends?

The badge felt heavy riding on his coat, like a responsibility not lived up to. But he didn't take it off. It felt too good to be wearing it again.

"He gonna be here in the morning, you think?" Jack asked as he snuggled in beside his wife. She nestled close and kissed the cap of his shoulder.

"I think he will."

"I don't know. I wish I could be that sure. You didn't see the way he looked sitting in that jail cell, like he was waiting to hang. Like he deserved to hang."

"He's confused, Jack, lost and hurt and confused."

"He's a grown man, Em, not some little kid."

Man. Child. Emily didn't see much difference between the two. Both needed love and careful nurturing. Both needed the security of a place to belong in order to roam free and strong. It had been that way with Jack when she met him and it was that way with Billy now.

"Are you taking him back into the rangers?"

"I don't know that, either. I never thought I'd admit I couldn't trust him. I'd have put my life in his hands without the slightest doubt. I *have* put my life in his hands. I wish I knew if he crossed that line."

"Does it matter now that he's here?"

"Of course it matters!"

"How many times have you crossed that line between right and wrong and been forgiven? By Billy? By your family? By your own conscience?"

He was silent for a moment. "I get your point, Em. What am I supposed to do? Welcome him back into the company without questions? Turn him over to my baby sister without making sure he's not gonna hurt her?"

"Yes, that's exactly what I want you to do."

"Emily—"

"Jack, haven't you said all along that he's the best ranger you've ever commanded?"

"Yes . . ."

"And hasn't he been a friend to you, one who'd stick by you through the lean times when you didn't think anyone would?"

"Yes."

"If you don't take him back unconditionally, you're not going to get him back. You push what he may or may not have done in his face, and whether he's guilty or not, he's going to be gone. Is that what you want?"

"No."

Emily exhaled in relief and hugged him tight. "I love you, Jack. You're a good man."

"Yeah, well, good and smart aren't the same thing and often as not become good and dead."

"Oh, you don't believe that."

He rolled up on his side so he could command her kiss. It was long and filled with descriptive passion. "So, what am I supposed to do with my renegade ranger? Turn him loose in with the others and take my chances?"

"No. I've got a better idea."

"Christmas at Harmon's? Now, Jack, I don't know about that." Billy was beginning to regret staying overnight when greeted with this particularly unpleasant news.

"The whole family goes over for the week. He's got tons of room to put us up. Emily thought it'd give everyone a chance to know you better."

Billy smiled thinly. "Remind me to thank her for thinking of me."

Jack grinned. He could understand why the idea of days and nights under Harm Bass's roof might put a terrible distress into a fellow. Especially if that fellow wasn't one Harm was particularly fond of. But it would give him a chance to keep an eye on his friend and on Billy's relationship with his sister.

"You mean to just pack up and go?"

"Right after breakfast. Shouldn't take you too long, seeing as how you don't have much to put together. You said yourself Gant was planning to swing down into Mexico till the first of the year, so I figured I'd take some time off. It's not like the boys won't know where to find me if they need me. And you could use a breather before you get back to ranging work."

"I don't know, Jack. If I had my choice—"

"I'm not giving you one."

Jack fixed him with a level stare. *He knows!* Awareness leapt through Billy like a shock of wildfire. How much he couldn't guess, but he sure as hell knew something or he wouldn't be so grimly determined about him making this trip.

Jack went on as if that spark of tension hadn't jumped between them. "We'll swing on by my mama's and pick up Sarah on the way over."

Sarah. That was another thing Billy hadn't counted on. Seeing Sarah again. Anticipation spiked hotly, then was tempered by a cooler caution. What if she decided to spill everything to Jack? Wouldn't he be smarter to light out while he could, rather than trust to her discretion? He'd cut her loose from any obligation to him, so why should he expect her to protect him against her family? He'd be crazy to take the chance.

"Jack, I'm gonna need some things from town. Have I got time to ride on over and pick 'em up? Or will Sheriff Lowe clap me back in jail the minute he sees me?"

Jack hesitated and Billy saw a whole world of reluctance in his gaze. Then, surprisingly, Jack said, "I explained things to Calvin. Go on. It'll probably take Emily an hour or so to try to stuff the entire house into the back of the wagon. I want us to pull out no later than ten. If you're not back by then . . . you can catch up on the trail."

"Sure, Jack." Billy took a slow step back, easing toward the door and separation from this man who offered both freedom and forgiveness. What he hadn't anticipated was how hard it was going to be to break eye contact. Jack held him with his pale-eyed gaze, a compelling stare that reminded Billy of all the things they'd been to one another. He couldn't move.

"Daddy?" Little Carson Bass burst into the room with a youngster's thoughtlessness, and the mood was broken as Jack bent to scoop him up. "Mama wants to know if she can borrow you for a minute."

Billy retreated another step, his eyes filled up with that image of how family should be. "See ya, Jack."

Over the boy's head, Jack affixed him with another intense look as he told him, "You take care."

"I will." He turned and was gone.

Jack stood there for a long while, his arms full of four-year-old, his heart full of anguish.

"Where's Billy?" Emily asked as she finally came to see if her message had been delivered.

"I let him go."

Her husband's aching reply told her everything. "Oh, Jack."

"Guess it's up to him now." He pressed his face into his son's silky hair and inhaled sharply. The breath cut through his chest like his uncle's big blade. Then he set the boy down. "Well, let's get a move on."

As they pulled out of the ranger yard, family packed into an overcrowded buckboard with Jack handling the reins, Emily put her hand over her husband's for a reassuring squeeze. His glance was poignant, filled with disappointed misery. He'd guessed wrong. And he'd spend the holiday knowing that when it was over, he'd have to send out a detail after his best friend.

They'd gone about a mile when Kenitay shouted, "Hey, Ranger Bill."

Jack glanced around to see Billy flanking the wagon on horseback. Billy touched his fingertips to the brim of his Stetson in a silent salute and Jack turned back to the team, struggling to suppress his grin of relief. It was going to be a great holiday after all.

Sarah blotted her face with a damp towel and climbed up off her knees. Her stomach slowly calmed from its violent roiling into a quivery distress now that her morning ritual was complete. Feeling faint and feverish as the sensation of dizziness ebbed, she took a grateful breath and wondered how long this particular torture would continue. Surely a month hanging over the commode was suffering enough for what her mother called the joys of childbirth. She couldn't wait to get to the joy of it, because this part was sheer hell.

"Company coming in," Jeffrey sang out, following that with a gladsome, "It's Jack!"

Mopping her damp brow, Sarah dragged herself out onto the porch. The cool air was the snap she needed to revive her. Pushing damp tendrils of hair from her forehead, she plastered on a smile and prepared to meet her brother and his family. Though she saw their visit as a painful reminder of what she'd lost, she was determined to get through it gracefully even if it killed her.

But as it turned out, it was shock that almost killed her. For riding escort for Jack was his second in command, Billy Cooper.

He looked much the same as he had that first time she saw him ride in. He'd grabbed up her heart then and he still did now. Big, blond, and handsome, he was every young girl's dream and every woman's desire. His hat was tipped to shade his face and his expression, but she could make out the uncompromising line of his mouth. He wasn't smiling. Still, he looked marvelous: tanned, toned, and tawny. And it was then she realized how she must look to him.

Billy saw her come out of the house and tender emotion clogged his chest. His woman, his wife, with a life they'd created between them growing inside her. Expectation and excitement made for an edgy combination, and suddenly all he wanted to do was swing down from the saddle and snatch her up tight in his arms. She was staring up at him through round, startled eyes. He was just beginning to smile in response, the words *I love you, Sarah Cooper* spilling over the guarded walls of his heart, when her expression changed to one of stricken dread and she bolted back inside the house.

All his fragile hopes came tumbling down. Because she wasn't in the least bit happy to see him.

Chapter Nineteen

Sarah was raking her brush through the snarl of her hair when she heard a man's heavy step behind her. She spun, an expectant smile on her face, but it was only Jack in her doorway and her expression fell.

"Hey, little sister, you could have lit up a room with that smile. Wish it was for me."

She came to him, offering an exuberant hug by way of apology. "It's good to see you, Jack."

"But better to see him. I guess I can live with that."

"Oh, thank you for bringing him." Then her gaze narrowed suspiciously. "You didn't have to use force, did you?"

"Now, that's no way for a pretty new bride to talk." Jack stepped back to regard her with the tender tease of a smile, thinking how fragile and vulnerable she looked. If Billy Cooper didn't do right by her, he'd beat the fool senseless.

"A new bride that got a husband at knife point, you mean."

"The how's not as important as the why. You're not in love with that wild kid, are you?" Her shining gaze was his answer. "Oh, Sarah, I hope you know what you're getting into."

"I love him, Jack, and I want to make him happy."

"Then you'd better hang on tight, little sister."

She stiffened at the subtle warning in his tone. "What do you mean by that?"

"Billy said there was something you were going to tell me. What might that be?"

Her gaze dropped to his top shirt button. "Nothing."

His big hand skimmed along her stubborn jaw, lifting her head up gently. "Sarah, be careful. I'd hate to see either of you get hurt."

She returned his look without so much as a telltale blink and he marveled at his sister's sudden tough maturity. Covering for an outlaw husband would do that to a carefree young girl. But what could he tell her that she didn't already know?

"He's out front, Sarah, looking like his best dog up and left him. Why don't you go fetch him and introduce him proper to the folks?"

She gave him a quick squeeze about the neck. "I love you, Jack, and I take back everything I ever said about you."

He chuckled warmly. "Now, that's a comforting thought." He gave her a firm swat on the bottom to get her moving.

Emily and the boys had Rebecca and Will occupied in the front room. Sarah wound through them with welcoming nods and headed for the porch. Billy was there in the sun-washed yard, loitering next to his horse, looking uncomfortable and excluded. As if he were considering hopping aboard and heading out fast. He gave her a guarded smile when she approached.

"Hello, Billy."

"Sarah."

"I can't say I expected to see you here."

"Well, my plans got changed real suddenlike."

She frowned slightly. "Jack promised he didn't prod you here at gunpoint."

He smiled back. It was a wry gesture. "More like with a noose dangling over my head."

"Oh."

Her magnificent dark eyes clouded up and Billy entertained a brief hope that perhaps she wasn't as indifferent as she pretended. His tone lowered conspiratorially.

"You didn't say anything to Jack. Why?"

Her head assumed a cocky tilt that smacked of Bass pride. "You couldn't very well provide for me dancing from the end of a rope, now, could you?"

"Guess not."

Sarah came up beside him. His whole body had gone rigid

from the effect of her nearness. He tensed as her hand tucked into the bend of his elbow. She gave a tug.

"Come inside."

Her fingertips caressed along the swell of his forearm, and it was that inciting touch more than her words that had him walking tame at her side to join the others in the house.

"Mama, Daddy, you know my husband, Corporal William T. Cooper, of Jack's ranger company."

An awkward moment of silence stretched out as the elder Bass couple scrutinized their daughter's forced partner in marriage. Angered by their rudeness in refusing him welcome, Sarah clutched his arm tighter. Her chin took a haughty notch upward.

"Now that he's here, I'll be leaving with him. C'mon, Billy, you can help me get my things together."

As she towed him toward her room, Rebecca made a move to follow, but Will's hand clamped down on her arm to prevent it.

"Let her go. She made her choice."

"But, Will—"

"Let her go!"

"Well," Jack drawled, "this is real nice. Since there's not going to be any break-out-the-band greeting for a new member of our family, we might as well be heading on over to Uncle Harm's. You coming?"

Will bristled up, and Jack suspected the mood of the holidays was going straight to hell in a hurry.

"I'm not stepping foot over there. That interfering sonuvabitch owes me an apology and I'm not budging until I get one from him."

"Aw, Daddy, c'mon," Jeffrey coaxed with a touch of impatience. "It's Christmas. You and Uncle Harm have all next year to fight about stupid things."

Will shot his youngest a severing glance. "His pushing into our family affairs isn't a stupid thing. He ruined your sister's future."

"I think she pretty much did that on her own, Daddy. Can't you put aside the feuding until after—"

"If you want to go and make nice with him, you go. Take your mama if she wants to go. I don't need you here."

"Will," Rebecca petitioned softly.

"I said go if you want!"

Jack put his arm about his mother's waist. "I'll take you with us, Mama," he offered quietly.

Torn—just as she'd always been torn between brother and husband—Rebecca hesitated. Then she smiled up at her handsome son. "You go on, Jack. Tell Harmon we'll try to stop over later on."

Jack's smile was bittersweet. "I'll tell him. But he may just decide to come on over here and get you."

Her expression sobered. "Tell him that wouldn't be a good idea just now." She reached up to press a kiss against one lean cheek. "Have yourselves a good time. And tell Harmon—tell Harmon I love him."

"I'll do that, Mama." He released her, then took his youngest brother up for a hug. "See you later on, Jeff." Then he put out his hand to his stepfather. "Will." Jack waited with a look of infinite patience until the big ex-ranger took his hand for a firm shake. Then he turned to his family. "Let's get loaded up, all. We got to do some rearranging, because Sarah's probably got a million bags she can't live without."

She took only one, stuffed with the first things she could grab while tears blurred her vision. Billy waited restlessly just inside the door.

"I'm sorry, Sarah. I know I'm not what your folks had in mind. You don't need to tangle with them over it. You don't have to do this."

"What? Go with my husband? Of course I do." She stopped and looked back at him, a whole world of meaning in her eyes. "Unless you don't want me to."

"That's up to you, I guess."

He wouldn't give anything away. But when she thought of staying through Christmas in this tumultuous household, it didn't much matter if Billy was overjoyed with her company. She closed her bag with a determined snap. "That's everything."

"You travel light."

"I've got everything I need." Her dark gaze lifted to his lingering there in a tender foray of longing. He looked away uneasy with her display of desire.

"Let's go then."

With his arm locked abut her shoulders and her single bag in his hand, Billy guided her through the rest of the family without a glance at them. To hell with them all! He was filled with a burgeoning pride at her decision to come with him just as she'd said she would. He hadn't believed her. But then it wasn't as if they were going off alone. They were traveling on to her uncle's. That was hardly a huge step of faith. Still it warmed him considerably.

Rebecca followed them out and took Sarah up for a quick embrace. Then she leveled an unwavering gaze on Billy. When he didn't flinch or try to evade it, she smiled. Her soft kiss to his cheek was a surprise.

"Don't think badly of us, William. Sarah's father has a lot on his mind. Come back to see us again and we'll give you a proper welcome. Be good to her. That's all I ask."

"Yes, ma'am," he vowed in a husky rumble.

"Thank you, Mama," Sarah cried gratefully as she cast her arms around Rebecca for another emotional hug. Then she stepped back, smiling through her tears to say, "I'll see you soon."

And with Jack's family, they headed for Harmon's.

There, they found all the enthusiasm lacking from their greeting at Will's. Mainly because Harm wasn't there.

The children came together in a great noisy, squealing mass and darted off for the creek. Amanda ran down from the porch of her West Texas mansion to scatter kisses on Jack and share hugs with Emily and Sarah. Then she toed off in front of Billy, letting her gaze drag up from the tips of his boots to the untanned strip of his brow. She gave him a devilish grin.

"My, my, Mr. Cooper, you certainly have aged nicely. No wonder Sarah thought you were worth a second chance."

Before he could think of what to make of her words, Amanda curled an arm about his neck and drew him down, rubbing her soft cheek along his rougher one. Against his

ear, she whispered, "Make yourself at home, Billy, and don't
let Harmon scare you off. If he gets to growling too much,
you let me know and I'll give him a good smack on the nose."

The idea of this spunky little blonde dealing the fierce
Harm Bass a behave-yourself swat made Billy grin wide.
"Now I know where Sarah gets her brass from, ma'am."

"You don't stand much of a chance around this bunch
without brass, Billy. You remember that, and you and
Harmon will get along just fine."

"If you say so, Miz Bass."

"It's Amanda, and I do say so. I already like you, so what
chance does Harmon have even if he decides to be stubborn?" She linked her arm through Billy's to give him an elevated status amongst her guests. "Let's go inside. I'll get you
some coffee while I decide how to divide the upstairs rooms.
Are Will, Rebecca, and Jeffrey coming?"

"I don't think so, Amanda," Jack admitted sadly.

Billy stiffened, waiting to be condemned as the reason for
the family dissent. Instead, Amanda shook her head and gave
a savage sigh.

"Those two men . . . I'd like to tie their feet together, drape
them over a clothesline, and let them have at it. I can't see
why they don't just look past their pride and realize how
much they like each other. It's always something."

"Where is Uncle Harm?"

Amanda's mood dampened with worry. It was a slight
thing, that smothering of her spirit. "He's been gone for a
couple of days. I'm not sure when to expect him."

"Out hunting?"

"Out scalping Mexicans, for all I know." She didn't sound
bitter in that complaint, just concerned about his absence.
"He'll come in when he finds out you're here. Until then, we
might as well enjoy the peace. Emily, do you feel up to cooking? Maybe the scent of a good meal will draw him out."

The rest of the afternoon faded into evening and Billy
found himself relaxing. It was hard not to in Amanda Bass's
house. She made it easy to feel at home. Children ran in and
out. The women fussed in the kitchen and over the table. He

and Jack kicked back with strong coffee and a comfortable degree of silence between them, while trying to stay out of everyone's way. He liked Amanda. She was a truly genuine person of outspoken likes and dislikes. While Emily was of sturdy prairie stock, Amanda was a flighty eastern butterfly sneaking up on him with sudden hugs that were warm and mothering and made him blush to the roots of his hair. Anchoring her was a deep, determined strength, the kind it would take to love a man like Harm Bass. She and Emily were the kind of women a man was glad to come home to. Sarah took after them in different ways. And he'd be glad to come home to her if he could believe she'd be waiting there to love him.

They'd exchanged fewer than a dozen words to one another and none of them of an intimate nature. None of them preparing for the point when Amanda pushed open a bedroom door and said to the both of them, "This one's yours."

He could feel Jack's eyes on him as he ushered Sarah inside, a look that said: *That's my little sister you've got there, pard. Watch where you put your hands!* The fact that they were married seemed to make no difference, no more than the fact that she was already carrying his child. It was going to be a miserable visit, Billy decided as he closed the door.

Sarah didn't speak to him as she opened her bag and withdrew a heavy cotton nightdress. Without looking around at him, she stripped down to her practical underthings. He could feel his mouth growing drier with each layer she discarded. The remembered feel of her was enough to chafe his restraint. Then she was shimmying into her bedclothes and tucking under the covers.

"Good night."

Billy stood there feeling foolish and frustrated. Thoughts of a passionate evening scattered as she turned her back to him. He cursed softly under his breath as he levered out of his boots, then stripped down to his long johns. He'd just as soon not be in his bare skin if Harm Bass decided to take exception to him being there when he got home. Billy eased in on his side of the bed and lay back, regarding his wife's unyielding silhouette. His gaze traveled slowly along the tempting curves. His wife. His for the taking. But if he put a hand on her and she decided she

didn't like it, this wasn't exactly the kind of place he'd care to
have her start yelling about it. Not with a ranger brother across
the hall who slept with a .45 next to the pillow and a lethal-
tempered uncle creeping about somewhere with a razor-edged
knife. Better he just rein in his thoughts of passion and live to
do something about them later. He was her husband in name
but not yet in accepted fact. Not even by Sarah.

He lay there on his back, staring up at the dark ceiling, the
sound of Sarah's soft breathing driving him increasingly crazy.
He was just about to break down and do something about it
when he heard voices on the other side of the wall. Desire deflated in an instant. Harm was back.

"Where have you been?"

"Out. Is there any of what smells so good in the kitchen left
over?"

"If you wanted supper, you should have been here."

A soft laugh contradicted his wife's prickly tone. "I'm here
now. You didn't save me anything?"

"Oh, Harmon, you make me crazy!" That was followed by
the moaning rumbles of two people enjoying a very explicit kiss.

"Who's here?" Harm asked a bit breathlessly.

"Jack and Emily."

Billy tensed.

"Sarah and Billy."

Silence, then a low growl of "Did you put the two of them
in the same room?"

"Of course, in the same room. Harmon, they're married."

"Well, I can change that right quick!"

"You'll do no such a thing. I think you've done quite
enough meddling. Come back down here, Harmon. This
bed's a lot more comfortable than the barn."

Bed springs creaked and Billy exhaled.

"Now, then, isn't this better then curling up alone in your
bedroll." There was silence as she apparently worked to convince him it was. "Are you going to be friendly and polite in
the morning?"

"I'm always friendly and polite."

Billy snorted softly.

"In fact, I'm feeling real friendly and polite right now." The neighboring bed gave a few significant squeaks, and Harm's voice drawled, "Still want me to sleep out in the barn, little girl?"

"Ohhhh . . . . Harmon. Only if you take me with you."

From that point, the noises got a lot friendlier and extremely explicit. Billy flushed in the darkness of his own room, well aware of where Sarah had learned all those husky sounds of lovemaking she'd tormented him with in the outlaw shack.

Wondering if Sarah was awake and listening, Billy grew uncomfortably aroused. Just when he thought he'd have to head for the front porch and a dose of cold night air, the intimate sounds from the next room ended. He went limp with relief.

"I love you, Harmon," came Amanda's quiet claim.

Then a soft reply, one more tender than Billy had ever imagined a man's could be.

"You are my heart and soul, *shijii*. You are my life. What would I do without you?"

"You'll never know. I promise you that."

"I love you, Ammy."

Silence settled as the two of them settled in with one another. On the other side of the wall, lying next to the still and denying figure of his wife, Billy was tense and emotionally trembling. He was picturing what it would be like to be so much in love that his heart could open and allow such words to escape. Unable to visualize it with any degree of success, he spent a restless night under Harm Bass's roof.

The sounds of terrible sickness woke Billy from a fitful sleep. The space beside him was empty. He bolted upright in a panic, to find Sarah on hands and knees hanging over a chamber pot.

"Sarah?" He scooted out of bed and went to kneel down beside her. "Baby, what's wrong?"

When he put his hands on her shoulders, she shoved him away so hard he nearly toppled.

"Leave me alone. Get away." Her moans were low and wretched, and they completely terrified him. Convinced it must be something life threatening to have her heaving up her insides with such graphic spasms, Billy burst across the hall to bang on Jack's door.

"Emily? Emily!"

Bleary-eyed, she answered his frantic knocking, wearing one of Jack's shirts. "Billy, what is it?"

"It's Sarah. Something awful's wrong with her!"

Jack was up by then, and as a veteran husband and father, he took one listen and had it diagnosed. "Oh, for heaven's sake, it's just morning sickness. Go back to bed!" And Jack did, grumbling all the way.

Billy looked to Emily for confirmation. She smiled and rubbed his forearms.

"That's all it is. She's fine. Nothing to worry about."

"Are you sure?"

"Trust me. I'm sure."

He expelled a jerky breath. "Oh, God, I thought—"

She knew what he thought. One look at his pale, tortured face told her that. He'd thought Sarah was losing the baby.

"What's going on?" Harm muttered from his open doorway as Amanda peered over his shoulder.

"Nothing," Emily assured them. "Just a little expectant father jitters."

Billy wanted to disappear through the cracks in the floor just about then.

Harm shook his head in exasperation and closed his door.

"Well, now that I've made a fool of myself in front of everybody, I guess I'll go back to bed."

Emily smiled. She knew just the opposite was true. His frantic concern for his wife had probably anchored his place in the family as nothing else could. "Don't worry about it, William. Harmon and Jack are just remembering how crazy they acted the first time."

Billy gave her a weak, uncertain smile. "Sorry to wake you." Then he scuffled back into his borrowed bedroom like a shamed dog with its tail between its legs.

By then, Sarah was back under the covers and none too pleased with him.

"Thank you for humiliating me in from of my whole family. It wasn't enough to just wish I could die. Now, I'd like to kill you, too."

He lay down, feeling stupid and helpless and so relieved he wanted to weep in thanksgiving. Billy could think of no way to explain the fright that had overrode his common sense so he said nothing. He glanced at Sarah's rigid back. Uttering a quiet curse, he rolled up behind her and hauled her back against him within the curl of his embrace.

"Don't," came her irritable mutter. "Don't come near me. I look terrible."

He gave a soft chuckle. "You look beautiful to me."

"No, I don't."

"Okay, then I won't look. I just want to hold onto you for a minute. That all right?"

She was already drawing his arms in closer about her as she mumbled, "I guess so." Then she was aware of a slight tremor in his arms, a quiver that grew to an uncontrollable quaking. "Billy, are you all right?"

"Just glad to be holding you, is all."

"Oh." She liked the sound of that. Her mood softened toward him. "I'm sorry I scared you."

"No, I'm sorry. I just lost my head for a minute. I was afraid something was wrong with the baby."

The baby. Of course, Sarah thought morosely. He was worried about the baby. "The baby's fine. Just think of this morning as a pregnant woman's reveille. You'll get used to it." She felt the unmistakable pressure of his kiss atop her head and wished with all her heart that just a small part of his worry had been for her.

Billy stood on the front porch watching Harm and Jack dig. They'd been working at it for some time and both had their shirts off despite a temperature in the fifties. Something in that hard, physical labor appealed to him, and before he could think about it for too long, Billy strode across the yard to where the two men had edged out an eight-by-eight-by-three-foot square in the hard Texas soil.

"Give you a hand?"

Harm swiped a dirty forearm across his eyes and squinted up at him. It wasn't a particularly warm look, and that hole took on all the welcome of his own grave. Finally, without a word, Harm tossed his shovel. Billy caught it deftly. As he stepped down, Harm sat on the edge of the pit.

"I'll hold that for you," he offered, relieving Billy of his coffee, which he sipped while the younger man buried the spade in the ground. "Ammy decided she had to have a cold storage cellar. Figured I'd better get to it while I had some free labor."

After a dozen or so scoops, Billy broke a good sweat and peeled out of his shirt, too. Harm showed no inclination toward retrieving the shovel from him so he went back to work, toiling beside Jack in a companionable rhythm.

Harm sat idle with the empty cup in his hands. He watched Billy Cooper and had to admit to a grudging admiration. Damned if he wasn't starting to like the sassy kid. Of course, he wasn't about to let Billy know it. He'd treat Sarah better if he believed himself under the threat of a slow, lingering death at the merciless hands of her uncle.

Smiling to himself, Harm let his gaze lift to the hills. A disquieting stir came over him. He was motionless for a long moment, trying to get a hold of that uneasy feeling. His eyes scanned the rocky face of the Chisos.

"Harm, you gonna climb in here and get dirty, or you meaning to supervise?"

Harm grinned at Jack. "What do you think I invited you here for? I'm getting old and slow. Need to take it easy."

"Hah! Amanda's not going to let you get old and slow." He tossed a pick to him.

And as the three of them dug down in the unyielding earth, eyes just as cruel and hard watched them from above.

"Whatdaya think, Ray? He been playing us for fools?"

Ray Gant stared down at Billy, studying the way he worked alongside the Basses. His expression was thoughtful. "Don't know. Hate to kill him for nothing. Maybe it's time we gave ole Billy-boy a test to see what side he's really on."

Chapter Twenty

"Whoa! Don't you take another step!"

Harm stopped, his foot suspended above the second stair to his porch. Amanda stood at the top, arms akimbo, her freckled nose wrinkled up tight.

"The three of you could knock down a herd of longhorns at five hundred yard. Whew! You're not setting foot in my house until that stink is washed off you." She tossed her husband a batch of towels and a cake of soap, then gestured toward the creek.

Harm was tired, hungry, and in no mood to be barred entrance to his own home. Especially with Jack and Billy smirking behind his back. His brows lowered into a formidable line. "And just who was I trying so hard to please while getting into this . . . unpresentable state? Remind me to think twice before I do *anything* to please you again. Now get outta my way, so I can sit down to whatever Emily's been simmering in the kitchen all afternoon."

Jack made a cautioning noise and advised, "Uncle Harm, think we'd be wise to just get it over with. I did notice some of the ocotillo back there wilting whilst we were walking by."

He shot his nephew a jaundiced glance. "Maybe you let your wife dictate table manners to you, but I sit to mine any way I please."

"And it better please you to sit at it clean, or you're going to sit at it hungry," Amanda prophesied.

A cough of laughter had the bad luck to escape before Billy could catch it. Harm turned a skewering eye on him.

"You say something, boy?"

"No sir, Mr. Bass. Not a word. I was just on my way down to the creek to wash up for supper." He took the top towel and started in that direction, grinning because he knew there was no way the blustery Harm Bass was going to get past his bristled-up little wife.

"Where are you going?" Harm demanded of Jack.

"To wash up. I'm hungry."

Faced with total defection in the ranks, Harm glowered up at the smug barrier to his supper table. He started to spew an angry sentiment and she quickly cut him off.

"Your hot temper isn't going to get you past me, Harmon."

His blue eyes narrowed fiercely. "Well, then, maybe the cure for my hot temper is the same cure needed for your sharp tongue, woman."

He snatched her off the porch before she could manage a protest, the slap of her belly over his shoulder efficiently knocking the fight from her as he strode toward the crisp, fast-flowing water. But it was a short-lived quiet.

"Harmon!" she wheezed. "Harmon Bass, you put me down! Don't you dare drop me in that water! I'll freeze!"

"Oh, so it's all right for me to frostbite my tough ole Texas hide but not for you to chill your silky New York City skin."

"Harmon, I'm warning you!"

"I must be going deaf, 'cause I surely didn't hear what might be taken for a threat."

He waded out into the creek with Amanda hanging on to the back of his belt for dear life.

"Harmon Bass, I'm going to tan that tough hide and make a pair of boots out of you!"

"What was that, little girl?" He jerked her loose and brought her down in front of him, holding her in the wrap of his arms so only the hem of her dress trailed in the water. "You got something to say to me?" He waited, eyes going big and beguiling. Her annoyance with him blew out like a spring storm. Slowly, her fingertips charted the angles of his face and she leaned in to kiss him.

From where he stood on the bank, watching, Billy thought they possessed amazing breath control, because they didn't break off for an astounding length of time. Then Amanda was all soft purring contentment and Harm was the one with the smug smile.

"Now can I come sit at my table?"

"Ummmm, you can sit at the table any way you please . . . as soon as you wash." And she kissed him again, a slow appeasing slide of the lips that left him smiling.

"I thought you said you couldn't stand the smell of me!"

"But the taste of you is something else altogether."

"Seeing as how you put it that way . . ." He waded up to the shore to set her down on dry land. Their stares engaged in a moment of sensual sparring, then he let her go.

Amanda's palms rubbed over denim-clad hips. "Now you're going to have to get into some dry clothes, too. Hurry up and get scrubbed, and I'll help you change before dinner." The promise in that simple statement smoldered.

Harm watched her walk back to the house, the sizzle never leaving his eyes, and he muttered to his companions, "No amount a' pride is worth the fill of a good dinner."

Jack laughed, noting the way his uncle's gaze focused on the sway of Amanda's hips. "Or the feel of a good woman."

Billy said nothing. He was rather dazed by the whole thing. A smiling, playful Harm Bass. Now that was something he'd never expected to see. But it was more than that. It was the tender affection snuggled up beneath the surface sensuality, the casual intimacy of a man and a woman sure in one another's love.

How he'd like to be teased and taunted and eventually tamed like that . . . by Sarah Cooper.

Must be heat exhaustion, he told himself as he knelt to plunge his head in the mind-clearing water. But funny thing was, the desire didn't leave him. And it wasn't because the water wasn't cold enough.

The feeling was just too strong to wash away.

And over dinner, it kept intensifying. Sarah sat beside him, and every time she turned her head, he got a tantalizing sniff of something light and floral that she'd used in washing her hair. When she passed the dishes, their hands brushed unintentionally and that contact started a brushfire of desire inside him. Billy watched Harm and Amanda and Jack and Emily and the tableful of kids, and he realized this was what a family was supposed to be, not the cold, scary surroundings he'd grown up within. Even Harm was speaking to him civilly. Of course it was only to say pass the potatoes and no thanks to the peas, but at least he wasn't growling and spreading his butter as if he were wishing he were filleting Billy's flesh.

By the time Billy pushed back from the table, he was filled up on all sorts of things more savory than Emily's fine cooking. He excused himself to go outside and let them digest at a slow, savoring pace.

Sarah paused in her clearing of the table to watch him. His was such a lonely posture there at the edge of the porch. She ached to draw him in from that self-isolating stance but she didn't know how. Instinct told her to give him space, to give him time, but her heart was eager to include him. She couldn't force him to fit into her family any more than she could force him to care about her. She'd been foolish to believe that once upon a time. Now she was more cautious with her outpouring of emotion. Her pride wouldn't let her ask why he'd come to spend the holidays with her. She was afraid she wouldn't like the answer. What did it matter now that he was here?

"You could have done worse, you know."

Harm circled her shoulders for a light squeeze and she snuggled into his side with a soft "I know."

"He's got the makings of a good man. Maybe all he needs is a good woman behind him."

"Like you did?"

"Don't get sassy, little girl. Yeah, like I did."

There was a sudden childish cry of hurt and Billy vaulted over the porch rail. Becca. Harm and Sarah rushed out of the house to see Billy kneeling down next to her in the side yard, examining the girl's scraped elbow. When Harm started forward, Sarah grabbed on to still him.

Speaking soothingly and smiling often, Billy used his handkerchief to dry the child's copious tears before making a loose binding about the raw skin. He said something and Becca's arms went about his neck. Then he stood and carried her easily back to the house, where he shifted her over into her father's care.

"Just scuffed a little skin off, is all," Billy told him. "But she's being mighty brave about it, aren't you, sweetheart?"

She gave him a fragile smile, and over the top of her blond head, Harm's stare was carefully gauging.

"I'll take her on in and let her mama fuss over it. C'mon, *shijii*, you can show off your battle wounds to your sister."

When he'd carried her inside, Sarah smiled up at Billy.

"I've never known Uncle Harmon to let anyone pick up one of his kids unless it was one of us."

Billy couldn't miss the significance of that but he chose to make light of it. "Well, I just can't stand to see a little one crying. 'Bout breaks my heart in two to think of one of 'em scared or hurting."

She touched his arm and he went completely still.

"You've got a big heart, Billy Cooper."

"When it comes to kids. I'd have a dozen of 'em if I could."

"I thought we'd settled on six. Or at least this one to start with." She put her other hand on her stomach and his gaze went there, lingering. He reached tentatively to ease his fingers over the backs of hers, rubbing them slowly until hers spread and invited his to intertwine. He took a sighing breath and stared out over her uncle's property, his gaze pensive and sad.

"What are you thinking?"

"Hmmm? Oh, 'bout how funny it feels being swallowed up in your family, and how different my sister and I might have turned out if ours had been anything like it." He paused and gave Sarah a cautious glance, but she was looking up with a tender empathy and the words just came pouring out of him.

"I was thinking 'bout my little niece and nephew and 'bout how hard they have it. Julie, my sister, she makes a living off the sheets, and when she's not working, she's drinking and she don't spend any kinda time with her kids. Last time I was there, they were living no better than dirty little animals. I don't blame Julie. She don't really know no better. She's raising 'em like we was raised, but kids deserve better than that. They deserve to feel safe and loved. I keep thinking Jessie'll grow up to be a whore like her mama and Jed'll end up on a rope like—" He broke off, looking anguished and uncomfortable. "Jus' wish there was something I could do, is all."

Sarah's suggestion was unplanned and unexpected. "You could send for them."

"What?"

"Send for them. They could live with us."

He stared down at her, stunned, not knowing what to say.

"I mean, I grew up with family all around me. I'm used to living in the middle of a mob. I help Amanda raise her kids. It wouldn't be any bother at all. Look at Uncle Harm and Jack and Kenitay; half of us have other names and belong to someone else, and yet we're still all family. I wouldn't mind . . ."

The sudden crush of his kiss silenced her. It was hot and hard and hurried, and when he lifted up, Sarah was too dazed to do more than draw a ragged little breath.

In looking down on her, Billy saw absolutely everything in the world he wanted. He took a step closer and raised his hand, letting his knuckles trail gently over the smooth curve of her cheek. Again, she managed to take him unaware with her outspoken candor.

"Trust me, Billy."

Her sudden impassioned claim startled him. "What?"

"Trust me. I won't hurt you. Let me give you a place to belong."

He sucked in a quick breath and unconsciously withdrew that step. How had she known? How had this wild little West Texas girl known just what he needed to hear? Panic and wariness and a sudden crazy hope churned inside him.

Sarah was watching his face, trying to judge his reaction by the subtle shifts in his expression. She frowned unhappily. "I've done it again, haven't I?"

"What?" came his faint whisper.

"Tried to be the rescuer and made a mess of it. You're drowning, I jump in to save you, and end up pushing you under so you sink that much faster. I just can't seem to get it right." She blinked hard to discourage the amassing brightness in her eyes, but before the first glimmer could escape, his thumb was sketching the swell of her cheek. Her lashes flickered and finally sank closed as he bent to kiss her again, slowly and sweetly.

"You got it right this time," he whispered against her lips.

She melted against him, her body going lax with longing. Her hands pushed inside his long coat, rubbing and restlessly kneading the taut flesh over his ribs and waist. Her fingers hooked in the band of his jeans, tugging him up tight to the yielding fit of her. His response was immediate. And massive.

"Billy, would you come upstairs with me?"

He stiffened. The words were reminiscent of other times, other places, other women. And when he glanced inside, he was reminded of other factors, like the rest of the Bass family. There wasn't exactly any privacy.

Sarah was surprised when he gripped her hand and tugged her off the porch. She followed without protest as he led her down to the barn. Inside, there was a warm, pungent aroma of straw, leather, grain, and animals. He nodded toward the loft and she started up, even as her anticipation heightened. And under the low ceiling braces upon a prickly bed of sweet-smelling hay, she waited for him to join her.

The top of his tousled head appeared first, as mussed and golden as the shafts she knelt upon. Then she could see his eyes and all thoughts of the evening chill left her. The heat of his gaze promised a warmth like no other. He tossed up a bundle of blankets.

"Spread those out," was all he said, and she hurried to comply.

When she was bent over, smoothing a far corner, his arm

scooped around her waist. He hauled her up on her knees and against his greater size and strength, fitting her back to front between his spraddled thighs. Billy encouraged Sarah to let her head drop upon his shoulder, his mouth moving with infinite patience along her jaw, against her temple and throat, where her pulse pounded an urgent tempo. Her back arched away from his firm body when his hands skimmed up to cup and fondle her breasts. As a shudder of expectation claimed her, he began to unbutton her dress.

He was slow. So slow she wanted to push his hands aside and race down those stubborn little fastenings on her own. But there was something undeniably sensuous about him doing it. Calico was eased from the slope of her shoulders and his kisses burned upon bared skin.

She was as sweet as he remembered but he couldn't recall her feeling so damned fragile before. Her bones felt so tiny and breakable, her frame almost childlike as it undulated against him with what could only be described as womanly intention. He couldn't bear the thought that he might bruise her, so he gentled his touch even more, letting his fingers pluck at the laces of her chemise and ease underneath to glide on satiny flesh. Sarah sighed his name and moved impatiently against his palms. Her head tossed back and forth along his shoulder as his hands settled lower, drawing slow circles down the curve of her jerking torso, changing to long, soothing strokes over the concave of her belly.

When he nudged beneath the linen of her drawers, her breath altered into a series of panting whimpers. With the pressure of his palms, he pushed her thighs apart, tenting them wide alongside the spread of his own. Sarah began clutching at his forearms as he massaged her with the heel of one hand while his fingers delved deep, discovering a ready dampness and hot compliance. She tried to turn toward him but his other arm curled tight about her waist, anchoring her back against him as he continued to tempt and toy with her. It was maddening play, punctuated by the flickering trace of his tongue around the whorl of her ear.

Sarah trembled within the tender cage of his embrace, feel-

264   *Dana Ransom*

ing her will fracture. An involuntary cry tore from her as sudden jolts of sensation wracked her body.

After he'd pursued those tremulous spasms to their end, Billy held her to him, gratified by each shivery breath and nerveless tremor.

"Oh, Billy," she breathed with a rapturous languor. "Oh, Billy, that was nice."

"Nice, huh?" He nuzzled her glistening throat, tasting the thunder of her heartbeats. "Well, I'm not through impressing you yet."

He turned her in his arms and went down with her to their makeshift pallet. Instead of heading for her lips, though, he kissed his way around the graceful sweep of her collarbone, fastening with a tender violence upon one budded nipple. Sarah gasped, surprised that arousal could leap so quick within a form completely spent by satisfaction. She wound her fingers through his hair, waking once more to passion. She arched and writhed as his purposefully lazy touch coaxed her back toward that breathtaking pinnacle. Low illicit moans gusted up from the back of her throat, husky with desire, raw with need. He had her knees shaking and her soul quaking, and he had yet to take off his boots!

"Billy, Billy, please," she keened in a wild, despairing voice. But before she could communicate her want to come to this conclusion with him, it was rocketing through her with the heat of a shooting star, dazzling in its force and brilliance. As the streaks of sensations ran their splendid course and faded to a sated lethargy, Sarah looked up at the man she'd married, the man who was still such a stranger to her, and murmured, "I love you, Billy Cooper. I wish you'd believe that."

He didn't reply. Instead, he let his fingertips stroke back through her tangled hair, feathering it away from her damp brow. His expression was inscrutable.

"Did you mean what you said about taking in my sister's kids?"

"Yes."

"We don't even have a place to live."

"We can find one. Was the money you sent me stolen?"

He frowned slightly at the mention of the money. "Not from anyone who earned it honestly."

She accepted that. "Then we have enough to get ourselves a place." With an endearing touch of shyness, she added, "I want us to be a family, Billy. You, me, and our baby. Is there any chance that you might come to love—"

His kiss cut off the rest. It wasn't an answer but it certainly wasn't a refusal. He kissed her over and over until her mouth was bruised, her mind was dazed, and her heart was palpitating with quivers of hope.

"Please love me, Billy," she panted as he broke away long enough to shed his clothes. He gave a curse as his gunbelt, britches, and a boot slid over the edge of the loft to the floor below. But as soon as he stretched out over the supple figure of his wife, he forgot what he'd lost and concentrated on the treasure he'd found.

She closed around him like a furnace, scalding his senses, rewarding him for the time he'd taken to stoke her passions. He meant to keep feeding that fire with long, deep strokes, but soon the blaze was out of his control. Her response flared white-hot as urgent little cries were gasped against his shoulder and her hips lifted to make the most of each upward thrust. An explosive blast of pleasure roared through him and into her, even as her body surrendered to fitful waves of equal intensity. His groan was soul-deep and satisfied.

It was a long while before his mind cleared enough for even the most sluggish thoughts. But he was smiling as he eased over onto his side, holding her close so he wouldn't have to give up the feel of her around him. With eyes closed and muscles in a state of collapse, Billy muttered, "Oh, baby, we are good together, aren't we?"

"Mmmm-hmmm," was all she could manage.

In the stable area below, Leisha slipped inside with Kenitay in tow, meaning to show him the new foal dropped earlier that day. She paused and lifted a man's boot out of the straw. Abruptly, Kenitay grinned wide and put a shushing finger to his lips. He picked up Billy's denims and waggled his dark brow suggestively. Leisha jointed him in a devilish smile and together they toted their findings back to the house.

Everyone, with two obvious exceptions, was gathered in the parlor when Leisha announced, "Daddy, look what we found in the barn. Someone must have left them out there."

Harm came up off his seat with a thunderous expression, Amanda hanging on his arm as ballast.

"Harmon! Harmon, don't you dare do anything."

It was Jack who strode over to the two smirking youngsters. He tried to look harsh with displeasure, but it was hard not to crack a little smile when he relieved his stepson of Billy's pants. "Well, I'm sure whoever these belong to didn't get far. I'll take care of it. You two troublemakers get ready for bed and hope he's got a sense of humor."

Jack strode down to the barn. It was quiet and musty, with no obvious signs of illicit goings-on. Until he cleared his throat and a flurry of straw filtered down from above his head.

"Lose something, pard?"

He gave the boot an overhanded toss and was amused by his sister's yelp upon impact. There was a long silence, then Billy called, "You find anything else down there?"

Jack flung up his jeans. "Man oughtn't to forget where he drops his pants, if you know what I mean."

A lot more straw siphoned down and he could hear Sarah giggling. Pretty soon, his sister's skirts swept out over the ladder as she started down. Jack waited, then caught her waist to swing her to the floor.

" 'Evening, Jack. Going out for a ride?"

"No." He picked bits of hay from her hair. "But it looks like you just got in from one."

Her grin was wicked. Sarah pressed a quick kiss to his cheek and went racing up toward the house.

Jack glanced upward and was able to step out of the way as one of Billy's boots came plummeting down on the wake of a foul oath.

"Wasn't interrupting anything, was I?" he called up cheerfully.

"If you had been, I'da shot you where you stand."

"Oh, I don't think so." Jack hefted his friend's gunbelt in his hand and watched his half-shod partner climb down. Billy glowered at him and stuffed on his second boot. He was still grinning wide. "Nice night."

"It was," Billy grumbled. "She is my wife, you know."

Jack suddenly sobered. "Yeah, I know. I wasn't sure I liked the idea at first but I'm feeling different about it now." He put out his hand. "Sorry I'm late about getting to this."

Billy stared at that outstretched offer of acceptance. It was way too late in coming to make up for all the hurt and all the wrong things, but . . . "Awww, hell." He took his friend's hand and pumped it hard. "Thanks, Jack."

Jack went one step further, stepping in to hug him up tight and slap his back. "Welcome to the family. Kinda hard to find any privacy, but you'll get used to it."

What Billy couldn't get used to was the sudden swell of panic and distress. Good God, this fine man had no idea what he was embracing! He jerked away, wild with agitation.

"Jack, there are some things I got to tell you! Some of the things I did—"

Jack was quick to put us his hand to stop him. "I don't need to hear it, Billy. It's enough to know you were gonna tell me. Let it go, all right? All right?"

Billy took several ragged breathes, then finally he nodded. "All right, Jack," he agreed hoarsely.

"There. Now that that's been said, let's go on up to the house and see if we can talk Harm into breaking out any of that Apache beer he's got hoarded." He banded Billy's shoulders with the easy drape of his arm. "Sound good?"

"Sounds great."

"C'mon, then. Did I ever tell you my sister can't sew a stitch?"

"Yeah, but she makes a damned fine field dressing."

And the two of them left the barn, walking side by side toward the lights of the house.

Chapter Twenty-one

It was Christmas Eve morning, Billy realized as he heard the excited scamper of the Bass children out in the hall. But he had no time to see what had them up and running so early. He was holding his wife's head over the commode.

"There. Feel better?" he soothed when the wracking spasms ceased.

"Leave me alone," Sarah moaned. "Just go away."

"I'm not going away, so just get used to it." He was massaging her shoulders, awed by the delicate feel of them in his big hands. She yielded to his touch for a moment, then shrugged away.

"Don't. Just let me alone. I want to die with some dignity."

He smiled as he blotted her face with a cool, wet cloth. "I'm not gonna let that happen. What can I do for you?"

"Shoot me."

"Besides that."

"Find some other way to get the other five kids, 'cause I don't want to go through this again."

His smile faded but he wasn't discouraged. He sat cross-legged on the floor and drew her up into his lap, cradling her there upon his chest. She snuggled in willingly enough.

"You don't have to do this, Billy."

"Hush. I want to."

That seemed to satisfy her, because she made a contented little sound that rubbed raw on his emotions and she nestled her head beneath his chin. He began to rock her gently. A tender confusion settled into his heart. His wife, his child, his future. Billy was scared to death of all three things yet wanted them so fiercely it hurt. But having them meant trusting her. And he wasn't quite ready to let that final barrier down. She was too close, nudging under the safeguards he'd erected. He needed a distance that would bring a return of sanity along with it.

Billy stood with Sarah still in his arms and he carried her back to their bed. He laid her down on the mussed sheets, trying to ignore the sudden puzzlement and disappointment in her eyes when he pulled the covers over her instead of covering her with himself.

"You just rest easy now. I'll be back in a minute."

Sarah regarded him through big dark eyes and said nothing. He yanked on his clothes in a hurry and left the room.

Billy was relieved to find Emily in the kitchen. After exchanging good mornings, he worked up the courage to ask, "Miz Emily, what's good for morning sickness?"

He cringed as Jack's hand slapped between his shoulder blades.

"Sarah got you suffering from it, too?" his lieutenant asked as he pushed by him to fix a warm kiss on his wife. Emily gave him a chiding look.

"Jack, behave."

"Tolerance," Jack continued. "A lot of tolerance and a long patrol out on the flat lands until she's over it. That's what I'd recommend."

Emily socked him in the ribs with her elbow. "Jack Bass, you know darn well you spoiled me rotten through every minute of mine."

"Yeah ... well, it was that or have you make my life a nightmare." He was smiling as he said that, so she didn't hit him with the skillet she was holding.

A few minutes later, armed with a tray of toast and tea, which Emily assured him would stay down when it went down, Billy was headed back upstairs. As he ascended, he came face to face with Sarah. She was dressed and pretty and looking no worse for the wear. She glanced at the tray in his hands, then up at him.

"What's that for?"

"You. I asked Emily what you might like and she said—"

He never got the rest of it out. Sarah's eyes pooled up damply and her arms went flying around his neck. He maneuvered the tray aside so she could crush up against him and fasten upon his mouth with a grateful passion.

"I'll take that for you, pard," Jack drawled, relieving him of the tray so he could hold his wife in his arms. "Doesn't look like she'll be wanting it any time soon. Lots of bed rest is good for morning sickness, too. You might want to give that a try."

Without reply or breaking from Sarah's urgent kisses, Billy carried her back upstairs.

The bed rest worked just fine.

Afterwards, when Sarah was cuddling contentedly in his arms, smiling her pleasure, Billy thought to ask, "It's awful quiet this morning. Where'd all the kids go?"

Sarah was stroking his forearms where they banded about her. "Mmmm. What? Oh, the kids. Uncle Harm took them out to get a tree. Amanda insists on it. She does Christmas in a big way, the way her family used to in the East. It's a lot of fun. Uncle Harm grumbles but I think he enjoys it as much as she does. Emily always cooks up a feast for tomorrow and we gorge until we can't move. Then we lay around groaning, swearing we'll never get so carried away again. Kinda like making love. You can't wait for it to happen, it's over too quick, then you're looking forward to the next time." She tipped back her head to press a kiss on his chin. He gave a vague smile but his gaze was miles away.

Sarah watched him for a minute, feeling that disquieting stir of panic she experienced every time that remoteness overtook him.

"You give each other gifts and stuff?" Billy asked with an odd quiet.

"The kids do, and Amanda always makes a fuss over everybody. Emily usually makes things. She does beautiful stitchery. Me, I can't make a seam."

"So Jack told me."

"Jack told you? That brother of mine's getting a pretty big mouth on him!" Billy smiled and she rubbed his warm cheek with her palm. Her gaze softened. "I'm sorry I didn't have a chance to get you anything. I—I wasn't sure you'd be here."

His hand did a slow revolution over her abdomen. "I can't imagine getting anything better'n this, morning sickness and all."

"I love you, Billy." Sarah waited a beat, and when he didn't reply in kind, she stretched up to kiss him gently on the mouth. Fearful shadows crowded in behind his eyes, which she pretended not to notice as she snuggled back upon his chest. Silently, Sarah vowed to herself that the gift she'd give him this Christmas would be her love, and hopefully, he'd return it, if not this year, then next. Or the one after. However long it took.

When Harm returned with a passable-looking pine, the day's peace ended. The big house filled up with noise and activity. Wonderful smells drifted out of the kitchen and in the front parlor; the kids clamored for a chance to hang Amanda's delicate blown glass Christmas bulbs she'd had shipped from the East. Normally, Sarah would have been in the thick of it but this year she stood back, watching the cheerful goings-on from her husband's side. She could tell he was overwhelmed by it all; by the crowd of family, by the din of excitement, by the feeling of warmth and expectation. She stayed close to his side, hoping to ease him into the festive flow. But the more Billy observed, the more he withdrew.

Or at least he tried to, until sweet little Becca Bass came up to catch onto his hand. Sarah saw his mood melt down like an early spring thaw in high country.

"Ranger Billy, could you lift me up so I can hang this in the doorway?"

"Sure can, sweetheart." He hoisted the child and balanced her carefully, while she attached a green sprig with its festoon of red ribbons to a nail left in the molding, apparently for that purpose. He eased her down until they were eye to eye. "What is that?"

"Mistletoe." She canted a shy glance up at him, then looked to Sarah, who was watching them with a smile on her face. "When you're standing under it, you have to kiss a pretty girl."

"Like this?" he cupped her cheek in his palm and touched a light kiss to her brow. She turned the color of those scarlet ribbons and beamed with an embarrassed pleasure.

"You're supposed to kiss Cousin Sarah," she informed him in a conspiratorial whisper.

"Oh!" He grinned at her, dimples creasing deep. "You mean like this?" He bent and dropped a kiss on Sarah's forehead. Becca scowled at him.

"No, I mean a *real* kiss, like the way my mama and daddy do. Mama says Daddy's kisses curl her toes." She looked down at Sarah's feet, then back up at him patiently.

Sarah smiled up at Billy and lifted her face obligingly, expecting a chaste peck on the lips. What she got was a slow, searing brand that sent her senses spinning and, yes, her toes curling. She was breathless by the time he straightened and demanded of the critical seven-year-old, "How was that?"

"It'll do. With about ten years of practice. Keep working at it, Ranger Billy." Then her arms cinched up tight around his neck.

There was a moment of stark surprise in his face, which was overcome by emotions too complex to unravel. He gave the slight figure a gentle squeeze and set her down quick. As soon as she raced off, Billy was turning toward the door.

"I'm gonna get some fresh air. It's kinda stuffy in here."

It wasn't easy but Sarah let him go, her heart aching for the turmoil in his soul.

"Wear hard on a man, don't they?"

Harm's observation startled Billy. He rubbed the back of

his hand across his face and glanced around as Harm settled on his elbows at the rail beside him. "What's that?"

"Kids."

"Yeah, they do. You're a lucky man, Mr. Bass."

Harm smiled blandly as his gaze scanned the mountains rising up out of his side yard. "You wouldn't have thought so if you'd seen me at your age."

Billy waited for him to continue, somewhat cautious with the man's casual camaraderie. He wouldn't have believed Harm Bass would seek out his company, let alone deign to confide in him.

"It was the kids who kept bringing me back in. Jack, Sarah, Sid, and Jeffrey. God, I loved those kids. They had all the goodness in them that I'd lost. I remember Becky telling me that I couldn't come back unless I mended my ways. The thought of that just about killed me. Got me thinking about what was important. Then there was Amanda. She finished me off. I didn't stand a chance."

Billy said nothing. He was wondering why Harm was telling him all these things.

Then Harm cut to it.

"You miss your family?"

Billy snapped back in alarm, as if Harm had struck him unfairly. "What?"

"Your family? And don't bother telling me you don't have one. A man without a family doesn't look at another man's the way you do mine."

"I have one," Billy admitted softly. "I just haven't seen them for a while."

"Ammy calls me a romantic. Maybe that's so, but I think a man ought to be with his family this time of year."

"Why? To put up a tree and buy things for everybody? That don't make a family, Mr. Bass." The sudden rush of his own anger surprised him, but Harm didn't look surprised. He looked the soul of understanding and that made Billy all the angrier. "When I was a kid, we had nothing but nothing. We didn't have no fancy colored baubles to hang on trees or pretty paper to wrap up gifts. We had nothing. Look at all you got. What do you know about it?"

"Everything. 'Cause we didn't have anything, either. The only thing we could give was from in here." He put his hand over his heart. Billy took a step back, taking Harm's meaning with an uncomfortable panic.

"Well, we didn't have any of that, either."

Harm gave him a long look. "I don't believe you. A man who's never known love can't give love."

The panic just kept intensifying. Billy covered it with gruff bravado. "You want to know something about my *loving* family, Mr. Bass? My mama got trapped into marrying my daddy 'cause he got her with child. She was from a well-to-do family and wanted no part of what he was, which was dirt-poor and hardworking. He broke his back trying to please her. She hated him. She gave him two kids and she hated us because we tied her to him. He hated us because he couldn't make himself hate her. How's that for a warm family feeling?

"As for your fine romantic holidays, I remember wanting to give my mama something special, thinking maybe if I got her something nice like she'd been used to, she'd smile a little and just maybe start to take a liking to me. I got me a job cleaning up the mercantile so's I could buy her this ring I thought she might fancy. But when the time came to get paid, the store owner would only give me half of what he'd promised. It wasn't enough. I figured I'd earned that ring fair so I stole it. And when I gave it to my mama, she took one look, called it junk, and tossed it away."

He paused then, a protective toughness hardening his expression. "The store owner came out the next morning with the sheriff, saying I'd run off with a bunch of stuff. I never did and told him so. But hell, they wouldn't believe me, not one of them no-account Coopers. Not when they found the ring. They figured I just hid the rest better. My daddy, he beat me until I couldn't stand up, trying to get me to tell him where the other things were. There was nothing I could tell him to make him stop. I didn't have them. Then he paid that man for things I'd never stolen to keep them from taking me off with them. I never forgave him for not believing me. But his whipping didn't hurt me half as bad as Mama's words. And I never, ever got the urge to give nobody anything after that. So excuse me if I don't get all sentimental over such things now. I don't want no part of 'em."

No part of them? He was lying. Harm could see it plain in the defiant stare but he didn't argue the bold words. All he'd say was, "Think you've had a pretty hard time of it, huh?" And he gave Billy a look that foretold of stories that would make his own pale in comparison. But Harm made no judgments. "Well, maybe you did. Don't judge all of life on what little you've lived, boy."

Harm went back inside and Billy stood there on the cold windswept porch for a while, struggling to suppress his longing to believe those words.

A man's who's never known love can't give love.

Was that true as well? Was that why he couldn't commit to a wife who clearly loved him? To a family who were trying to accept him? Was that why he'd found it so easy to fall in with the likes of Ray Gant, who played upon that empty cavern in his soul?

But he had known love. He had known the bond of family. Not from his mother. Only sporadically from his father. But Julie had loved him. Theirs had been a desperate sort of affinity, the two of them against all the unfairness life had handed out. He could remember Julie caring for him when he was sick. He could remember her holding him tight as the two of them cowered under the bed, trying to become invisible while their father reeled through one of his drunken rampages. It had been the two of them right up until the time that stranger had come to tell them their daddy had been killed in town. In a matter of minutes, she'd had her meager belongings packed. Julie told him in a new, hard voice that she wouldn't spend another second on a farm that had been as ungiving as their folks. She moved into town, leaving Billy to do as he pleased. He'd been just shy of thirteen years old. He hadn't known what to do! She was all he had in the world and there was no place for him above the saloon, where she took to selling her fifteen-year-old soul.

What did he know about love, except that it always abandoned you when you needed it the most? If that was the case, he'd be better off steering clear of it.

Billy tried to keep telling that to himself when he went back inside and found the Bass family gathered around a cozy fireplace while Jack read the words of the Christmas story. Sarah looked up and smiled when she saw him, patting the sofa cushion next to her. When he sank down, Becca came to burrow in between them, bringing that state of anguished panic back to his heart. He looked around him, to where Harm sat on the floor, one arm around his wife, his other about his elder daughter, his son curled up and dozing in his lap. Jack cuddled Emily and Carson, and Kenitay lounged at their feet. There was a solidity to all he saw that defied the determined loneliness of his life. It beckoned to him as seductively as his wife's kisses and was proving just as hard to resist. He wanted to believe what he felt, he wanted to fit into what he saw.

And as if she understood, Sarah sent her fingertips gliding over the backs of his until they met in a tight, possessive tangle. Her head nudged against his shoulder and he opened his arm to draw her in close.

I love you, Sarah Cooper. The realization beat strong within him, but he hadn't the courage to speak the words. Instead, he tried to show her by the warmth of his embrace and, later, by the sweetness of his kiss as they lay entwined upon their bed. It wasn't the need for physical gratification that rose so insistently within him, it was the need for an intimate union of spirit. She didn't seem disappointed in his desire just to hold her. Her sigh gave away a soul-deep satisfaction as he tucked her up close and whispered good night.

And her reply both soothed and chafed his heart.

"I love you, Billy."

Still, he couldn't answer.

* * *

It was early and the chill woke Sarah. Her bare feet were uncovered and freezing. She tucked them back under the blanket, nudging them up against Billy's for warmth. The icy contact startled a jump out of him along with an unfriendly grumble, but he didn't awaken. Curled up beside him, Sarah couldn't go back to sleep.

She heard the sounds of someone stirring, and recognizing the pattern of Harm's Apache stealth, Sarah wondered what he was doing up and about before dawn. She followed the soft echo of his footsteps down the stairs and listened to the swing of the front door. Then silence settled once more. The kind of silence she needed for the depth of thought required of her. Soon the house would be waking to the excitement of Christmas Day and she'd have no further time for reflection.

She had to decide what to do about Billy.

What was she going to do if he went back with Ray Gant? She'd been afraid to ask his plans. He had his ranger star pinned to his coat, but he'd never actually said he was going back to serve under her brother. Jack seemed to think he was, but then her brother didn't know how close he'd come to losing him altogether. Sarah had never breathed a word about Billy's defection. She'd never examined her reasonings but suspected it had something to do with protecting her own. It was that same instinct that had gotten her into trouble in the first place back on that interrupted train ride from Austin.

The day peeked through with a weak graying tint brightening across the bed linens. Billy was asleep on his side with his back to her. She could see the unruly tousle of his blond hair and the golden contours of one bared shoulder. Sarah fought the need to sample that sleek curve. She didn't want to wake him just yet. Not when her thoughts were still so troubled.

Oddly enough, she was remembering Jack's dog. It had shown up on their ranch one day, starved and abused, nothing but ribs and great frightened eyes. It had taken an entire hour for Jack to coax it up to the porch with the offer of food. After one taste, it had darted off to safety and sat there on it skinny haunches, hungry yet too wary to give in and trust that outstretched hand. Jack had been patient. It took a week but the animal finally crept close enough to eat from his hand. Even then, it was ever watchful should that hand of kindness turn to one of cruelty. Their mother said the dog reminded her of her always-wary brother, Harmon. Jack named the dog Hank because he didn't think his uncle would be amused to have a scrawny stray as a namesake.

Jack spent his every spare minute with that dog, grooming him, gentling him, trying to earn its illusive trust. Sarah had never seen an animal so stingy with its affection. It would always show up for food, would trot at Jack's heels and even lie beside his bed, but it would never submit to petting. It always cringed beneath Jack's hand, as if anticipating the unexpected blow.

And then one day the dog came dragging in, nearly gutted from an encounter with a javelina. Try as he might, Jack couldn't get close enough to tend the animal's ghastly wounds. Whenever he'd reach out, the dog would snarl and try to bite him, too afraid and hurt and haunted by bad experiences to trust him. Though it had known to come to him, its fear was greater than its faith in the kindness Jack had always shown. It crawled under the porch and died there in misery because it wouldn't accept help.

That frightened, mistrustful dog didn't make her think of her Uncle Harmon. Sarah saw that dark caution in Billy Cooper and she couldn't bear the thought of him coming to the same terrible end.

She'd done everything she could to make him trust and love her. Had she the courage to test the fragile bond between them? She'd know soon enough, for their idyllic stay at Harm's was about to end. Then she'd discover which way Billy Cooper meant to go.

His skin was warm. It shifted over the hard steel of his muscles beneath the movement of her palm. Sarah marveled at the feel of him, thrilled that this strong, gorgeous male creature was hers. In name, at least.

Billy muttered quietly and rolled onto his back. She had a

moment to admire the fine angles of his face before his eyes opened, fixing her with a curious dark gaze.

"Were you wanting something, Mrs. Cooper?"

Mrs. Cooper. Her heart jerked at that. Sarah lifted up on an elbow so she could look down at him. Her smile was deliberately provoking. "Depends on what you planned to offer, Mr. Cooper."

Her fingertip traced the bend of his smile and she saw the flicker of caution come into his eyes. That wasn't what she'd hoped to see. Disheartened, Sarah withdrew her hand. When she did, his brows lowered in a pucker of disappointment. She wished he'd make up his mind. Did he welcome her affection or was it just the physical satiation he sought? While she had no complaints about the latter, it was the former she longed to share with him.

"Feeling all right?"

"So far, so good."

He reached up to rub his knuckles along her jaw, opening his hand when he came to her neck, so he could thread his fingers through the spill of her hair. His gaze had become a smolder of expectant passion. But that was lust, not love.

"Then why don't you come down here and wish me a proper good morning?"

When she didn't move right away, his fingers curled, locking her tresses around them so that when he pulled gently downward, she had no choice but to follow. Right down to the soft part of his mouth. It didn't take him long to notice her lack of response. His grip eased so she could withdraw if she wanted. She did, but only a few inches.

"Baby, what's wrong?"

Sarah had no chance to answer, for just then the halls came alive with noisy children. There was an impatient pounding on their door and Carson's childish call of "Aunt Sarah, come see what Uncle Harmon got for Aunt Amanda!"

Smiling regretfully, Sarah got up to dress, moving slowly lest her usual queasiness assert itself. Billy lay watching her for a time, as if trying to figure out something, then he rolled out to pull on his clothes. His mood was distant and she could feel his uncertainty, but there was no time to soothe it as the Christmas spirit overtook the household.

Harm's gift to his wife was tethered to the front porch post: a deep-chested palomino that shone gold and silver in the morning light.

"Oh, Harmon! He's beautiful!"

"She," he corrected. "Got her down in Chihuahua City."

"So that's where you were. Why didn't you tell me?" Amanda's arms whipped about his neck for a choking squeeze. Then she leaned back and eyed him suspiciously. "You paid for this horse, right?"

"Ammy!" He sounded shocked that she would suggest he'd reverted to his Apache roots. "I've got papers if you want to see them."

She smiled and kissed him hard. "That's all right. I believe you. . . . You can show them to me later. I'm going to call her Golden Promises."

Harmon looked pained. He didn't share his wife's affinity for making animals into pets. "If you like."

Just about then, the Bass children discovered their presents and began to tear into them. That bit of excited savagery lasted only a few short minutes. When the kids settled down to enjoy their new possessions, the adults began to think more seriously about coffee and breakfast.

Once the parlor had emptied of all but wrapping paper scraps, Sarah headed for the kitchen. Tugging on her hand, Billy whispered, "Hey, I got something for you."

"Really?" She was so surprised, she just stared at him for a long minute.

"Well, it's nothing much." He looked alternately shy and mischievous, but beneath his facade, she sensed an undercurrent of agitation and uneasy dread. As if he were just waiting for her to hurt him. *Can't you trust me?* she wanted to wail, but she settled for a playful mood that wouldn't threaten his cautious overture.

"Well, what is it? What is it? Show me! Don't tease. Is is in there?"

He held his saddlebag up out of her reach. "Now, hold on

a minute. You're worse than the kids." He brought it down and she snatched it out of his hands. "It's in that side." Billy waited, gut tensed, for her reaction.

At first she was mystified, then she looked up with a slight frown and he froze up inside.

"You rat," she said softly. "All this time you let me think you gave it to Luisa. I ought to strangle you, Billy Cooper!" She pulled her petticoat, the one she'd thrown in his face, out of his saddle pack and crushed it to her. Tears glimmered in her dark gaze.

"I couldn't imagine wanting to take if off anyone but you," he told her in a guarded tone, still not quite sure of her reception.

With an emotional little cry, she flung her arms about him, hugging hard, all the wariness melting from around his heart.

"Oh, Billy, thank you. You couldn't have given me a better gift!"

Yes, he could, and he realized what it was in that instant. Holding her tight because he wasn't quite brave enough to look her in the eye when he said it, Billy gave her what she wanted most, in a rather hoarse whisper.

"I love you, Sarah."

Chapter Twenty-two

Sarah went completely still in his arms. Then, very slowly, she inched away.

"What?"

He couldn't force himself to repeat it so he told her, "Merry Christmas, baby," and dropped a gentle kiss on her surprised, relaxed lips. As if waking to the reality of his words, she gave a muffled squeal of delight. Her hands flew up to clasp his face and she returned his kiss with a voracious fervor.

"Uncle Billy, you're supposed to do that over here under the mistletoe," interrupted Carson Bass in a sober tone.

Sarah came down from her toes to explain, rather breathlessly, "It was too far to walk."

Carson looked at the two of them with a peculiar smile, then went to unearth one of his gifts from beneath the mountain of discarded wrapping. "This was all I wanted. You can go back to kissing her if you like."

"Thanks, pard, don't mind if I do."

He'd just settled leisurely upon her lips, when Leisha cleared her throat. "Mama wants to know if you want bacon or biscuits and gravy."

Sarah sagged against her husband's chest, her stomach doing a traitorous roll at the thought of eating. "Neither," she said weakly.

"How do you like your eggs?" Leisha persisted.

Feeling her fingers clutch spasmodically in his shirt, Billy told the girl, "She'd like them in a couple of hours."

"How about—"

"How about I take care of it, Leisha?"

She gave him a look of cool injury and said, "Do whatever you like, Ranger Cooper," then she swept from the room. Her hauteur was quite the contrast to the pristine white dress she was wearing.

"If she ain't the spitting image of her daddy," Billy muttered, then he looked down at Sarah's bowed head. "You all right, baby girl?"

Her head shook and a very explicit groan rumbled out. "Please don't take this personally, but if I don't get upstairs right this second, I'm going to do something very disgraceful on your new boots."

"Do you want me to—"

"I want you to stay down here. Please. I'm going to lie down."

"Are you sure—"

"Yes, very!"

"I could come up—"

"No! Have breakfast with the rest of the family. I'll be down later." She gave a reluctant push away from him. The sallowness of her complexion convinced him of her urgency. Then abruptly she hugged him tight and murmured fiercely, "Oh, Billy Cooper, I love you so much!"

"I love . . . you, too." But she'd already darted for the stairs and he could hear the frantic patter of her feet as she raced for their room.

Billy stood adrift for a long while, wondering what to do. He felt uncomfortable rejoining the Basses without Sarah, even as he wore the tokens of their acceptance. From Emily, he'd received a richly patterned vest with a satin back, which made him feel quite dapper. Kenitay presented him with a belt of leather and snakeskin he'd made himself. Jack had helped with the tooling and Harm with the snake, he said proudly, and Billy was so choked up he could barely muster a smile. But it was Amanda's gift that stunned him speechless. She'd ordered fancy stitched boots for both him and Jack from a bootmaker in Houston, using an old discarded pair for reference. He'd never seen such fine workmanship, and when he pulled them on and they snuggled up to the calf of his leg, Billy grinned wide, thinking that nothing had ever fit him better—except perhaps his wife. Sarah had given him a purely wicked look, as if she knew exactly what he was thinking.

Lord above, he loved that woman and her family!

Admitting it made him jittery as hell. All the newfound affection was closing in around him with a smothering intensity. He needed to take a step back so he could study the changes in his life with a bit more detachment. Otherwise, he'd be weeping his gratitude all over the bunch of them.

Deciding that the cold morning air would suit him better than the warmth of the family table, Billy headed for the door but found Harm and Amanda blocking his exit. Harm was staring out to the west, his face an expressionless mask. Amanda was far less adept at concealing her emotions. She was clearly upset.

"Harmon, the day's young. They could be on their way even now."

"They would have been here last night if they were coming. Damn Will and his stubborn pride, anyway."

"Harmon . . ."

"I know, it's my fault, too. But Ammy, Becky and I have always managed to spend some part of Christmas together! I can't believe he wouldn't let her be with the family. It's not just me, it's Jack and Sarah, too, and our kids and theirs. I'm gonna go get 'em."

"Harmon, wait."

"No. They belong here with us."

"What are you going to do? Invite him over for Christmas dinner at knife point?"

Harm gave a massive sigh. "No. I thought maybe I'd make whatever apology it takes. If he wants me on my knees, I'll get down on 'em. At least until the holiday's over."

Amanda gave him a shrewd look. "Really? You'd go crawling to Will Bass? I don't believe you, Harmon. Maybe I'll just ride along with you."

"Ammy, we've got a whole houseful of guests!"

"Well, they're not going to miss my cooking."

"Ammy . . ."

"I'll ride along with him, Mrs. Bass."

They both turned toward Billy in surprise. Then Harm frowned and Amanda beamed wide.

"Why, that's very kind of you to offer, Billy. But Sarah—"

"Sarah's feeling poorly and wants to be left alone. I'd just as soon be out doing something."

"Well, you'll be doing something if you can keep Harmon from coming back with his brother-in-law's hair. Watch your own, too."

"Yes, ma'am," Billy assured her somewhat uneasily. A ride with Harm Bass would definitely take his mind off anything else the future might bring. He'd be too busy wondering if he had a future to worry about. "Tell Sarah I'll be back soon and—and that I meant what I said this morning."

Amanda smiled as if she knew exactly what had passed between them. "Why, I'd be happy to, Mr. Cooper. Harmon, you watch over him or Sarah just might come after your hair."

Harm made a discounting sound and gave Billy a narrow glance. "If you're coming, get a move on."

"Yes sir, Mr. Bass." He snatched up his coat and followed the small Texan's strides down to the barn.

The air was cold and the company colder, but Billy enjoyed the hard ride. There was no need to worry about keeping up his end of the conversation. Harm was certainly no conversationalist. He was a man of singular concentration and entertaining his new nephew was not a priority. Billy didn't mind. He figured Harm was sweating the humbling to come. That had to sit sorely with a man of his pride, and it was a powerful testimony to how much family meant in terms of self-sacrifice.

Harm reined in so suddenly Billy's horse shot by him and Billy found himself staring back over his shoulder. He brought his mount around in a wide circle and by then Harm was standing in the stirrups, studying the horizon through the high-powered binoculars Amanda had given him that morning as a gift.

"What is it, Mr. Bass?"

Harm yanked the strap over his head and tossed the binoculars to Billy even as he was lashing back with his heels to startle his horse into a gallop. It took Billy a moment to figure out how to focus, then things were all too clear.

Smoke. Lots of it.

The only thing within miles around that could send up that large a cloud of smoke was Rebecca and Will Bass's ranch.

The barn was ablaze. One look told them there was no saving it. From inside came the shriek of terrified animals still in their stalls.

Harm barreled into the yard and swung down from the saddle without slowing or benefit of stirrups. He was running even as he hit the ground.

"Will?" he shouted, casting a quick look about the place. There was no one in sight. "Jeffrey? Becky?" Then he was through the open barn door and he couldn't manage any further words in the thick cut of smoke. He had his knife out and he slashed through the gate ties, pushing them wide so the frantic stock could escape. By the time he'd cleared them all out, Harm was choking and blinking hard against the stinging in his eyes. The first few pulls of fresh air sent him into paroxysms of coughing. Wiping his streaming eyes on a grimy sleeve, he looked about more carefully. Billy had gone up to the house. It was quiet. Maybe they'd already left, and somehow he and Billy had missed them on the trail. . . .

Then he noticed the unsettled dust in the yard, a stirring made by many horses, many men.

"Becky?" It came out soft, almost sounding like a prayer. He started for the house, his stride increasing, his pace quickening, until he was running full out by the time he hit the steps. He charged up them just as Billy came out the door. The boy's face was white, his expression stark. Harm didn't want to believe what that look told him.

They were all dead.

"No! Becky!"

He collided with the solid brace of Billy's forearm barring

his entry into the house, the impact against his chest knocking the wind from him. The next thing he knew, the kid had him in a tight hold and was turning him away.

"You don't want to go in there, Mr. Bass. Please don't go in."

Pain and terror forced air back into his lungs and he was able to struggle, wildly, ferociously, within the restraining band. "No! Let me go! You let me go!" All manner of curses—Apache, Spanish, English—snarled from him as he twisted to free himself. And between those savage oaths, low wails of anguish arose from a shredded soul.

"Easy. Easy now, Mr. Bass. I'll let you go as soon as you calm down."

But it didn't seem as if that were going to occur, and Billy was afraid of what might happen if Harm, in such an irrational state, were to view his family.

Then abruptly Harm went limp against him, his fight gone, the breath jerking from him in hoarse sobs that dwindled down to a quiet panting. Billy could feel the power of the man gathering into an intense calm.

"Cooper, you let me go right now or I'll kill you where you stand."

That sounded pretty damned rational to Billy. He let the man go, unable to do anything except follow him inside.

Harm stopped almost at once, then took a stunned step backward, bumping into Billy, who was right behind him. He made a low sound in the back of his throat, a sound so wounded, Billy was moved to offer, "You don't have to do this. I can take care of them."

After several labored attempts at speech, Harm said, "No, I'm all right."

Sure he was. What man would be all right when confronted with the members of his own family slain in such brutal fashion? But Harm walked forward without hesitation, dropping down on one knee between the chairs that held his brother-in-law and nephew, both still tied where they'd been fatally shot. With a hand upon each of them, he said in a quiet, lethal voice, "I will not rest until I have avenged you."

Billy felt the hair prickle along his forearms.

Slowly, Harm stood, and for just a moment, his taut control buckled. He hugged Jeffrey's head to him and bowed his own, but he made no sound of grief. Then, taking a deep, steadying breath, he stepped away and asked, "Where is my sister?"

"She's in there, Mr. Bass." Harm followed his indication back to the bedroom she'd shared with her husband. Despite the terror that shadowed his expression, he went forward.

Billy didn't go with him. Some things were just too private. He hadn't known these people well. There was no great sense of loss the way there would have been had it been Harm's or Jack's family. But Billy was thinking of Sarah, of how the news was going to devastate her, and that made the pain very personal.

Someone had invaded these people's home, had bound them and killed them, and Billy knew damned well who it was.

It was then he found a packet left negligently atop the table next to the breakfast dishes. Printed on the outside in bold letters was the name Billy Cooper. He stared at it for a moment, too surprised to act, his heart pounding wildly. Then he heard Harm returning and he snatched the packet up, stuffing it away in the pocket of his coat.

Harm had wrapped his sister's body in the spread from her bed. He carried her in his arms, his face totally void of emotion. Billy stepped back, giving him room to pass, not wanting to interfere even as Harm walked down to the barn. It was an inferno by then, the roof a sheet of flame, timbers cracking and popping as they readied to give way. And Harm walked right inside.

Billy stared, aghast. "Oh, my God! Mr. Bass—" He took a few steps, then realized there was nothing he could do. He waited on the porch, heart crowding up in his throat as he tried to push down the horror of having to ride back to Amanda and tell her that her husband was dead, too.

Then Harm emerged, his arms empty, having left Rebecca within what would become her funeral pyre. He walked slowly, reeling slightly, but he never looked back. Not even when the roof joists caved in with a tremendous roar, sending out a burst of heat that knocked him to his hands and knees with a forceful push. He stayed there for a time, on all fours, his head hanging down against the backdrop of flames. Finally, he rocked back on his heels and, with his big bladed knife, began to cut off handfuls of his hair until it was little more than a short black stubble.

Uneasy with it all, Billy finally approached him, cautious and concerned by the blankness of the stare that lifted when he called Harm's name.

"Mr. Bass, what do you want done with the other two?"

Harm continued to gaze up at him, his eyes blue as the Texas sky in summer and just as vacant.

"Mr. Bass, they need to be buried. Do you want to take them back to your place? We can't leave them here. Do you want me to take care of it?"

Looking into his eyes was like looking into a lonely hell.

"Mr. Bass? Can you hear me? Do you want me to take care of them?"

Harm nodded once and Billy returned to the house, glad to be doing something. Harm had him spooked. He prepared the bodies of father and son for travel with a crisp efficiency. It wasn't the first time he'd readied the dead for burial and he did it without any undo thought or emotion. It was better that way, not to think or feel. It was better not to dwell on the thought of Sarah's grieving or on the sonsofbitches who'd done this to her family.

He went outside to round up one of the horses Harm had freed from the barn. A nervous glance showed Harm still kneeling, his gaze unfocused, his features as stoic as the wind-tortured buttes. Billy slipped a bridle on the horse and tethered it to the front porch. He brought the carefully wrapped bodies out one at a time and strapped them securely on the animal's back. That done, he went back up on the porch to close up the empty house, and when he turned, he found Harm standing there right behind him. He gave a startled gasp, for he hadn't heard the man come up onto the porch.

"I want your word you will never tell anyone how we found her." There was a queer sort of flatness to his tone, as if there were no life to it.

"But, Mr. Bass—"

"Your word!"

"All right. You've got it." Anything to escape the sudden intensity flaring in the feverish blue eyes. "Are you ready to go, Mr. Bass, or was there something you wanted to get from the house?"

Harm's stare moved past him, lingering over the place that held so many memories, and he shook his head. "No. There's nothing for me here. And it's Harmon. Just Harmon. My name's not Bass. Not anymore."

"Whatever you say," Billy murmured to placate him. He was wondering if Harm Bass had slipped beyond sanity.

The ride back was slow, out of respect for those they carried. It gave Billy plenty of time to build up to the terrible dread of what was to come. He'd experienced no great trauma at the loss of his parents, at least none that manifested itself in purging sorrow. His grief was more a slow festering of emotion. He didn't know how to go about consoling Sarah or, indeed, how to handle his own reaction to her distress. How simple things would be if he had no ties to these people, if he was still just Jack's second in command who could pay his condolences and back away without sharing in the remorse. But that wasn't the case. He was involved whether he was ready for it or not, whether they wanted him to be or not.

And the minute they rode up into the front yard, he knew he wasn't ready. His insides were in knots, his emotions a raw ache of tension. He would rather have been anywhere, doing anything, than here doing this. But he swung down, tied off the horses, and waited for Harm.

Harm sat his saddle for a long moment, his newly shorn head bowed, his eyes closed. His face was black with soot and scored by runnels of tears Billy hadn't seen him shedding.

"Mr. B—, do you want me to break it to them?" Billy offered quietly, thinking how awful it must be for him.

Harm drew a slow, composing breath and shook his head. "I'll do it." He stepped down and Billy was struck anew by the slightness of this man who cast such a huge shadow. He'd never been so awed by anyone. He followed Harm up the steps, pausing behind him when the older man stopped to garner the rest of his courage. Then they went inside.

Emily and Amanda saw them first and both knew immediately, Emily because she recognized the Apache signs of mourning and Amanda because she knew her husband. They'd been setting the table for a late lunch and all activity ceased.

"Hey, Uncle Harm, it's about time you two got back. I'm—" Jack broke off as he entered the room. His gaze took in his uncle's expression and the crudely cropped hair. He looked to Billy and got the same grim answer. He drew a harsh breath.

"Jack," Harm began softly, then the rest of what he'd meant to say dammed up tight in his throat. He made a sound that wasn't a word but said everything.

Jack stood as if rooted, understanding coming over him in a huge sob. "No. Uncle Harm, they can't be dead. They can't be—"

Harm caught him up in a tight embrace, supporting him when his knees went weak. He didn't say anything, just held tight, his eyes closed, his cheek pressed to Jack's hair while his nephew struggled with his shock.

"H—how could that be? We just saw them. W—what happened?" He lifted his head but Harm wouldn't look at him. He turned to Billy, who made the explanation as gentle as possible.

"They were shot, Jack, by that same bunch terrorizing the area."

"Will? Mama? Jeffrey, too?" His features crumpled.

"I'm sorry, Jack."

The commotion brought the children in. Leisha and Kenitay took the news with stoic faces. Becca ran to her mother in tears. Carson and Randall, who were too young to understand what was happening, clung to Amanda's skirt for reassurance. Billy stood back, an outsider to their pain, until he saw Sarah. She froze in the doorway, taking in the significance of her uncle's hair and her brother's tears.

"Where are they?"

"We brought your father and brother here for burial," Billy

told her, and she was running past him and out the door before he could intercept her.

By the time he joined her in the yard, she was hugging the blanketed forms draped over the extra horse. He slowed, trying to think of something to say that went beyond "I'm sorry." Then she looked up and he could see her eyes were dry. And angry.

"Where's my mother?"

"Your uncle saw to her already."

"What do you mean, saw to her? He buried her?"

"Yes." In a way.

"Why didn't he bring her with them?"

"I don't know, Sarah. You'll have to ask him."

"I wanted to see her. I wanted to say goodbye. How could you let him take that from me?"

"Sarah, it wasn't my place—"

"What do you mean? Of course it was!"

Billy clamped his lips together and said nothing. That incensed her all the more. She rounded on him in a hysterical fury.

"You should have been thinking of me instead of cowering in front of my uncle. How could you have let him bury my mama without me being there?" Then she went still and very pale. "What did they do to her?"

"Nothing, Sarah."

"Then why didn't Uncle Harmon want us to see her?"

"I can't say."

"Can't say or won't say? What did they do to my mama?"

When he didn't answer, she slapped him. With all her frustration and pain backing it, the blow rocked him.

"Sarah, that's enough."

She turned to Harm, panting wildly, eyes tearing up in an agony of imaginings. "What did they do to my mama?"

Harm came down off the porch to where she was standing and he put his hands upon her shoulders. "They did nothing, *shijii*. Your mama didn't give them the chance."

She looked up into his eyes, searching them in a desper-

ate confusion. "What do you mean? I don't—I don't understand."

His hands came up to cradle her face, his thumbs stroking
away the dampness from her cheeks. "What was done to your
mama was done a long time ago by the same kind of men who
came to our house when we were little more than kids. Our
mama didn't survive that visit. Becky and I did, but we always
kept the reminders of it. I went half crazy and walked in a
nightmare until Amanda woke me from it. And Becky, she
had—"

"Jack. She had Jack, didn't she?"

Harm nodded. "That's why she held you in so tight. She
didn't want you getting hurt like we were hurt. And that's
why she did what she did today."

Sarah gasped. "Oh, my God, Uncle Harmon, she killed
herself, didn't she?"

His hands eased back through her hair in a soothing gesture. "Little girl, don't you ever think bad of your mama. She
was so brave and she loved you so much."

"Then how could she have done such a thing?"

"I guess that was a part of her past she couldn't bear to go
back to. I couldn't put her in the ground, Sarah. I just couldn't.
I'm sorry if I robbed you of your chance to say goodbye. I just
couldn't see her buried in some dark grave. She'd have understood. I hope you can forgive me." Then his voice altered subtly, growing thick and punishing. "I should have been there. I
should have been there the first time and I should have been
there this time. I let her down, Sarah. I let her die."

Sarah cast her arms about his neck, hugging fiercely to him.
"No, that's not true. It's not true. It's not your fault, Uncle
Harm. How could you say that? How could you think it?
Mama loved you. She loved you as much as she loved Daddy,
and she'd be madder than hell if she heard you talking like
this!"

Harm kissed her temple and stepped away. His bland smile
said he wasn't totally convinced.

* * *

Will and Jeffrey Bass were buried in the hole already dug for Amanda's cold storage cellar. It was done without ceremony and with few demonstrative tears, from a West Texas family too hardened by troubles to give much away. There was no time to wait for Sidney Bass to make the trip from school. He'd be given the news by wire. Not the way any of them would have chosen to do it, but there was no other choice. The men in the Bass family had revenge to occupy them and it didn't allow time for bearing bad news. Being a Bass, Sidney would understand and he would come home to pay his respects as soon as he was able.

After the silent grave-side vigil, they went their separate ways to do what needed doing and to grieve in their own fashion. Harm headed off to be alone and Amanda reined in his children to keep them from following him. She went back to the wash she'd started that morning and Emily began fixing a supper meal no one would feel like eating. While Sarah distracted the kids in a silly game, Jack sat on the front steps drowning in his misery.

"Hey, stand some company?"

"If you can stand mine."

Billy dropped down beside him and spent a few awkward moments trying to think of what to say, wishing there were something he could do to ease his friend's hurt. He hoped that by just being there, a willing listener would be enough.

"Will and I weren't as close as I wish we had been, not like me and Uncle Harm, but I had a lot of respect for that man. He taught me what was right and how not to back down from seeing it done. He made me want to be a ranger because he made it sound like that was the best a man could be. What good did it do him? I couldn't do a damned thing to stop them from killing him." His voice caught up painfully and for a moment he was silent, head and hands hanging down as limply as his spirits.

"You're doing your best, Jack. That's all he'd expect from you."

"My best. It's not half good enough! Not when men like Gant can run loose doing pretty much whatever they please.

I hate this job. The local law has got maybe five miles of trouble to worry over, a sheriff thirty, but we've got five hundred to a thousand of outlaw-packed hell and we can't be every place at once. And the one place I should have been I wasn't. How am I supposed to protect the state of Texas when I can't even keep my family safe?"

"Jack—"

Jack put his hand over the one Billy pressed atop his shoulder. "Don't mind me. I'm just whining 'cause I hate being helpless. I'll be better tomorrow. Tomorrow I'm riding back to camp, and I'm gonna grab up every man and we're gonna see every one of those bastards dead." He glanced up through hard, glittery eyes. "Are you with me?"

Billy's fingers tightened. "All the way, Jack."

It was late and it was cold, but Sarah was numb to both those facts as she slowly rocked on the porch swing. The house was strangely quiet, the kids in bed, Jack and Billy whispering business over the table, Emily and Amanda finishing up the dishes, and Harm still out somewhere in the gathering darkness.

She hurt so bad she didn't know how to begin to resolve it. It was an overwhelming pain, one without a beginning or an end. She couldn't seem to cry. Her eyes burned from the lack of tears and her heart ached from the lack of focused grieving.

"Hey."

Sarah looked up to see Billy lingering beside the swing. He offered a thin smile but nothing else. How could she have struck him?

"Billy, I'm sorry I—"

He held up his hand. "Don't. It's all right."

If it was all right, why was he keeping a careful distance?

"Billy, could you sit with me for a while?"

Wordlessly, he came to settle on the swing beside her. His arm assumed a drape along the back but he didn't touch her. His caution made her feel more alone than ever. Unhappily, she touched his cheek. He gave a start but didn't pull away.

"I hurt you after I promised I wouldn't."

Again the tight smile. "You didn't hurt me, Sarah."

"Then why are you acting so strange?"

" 'Cause I'm hurting for you, and I don't know what to do about it. What can I do?"

"You can hold me."

"I can do that." His arm slid around her, coaxing her up close. She leaned into his warmth and strength, finding comfort there, the kind of comfort no amount of words could bring. With her face burrowed into the folds of his coat, the tears finally came.

"I want my mama."

His embrace tightened. His other arm scooped beneath her knees and she found herself lifted up onto his lap like a child about to be cradled and soothed. His low voice crooned in a gentle vibration.

"You're gonna be a mama soon yourself. And you can give back all the love yours gave to you. I think that'd make her real happy."

"I wasn't a very good daughter. I vexed her plenty. There are so many things I wish I could take back. So many things I wish I'd said. I never told her I loved you. It would have made her happy to know that. Billy, I never thought losing her would make me feel so alone."

"You're not alone, baby. I'm here. I'll be here as long as you need me."

"I think I'm probably going to need you forever." She leaned back and looked up at him with a timid expectation. He smiled with a hint of dimples showing. It was the sweetest smile she'd ever seen.

"That'd be all right with me," he told her.

She tucked her head again and listened to the steady drum of his heart. And with that primal beat arose a basic passion within her.

"When Uncle Harm gets back, we're going to track down the men that did this to my family. And when we find them, I'm going to help him kill them."

She felt Billy's recoil. "Your uncle would never go along with such a thing."

"Uncle Harmon understands the right to revenge. He won't refuse me."

"Well, I am! Sarah, what're you thinking? If your uncle allows it, he's gonna have to deal with me!"

She tried to pull back but he wouldn't let go. A sudden outrage overruled her distress. "You have no right—"

"I have every right, Sarah Cooper! You said so yourself. It's up to me to look out for you, and I mean to. I'll see them that did this are made to pay for it. I give you my word."

She sat back so she could study his features. His was a strong, determined face and his dark eyes were steeped in sincerity. He would see to her revenge.

"I love you, Billy," she told him gruffly, before giving him a hard, affirming kiss. Then she stood. "I'm going up to bed. Are you coming?"

She made it sound like part plea, part reward. He drew her down for another kiss, this one full of a torturing tenderness.

"I'll be up in a minute. You go ahead."

After she was gone, Billy sucked in a stabilizing breath. Amazing how far into her family he'd been pulled with two simple questions. *Are you with me? Are you coming?* And he'd answered yes to both without hesitation.

With a sudden recollection, he reached into his coat pocket and drew out the packet addressed to him. He studied it for a moment, almost afraid to find out what it contained. He didn't recognize the writing and thought it odd that Will Bass would have given him a gift. The man had had no use for him, of that he was sure. Finally, deciding the only way to know for sure was to look, he opened the missive.

He stared at it, not understanding. Then understanding all too well.

It was a deed of sale for Will Bass's property made over in his name and properly signed. And tucked in with it on a separate scrap of paper was another note, this one brief and soul-shaking.

Merry Christmas, Billy-boy.

Chapter Twenty-three

Amanda Bass was panicking. From beneath the warm mound of the bed covers, she lay watching her husband. For the last few hours he'd done nothing but stand at the window looking out into the night. He'd come home wet, cold, and smelling of sage smoke. She understood his methods of grieving and those things didn't bother her. His manner was what bothered her.

He hadn't spoken a word to her. He hadn't asked after anyone in the family. He hadn't looked in on his children. He'd allowed her to coax him upstairs to the room they'd shared for ten years. He'd let her undress him and towel dry his chilled skin and ragged hair. But he hadn't so much as looked at her or acknowledged her expression of regret. Whatever he'd locked up behind the blank blue of his stare, he wasn't willing to share with her. For the first time in ten years, he'd shut himself off from her emotionally and she didn't know how to reach him.

She knew the minute she closed her eyes, he'd be gone.

"Now would be a good time for you to take the kids up to New York for a visit."

His sudden words startled her. But their connotation terrified. If he wanted her gone, she knew the reason. He'd told her once that he didn't want her there to watch him die.

"I'll go if you'll go with me."

"No."

"Then I guess I'll stay."

No response.

She couldn't stand it any more. She went to him but embracing him was like hugging to sun-warmed rock. She didn't make the slightest impression.

"I love you, Harmon. I know how you must be hurting."

"Do you?"

"I've lost family, too."

"I know you have. But you've never had to live with knowing they were so scared and desperate that they'd rather put a bullet in their own head then risk another minute of living. I know how bad that feeling is. If it hadn't been for Becky needing me, I'd have stayed in that box with my mama, because I surely didn't want to go on after what I'd seen and after what had been done to me. I fought because my sister needed me. She doesn't need me anymore. They went and took her anyway. I went through all of it for nothing."

"I need you, Harmon."

"No, little girl. You've never needed me. You're the strongest, bravest woman I've ever known."

"Not without you, Harmon. Not without you."

He looked at her then. His gaze was calm and empty. And behind it lurked the madness of his past, the wildness that had never been bred out of him. The soul that she could tame but never conquer. He'd only let her think she had. Now, he was denying her any control at all and she knew she was losing him.

"Don't go."

"You know I have to, Ammy."

"No, you don't. You have your own family to take care of. No one expects you to take on the world by yourself. You can't win, Harmon."

"It doesn't matter."

"It matters to me!" She grabbed his face between her palms and shook him hard, but the mild remoteness never faltered from his stare. "I've never begged you for anything but I'm begging you now. Don't go. Don't do this. If you leave to pursue this vengeance, you won't be coming back. I know it. I feel it and so do you, otherwise you wouldn't be acting like this."

"I love you, Ammy."

"Then don't do this to me. I've loved you since the minute I saw you. I made you my life. I gave you three children. I let you come and go without question, without doubts. I've never made any selfish demands on you but I'm making this one. If you have to go, go with Jack and the rangers, not alone. You're not infallible, Harmon. You're not your own legend. If you go after them by yourself and outside the law, they'll kill you."

"But I'll be taking a fair share of them with me."

"Do you think I care about that? Do you think your children are going to care? Do you think that's what Rebecca wants from you?"

"It's what I have to do."

She shoved away from him hard, her eyes ablaze, her chin quivering with fright. Her tone was Texas tough. "Then you go. And don't look back. Don't come back. Throw away ten years and three children. Walk away from the love I've given you as if it never mattered to you at all. From this moment on, I'll curse the day I met you!" With that, she flung herself facedown on the bed, sobbing loudly so she wouldn't have to hear him leaving.

After a minute of wild weeping, Amanda caught her breath and realized she might never see him again. How could she send him away with her words of anger weighing on his heart?

"Harm . . ." She rolled over with that desperate entreaty on her lips. Then his mouth was there to swallow up the sound as he stretched out over her.

"Love me, Amanda. Say you'll always love me."

"Always. Oh, Harmon, you promise me you'll be careful."

"I'll do everything I can to come back to you."

"And if you can't?"

"Then you'll still have my soul."

"I don't want your soul. I want this." She kissed him hard. "And this." She grabbed his hips and rubbed him roughly against her. "I want to make you crazy with my talking. I want to hear you complain about my meals. I want to sleep with you beside me and have you love me until I'm bowlegged. I want those things for thirty, forty more years." She was sobbing and he was kissing up the tears with a fierce tenderness. "Love me, Harmon. Make love to me for as long as you can. Just promise me that I won't see you leave. I couldn't bear to say goodbye to you."

"I promise. And I love you."

And for two more hours, he did just that. And the second she surrendered to a reluctant slumber, he was up and gone.

The horse gave a low nicker when saddle leather slapped down.

"Shhhh. Whoa, boy," Billy murmured as he jerked up the double girth. That secured, he turned to reach for the reins and found a knife blade at his throat.

"Going somewhere, boy?"

Billy went completely still. "Yessir, I am. Got some business to attend."

"Mind me asking what kind?"

"Would it matter if I did?"

"Not if you want to go on breathing under my roof."

"Family business."

"Yours or mine?"

"Ours."

Harm lowered his blade. "If you're stealing a horse, the bay's a good choice. More bottom to him, and you'll need the extra if you expect to outrun me."

"I'm asking you to stay out of it."

"Why should I?"

"I let you go this morning when you asked me, now I'm wanting you to return the favor."

Harm's eyes narrowed at the reference as they did a suspicious once-over of his niece's husband. "What are you up to, kid? I can't believe you're sneaking out on Sarah when she needs you most, so you must have some pretty damned good reason. Let's hear it."

"Like I said, it's my—"

"Business. Yeah, that's what I thought you said. Well, if you want to get to it, you'd better come clean, 'cause there's no way you're going to get past me until you do."

Billy eyeballed the distance to the door and weighed what he could see of Harm Bass. He wasn't fooled by the wiry compactness. He knew the man was tougher than hardtack.

"I don't want to tangle with you, Mr. Bass."

"Consider us tangled. If you'd quit being so hardheaded and prideful for just one minute, you might figure out that I'm kind of a handy fella to have on your side."

"There's nothing I'd like better, Mr. Bass, but it ain't gonna happen. Not when I'm the reason for what took place over at your sister's."

Harm drew a low, hissing breath. It sounded like steel rubbing across a whetstone. "Son, you'd better explain that real good."

Wordlessly, Billy handed him the bill of sale, watching the black brows furrow as he read it over. Blue eyes lifted in question.

"I don't understand."

Billy gave him the note. "It's from Ray Gant. I told him I needed a place to set Sarah up. He got me her folks' ranch."

Harm was silent for a moment, digesting that. Then he looked up again, and Billy knew he was within dying distance of the most dangerous creature ever bred in the scorch of West Texas.

"Gant killed them so you could have their spread?"

"That, and to test my loyalty to him."

Harm moved so fast Billy never had a chance to cry out. Strong fingers closed about Billy's windpipe, clamping off air with one hard squeeze. Before he could resist, Harm had him slammed back against the rails of the stall, his knife blade poised to perforate his middle.

"You *cabron*, if I find out you had a hand in what they did—"

"Either kill me or hear me out. I ain't gonna talk to you whilst you're fixing to skewer my gizzard."

Harm backed down a cautious degree. "Talk."

And Billy did. He told Harm everything—about his flirtation with joining Gant's gang, about what happened with Elena Lowe, about how Jack forgave him his weakness. And Harm listened with an inscrutable front before speaking. If there was anyone who could help him sort out the mess he was in, Billy realized all at once, it was this man. If he could get Harm to believe him and believe in him.

"And so, after hearing all this, you're asking me to accept that you want no part of Gant and are just riding on outta here to tell him so?"

"No, I'm telling you I'm riding outta here to see the sonuvabitch hangs for hurting my best friend and making my wife cry."

Billy could see the gears of thought spinning and meshing behind the level cut of his stare. "So you're doing this for Jack and Sarah?"

"I'm doing it for me, Mr. Bass. 'Cause I'd be a damned fool to pass up on what I found here."

"So why you down here sneaking off like a thief instead of talking to Jack?"

"Don't get me wrong. Jack's the best kinda man in the world to ride with, but he's set in his ways. There's no way he'd agree to what I have in mind."

Harm nodded. "Jack's a good man. He wants to do things the right way, but you and me, we're not that close to sainthood, are we?" Harm smiled at him, a slow, spreading smile that implied a shared ground. "We do things the hard way, 'cause it's the danger, not the duty we lean toward. Am I right?"

Billy smiled back, overcome by a knee-weakening relief. "Yessir, Mr. Bass."

"Harmon," he corrected easily. "Call me Harmon."

"Yessir, Uncle Harmon."

"Don't get sassy with me, boy."

"I ain't one to mess with *The* Harmon Bass."

"Smart kid. So, what you got in mind?"

It was on the cusp of daybreak when Harm cozied back under his blankets and curled up to the warm figure of his wife. He'd just closed his eyes in hopes of a few hours' sleep, when he felt Amanda jerk to wakefulness. He opened his eyes to meet her startled gaze. Her features were still swollen from weeping and his heart gave a tender turn.

"Harmon, what are you doing here?"

"Last I knew, this was still my bed unless you went out and replaced me already."

Amanda forced a jerky swallow and a smile. "As if anyone else would put up with me." Her fingertips were trembling as they touched his face. "Does this mean you're not going?"

"It means I'm an old man who likes sleeping with his old wife and who needs some rest before riding with Jack in the morning."

"You're leaving with Jack?"

"That's what I said. Now, you gonna let me get some shut-eye?"

She started to nod, but her eyes welled up and her arms encircled him for a constricting squeeze. "Oh, Harmon, I was so afraid for you." He held her tight until her tremors ran their course. Then she was studying him. "Why did you come back?"

"Seems I ran into that Cooper kid down in the barn and we got to talking. He asked me to take care of Sarah for him whilst he was seeing to some business and I couldn't very well say no."

"What kind of business, Harmon?"

"Family business. He called me Uncle Harmon. Sassy kid." He sounded as if that pleased the hell out of him. And Amanda understood more than that. If her husband was turning over the brunt of his revenge to Billy Cooper, he must have felt the young ranger had the stronger claim to it. She didn't ask why. She didn't care why. Harm had stepped off his lethal path to self-destruction and she could be nothing but grateful to Billy. And more than a little concerned about him.

"Billy's not going to go off and get himself killed, is he?"

"I wouldn't worry about him. He's a tough kid with a lot to prove before he can settle down into a respectable family man like me."

"You're hardly the soul of marital sobriety, Mr. Bass. How long will you be gone?"

"Not any longer than I have to be. So, until you've got this ole legend back sharing your bed, take to sleeping with a real big gun."

"I didn't think they came any bigger than the legend."

"Ammy!"

She reached down to prove her point. "See. I told you."

"Ammy, I was planning on getting some sleep," he grumbled, but his pattern of breathing had already altered encouragingly at the coaxing temptation of her touch.

"You can sleep in the saddle, Harmon."

"Yes, ma'am. I surely can. So why don't you do the riding while I'm still awake." He pulled her over him, then down to meet his kiss. And she complied with a fervor that had his toes curling.

Sarah was far from happy as she sat in the buggy waiting for Harm to say his goodbyes to his family. She could tell from her brother's expression that he wasn't pleased, either. Harm had come up with some vague reason for Billy being gone and neither of them were buying it. But no one could get anything out of Harm if he didn't want to give it, so it did no good to press for more detailed answers.

"We'll see that no coyotes come sniffing around whilst you're gone, Daddy." Big words from a little girl, but the carbine Leisha Bass handled so expertly made them sound more serious.

"Take care of your mama. You're the better shot." He bent

to kiss her smooth golden cheek, then moved on to Becca. Her arms wound about his neck for a tight hug.

"I'll miss you, Daddy."

"I'll be carrying you in my heart." He set her down and put out his hand to his small son. "You're the man of the house while I'm gone, Rand. You see to things for me."

"Yessir, Daddy," he piped up in an adult-sounding voice. As soon as his father looked away, Randall shot a smirking glance down at Leisha, who glowered back because no matter how bossy she got, she'd never be man of the house.

Harm paused before Amanda, not saying anything because they'd said and done everything possible over the course of the night. Amanda stepped up to him, placing her hands on his shoulders. His settled on her waist.

"Hurry up and kiss her, Harmon. I'd like to get home before dark."

Amanda smiled over at the impatient ranger. "Take care of him, Jack, and send him home to me."

"Well, I certainly don't plan to keep him hanging around my house eating up all my food. I'll send him packing as soon—as soon as we're done with what needs doing." That last was a grim reminder to them all of what their purpose was.

Amanda gave her husband a long look, then said strongly, "Make them pay for what they did, Harmon, and then you come back to me."

"I will."

"And you be—"

"I'll be careful. You be careful, too. Jack's gonna send over a couple of his ranger boys to keep watch over you until I get back. Ask who they are before shooting them outta the saddle. They don't need to be staying in the house. They aren't pets."

"I'll cook them a meal. That'll have them keeping their distance."

He gave a bland smile, not daring to agree. Then he kissed her, hard enough, long enough, and thorough enough to leave her speechless until he could mount up and wheel away.

"Goodbye, Amanda," Emily called. "You take care."

Jack tipped the brim of his Stetson to those on the porch, then his gaze lingered on the freshly filled grave. He jerked his horse about and headed after his uncle.

Sarah settled back for the tedious journey, well aware that during her stay at Harm's everything in her life had changed.

She was thinking about those changes when some time later Harm drew his horse up alongside the wagon and lifted Carson up to ride in front of him.

"Uncle Harm, when did Billy say he was going to be back?"

"He didn't, just that you were to wait for him at Emily's."

She stared at him narrowly. He was keeping something big behind those impassive blue eyes. "When are you going after Gant?"

He gave her a quick look.

"I'm not stupid, Uncle Harm. Well?"

"I'm riding out with Jack."

"With Jack?" That was a surprise. Her uncle didn't ride en masse when on a blood trail. It wasn't like him to let the rangers slow him down with their number or their slightly more civilized conventions. The rangers were an unforgiving bunch, but they had nothing on Harm Bass. "I thought that maybe you and I—"

"You thought wrong, little girl. You stay put or that husband of yours will have my hide. I don't want to go tangling with him again."

Sarah blinked. Harm backing down to Billy's demands? A sudden fierce pride rose within her, to think that her husband could wrest such a degree of respect from the barbed-wire-tough Harm Bass. Since when was her uncle concerned about what anyone else thought? So she asked him, and his answer confused her even more.

"He's your man, Sarah. You trust him and you do like he tells you if you expect him to stick by you." Then he nudged back his heels to send his horse into a canter, ending the conversation.

What were they up to? She didn't like secrets. And she

didn't like being treated like some fragile nuisance. If they weren't going to let her ride with them, she'd just have to think of some other way to make herself useful in bringing her parents' and brother's killer to justice. But first there was a long, lonely night to get through.

As the hours dragged by under Jack and Emily's roof, Sarah yearned for Billy Cooper to fill her arms and to keep the pain of loss at bay. He'd promised he'd be there as long as she needed him. Oh, she needed him now!

Where was he and why?

Calvin Lowe was making his rounds of Terlingua's streets when a slight figure separated from the shadows to walk at his side.

"You've got a way of making a fella swallow his heart, Harm. Be mindful that I'm getting on in years. You wouldn't want me to go keeling over, would you? What if I'da shot you?"

"Not likely." And Harm handed him back the revolver he'd plucked from its holster without the sheriff being aware of it. Cal replaced it with a chagrined smile.

"Had it been anyone but you that pulled that trick, I'd be handing in my badge and retiring."

"You'll never retire, Calvin. You're a lawman to the bone. 'Sides, Elena'd go crazy having you at home all day."

"That she would."

"How's she doing? The Cooper kid told me there was some rough stuff a while back."

"She's doing fine. How's the kid? I'd sure like to see him turn out all right."

"He will. I come to ask a favor of you, Calvin."

"Anything, Harm, you know that. Just ask it." The sheriff paused where the darkness fell deep beneath the porch overhang. He looked down at his friend, seeing the hard edge to him, feeling the raw tension coursing through him, sensing death in those things. He wouldn't want to be the one Harm Bass was after.

"It's personal, Calvin, and it's gotta be done quiet."

"We go back a long way, Harm. Whatever you want. Heard the news from one of the rangers just a bit ago. And Harmon, I sure as hell am sorry about Will and your sister and their boy."

The gentle words of sympathy caught Harm off guard. He took a quick step back and drew a ragged breath, trying desperately to override the huge swell of pain crowding inside, forcing its way up to choke him. He couldn't breathe past it, and suddenly, his chest was jerking with the effort. He tried to blink and, to his horror, a cascade of dampness flooded down his face. He made a small sound. It came tearing up from deep within him, where he'd struggled to keep the hurt controlled in darkness. But once that soft vulnerable cry escaped, there was no turning back the rush of grief. He let his friend take him up in a crushing embrace. He couldn't move. He couldn't do anything but wail with a wounded intensity until he'd sobbed his spirit dry.

And while he did, Calvin Lowe held him easily, murmuring, "Aw, dammit, Harm, I'm sorry. Cry it out, son, then we'll get down to the business of making those bastards the sorry ones."

"Well, lookee who's here. Howdy there, Billy. You have a nice visit with the in-laws, did you?"

Billy strode up to Ray Gant and leveled him with a single punch. There was a scrape of gunmetal in holster leather but Ray waved a calming hand. Then he sat on his rump rubbing his jaw, smiling up without signs of malice.

"Something on your mind, Billy-boy?"

"There was no call for what you did, Ray."

"You wanted a place, I got you one. Thought the little lady might feel more at home somewhere familiar. You got a problem with that?"

"I will if she ever finds out I had a part in it. Me, I don't give two hoots in hell that you killed 'em. They didn't much like me, anyway. But Sarah, she's right broken up about it and that don't please me none."

"So you refusing my gift?"

"No. Nice place. It'll do fine. Figure I'll tell her the old man willed it over as a belated wedding present. Just a coincidence that he happened to cash in right afterwards. By the way, how did you manage to get a tough ole bird like that to sign the place over?"

"Had a gun to the boy's head. Made him right cooperative. Kinda sorry the woman chose not to be. She was might fine-looking, a lot like your pretty little bride. Might have kept her around for a while." He put up his hand to Billy and waited, watching the other's expression. Billy finally took his hand and hauled him up. "Something different about you, boy."

"Yeah? What's that?"

"You got a look on you that's harder and hotter than hell."

"Comes from feeling the Bass boot heels on my throat while trying to make nice with them. Was worth it to have a few days with my woman. And I got these here fancy boots. They're something, huh?"

"That's another thing I was wondering about. You were looking mighty cozy alongside them."

Billy stiffened up. "And I suppose you'd have rather taken a noose over being sprung from jail? Kinda nice having relatives with that kind of power."

"I wouldn't have let myself get caught by going softhearted over some woman."

"That won't happen again. I'll be wanting my cut of the take, Ray."

Gant laughed at his brass. "Do you? Well, we'll have to talk on that some. Anybody following you that we ought to know about?"

"No. Got no reason to invite anyone along for the ride. I came as soon as I could get away clean, but I'm warning you, Ray, Harm Bass is gonna come looking. If you want, I'd be more than happy to take care of him."

"You leave Bass alone, Billy."

"Why? The man's dangerous."

"That's the way the boss man wants it."

"What you want to go protecting Harm Bass for?"

"Not me. My boss."

"And who might that be?"

Ray Gant smiled. "Someone who says Harm Bass and his ranch don't get touched. Someone who's got good reason not to want to mess with him again."

"McAllister?"

Gant's head snapped back and his eyes narrowed. "Where'd you hear that name?"

"From Bass."

"Well, you forget you heard it, hear?"

Billy shrugged. "Anything you say, Ray. Don't much care who's dishing out the pay as long as it's good." And he started to relax, thinking how easy it had been to slip back in with them.

The blow came so sudden, Billy had no time to prepare for it. Pain splintered along his jaw as the force sent him spinning. He should have known. He should have guessed there'd be some price to pay before he was taken back into the fold. He'd gone against Gant's authority and that couldn't be borne, not if a hard leader wanted to keep the respect of his men. Ray rubbed his knuckles as he ordered, "Pauly, Jasper, grab onto him."

Billy's arms were pinned as he reeled and started to stagger. He looked up at Gant through anxious eyes. Talking hurt, but it was better than dying. "Ray, I don't—"

Gant's fist buried deep in his middle, jackknifing him as sickness surged in great black waves. He was fighting the urge to retch as the next blow took him high on the cheekbone, followed by a backhanded smash that gashed his mouth against his teeth. His knees went out from under him then and he hung limp within the imprisoning grips. Gant's fingers clenched in his hair, wrenching his head up with a brutal twist.

"Don't you ever put a hand on me, Billy-boy. And when I tell you to do something, I expect it done. There ain't no rewards for a poorly done job. You understand, boy? Do you understand?"

He drew back his fist again and Billy retreated wildly, trying to escape the anticipated blow, cowering the way a boy had once cowered beneath a much greater threat. "No! Don't hit me. Please! I'm sorry. I'm sorry! I won't do it again!"

Ray lowered his hand. "Let him go." He caught Billy as he sagged on strengthless legs, supporting him gently. "I'm not gonna hurt you, Billy. But they will. You remember that. I'm gonna take care of you, just like I promised, but you have to do what I tell you. You understand that?"

"I'm sorry, Ray," he gulped out, leaning weakly against the other's strength. "I won't let you down again."

"I know you won't and I'm sorry I had to deal out such a hard lesson. You remember it. And you remember who cares about you. Remember who your friends are and what you owe 'em. Now go get yourself cleaned up. And Billy, good to have you back."

Gant released him and Billy dropped to hands and knees, crouching there, too dazed to move. He was shaken by a sickness of body and soul and by the terror of past intimidation. The last time he'd endured such a beating, he'd been no more than a helpless kid. He put an unsteady hand up to stem the flow of blood from his torn lip as his dark gaze lifted to fix on Ray Gant's back. If Gant had seen that look, he would have killed Billy on the spot rather than trust him another second. Because that look was simmering with a hurt and hate and a need for retribution that went far beyond the simple gut-level fear Ray Gant had been hoping to instill.

He remembered his friends and what he owed them, and he wouldn't forget again.

Chapter Twenty-four

Sarah waited until Harm rode out with Jack and a fifteen-man patrol, then she ran along the ranger barracks to where Billy kept his bunk. She wasn't stupid. She knew Billy had gone back to Ray Gant without Jack's knowledge. Why else would he have crept out of her bed without so much as a goodbye kiss? To wake alone and hear of his leaving from another wounded her to the soul. After all his beautiful words about love and family, and he still had no faith in her. As much as that hurt, it made her angry, too. Why he'd gone, she didn't know. Part of her believed it was to see to the revenge he'd promised her. She was almost certain it wasn't to run the outlaw trail. Almost. There was that small sliver of doubt just because he hadn't told her his intentions. Mistrust bred mistrust.

She wanted to get Ray Gant. He was the man behind the murder of her parents and brother. He was the man tempting her husband to do wrong. The sooner Gant was dead or in prison, the sooner she could concentrate on a life with her new husband and upcoming child. Revenge was something she'd learned of from her uncle and it was a provoking force. No way was Gant going to get away with what he'd done to her family. There had to be some way to make him pay the price and she was certain enforcing that payment would ease the raw anguish in her heart. Billy was out doing what he could—at least that's what she was hoping. So were Harm and Jack. Sarah couldn't stand being left behind and helplessly uninvolved. She hurt every bit as much as they did, maybe more. And her right to revenge was just as strong.

She didn't know what she expected to find in her search of Billy's belongings. Maybe nothing. Maybe a clue to where he'd gone or why. Everything he had—and it wasn't much— was stashed in a sack, where it had lain in disgrace since his supposed desertion of the ranger corps. The man she loved didn't carry around much of a past. A couple of well-worn shirts and denims. A pair of red flannels faded pink by repeated washings. Socks with holes in them. That affected her strangely. There was something lonely about socks with holes. It implied a neglect and pricked her with a sudden strong protectiveness. She had to take better care of him. And she'd start with a vengeance as soon as she found him—right after she chewed on him royally for deserting her without a word!

She was thinking she'd have Emily teach her how to darn, when she came across a packet of old letters. They were from Fort Stockton, written in a shaky female hand. They were from his sister Julie. They all started out the same way: *Dear Billy, Thank you for sending money. I tried to make it stretch but it didn't go near far enough. Jed needs shoes. . . . Jessie needs to go to the doctor for a cough. . . . I'm behind on our rent and the landlord's threatening to throw us out. . . . We got nothing to spend on food this month. . . .* The pleas went on and on. Sarah could well imagine Billy's tender heart being torn between his desire to provide for them and his certainty that all the money was going right down a whiskey bottle. She felt a certain sorrow for his sister's circumstance, but it was tempered with a deeper resentment that the woman would use Billy's love so shamelessly. Something else for her to take care of. She tucked one of the envelopes with a return address into her coat pocket just as she heard footsteps behind her.

"Moving him out, are you, Miss Sarah? Or I guess I should say Miz Cooper."

She turned to see Pete Meyers. "Hello, Pete. Just getting his things together."

"What's the boy up to these days? Sure miss having him around."

"He's fine, Pete."

His eyes chided her for the evasion. "Is he now? That why Jack had to go springing him from Cal Lowe's jail after Bob Westerly was shot and killed, and Elena Lowe nearly died in that robbery he took part in just before Christmas?"

"What?" A lump the size of a twenty-pound ice block dropped to the pit of her stomach. So that's what he'd meant by Jack bringing him for the holidays under the threat of a noose. He'd taken part in a killing. But had he taken part for the benefit of Ray Gant or the Texas Rangers? And wondering which way it was terrified her because of the effect it would have on his motives. If he'd done it for Jack, she could be secure in her trust of him now. If he'd done it for Gant, could she trust in him at all?

"Hated to see that boy go back to bad. Really thought there was a chance for him to turn himself around from a rustler to a ranger. Was hoping marrying you'd do the trick. But I guess you just can't wish the bad outta some folks."

"That's not true," Sarah protested, not wanting to believe it, not wanting to think that could apply to the man she'd married. "He hasn't gone back to bad. He only rode with Gant because Jack asked—" She saw Meyers's eyes go round and Sarah clamped her jaw shut—a bit too late.

"What's this?"

"Nothing," Sarah rushed nervously. "I shouldn't have said anything."

"Miz Cooper, I'm one of Billy's closest friends. If you're telling me I don't have to go crying for his lost soul, then I got cause to celebrate."

Sarah hesitated. Pete Meyers went as far back with the Rangers as her father's days. He knew Harm and Jack and was Billy's friend. And maybe he could tell her something that would help her help them.

"Billy never left the rangers. He and Jack planned it all out together. But now I'm afraid he's in some terrible trouble, and I've got to find out where he is and what he's doing before he gets himself killed."

"Could be we just might be able to arrange that for you, ma'am."

Sarah looked around in surprise to see Matt Cobb, the young ranger who was one of Billy's other bunkmates. He was usually all full of sass and swagger, but not now. Now he looked as grimly serious as the Colt .45 in his hand.

"Sounds like Billy Cooper's in a mess a trouble," Cobb concluded as he shut the door behind him.

Sarah made the connection with a sinking heart. Cobb was the man on the inside feeding information to Gant. She turned to Pete Meyers, only to find him staring at his boots with an uncomfortable intensity.

"Pete?"

"What're we gonna do with her now, Cobb?" he mumbled unhappily.

"Pete! I can't believe you're a party to this!"

"Sorry, Miz Cooper, but that's the way of it."

And Sarah realized there'd be no assistance coming from his direction.

Matt Cobb was smiling thinly. "You don't give us much of a choice, ma'am, seeing as how you blundered in and know who we are and what we been doing. I'm purely sorry to say we're gonna have to kill you."

"All right, Harmon, how much longer am I gonna have to wait until you tell me what's going on?"

They were two hours out of Will's ranch, following the tracks left by the marauders who'd killed him. The trail showed every intention of swinging down into Mexico, but Harm was in no hurry to run it. Jack was mystified and growing aggravated by his uncle's secrecy. He was anxious to catch up to those responsible and couldn't understand why the other man wasn't. Harm looked over at him, all bland Apache stoicism, and Jack was ready to choke him.

"Let's make some talk, Jack."

"It's about time," he grumbled, then to his patrol he

shouted, "Step down, boys. We're taking a minute to blow. Don't wander off."

Harm sauntered away from the gathering of Rangers to look back in the direction they'd come. Jack stood at his elbow, waiting, then prompting.

"Where's Billy, Uncle Harm?"

"Gone back to Gant."

"What? How do you know that?"

"He told me."

"And you didn't try to stop him?"

"He knew what he was doing."

"Well, why don't you tell me so I know!"

Harm gave him a long, steady look, then said carefully, "Gant left him a message at your folks' house."

"What kinda message?" Jack had gone very still.

"The kind written in blood. Smart man, Gant. Put the boy in a hell of a spot. Figured none of us would believe he wasn't in it from the get-go and that he'd never turn to us for any kind of help. He was almost right. He guessed if Billy came after him with us trailing, he'd know what side the kid was on right quick. Whoever is getting information to him from inside your camp is probably heading there even now to let him know that we're off in the wrong direction. Which is why I have a couple of Calvin's deputies watching to see who leaves."

"So we're following this trail—"

"To throw off suspicion. Billy figures the band'll split up a ways from here, with part of 'em heading below the border and the rest into the Chisos into hiding. He went direct into the hills, and if we don't show no sign of knowing what he's up to, maybe we can have our ringleader, our traitor, and our killers all in one."

Jack stared at him. He didn't look pleased. "Thank you very much for sharing this with me now."

"Billy figured you wouldn't let him go."

"Well, he's right about that!"

"Why don't you tell your boys to keep on this track till it hits the Rio Grande. A blind man should be able to follow it.

It's time we shaded off and hied it back to Terlingua to see who's left real sudden like."

Jack was still glaring. "You could have told me."

"Didn't want to compromise your integrity," Harm drawled with a mild smile.

"How long ago did they leave?" Jack demanded of the two shamefaced deputies.

"About three hours," one of them mumbled. "We're real sorry, Lieutenant Bass, but we didn't think nothing of it, them being with your sister and all."

Jack strode away from them without comment, going outside to join up with his uncle. He shook his head, still dazed by the news. "Pete Meyers. I can't believe it! Cobb doesn't come as a surprise. He was always a cool customer, but I've known Pete all my rangering days and I'da sworn no better man ever wore the badge." He gave a savage sigh of frustration. Billy's neat little plan wasn't coming together as tidy as they'd hoped. All because of one unforeseen problem. His ever-helpful and interfering sister, Sarah. "What now?"

Harm was looking outward across the dry plains to the hills beyond. To where Sarah was being dragged into danger and Billy nudged closer to death. "Now we get ourselves a couple of fresh horses and we ride 'em into the ground. Then we beat your sister good for not doing what she was told, and the two that took her, we kill slow and ugly."

And to all of that, Jack had only one thing to say. "Let's ride."

Sarah wasn't worried about dying at Ray Gant's hands. She was sure she was going to expire on the trail.

It was Pete Meyers's idea to take her along. He convinced Cobb that she would be valuable as a hostage should the Basses catch up to them. And he got the other thinking that Gant would be happy to decide her fate himself. Cobb was an arrogant kid, but he had a healthy fear of Ray Gant and a need to impress him. He'd be doing that by proving Billy Cooper a traitor in their ranks.

As soon as they were outside the ranger encampment, Sarah's wrists were bound to the saddle horn and the reins of her mount taken by Meyers. Then the two men more or less forgot about her as being a problem as they headed across the flatlands.

The queasiness rose in slow, insistent surges, until it roared into full-blown nausea. Sarah sagged in the saddle, dizzy and hot despite the cool temperature, and so sick she thought she might welcome a bullet. Finally, her moaning misery came to Cobb's attention.

"What's wrong with you?" When he got no answer, he glared at Meyers and demanded, "What the hell's wrong with her?"

Pete took one look at her greenish pallor and diagnosed, "Seems she's in a family way and faring poorly. You doing all right, Miz Cooper?"

"Could we stop a minute," she managed through clenched teeth.

"No stopping," Cobb ordered.

"Cobb, she looks in a bad way."

"Then shoot her and be done with it."

"I'm going to be sick," Sarah groaned pitifully, and Meyers, the father of four children, took it upon himself to rein in and ease her down.

"Meyers, you fool. Can't you see she's just faking to slow us down."

Just about then, Sarah had reached her limit of control and displayed, very graphically, that she wasn't faking anything. Scowling, Cobb turned away with a hard, insensitive man's typical disdain for female weakness, but Meyers knelt beside her, mopping her brow and offering his canteen when he figured she could keep water down.

"Cooper the daddy?"

Sarah nodded faintly. Her strength was gathering, but she was careful to continue the helpless role of feeble expectant mother. Her gaze focused on the revolver strapped on

Meyers's hip. She was wondering if she should try to take them now or wait until they took her closer to where Billy was. She couldn't let them get to the outlaw camp. They'd give away her husband's pretense and she couldn't allow that to happen. Protecting Billy and his unborn child were all important to her. And next to that was her lust for revenge against Gant, who had refused her mother an honorable death.

"Feeling better, ma'am? Feel up to riding?"

To her own death? Not likely. Sarah dredged up a wretched moan. "Not yet. I'm so faint. Maybe a little more water." She gulped it down greedily, ignoring Pete's cautioning, and as expected, it hit bottom and began to seethe like a turbulent sea in the pit of her empty stomach. Within seconds, she was heaving it up, to Meyers's dismay and Cobb's disgust.

"Please," she whimpered in fragile petition. "Please, can't I have a minute or two to rest?"

"What's the hurry, Cobb? I could go for some coffee and a smoke."

"You forgetting the lieutenant? We got his baby sister here."

"Jack's on his way to Mexico. It'll be days before he finds out we're gone and figures out the rest. And by then, I mean to be in another territory."

Cobb snorted. "Old woman. You sound like you're scared of them."

"Only a fool or a dead man wouldn't be. I've seen Harm Bass do things you wouldn't want to know about."

"He's just one man."

"That's all it takes when that one man's Harm Bass."

Cobb looked unconvinced. He went to scrounge up some burnable wood, while Meyers unrolled his bedding so Sarah could rest on it more comfortably.

"Why are you doing this, Pete? I thought you were my family's friend."

Meyers looked as miserable as she felt. "There's a lot of

things involved, ma'am. Too many to be talking on now. It's too late to change any of them things."

"Not if you help me. Please, Pete. I'm sure Jack would be willing to—"

"Shut up, girl," Cobb snapped harshly. "Don't go filling him with fool thoughts. He's in it as deep as I am and there's no going back. The only things the rangers got in mind for us is a strong rope and a short drop, so save your breath. Meyers, you wanted coffee. Get to grinding up some beans."

Sarah lay quiet, her eyes slitted to simulate closure. She watched the two men and she studied her surroundings. These two didn't know her. They saw a helpless woman with child. They didn't know she'd been trained to survive by the legend they feared. Sarah hesitated to act, not because she was afraid, but because she was waiting for the right moment.

It came sooner than she expected.

Cobb finished his coffee and came to stand over her. Through the fringe of her lashes, she saw his look take on a glaze she recognized all too well.

"Cooper's woman, huh? Bet he's got you well trained to answer a man's need for pleasuring."

Sarah didn't move. When he prodded her with his boot, she opened her eyes slowly, glaring at him fearlessly. "You touch me and he'll kill you."

"Hell, he ain't gonna live long enough to do any such thing."

That put a whisper of panic in her. Not for her own safety but for Billy's. She couldn't let these two compromise her husband. And they were getting too close to doing just that. Sarah rolled onto her back and splayed her knees slightly, just enough to get Cobb's attention on that seductive tenting of her skirt and the promise of what it covered.

"What about me?" she asked softly, her gaze taking on a speculative glitter. "Are you going to kill me, too? Or can I persuade you that I'm more valuable alive?"

Cobb wet suddenly dry lips and glanced from her ripe mouth to his glowering partner. "Meyers, take a long walk."

"What are you planning, Cobb? I don't want any part of this."

"Then don't watch," Cobb snarled.

Meyers hesitated. He looked from Sarah's seemingly willing form to the ranger turncoat who was undoing his belt. With an angry curse, he stomped away.

"Guess he didn't want to watch," Cobb smirked. "You know what that means."

Sarah smiled. "It means I'm going to have myself a real man."

"Wouldn't you know Billy'd pick himself a whore. Who'd a guessed as much of Gentleman Jack's little sister."

Sarah's eyes narrowed but her smile beckoned. "I don't want to talk about them. I want to concentrate on you." She wriggled her hips suggestively and Cobb couldn't unfasten his pants fast enough.

And that's where Sarah planted her foot, squarely into that eagerly parted fabric.

Cobb went down with a groan of exquisite pain. Sarah was up in an instant, hoping to grab his gun, but he fell on top of it. When she tried to roll him to one side as he writhed in misery, he struck her hard in the abdomen. Agony exploded through her, but her instincts for self-preservation were stronger. Cobb caught at her wrist, cursing her through his gritted teeth until she smashed her elbow as hard as she could against his mouth, bringing a satisfying spray of crimson and driving a goodly amount of his teeth down his throat. He let her go. And she ran. Pete Meyers suddenly appeared between her and the horses, so she sidetracked without pause.

Sarah had noted a deep gully in her earlier study of the land and she headed for it in desperate flight. Pain radiated through her middle but she ignored it as best she could to get to cover. Once she was safe, she could worry about the possible significance of that pain. Once she was hidden, she could gather her strength and do what had to be done. She wasn't going to run away. That never entered her mind. She had to kill or capture the two ranger turncoats. That was the only way she could protect her husband. She never considered the unlikelihood of that plan.

She was too much like her uncle to think of odds.

She darted along the twisting arroyo, certain Cobb would be in pursuit—as soon as he could stand. She had to find a strategic place to hole up, and she was busy searching for one when an arm caught her up about the waist. Her startled cry was cut off by a big hand clamping over her mouth. She was immediately fighting.

"Shhh! Sarah, stop it!"

Jack!

She went limp against him, darkness swimming up to overtake her senses. And for the first time in her life, she fainted dead away.

A gentle blotting of cool water upon her brow brought Sarah back to awareness. It was a terrible effort to drag her eyelids open. Her brother's features came into gradual focus.

"Jack."

"It's all right. Everything's all right now. Rest easy." He was holding her in the cradle of his arms. Hers went around his neck for a frantic squeeze.

"Oh, Jack, how did you get here in time? I thought you were on your way to Mexico."

"That's what we were hoping everyone would think."

"We?"

"Hey, little girl."

She sat up slightly to see her Uncle Harmon squatting Indian fashion nearby, with his carbine trained on their two securely bound prisoners. The movement brought a stab of pain and she grimaced.

"Sarah, are you all right?" Jack demanded.

"Cobb hit me," she gritted out, clutching at her aching belly.

"Let me see. Let me see!" Jack untucked her shirtwaist and eased it up carefully, exposing a nasty bruise just below her rib cage. His breath sucked in slow and a very dangerous look came over his handsome features. "Cobb did this?"

She nodded.

"He's dead."

"Not until you find out where Billy is! There's no time to be taking prisoners back to Terlingua."

"We were just about to get to that," Harm told her. Then his voice grew quiet. "And we won't be taking any prisoners back."

Sarah looked to Jack and his somber expression confirmed it. "Jack, Pete saved my life. Cobb wanted to kill me when I caught onto them. He didn't want me hurt." Her brother's look was uncompromising. "Jack, please. He's been your friend and Uncle Harm's for years."

"That can't matter, Sarah," Jack told her. An edge of remorse crept in beneath the toughness of his words. "We can't afford to let him go and we don't have the time to take him back."

"He's right, Miss Sarah," Pete put in, with a remarkable nonchalance for a man facing death at Harm Bass's hands. "I knew the risk. I appreciate the thought, though."

"What if he cooperates? What if he tells you everything you need to know?"

"I don't know nothing, Miss Sarah. You'll have to get that outta Cobb."

"My pleasure," Harm murmured. And his blue eyes glowed with a hot savagery.

"I ain't asking no favors of you boys 'cept that you make it quick."

Jack faltered, looking away from the man he'd ridden with for almost eight years. "I've no cause to keep you suffering, Pete." He drew his pistol. Sarah hung on his arm like a weight to his conscience.

"Jack . . ."

Harm stood. "I'll see to it, Jack." He nodded toward Meyers. "Let's take a walk."

"What about me?" Cobb yelped.

Harm turned to him with a cold smile. "I'll be right back for you. Don't go away."

Meyers walked from the makeshift camp in an almost companionable silence beside the part-Apache tracker. They'd shared too many trails for it to be otherwise.

"Here's fine," Harm said at last, and Pete stopped without argument.

"Harmon, I'd appreciate it if you got my things back to my family. They've been having a real hard time of it since my wife died. I've been paying some neighbors to look after the kids and I want to make sure they're all right."

"What happened to your wife?"

"Took sick about eight months ago with some female thing. Doctor took everything we had set aside and she still died. I ain't crying to you about it. I saw a chance to make some fast money to see them cared for and I took it. It was wrong and I don't make no apologies for my bad judgment. I'd go to my Maker without complaint if I knew you'd look out for them."

Harm nodded and drew his knife. "I will." And he made a quick slash.

Pete Meyers stared down at the severed ropes that had bound his wrists together. Then he looked up, bewildered.

"Go take care of your family," Harm told him. "If you head straight back for Terlingua, you can have your stuff cleared out and be gone before we get back."

"Harmon . . ."

"I don't ever want to see you again, Pete."

"You won't, Harm. And I won't be forgetting this."

Harm turned and walked away. When he returned to Jack and Sarah, he gave them an inscrutable glance and told them flatly, "He's gone."

It wasn't really a lie.

Jack gave a tortured sigh and bowed his head. Then he helped his sister stand. "You all right now, Sarah?"

She blinked the weakness from her eyes and gave him a steady look. "I'm ready to ride with you."

"I want you to go back to Terlingua." Before she could protest, he held up his hand. "I want you to go slow and easy and take care of that baby. I've lost too much family to let you take that kind of risk. Do this for me, Sarah. Please. I couldn't bear to be worrying over you. We'll see to Billy. You see to yourself."

She looked up into his grieving eyes, seeing an anguish there that matched the pain in her heart. She embraced him in a sudden rush of tender emotion. "I don't want you to worry, Jack. I'll see to what I have to."

"Thanks, little sister. We got some . . . things to take care of here, so you'd best go now."

"All right. I'll see you back at Emily's." She kissed one lean cheek and gently caressed the other. "You and Uncle Harm be careful."

"We will."

Then she went to hug her uncle with a fierce affection, whispering, "I'm counting on you, Uncle Harmon."

Though he didn't understand her reference, he was quick to answer, "You know you can, little girl."

Sarah mounted up without another protest, and casting a last hard look at Matt Cobb, she wheeled her horse away.

Harm waited until she was gone, then said quietly, "Let's get to it."

Cobb glared up at Harm Bass when he approached. "I'm not scared of you, friend."

"You should be, because I'm not your friend." He was carrying one of the long stakes the rangers used to tie down their horses. Cobb twisted frantically when Harm walked around behind him to kneel and drive the stake into the ground.

"What are you going to do?"

"I'm going to ask you some questions and you're going to answer them."

"Not likely," Cobb sneered with a shaky bravado.

Harm looked unconcerned. "Yes, you will. Eventually." And he kicked the ex-ranger over onto his back, wrestling his bound hands up to secure them to the stake. Cobb struggled, jerking against the bindings, remembering with awful clarity all the gruesome stories he'd heard about Harm Bass and his Apache methods of hurrying conversation.

"Lieutenant? . . . Jack! You're not going to let him do this, are you?"

Harm glanced back at his grim-faced nephew, and out of sympathy for Jack's soft white man's heart, he suggested, "Take a walk, Jack."

But Jack was seeing the clods of Texas earth being shoveled down atop his stepfather and brother, and a ruthless chill entered his pale eyes. "Ask the questions, Harmon. I want to hear the answers."

Harm gave him an assessing look, then nodded. He straddled Cobb's thighs, using his weight to anchor him to the ground, then, with an abrupt move, ripped open the man's shirt. Cobb's bare chest was heaving with panic. Harm drew his knife and very slowly ran his thumb along the blade. He sucked off the line of blood with a lethal relish. His features settled into calm, emotionless lines, like those of his Apache forbearers who viewed torture with an almost religious solemnity.

"I'm going to ask the questions," Harm told the man flatly. "You can answer now or you can answer when you're done screaming."

"They'll kill me if I say anything!"

"You're dead anyway."

Cobb's wild gaze flew to Jack, who said, "I can do it or my uncle can do it, depends on what you tell us."

The helpless man fixed his stare on the big blade of Harm's knife and he all but screamed, "You do it, Lieutenant. For God's sake, you do it!"

"Who are you working for?"

"Ray Gant."

"Who's Gant working for?"

"I don't know."

"Is it McAllister?"

"I don't know. Honest to God!"

"Where's Gant?"

"In the Chisos. I can show you!"

"Tell us. We can find him on our own."

Cobb told them. He told them everything they asked, and afterwards, Jack drew his pistol and put him to a merciful end without blinking an eye. In his own mind, he justified, *That was for my mother.* Then he collected the dead man's armaments and ranger star and looked about for a place to bury him decently.

"Leave him," Harm commanded. "Let him be a meal for those of his kind."

Jack bowed to the fitting nature of that end and mounted up. They were on their way into the foothills of the Chisos in a matter of minutes and hadn't gone far when Harm reined in with a low Apache curse.

"What is it, Uncle Harm?" Jack asked, perplexed by the intensity of his dark expression.

Harm pointed to a single set of tracks, heading ahead of them into the hills. "She doesn't listen very well."

"Who?"

"Your sister."

"Sarah?"

"She's going after Cooper. I should have known. Too much of her aunt's influence."

"But how does she expect to find them?"

Harm smiled tightly. "I taught her how to look."

Chapter Twenty-five

Sarah rode hard with her gaze fixed to the ground. It wasn't a difficult trail to follow. Heavy men made for heavy horses and a deep track. The pain in her middle had eased to a dull ache and there were none of the cramping spasms that would have had her fearing for the life of her child. The baby was a Bass and a Cooper, strong stuff. Her one goal was to find her child's father. If Billy was working for the rangers, she meant to help him against Gant. If he was with Gant, she would protect him to her very last breath against her family and himself. Like Jack, she'd lost too many to let go another.

This time, she spotted Gant's outposts before they saw her, and she was deep into their basin hideaway by the time the alarm sounded. She wasn't armed, so there was no reason to treat her rough, other than the fact that she'd snuck right in under their noses and they feared Gant's temper. One of the outlaws who rode down on her snatched her off her horse and threw her across his saddle. If it hadn't been for the child she carried, Sarah would have given him a notable fight. But they were taking her where she wanted to go so there was no purpose in struggling.

"Hello, in camp. Brought you something, Cooper."

Sarah had no chance to catch her balance as her escort gripped the waistband of her skirt and flung her off his horse. She landed hard, her backside taking most of the impact and her pride the rest. A pair of fancy stitched boots came into sight, and she followed them up a long, long stretch of denim-clad legs to a leather and snakeskin belt and tapestry vest. By the time she came to his face, her heart was pounding madly. Until she saw his expression. It was dark with fury, made even fiercer by the mottling of bruises.

"What the hell are you doing here?"

"Billy, I—"

"Are you trying to get me killed?"

"No, I—"

"You leading the rest of them right up here to shoot us down?"

"No! Jack and Uncle Harm are riding with the rangers down into Mexico."

"Then why aren't you with them?"

"Because I know the track of the bay you're riding. It has a cracked shoe. I came alone, Billy. I came because I wanted to be with you."

So that's why Harm was so helpful about offering him the bay, Billy thought to himself. So he'd be easier to trail. Smart man, Harm Bass. So why was he on his way to Mexico leaving his impetuous niece loose?

Aware that Gant and all his men were watching, Billy reached down to grab a handful of Sarah's jacket, hauling her to her feet. She weighed little more than nothing and looked so fragile and pale, it worried him half out of his mind thinking of her throwing herself into so much danger. But there was a toughness in her dark-eyed stare, the same grit and determination all the Basses possessed and shared with their women. She wasn't as delicate as she seemed.

"To be with me, huh? And what makes you think I want you here?" He made his tone deliberately cruel and he saw a flicker of uncertainty cloud her gaze.

"Before you left, you said—"

"I said a lot of things but I don't recall any of them being that I wanted you to follow me. Go home."

"No!"

"You heard me. I don't want you here. Go home."

Her chin quivered slightly, then firmed in a stubborn

square. "I don't have a home to go to. All I have is you. Billy, let me stay here with you."

"Drop," he told her in a sudden soft whisper.

"What?"

Then she saw his hand arc back and rush downward. He swung so his palm connected with little more than a sting, but she went down as if he'd hit her with a two-by-four, holding her cheek to hide the lack of intensity.

"That was to get your attention. Now, you listening to me? You do what I tell you and you keep your mouth shut about what I'm doing. I don't need no more trouble than I already got."

"Then I can stay?" she petitioned in a whispery voice.

"That ain't up to me," he growled. He turned to Ray Gant and waited on his judgment, while Sarah wound around his legs like an eager alley cat. The way her palms pushed up and down his thighs was waking an uncomfortable reaction.

Ray Gant considered the request, then drawled, "Well, now, Billy-boy, you know we all pretty much share everything here equally. You willing to do that with your woman?"

Billy felt Sarah press closer. He tried to smile, wanting to believe the other man was joshing with him. "Ray, she's not my woman, she's my wife. She's carrying my child. That ain't something a man wants passed around."

"You saying what's yours is too good for the likes of the rest of us?"

There was a grumble from the other men, who were beginning to look between Sarah Cooper and their own used-up whores in unfavoring comparison.

"That ain't what I'm saying at all." A deep, terrible uneasiness was starting to churn as he looked to Gant for some sign of his meaning. The outlaw leader's expression was calm, almost amiable, but his eyes were cold.

"Sounds like it to the rest of us, don't it, boys?"

There was an assenting murmur and Billy felt Sarah adhere to his leg in a clutching panic. He didn't dare look down at her.

"Ray . . . please. This ain't funny."

"Am I laughing? Any of the boys laughing?"

"Don't do this."

"You asking me for a special favor, Billy? Was a time when I might have been willing to grant you one. Was a time when I'd have done just about anything for you. I don't know about now, Billy. This little gal's already cost us Joe Beals. I'm not willing to risk any more men for her sake. Figure if you share her out, won't nobody be jealous and do something stupid enough to die for."

"Then let me send her away."

"She already knows where we are. It'd be easier and safer to just kill her."

Billy's hand dropped down atop Sarah's head, his fingers curling, clenching in her hair. "I'm not going to let you do that." That was said quietly but with an incredible amount of strength behind it.

"Then you should be willing to do just about anything to keep her alive, shouldn't you?"

"She's my wife, Ray. She's not a whore."

"Maybe I ought to be the judge of that. I seem to recall you saying you'd go along with whatever I told you, Billy. You saying now that ain't so?"

Sarah could sense the dangerous tension gathering. In a few seconds, there'd be gunplay and her husband would be dead. There was no getting around it. She could tell by the cold glaze in Gant's eyes that no less than complete capitulation to his wishes before the rest of his men would satisfy him. He wouldn't tolerate Billy's challenge of his authority. And that meant he'd give her over or Gant would have to kill him. She couldn't let that happen.

Sarah stood, sliding up along Billy's side until she was tucked securely under his arm and against his rib cage. She could feel the frantic rock of his breathing. She put her hand on his shirtfront and rubbed gently.

"It's all right, Billy."

He looked down at her in surprise. "What?"

"It's not worth dying over."

"Sarah—"

"Listen to her, Billy-boy. She's making sense. Me and your little wife are going to get better acquainted, then I'll let you know what I've decided to do about her."

"No!"

Sarah pressed both of her hands against his chest when he took a fierce stride forward. "Billy, listen to me. It doesn't mean anything. It doesn't matter."

Billy and Ray Gant had locked gazes, and the unspoken struggle between them was a potentially deadly one. Then Ray drawled, "What's it gonna be, Billy?" and Billy's hands tightened up possessively on Sarah's arms. Gant was asking if he'd casually hand over his wife for another man's pleasure. Well, he wasn't going to! They would kill him first before he'd ever let anyone put a hand on Sarah!

Her hand slipped over the backs of his, squeezing first, then gently prying them off. Her dark gaze was uplifted, searching his out, seeking to convey some calm, some control into his fevered state of fury. Don't, her steady stare seemed to say. Don't fight. And he understood then, even as he hated the logic that would keep them both alive.

He released her and growled with all the gruff resignation he could muster, "Go with him. I guess it don't matter all that much."

But Sarah could see that it did. She could feel the terrible frustration trembling through him as his hands fell away and she knew she couldn't falter. If she showed the slightest hesitation, he'd jump to her protection with fatal results. One of the other lessons her uncle had taught her was to live to fight another day. Nothing was more important than that, than keeping her husband and her baby alive. Even enduring what the outlaw leader had in mind.

She turned away from her husband and walked proudly up to Ray Gant, asking in a gritty voice, "Do we drop right here or what?"

He laughed at her audacity. "My tent's a little more private for what I had in mind." He went ahead of her, giving her a broad, tempting view of his unprotected back, and she wished for something, anything, to thrust into the middle of it.

The inside of the tent was fairly weather-tight, with the musty smell of long-stored canvas. There was an old army cot set up beneath the steep slant of one side and that's where Sarah's gaze riveted in sudden horrified dismay.

Seeing her expression, Ray drawled, "You know if you yell out and he comes busting in here, I'll kill him, don't you?"

"Yes. I'm not going to yell out."

"Unbutton your shirt." He said it indifferently, as if telling her to pour him coffee. She obeyed, fingers shaking but spine starched with resolve. "Take it off and what's under it, too."

She was bare to the waist before he even bothered to look at her. Then it was with a passionless assessment.

"You're a very fine-looking female, even if you are a bit on the skinny side. No wonder Billy sets such store by you."

When he didn't grab for her right away, Sarah grew bolder. "I thought Billy was your friend."

"My friend? I guess you could say he is."

"Then why are you doing this?"

"I like Billy. He's a bright kid, good with guns, quick with his head, slow on the temper. If I was the kind who needed friends, he'd be the kind I'd pick."

"And that's why you want to rape his wife?"

He gave another soft laugh. "Rape you? You came in here willingly enough. That's because you're a smart girl and you don't want him getting himself hurt over something that's done and forgotten in a matter of minutes. That's what I'm counting on, you being a smart girl." And he reached for her then. It took all Sarah's courage to stand firm as his fingertips sketched along her shoulders and down to the swell of her breasts. He didn't follow with his gaze, though, which he had locked into hers. His eyes were shrewd, chill, without any sign of a man aroused by the anticipation of having a woman. It was an all-business look of a man striking a deal.

"I need to know I can trust him. And I can trust him if he's worried about you, if he knows you'll be safe as long as he does what I want him to."

She gave a gasp as his thumbs rubbed across her nipples

but she quickly bit back the sound. Her shivering wasn't as easy to control.

"Have you ever been with anyone but him?" His question sounded almost gentle with concern.

Sarah shook her head stiffly.

"You wouldn't be much good as a whore then. Though these boys'd give you plenty of experience in a hurry."

She shuddered at that thought but made no comment.

"You want to lie down with me or do you want a drink?"

She was too surprised by the choice to answer at first, then she muttered, "I'll take the drink."

Ray smiled wryly, then stepped back. Her exposed skin immediately erupted into gooseflesh. He hoisted a bottle and took a deep swallow. He passed it to her and she did the same, blinking against the burn of it.

"Can I put my shirt back on?" she ventured cautiously, and when he shrugged, she quickly wriggled back into it.

"Now then," he continued in that same conversational tone, "just so we understand each other." He snatched up a handful of her hair and, sudden as a snake strike, roped it around his wrist, yanking hard upon the roots. Sarah's eyes watered but she didn't cry out. He dragged her up against his chest and smashed his mouth down over hers. The sudden revulsion made her squirm, but he had no intention of making it last. It was just a lesson. A warning. He let her go and she surged back, panting wildly.

"I could take you and I could hurt you bad. I could fix it so you'd be no good to anyone, not even Billy anymore. I could make it so no man ever wanted to look at you again."

"Like you did Chonita?" she hissed in careless contempt.

"Oh, much, much worse than that. Chonita still has teeth and she can lie with a man without screaming. You won't be able to say the same when I'm through with you. You make sure Billy-boy minds his manners or we'll have ourselves another talk. After that, you'll be ready to put a bullet in your head. Just like your mama did."

Before Sarah could react to his words, he threw up the tent flap and strode out.

Billy was standing where he'd left him, posture taut and eyes black with tortured emotion. Gant spoke to the others but his gaze never left Billy's.

"You ain't missing nothing, boys. She's strictly a one-man ride and not worth the trouble. So if I hear of anyone pestering her, I kill him. That clear to everyone?"

Billy was still staring at him murderously, his restraint fraying under the strain of not knowing. Ray smiled and gestured toward the tent.

"Help yourself to my accommodations, Billy. She's all yours."

Billy waited until Ray had sauntered back to the fire, before he crossed to the tent. He was a mass of angry panic, unsure of what he'd find or how Sarah would receive him. How was he going to treat her after knowing he'd let another man take her? Like nothing had happened? He wished it could be that easy to pretend nothing had!

She was standing with her back to him, her arms wrapped in a tight hug about her slender figure. His agonized gaze took in the sight of her untucked blouse and the delicate underpinnings that still lay forgotten upon the ground. Rage, darker and more violent that he'd ever imagined, leapt within him, choking out reason as he took a hold of her shoulder. His grip must have been stronger that he intended, for she made a small sound and winced away. She spun toward him, her eyes large and alarmed. Her kiss-bruised lips parted but no words came. He was busy taking in the way her blouse was buttoned up wrong.

"That sonuvabitch! I'm gonna kill him!" Billy roared. The man had taken what was his and he'd allowed it! The shame of that, the guilt of knowing he'd failed to protect the woman he loved, was too much. But as he started to reach for his gun, even as he pivoted toward the tent flap, Sarah had him by the arms, restraining him.

"No! Billy, no! It's all right. Nothing happened!"

"Nothing? It don't look like nothing to me! Goddammit! Did he hurt you? I don't know what I was thinking. I can't believe I let him touch you. I should have—"

"What?" she demanded, trying to force reason. "What should you have done? Gotten yourself killed? No! You did the only thing you could. Anything else would have been just plain stupid."

She made it sound so sensible, so right. Then why were his insides quivering with agitation and his heart jerking around like crazy? Because the sight of her walking off with Gant had made him think and feel the way he had when he'd watched his sister saunter upstairs, arm in arm with a cowboy in a smoky Fort Stockton saloon.

"I should have been able to protect you."

"You did, Billy. You protected me by not letting him kill you. If you'd died, I'd have been spread under each and every one of them by morning."

"Instead of just under Gant." That was spat out so bitterly, Sarah nearly gave way to tears.

"He didn't touch me, Billy. He didn't do anything. He just wanted to scare me to control you. That's all. It was for the power, not anything to do with passion."

He stared at her, belief and relief flickering, mingling, overwhelming all else. "I thought . . . I couldn't stand thinking . . . I don't know what I would have done."

"What would you have done?" Sarah took a step back, becoming strangely reserved. "What would you have done if he had lain with me? Would you have walked away from me in disgust?" All she could think of was her mother, pregnant with her would-be murderer's child, wondering if any man would ever want her. Of the torment in Jack's voice when he'd cried out, *What do you see when you look at me?* Would Billy Cooper ever have looked at her the same if she'd done what she'd been prepared to do to save their lives?

He didn't answer right away. He was looking at her with a strange intensity. Then he put his hand to her cheek, cupping the curve of it in a gently hollow. His voice was soul-wrenchingly tender.

"I'd have thanked God that I married the bravest woman in all West Texas and that she loved me enough to be willing to pay such a price."

Her arms went around his middle, cinching up tight. His banded her shoulders. They were shaking with the fervor of the embrace.

"I love you, baby," he told her with forceful feeling, letting go all he'd had to hold in check since she'd looked up from a sprawl at his feet. He hugged her, relishing the feel of her fit against him. Wanting that fit to become much more personal but wanting even more for her to know how much he cared for her. And because he cared, he was reminded of an earlier question. "Now what I need to know is what the hell you're doing here?"

She lifted her head back to look up at him and her eyes clouded with concern. "Oh, your poor face! Who hurt you? Oh, Billy . . ."

"Forget my face," he growled, but she'd already come up on tiptoes to lightly kiss the colorful split on his cheekbone, the lump at the strong angle of his jaw, and finally, the swelling at the corner of his mouth. She lingered at that last spot until his lips parted and allowed a soft moan to escape.

"Billy, make love to me."

It should have sounded like a ridiculous request, considering. But it didn't. It sounded right even if a little desperate. And he was anxious to comply because she was his and he loved her, and he wanted that claim to be as deep and certain as the child she was carrying. Because he'd been scared to death over her, he'd missed her every second they'd been apart, and he wanted the hot sweetness of their union to drive all else away. If only for a little while.

His hands were on the buttons of her blouse. When he eased it from her shoulders, he froze, his stare drawn to the discoloration beneath her breastbone.

"What the hell happened? Baby, are you all right?"

"I'm fine, Matt Cobb hit me when I was trying to get away. I hit him harder." That was said with a grim satisfaction, the way a Bass would say it.

"Cobb?"

"He and—he and Pete Meyers were the ones working with

Gant. I found out about it and they were bringing me here to expose you."

She watched his features as he digested that information. She could see his distress and disbelief and, ultimately, his anguished acceptance. Then his thoughts circled back to her. "And Cobb hit you? I'm gonna kill that—"

"Uncle Harm took care of it for you."

"Harm? I thought he and Jack—"

"Are right behind me. I had to come ahead to warn you in case—" She broke off suddenly, her gaze dropping away from his as she remembered what her thinking had been.

Now he was watching her. "In case what, Sarah? Warn of what? That Jack and Harm were coming? Sarah, did you think I was riding with Gant for real?"

Her head came up proudly and she declared, "It didn't matter."

"Didn't matter?"

"You're my husband and I love you. It didn't matter why you were here, just that I be here with you."

"You don't trust me at all, do you?"

"About as much as you trust me, or you wouldn't have gone sneaking off out of our bed without a simple goodbye."

"Sarah, I didn't want you involved. I told you I was coming for Gant. I told you I would see to him because of what he did to you and your family. Didn't you believe me? Did you think that I'd join right up with them again after what they did to you?"

"That's not important," she insisted, but his expression said it was and so did his flat words.

"It is to me."

And then he turned and left her.

He strode to the fire, where the others had gathered to cut the chill with its heat and whiskey and the first available woman. He took the bottle Tom Benton held up to him with a mumble of thanks, before glancing over toward where Ray Gant was sitting. Billy was still upset enough to think about drawing his gun and blasting a hole through the other man, but he was calm enough to know it would be sheer foolishness. Ray had made his point crystal clear. He gave the bottle a slight hoist and nodded his head in nearly imperceptible thanks. *Yeah, thanks for making me out a failure and a coward in front of my wife. Bad enough she already thinks the worst!*

Gant smiled as if he could read the turmoil and carefully leashed anger in the younger man. But he didn't mind because he could also feel the submission. And that's what he'd wanted, to humble Billy Cooper into helplessness with just the right emotional lever. From the looks of it, he'd succeeded.

Sarah lay curled on the borrowed cot, shivering with cold and loneliness. Why had she let Billy think she didn't have faith in him? If that were the case, would she be here, placing herself and her unborn child in jeopardy? She argued the point back and forth, on the one hand chiding herself for not having blanket trust in the man she'd married and on the other holding up experience as her rationale. He'd known a confusion of loyalties before. He'd gone so far as to be involved in the robbing and killing of Bob Westerly. She was almost certain that had been serious business and not part of his ranger cover. Why else would he have behaved as he did when Jack brought him home? He'd been on a fragile edge then and what had she done? Pushed him right over it with her failure to have faith.

He was here because of her. He was here to stake his place in her family. Why had she ever let him think he needed to make such a sacrifice? His proclamation of love had been enough. Or had it? If it had, would she have harbored even the slightest suspicion that he was here for reasons of gain rather than of righteous glory? She'd doubted him, and in his eyes, that was worse than not loving him. He'd needed her confidence in his basic goodness while he struggled to establish it, and she'd failed him. She'd hurt him after she'd promised not to, and she didn't know if he would ever believe in her again.

The patter of icy rain on the canvas overhead echoed the beat of misery in her heart. The change in weather broke up the noisy gathering of men and sent them seeking their bed covers. Sarah knew a second of paralyzing terror as the tent flap flew up. What if Ray Gant had decided to take back these quarters? She'd rather sleep out in the elements than under the same roof with him! Then she heard Billy's low curse as his head struck the center pole and sent the whole structure shuddering.

She lay still, listening to him disrobe in the dark. There was plenty of hesitation in the movements. Finally, she heard him feel his way over to the cot, and there was a rush of frigid air as he lifted the blankets and scooted into the tight space beside her.

She'd wanted to welcome him graciously, but the touch of his clamminess against her wrought an objecting yelp and his immediate apology.

"I'm sorry. If you don't want me here with you . . ."

She grabbed onto his arm and wrapped it close around her. "You were cold, is all. Ease up and I'll warm you."

Cautiously, he nudged in against her, fitting along the sleek line of her back and flanks and tucking his long legs up behind hers. They lay like that for a long moment, comfortable yet awkward with one another. Each was trying to find a way to broach the silence with the right words, until Billy finally did so with a gentle touch.

He brushed the hair away from her face with the stroke of his fingertips and settled a kiss upon her temple. Her breath came sighing out in response and her body arched in a sensuous invitation, one he couldn't refuse. His hand soothed along the angle of her arm where it fit the dip of her waist, then his palm skimmed her hip and down her thigh. She was wearing her chemise, no more a barrier than his own long johns. He wanted her in a hurry but he made himself go slow. She was worth the frustration of waiting.

But she didn't want to wait. She directed his hand down to the damp delta where desires throbbed and needed tending. His breath stroked warm and fast along her cheek, echoing the rhythmic pace he set to build her passions. It wasn't long

before her hard completing spasms had the cot joints creaking.

"I love you, baby." The words came so easily now, he
couldn't imagine having once struggled to even frame them up
within his mind. "All I want is to make everything so good for
you."

"Then don't stop now." And she moved against him, her
buttocks pressing with urgent insinuation into his hardness.
With a bit of eager fumbling to free himself from the confines
of flannel, Billy nudged his knee between hers, using the contour of the cot to enhance their closeness as he sank himself
deep and drove them both to a quick and explosive climax.
His hand clasped over her mouth as her cries threatened to
intensify in tandem with their pleasure. Then came the drain-
ing ebb of ecstasy, and he continued to hold her while his
mind spun in a desperate search for answers.

How was he going to get her away from here and convince
her that all he wanted in the world was to hold her in the tender aftermath of their loving while his child moved beneath
his hands?

Chapter Twenty-six

Sarah awoke cold and alone, wishing for her husband's comforting heat beside her. Wishing even more that she was lying in the bed they'd share for the rest of their lives, in a home made just for them and their six children. And she wondered if that particular dream would ever come true. He'd given her no definite promises on which to cling. Their lovemaking had been powerful and satisfying, and Billy had told her more than once how much he loved her. She believed him. She wanted to believe in her future with him with an equal certainty. And as soon as Harm and Jack stepped in to help rid them of the threat of Ray Gant, she'd concentrate all her efforts toward that end. Nothing had been easy for them since they'd met and mated and been forced to marry. Soon they'd have the baby to come between them. Maybe they could go someplace, just the two of them, perhaps to Austin or New Orleans. Someplace they could get to know and trust without the pressure of Texas and the Bass family weighing down on them. A week or two of nothing but loving upon which to build their future.

But first they had to have a future. And when her uncle and brother came calling, she didn't want to be caught lying naked and unprepared inside a tent. She wanted to be ready to lend a hand.

The first thing Sarah did after ducking out under the tent flap was to look for Billy. As soon as she saw him sipping coffee at the fire with several *compadres* and located Gant nearby, she felt safe to see to her needs in the thick scrubs surrounding the camp. She needed a gun and wondered if Billy could get one for her. Walking around the edges of the outlaw camp unarmed was like going barefoot around a snake pit.

She found a tiny stream and went to wash up. The cold water was like a hard slap to the senses. When she straightened, she was thrilled to see Chonita, who was bearing a load of wash with the intention of soaping it in the chill current. The two women exchanged a quick embrace.

"I heard you were back with *Senor* Cooper. He is a good man. He should not be here."

"He is a good man—my man—and he won't be here long." Sarah looked at the other woman, feeling a debt owed for the mars on her pretty face at Gant's cruel hand. "Chonita, stay down here by the stream this morning."

"Why?"

"Don't ask questions I can't answer. Just stay down here and out of sight when the shooting starts."

"Shooting?" Chonita gasped. "What is going to happen?"

"Yes," drawled another voice. "What is going to happen?" Sarah turned to face Luisa's suspicious black eyes.

"What shooting?" the whore demanded. "You bring trouble, *puta*. Now I make plenty of trouble for you."

The vindictive woman whirled toward the camp and Sarah recognized the danger in what the whore had overheard. She gripped Luisa's arm and jerked her back about, and before the woman could shriek in fury, Sarah swung with all her might. Her fist connected with a knuckle-splintering force against the other's jaw and Luisa collapsed like an armload of discarded dirty laundry.

Rubbing her aching hand, Sarah glanced around for something with which to bind the woman. Chonita was quick to rip apart one of the shirts she'd been about to wash, tying one strip around the unconscious woman's ankles, one about her wrists, and another over her mouth.

"That will keep her here and quiet," Chonita vowed with grim pleasure. "I will stay and make sure she causes no trouble."

Sarah thanked her with a smile and hurried back to camp before she was missed and Gant sent someone searching. The man's eyes fixed on her the second she stepped into the clearing so she knew he'd noted her absence. Giving him an unwavering stare, she walked up to her husband. She went down on her knees behind him, leaning against his back and resting her cheek upon his shoulder. When he didn't respond, she nuzzled his neck and ear and finally whispered, "Get ready for company. I'll watch your back. Billy . . . I love you."

That had him turning toward her and her palm slipped along his jaw, holding his face so she could press an urgent kiss upon him. Their eyes met and held for a long moment before a commotion at the edge of camp pulled their attention from one another. Then both were rising to their feet in surprise and dismay.

Shad Randolph was marching a man into the camp at gunpoint.

And that man was Jack Bass.

"Who you got there, Shad?" Gant called out when the prisoner was brought to stand on the far side of the fire.

"Ranger. Caught him sneaking around. Want I should cash him in?"

"No," Gant said, seeing how Sarah surged forward at the suggestion before Billy grabbed her. The outlaw leader's eyes narrowed thoughtfully as he strode up to Billy's side. "Someone you know, Billy-boy?"

"My lieutenant," Billy told him.

Gant looked from Sarah to the stony-faced ranger. "Could it be we got us one of the Basses?"

"He's my brother," Sarah hissed. "Don't kill him. Don't you dare! Every ranger in the territory will be out for your scalp, not to mention my Uncle Harmon leading the way."

"If they're not already. Who's with you, Ranger?"

"No one," Jack stated flatly. "I came to get my sister. She's running with bad company."

"You want to go with him, girl?" Gant asked, glancing at Sarah with a curious lift of one brow.

She cast an appeal up at her husband. But Billy's face was

expressionless, no help there at all. She looked to Jack, her heart in a turmoil. He met her gaze without blinking. If she went with him, would they let them go or kill them both? It was doubtful they'd let a ranger live, in any case. She'd have a better chance prolonging that treasured life if she stayed where she was. Sarah took a tremendous risk and entwined her arm about Billy's.

"Guess she ain't interested in going anywhere with you, Ranger. Looks like she prefers bad company to yours."

There was an echo of rough laughter from around the fire. Jack's steady gaze never left Ray Gant. He ignored Billy as if he was of no consequence. When he spoke, his tone was strong enough to carry the incredulous message.

"I suggest you all lay down your arms, 'cause I'm arresting you in the name of the state of Texas."

"Just you?" Shad scoffed, prodding his kidney with his pistol.

"Don't take more than one ranger to deal with the likes of you."

No one laughed because the sure way he said it spooked them plenty.

Observing the reaction of his men, Gant drawled, "You're trouble, Ranger. You'd best be saying your prayers."

"Billy?" Sarah murmured uneasily. "He's my brother. Don't let them kill him." Her mind was spinning fast. Billy had his gun. If she could grab on quick to another, they'd have all of maybe three seconds to take on nine badmen. If they were fast and lucky . . .

"Oh, we ain't gonna kill him, Miz Cooper," Gant drawled. "We'll let Billy take care of it for us." He drew one of his matched sidearms, passing it butt first to Jack Bass's best friend and brother-in-law. "Unless you got a problem with that, Billy?"

There was a moment of hesitation. Ray Gant waited, smiling expectantly. Sarah's gaze flew between brother and husband. "Billy," she petitioned worried.

"No. No problem," Billy answered as he took the gun.

Gant laughed. "Didn't think so. Wouldn't think killing one

brother would mean any more to you than letting us do away with her folks and the other one so you could have a clear shot at their ranch." He took in Sarah's astonishment. "Oh, he didn't tell you that while he was cozied up over Christmas dinner, we was busy getting a place for the two of you to settle into? Just a reward for being such a good and loyal right-hand man."

Sarah took a step back from Billy's side. Her gaze had gone wide and dazed. "No."

"Oh, yeah," Gant insisted. "After you kill this one, Billy, me and the boys will help you move on into your new house. Might even throw you and your little bride a housewarming party. Then you can take as long as you like breaking her into the idea of staying with you. I'm not sure I envy you that. You'll have to sleep with one eye open for a while." Then his voice sharpened into a command. "Kill him, Billy."

Billy raised the gun without pause, sighting in carefully on his stoic friend. "Sorry to drop you on the spot like this, Jack. Change in plans. No hard feelings." And he fired.

Sarah let out a scream as her brother clutched his chest, his expression one of surprise as he spun and fell facedown and lay there, unmoving.

"Jack!"

She started to run forward when Billy caught her wrist, jerking her up. She turned on him in horror.

"Ain't nothing you can do for him now."

With a ferocious snarl, she lunged at him, hitting him with her fists, slapping him, trying to claw at his eyes. He had his hands full trying to hang on to her and avoid any real damage.

"Sarah, stop it!," he snapped. "Stop! Don't make me hurt you."

"Hurt me?" she cried fiercely. "You're going to have to kill me if you want to close both your eyes again. 'Cause the minute you do, you're dead! Do you hear me! You're dead!"

"Sarah!" His hand clenched in the hair at the nape of her neck, twisting until all the slack was gone and she was held helpless. He pulled her up close, so their faces were scant inches apart. And he told her with a quiet urgency, "Trust me!"

Her breath was coming in tortured sobs as emotions tore up from a broken heart. He'd killed her brother! He'd known her family was going to die and he'd done nothing! My God, what had she married?

Then their stares locked and she couldn't look away. *Trust me!* She took a hitching grab for air, tremors of shock running through her.

She remembered a grinning Billy Cooper sitting on his horse in her uncle's front yard. The look on his face when he'd stood under the mistletoe with Becca in his arms. The anguish in his voice when he'd said, *It matters to me!*

Trust me!

And suddenly, she did.

The fight drained from her and she went limp in his arms as if in a swoon. He eased her down carefully to the ground, bending close enough to whisper, "Watch my back, Sarah. I love you." Then he pressed Gant's gun covertly into her hand before straightening.

As he came up, Shad Randolph was prodding Jack with his boot. "Hey, Ray, he ain't—"

Abruptly, Jack rolled, catching the outlaw's feet and sweeping them out from under him. The ranger came up with Shad's gun, the bandit wrestled as a shield in front of him.

"Sonuva—"

Billy's pistol jabbed into Ray Gant's ribs before he could finish the phrase. The other half-dozen men at the fire went for pistol grips, until Harm Bass's terse tone rang down on them like the bead of his carbine from above.

"Don't nobody who wants to go on living so much as breathe deep!"

None did.

Gant's gaze flew along the ridges.

"Lookin' for help?" Harm drawled as he hopped down off the outcroppings above. In one hand, he held his carbine. From the other dangled four gunbelts. "Don't bother. We been here for a while." He tossed the gunbelts into a pile and gestured to the others with the bore of his rifle. "Why don't the rest of you add yours to it."

Hardware added up to a considerable stack real quick.

"Now, you all just sit yourselves down and stick out your hands so's I can truss you up proper." He passed Sarah his carbine. "Hold this, little girl. Blast any of them that moves."

Harm ran an efficient rope to bind up the remaining outlaws, until all but Ray Gant and Shad Randolph were neatly subdued.

"You all right, Jack?"

"Yessir, Uncle Harm."

"Want to add your varmint to the bunch?"

"Sit," Jack advised with the prod of his pistol, and Randolph sat. Then Jack's arms were filled with his teary-eyed sister, who was intent on kissing him all over his face in weepy thanksgiving. "Sarah! You're drowning me!" But despite his complaints, he was hugging her tight. "You're just doing this to keep me from beating you but good and it ain't gonna work." He kept his arm about her in an affectionate circle as he eyed Ray Gant.

"We got some unfinished business with you, mister."

Sarah glanced up at her brother. She'd never heard such a menacing sound come from him.

Gant shrugged. "So hang me. But when I climb up on that gallows, Billy here is going up and dropping down with me, 'cause he's guilty as hell of the same things I am. You think about that."

"Corporal Cooper was working with the full knowledge of the Texas Rangers under my orders," Jack stated. "And I'll testify to that in court."

"And you gonna swear it on a stack a Bibles, too? He was playing both ends for his own benefit and you know it, Ranger. When I get done talking, everybody's gonna know it." He gave Billy a cold, shrewd look. "'Less, of course, you let me go, then it'll be our little secret."

"I'd rather hang," Billy told him. He was very aware that Sarah hadn't come back over to his side. She was hanging on to Jack, doing everything she could to keep their eyes from meeting, obviously shaken by Ray Gant's words. If she didn't care what happened to him, he'd just as soon hang, anyway.

"I don't think we have to worry about it coming to that," Harm mentioned casually. "See, Gant, when you get done talking to us, you aren't talking to anyone ever again about anything."

"And what makes you think I got anything to say to you, Bass?"

"Your friend Cobb had plenty to say."

Gant smiled, not at all intimidated. "Well, I ain't Cobb. And I ain't saying nothing to you."

"Who paid you off, Gant?" Jack asked with all the authority of Texas behind him.

"I don't know what you're talking about, Ranger."

"McAllister," Billy put in.

"Did he tell you that?" Harm demanded.

"I didn't tell him nothing."

"Not in so many words," Billy amended.

"Not in any words," Gant clarified.

"Uncle Harm, we need more than that to go after him legally," Jack interrupted, but Harm wasn't listening.

"Did he tell you to murder my family?" Harm rumbled with a lethal quiet.

"Nobody told me to do that. I did it for my friend Billy. That's what friends are for, after all. He wanted money and I gave him a way to earn it. He wanted a place for his little lady and I got him just what he asked for."

Billy saw his whole future drain away as fast as the color from Sarah's cheeks. "That's a lie! Ray, I had no part in that!"

"That why you're carrying around the deed to the property? A wedding present from your dearly departed father-in-law, was it?"

"You bastard, you know it wasn't me—"

The instant Billy let down his guard in anger, Gant had him, one arm snaking around his neck to haul him up in front of him, the other wrenching away the gun and cramming it under Billy's chin. The hammer clicked back.

"Now then, I'm taking a little ride, and if I see any of you twitch, I'll blow this boy's head clean off. You might be right fond of him, but he don't mean a damned thing to me. Move with me real easy, Billy-boy, less you want your brains viewing daylight."

Gant started to backpedal, his gaze darting between Harm's empty hands and the gun Jack held out away from his body. When Billy balked, Ray pressed the muzzle of his .45 up against his temple.

"Don't test me, boy. You know I'll do it."

"Drop."

The word came soft and suddenly from Sarah. When Gant started to look to her in question, Billy let all six feet four, two hundred plus pounds go lax, dragging his captor off balance. And the minute Gant tried to readjust, Sarah Cooper put a bullet in the center of his forehead.

"Just like my mama," she said in a small, cold voice as the smoking pistol was lowered to her side. Then consequence sank deep as she regarded his still form stretched out upon the ground. Her gaze swung about in terrible anguish. "I'm sorry, Uncle Harmon. I know you wanted to get information from him, but I just couldn't see him getting away. Not after what he did."

Harm stepped up and scooped her into a close embrace as shivers of delayed shock and grim justice shook through her. "You did just fine, little girl. He wouldn't have told me anything. Some men can't be persuaded by any means. Nice shot. Your daddy'd been proud."

While Harm comforted Sarah, Jack crossed over to Billy. "You all right, pard?"

Billy nodded, but his troubled gaze never left his wife. "He was right, Jack. I'm as guilty as he was. I got no right to wear a ranger star. I wasn't under your orders when I rode on a half-dozen raids or when Bob Westerly was killed or even when I came here." Then his eyes fixed on Jack's. "But I didn't have anything to do with your folks, Jack. I swear to God! If I'da had any idea . . ."

Jack nodded, believing him.

Billy waited for a sign that Sarah, too, had heard and believed him but she was lost in Harm's embrace and he couldn't be sure she was even listening. His spirit sank into helpless despair. "I think I ought to resign from the company."

"That what you think?" Jack gave him a long, careful scrutiny, displaying no sympathy for his position. "Well, that's about the most selfish, single-sighted thing I've ever heard!"

Billy gaped at him.

"Just when I need you most, you up and quit on me. I've always counted on you to be there to back me up. I expected you to be riding with me when we join up with the boys and corral the rest of this bunch down in Mexico. If you go walking off, how do you expect to support my sister? You'll have to come up with plenty of money to eat out at the hotel, 'cause her cooking will kill you quick."

"Jack . . ."

"You want to quit you quit, but I'll always consider you the finest man I've ever ridden with. What happened is done with, over. I'm not going to hold that against you. I put you in here with Gant. A man like that can warp even the best man's mind. I should have known you were drowning and pulled you out sooner. It's my fault you—"

Billy grabbed him up in a hug so tight, the rest of the words were squeezed out of him. Then the ranger corporal stepped back with a gruff "When are we leaving?"

"Leaving?"

"For Mexico."

Jack grinned at him. "Now would be nice." He looked over his shoulder. "Uncle Harmon, you think you can get this sorry-looking bunch back to Terlingua?"

"With Sarah riding shotgun, I can guarantee they'll get there still wearing all their hair. What do you say, little girl? You gonna back me up?"

"Sure, Uncle Harm," was her too-quiet reply.

Harm looked between her and Billy, then suggested, "Jack help me get these *hombres* mounted up and lashed down good, 'cause if they try to run off, I just might not be able to control myself." He glared at the tethered badmen and they blanched as one.

While the two Bass men went to round up the horses, Billy waited uneasily for Sarah's reaction. She surprised him with her chilly demand.

"I want the deed to my family's ranch."

He handed it over without a word in his own defense. She glanced at the note from Ray Gant and a faint quiver of her chin was quickly stilled.

"Sarah . . ."

He reached out, and she shied away in a confusion of hurt and upset. "Why didn't you tell me? I'd have rather heard it from you than from . . . him. Were you so sure I wouldn't believe you?"

"I wanted to set things square. I'd done so many wrong things . . ."

What had Emily said to him? It came back suddenly. Something about the worst things happening for the best. That's what he had with Sarah, a very right thing built on a lot of wrong ones. The way he'd taken her that first time, the way they'd been married, the lies he'd told her, the truth he hadn't confided, the path he'd wandered in anger, the love for her he hadn't surrendered to until the last possible moment. Wrong things that led to the one right thing standing before him. As she'd always been there since that very first kiss. She'd come after him, once to save his soul, once to save his life. She'd come to him when he called her, even though she rejected the life he'd offered her then. Rightly so. Still, she'd waited, holding to her faith in him. With her, it had been a lot of small cautious steps forward and several hurried retreats. But hadn't she taken the final one when she looked up proudly to declare it didn't matter what he'd done, who he was? And again when he'd asked for her trust and she'd given it.

Was that still true?

He'd been so sure she was going to fail him that he was the one who ended up disappointing her.

"Sarah, when Jack and I finish in Mexico, do you want me to come back to you?"

She stared up at him in an unsettling silence. Her expression betrayed the pain of a broken heart. A heart he'd wounded with his secrets and torn apart with his lack of faith. He wasn't sure he knew how to mend it. A nervous terror clenched inside him, warning him not to speak, but he had to say it. He had to give her the choice that was denied her before.

"I don't have to come back if you'd rather I didn't." Billy waited, sweating her reply.

She had the deed clutched to her chest. It stood between them more effectively than a ten-foot wall, a symbol of all their misunderstandings, all their insecurities. Her family's blood saturated that curl of paper and was neatly bound in Ray Gant's lies. There was nothing he could ever do to take the stain away.

She wouldn't answer. Well, that was it. That said everything. Holding to his pride when his heart failed him, Billy nodded grimly and turned away. As he began to walk toward where Jack was waiting, already mounted and holding his horse, Sarah's quiet words stilled him.

"Come back to me."

And just when hope began to blossom, her next words provided an unpromising caution.

"And we'll settle things."

Words vague enough to send him riding away without knowing to what he'd return.

Sarah stood stiff and still, watching her brother and her husband until they were out of sight. Then she felt Harm's palm glide along her bravely squared shoulders and her fragile body trembled in vulnerable suggestion.

"It takes a strong man to pull out of a past as bad as the one he's walked."

"Has he, Uncle Harm?"

"It doesn't matter what I think, little girl. What do you think?"

"All my life I've had the security of my family around me

and I just figured my future would be stable forever. Now he's my future and he's not safe."

"And that scares you?"

"Yes . . . and no. It's like holding a match, watching it burn, enjoying the beauty of the flame and the feel of the heat, and knowing at the same time how bad it's going to hurt when it burns down. Oh, Uncle Harmon, I don't know if I'm what he needs. I want to be a good wife and give him a good home the way Emily has for Jack, but I'm just no good at those things. I can't sew, I can't cook, I hate just about everything there is to housework. I'd rather be out riding with him, then home waiting on him. I can shoot and track and love his kids, but I don't know if I have the strength to hold on to him."

"Have you asked him what he wants?"

She looked around at Harm. Her eyes held a vulnerable glimmer "I'm afraid to." She had asked once and he'd said all she had to be was a good mother. He hadn't said a thing about his own needs. It was as if he didn't think they were important enough to be considered. But they were important to her. A lot had changed since then, and she knew there had to be more than just sound maternal instincts involved in the care and comforting of Billy Cooper.

"Well, you ask and you might just be surprised at what you hear. You give him babies, you give him love, you give him a place to come home to; something tells me that'll be enough. Why do you think I've been going back to the same woman for ten years? It sure as hell isn't my love of her cooking!"

Sarah smiled at that but her mood was still pensive. Because there was more at stake than those basic things. It had to start with forgiveness. And she didn't know if the well of her love was deep enough to yield up that special healing.

Chapter Twenty-seven

He came in tired and dirty and so cold to the bone from the January chill, all he could think about was a hot bath, clean sheets, and a long sleep. Thankfully, he was too exhausted to think of the two empty bunks in his barracks. All his concentration was focused on his own. He sat on the edge and dropped back, expecting the comforting yield of his mattress. Instead, he got a startled yell and an elbow in the ribs.

"Hey! What're you doing? You got the wrong bunk, pard?"

Billy jumped to his feet and glanced around him. No, it was his bed. And he didn't recognize the fresh scrubbed face of the boy sleeping in it. "If there's a mistake, you've made it. I've been sleeping there for nearly four years and just got it broke in right. Now, I'm tired, so don't—"

"You're Cooper." The boy sat up and stuck out his hand. "Name's July Ketchum and I'm right pleased to meetcha. Me an' a couple other boys just signed on under Captain Bass."

"Lieutenant," he corrected.

"What's that, Sergeant?"

"It's corporal." Billy stared at him groggily, suddenly in no mood for word games. "Whatever. Get outta my bed."

The boy laughed. "How long you been out there, Sarge? If I had a wife as pretty as yours, I surely wouldn't want to share my sheets with no ranger private, even if I ain't so bad to look at. Why don't you go on home, sir?"

"Home?" That word touched off a bittersweet chord but he shook it off. Had he gone suddenly stupid? Nothing was making much sense to him. He'd planned on looking Sarah up in the morning, when his mind was clearer and he was a whole lot cleaner. When he'd garnered the needed courage to hear what she had to say. Then he realized he had no idea where to look for her. Probably at Jack's. She'd seek refuge with her family. "My stuff already over at Jack's?"

July Ketchum was beginning to frown, as if he were talking to some loony. "I suspect it'd be at your ranch, Sergeant Cooper. Along with your wife. You remember her?"

"Don't get sassy with me, boy. A man don't forget his own wife."

"Jus' where he put her?" July grinned at him. "If you done forgot how to get home, I'd be happy to give you an escort. Be nice to get a meal from your housekeeper. Dang fine cook."

Was he in the right place? Billy looked around and everything was familiar except this kid and his own confusion. Rather than appear the total idiot, he mumbled, "Well, nice meeting you, Private. See ya in the morning."

"You mean next week."

Billy blinked. "Next week? Are you going somewheres?"

The boy started to laugh. "No, you are. I get it. You're jus' pulling my leg. You're a real kidder, Sarge. A real kidder. Had me going for a second." And chuckling, he laid back in Billy's bunk.

Home, a housekeeper, a week doing something he didn't know about. Sergeant? In the three weeks he'd been gone, either the world had gone crazy or he had!

If home was on a ranch, he had a pretty good idea what that meant. Sarah was out at her folks' place, which meant a good stretch of riding before getting any rest and confronting a good deal of guilt he'd hoped to forestall just a bit longer. He'd escaped all thoughts of it while out hunting down the rest of Gant's gang. He'd been a simple ranger then, following orders, living lean and hard under his best friend's leadership. It had felt good, cleansing somehow. He hadn't thought of himself as married into the Bass family or as an accomplice to Ray Gant's crimes. He'd been Corporal Billy Cooper again and he'd liked it.

Now, he had the rest of his responsibilities to face.

And all his fears.

It was completely dark by the time he reined in outside Will Bass's adobe home. Beyond it lay the shadow of the gutted-out barn. Why had she come here unless it was to punish him? There was a light burning inside the house, so he tied off his horse and stepped reluctantly onto the porch. What would he say to her? How could he convince her to have faith in their future when he hadn't seen fit to have faith in the present? Maybe he'd find she'd missed him so much words wouldn't be necessary.

He didn't expect Chonita to greet him at the door.

"Welcome home, *Senor* Cooper. Do you wish some hot food or just some water for a bath?" She reached for his coat and he handed it to her in a daze.

"Is Sarah here?"

"She has already gone to bed. She works very hard, that girl. The little one makes her tire quickly, but she will not listen and rest." The Mexican woman clucked in fond exasperation. "Can I make you some supper?"

"No. Thanks. I just want to wash up and turn in."

"There's hot water on the stove and clean towels. If you don't need me for anything, I'll go to bed, too."

"Uh . . . Chonita? Where's my wife?"

"Oh, she is in the front bedroom. Good night, *Senor* Cooper."

He mumbled good night and went to wash three weeks of dirt off him, but the film of confusion lingered. Then one thought surfaced: After weeks of sleeping on the cold ground listening to the snores of his companions, tonight he had a bed and a woman waiting. So what was he doing standing like a lost fool in the kitchen terrified of what his reception was going to be?

Just the soft sound of Sarah's breathing was enough to fill him with a hot, hot ache. He left his clothes on a chair by the door and crossed to the bed on silent bare feet. He could see the shape of her outlined by pale moonlight—sleek, feminine.

His. He was under the covers, as eager and nervous as a boy on his first trip to an upstairs room.

"Sarah? Baby, I'm back. I'm . . . home."

Home.

Just as the suggestion of that was sinking deep, Sarah muttered and rolled up against him. Her cheek burrowed into his shoulder, and one slender arm curved over his ribs and around his middle.

"You've got the longest legs I've ever seen," was what he thought he heard her mumble.

"What? Sarah?"

But she was fast asleep, sighing like a contented child in the curl of his embrace. He was startled to discover a great swell of tenderness overtaking his agitation and cooling his desire, amazed as well that it was suddenly enough just to hold her close, to know she'd be there in the morning. And in the morning . . . well, they'd both be rested enough for a proper greeting then!

Billy settled in and let his eyes close, and when he opened them again, it was daylight.

Sarah was stretched out along him, nestled in like a kitten. He knew exactly when she started to wake, because her palm pushed up and down his chest with heart-jerking, groin-tightening results. She made a happy little purring sound, then suddenly her dark head jerked up.

"Billy! Oh! When did you get in?"

"Last night." He liked the way astonishment and joy had her dark eyes gleaming. It got him hoping all sorts of things.

"Last night? Why didn't you wake me up? I should have made you dinner and—"

"Chonita let me in and I tried to wake you up, but the only thing you could talk about was my legs."

"Your—?" She blushed prettily, then looked angry with herself. "I wanted to give you a proper welcome. One you'd remember."

His fingertips stroked along her cheek. "You did."

And just as desire was beginning to heat up from its tender simmer, she was up and over him and *out* of bed!

"Sarah?"

"What time is it? I can't believe I slept so late!" She was running out of the room, her nightgown trailing in a flutter. "Chonita, can you make coffee while I get cleaned up?"

Billy sagged back into the pillows, the feeling of stepping into some sort of insanity slipping back over him. "Sarah?"

She popped her head back in. "Yes?"

"What are you doing?"

"Get up! We've got a train to catch."

"A—" But she was gone again. A train? He finally gave up trying to make sense of it and arose from the bed he'd hoped to linger in all morning. But without his wife in it, it lost much of its appeal.

Billy wandered into the kitchen, filling his nose with the delicious scent of steak and eggs and hot coffee.

"Good morning, *Senor* Cooper. Did you sleep well?"

"Fine. Thanks. Ah, Chonita, do you have any idea where we're going on a train?"

"To Austin," she told him, giving him that pitying look one usually reserved for an imbecile. "Eat some breakfast. It's a long stage ride to Marathon."

"What's in Marathon?"

"The train."

"I give up." So he sat and he ate and he didn't ask any more questions. By the time his plate was clean, Sarah came bustling back in, agitated with urgency. Her flittering around made him nervous. He wanted to grab on to her and hold her tight, to beg some sign from her that she wanted him here. But she wasn't looking at him and her manner was more than just flighty; it was determinedly evasive.

"Are you finished? You've got time to shave, then we'd better—"

He caught her hand and put her palm to his bristly cheek, and abruptly, she lost her train of thought. Her fingertips charted the line of his facial bones and her thumb followed the sensuous curve of his upper lip. His eyelids drooped to a sultry half-mast, and when he sucked in the pad of her thumb to lave it wetly, Sarah lost some of her self-control. But it was all too quickly recovered.

"B—Billy, we have to go."

He stood and her gaze galloped over him in a reckless rush. "You look . . . nice." Her palms rested against the back of his thighs, rubbing up to the seat of his denims in wicked appreciation. She leaned against him in a moment of weakness, breathing in the starched freshness of his shirt and the warm scent of his skin. Her will trembled, then she jerked back. "You shave, I'll load the buggy."

When she started away, he caught her wrist again. When she stiffened up, he released her. "Sarah, where are we going?"

"To Austin."

"I know that. Why?"

"Amanda bought us travel tickets and a suite in the city's best hotel. For our honeymoon." That last was said with a regrettable lack of emotion.

"Oh."

"All the arrangements were confirmed yesterday when we were waiting for you to get in. Emily assured me that Jack would agree to give you time off. I thought it would be good for us to get away from here for a while . . . to decide what we're going to do from now on. Is—is that all right with you?"

He blinked. "Fine by me." God, why couldn't she give him some kind of reassurance?

Her look went all cool again. "Good. Then shave and let's go."

Damn. She sure made it hard for a man to hold to any kind of expectations.

By the time they reached the stage stop in Terlingua, he'd told her all about the excursion into Mexico and their victorious return with the remaining outlaws. She was a good listener, asking smart questions and applauding his bravery at the appropriate times. She made him feel good about what he'd done, in fact, almost heroic. He liked that. Her admiration meant more than any medal or commendation ever could. He never did get around to asking all the questions he had, though.

Once they were crowded onto the stage between a noisy and ill-mannered family with three kids and their asthmatic grandmother, there was no chance for more talking. Billy liked most kids, but these he found overbearing and obnoxious. And once their harried mother found out that Sarah was expecting, she regaled them with horror stories of how she'd almost died during each one of her children's births, going on and on in graphic detail until their only defense was to feign sleep. When Sarah finally relaxed enough to slumber against him, Billy studied her fragile form in increasing panic as the words the woman spoke sank deep. What if something unforeseen should happen and he were to lose her? Of all the perils they'd survived together, the thought of meeting death while bringing in life scared him more than any of them— because he was completely helpless. All the hard work fell on Sarah and he could only pray she was up to it. Billy decided on that long, nearly sleepless night that it was hell caring about someone.

What if she refused to let him be there when the time came for the birth of their child? What if she'd decided she didn't need him?

The full moon allowed the coach to roll day and night, and by the time they got to Marathon, the passengers were sore and grumpy and covered with travel grime. Sarah was too droopy to do more than collapse on a seat at the train station, saying she'd wait while Billy made some quick purchases. He returned in time to see the locomotive steam to a stop in a cinder-studded cloud and to help his wife aboard to find their seats. They sat side by side for a moment, then she asked, "I thought you did some shopping."

"I did."

"Well, you didn't buy anything very big. What did you get? New socks?"

"Socks? What's wrong with my socks?"

"Nothing, if you don't mind your toes sticking through the ends of them."

"Well, if you'd rather I took back what I got you and bought me some socks instead, I guess I could—"

"You bought something for me?"

He sat for an uncomfortable minute, then glanced at her, seeing nothing but anticipation and appreciation on her face. Still, it was hard to swallow down his apprehension. "Gimme your hand. No, the other one."

She looked down in surprise at the ring he slipped on the third finger of her left hand. It was made up of twin bands of gold and silver braided together in an unbroken circle. The longer she stared, the more nervous he got.

"I couldn't afford nothing with sparklers on it, but that there kinda reminded me of us—you being the gold, all soft and warm, and me the silver, flashy and quick to tarnish." His dimples creased deeply, then he got very serious. "I wanted you to have something permanent." He wanted what they had to be permanent.

Sarah made a small sound, then her arms flew about his neck. She didn't say anything, and he was aware that though she'd accepted the ring, she hadn't accepted his invitation to a future together. It wasn't much of a consolation and he was still scared to death.

"You know what else?" he ventured.

"What?" she sniffled, drawing back slightly.

"You haven't given me a kiss since I've been back."

She let her gaze linger over his face. He was sure everything inside him was written there as plain as newspaper headlines while hers was a frustratingly blank page. Just as she started to lean toward him, they were aware of a throat being cleared.

"Hey, don't mind me."

"Uncle Harmon, what are you doing here?" Sarah squeaked out in dismay as Billy jumped back from her.

"Got some business in Austin and thought I might ride along."

Billy ground his teeth. The last thing he needed was the overbearing presence of Harm Bass when they were already on such tenuous ground. What kind of business would take him to Austin, if not to watch out for his favorite niece? It was hard to get over the sense of defeat that just kept mounting. Billy thought he and Harm had struck a truce. Apparently, he was wrong.

"Where are you staying, Uncle Harm?" Sarah was asking as she twisted the ring on her finger.

"Not with us," Billy said with a teeth-baring smile. "Right, Uncle Harm?"

He dropped down in the seat opposite and nudged his moccasined feet up onto the seat between them. "Thought I might bunk down at the foot of your bed," he told them, then leaned back against the cushions and tipped his hat down to shade his smile. He seemed to go to sleep almost at once.

"Would you mind if I rolled him out at the next water stop?" Billy whispered to his wife.

"I'm a very light sleeper," Harm warned without opening his eyes.

"Better keep one eye open," Billy suggested.

Then he sat stiffly beside his equally rigid bride, while Harm Bass snoozed contentedly all the way to Austin.

Harm disappeared in the train depot and Billy was in no hurry to find him. He hailed a rig to take them to their hotel and was quick about getting his wife behind a locked door. Sarah swept through the room raving about its opulence but subtly skirting the big bed to throw open the terrace doors.

"Oh, Billy, look at the view! Don't you just love all of it!"

"Desperately," he growled, unable to stand another second of the distance between them. He stepped up behind her, curling one arm gently about her waist. She went very still but didn't try to pull free. Slowly, he lifted the veil of her black hair off her neck so he could chain a row of hot kisses. Her soft moan of surrender was immediate and sent a scalding shiver all the way to his toes.

"I hear this place has the finest sheets in Austin," she whispered huskily.

"Let's get a look at them."

She revolved in his embrace, her dark eyes lifting to his. He saw passion to rival his own in them, but still that edge of restraint. "I understand that in order to appreciate the quality you have to stretch out on them with nothing on." She started boldly down his shirt buttons and his heart was banging underneath.

"And just where did you hear that?" he asked in a nearly failing voice.

"From Amanda."

"Figures."

"Meaning what?"

"Meaning you go ahead and listen to whatever she tells you. If she can hang on to that husband of hers for ten years, could be she knows something worth sharing."

Her palms rested on his bare chest, as if to test the rapid thunder of his desire. When he dipped down to claim her lips, they parted without hesitation. She tasted as sweet as the promise of forever. It was what he'd starved for these three long weeks. It was what he'd longed for all his life.

Their kisses intensified and their movements grew increasingly hurried with every layer of clothing shed, until there was nothing but bare skin and the anticipation of fine sheets. Billy lifted Sarah up in his arms and was about to deposit her on the bed, when there was a knock at the door.

"What?" he all but snarled.

"Room service." Harmon.

Sarah answered breathlessly. "Uncle Harmon, could you go away for a while. Please!"

"How long before you're done with ... whatever you're doing?"

"Four days," Billy told him.

"A half hour," Sarah modified.

"An hour," Billy concluded.,

"I'll be downstairs having some coffee."

"Order up a pot of it, Harmon."

And the funny thing was, neither of them could remember a thing about the feel of the sheets.

* * *

Harm looked up from his fourth cup of coffee to give his niece and her husband a mild look. They both had a flush about them that was unmistakable. He'd begun to wonder but now was reassured.

"I ordered us lunch. I told them not to hurry," Harm told them with a bland smile. Sarah bent to press a warm kiss to his cheek, then settled in beside Billy, who was so smug with satisfaction, Harm felt vindicated for the action he'd taken back in a Presidio hotel room when he'd encouraged romance at knife point. He was watching them flirt shyly with one another when the arrival of a well-dressed businessman caught his attention. Setting his cup down very carefully, he stood and remarked smoothly, "There's my business. I'll be right back."

The businessman was seated with deference. He ordered an expensive bottle of wine and looked over the menu. He was handsome in a dark, distinguished fashion, his face and hands weathered in a way not consistent with his fine clothes. Nor was the power of his body in keeping with his sophisticated manner. No lazy philanthropist or desk-occupying lobbyist could claim such a lean, tough look. It was a veneer of gentility over the spareness prison life gave a man. And that's where Russell McAllister had spent the last nine years.

His steak came and he shook out his linen napkin to place it across his lap. As he reached for his table knife, a brown hand closed over the handle, lifting the sharp utensil with a lethal familiarity. McAllister stopped breathing.

"That's a fine-looking cut of meat."

McAllister lifted his blue eyes to meet those of a shared color. "What do you want?" His voice was surprisingly even.

"Just thought I'd stop on over and say howdy. Never got around to visiting you in prison and were never one for writing letters. Can't imagine what I'd have to say to you anyway: 'Hello, Daddy?' "

"Say your peace and let me get on with my meal, Mr. Bass."

"So formal. All right. If you want it that way. Let me cut

to the quick of it. Gant's dead, and if I could prove you had anything to do with my sister and her husband and son dying, you'd be dead, too."

"I don't know what you're talking about. I served my time, Mr. Bass. If you think to harass me, be warned I still have some very influential friends."

"I'm not here to make a nuisance of myself. I just dropped by to give you a friendly, son to father piece of advice. You go near my family and I won't need any evidence to come after you."

"It may surprise you to know that your family is the furthest thing from my mind. I'm a legitimate businessman—"

"Who's making money paying scum like Cates and Gant to run off or murder folks to get their property. A fine upstanding business venture you got there. One I'm glad I'm not inheriting."

"You said you'd be quick."

"Stay away from me and mine. I get wind of you anywhere in the Bend and I'll come after you, law or no law. And I'll make steaks outta you." He stabbed the point of the knife into the cut of beef and left it there quivering. Just as McAllister was quivering as Harm strode away.

As much as she'd have liked spending all four days in bed with a husband who was willing to give his all to see her satisfied, Sarah paid visits to her brother Sidney and to her father's family. Harm said a few words of regret, then headed back for Blue Creek, apparently having concluded whatever brought him to Austin. She'd almost begun to wonder if he'd come along to play chaperon. Billy stayed beside her, oddly restrained but a silent support, and back in their room, he kissed her tears away.

On their third day, Billy received a summons to ranger headquarters, where he was promoted to acting sergeant under the command of newly appointed Captain Jack Bass. Apparently, he was the only one surprised by the news, because a bottle of champagne was waiting in their room. He and Sarah spent that night and the entire next day without ever leaving their bed—celebrating.

While lounging around on those fine sheets, Billy laughed and teased her as mercilessly as the young ranger who'd ridden into her uncle's and snatched away her heart. It was as if all the shadows had been wiped from his memory, and he was hoping she'd come to treasure the fun-loving man who emerged . . . the man who wanted to spend the rest of his life with her. Their time together was a wonderful respite but it couldn't last forever.

Somehow, they never got around to talking about the future. It was almost as if they didn't want doubts to spoil the happiness they took from one another.

But on their way back from Terlingua, their easy mood increased in tension as the questions Billy had forgotten resurfaced. He brought them up cautiously, while keeping a careful eye on her expression.

"I never did ask why Chonita is staying with us." He'd been wondering if Sarah had invited her there to act as a buffer between them.

Sarah slid a glance at him. "She didn't have anyplace to go, Billy. After all she did for us, I couldn't see letting her go to work as a . . . for a living. She's a wonderful cook and she loves kids. She said she'd be happy to watch our first through sixth when I go out riding after you."

"What? Now, Sarah, you can't—"

But she was grinning at him and he wasn't sure if she was serious, so he decided it wasn't the time to argue the point. He loved it when she smiled, and she was intimating that she was interested in making children two through six with him. That was something. Her generosity pleased him, and so did her capacity for forgiveness of the fallen. He wondered how far it extended. To him? Or was that too much to expect?

"How much we paying her?"

"Nothing. She's staying on for room and board."

"Sounds like a fine deal to me. She'll be company for you when I'm gone."

Her gaze cut over to him again, then darted away apprehensively. Did she think he meant to leave her? Why in God's name would he ever do that? She was carrying his child. She was holding his love. She was everything he'd ever dreamed a good life could offer. And she had yet to state she'd made a firm place for him within it. The tentative nature of their relationship had to be settled before any more emotions were at risk.

"About the ranch . . ." he broached gingerly.

"It's mine. Jack has his own place and Sidney plans to stay in Austin." She didn't mention the deed in his name so neither did he. He was chafing with anxiety, wishing she'd just come out with it. Did she want him there or not?

"There's a lot of upkeep to a ranch, Sarah. I don't know how much help I'm gonna be."

"That's where the six kids come in." She smiled fleetingly, and he felt even more strongly that she wasn't telling him the whole truth. "It'll be a good place for you to retire to when you quit the rangers someday."

There was that suggestion of shared paths again. Billy was breathing so quick in expectation, he felt light-headed. "It don't bother you, being there?" he asked gently.

"No. I thought it would, but it makes them feel closer. There are so many good memories in those rooms. I couldn't bear to think of strangers living in them."

Finally, he got right to it.

"What about me living in them?" Did she still think about his connection with Gant and the killing of her family? he wondered. If so, how could she stand the thought of him using those rooms?

She looked truly surprised at his question, then dreadfully dismayed. "If you'd rather we moved someplace else, I guess we could. We could sell the ranch and——"

Her eyes had lowered to hide her anguish. He freed one hand from the reins of their buggy and slipped it over hers. "It'll make a good home if it makes you happy, baby. I'll do my best to work it on my time off and we'll make ends meet."

She smiled at him, a purely glorious gesture of relief, and his heart melted. Then she was looking ahead toward the homestead they approached. And it was more with a look of apprehension than one of anticipation.

Billy drew the buggy up at the front porch. He saw a flutter of wash on the line. Clothes too small to belong to an adult. "What's going on, Sarah? We got Harm and his family living over here now?"

"No."

That was the most evasive answer he'd ever heard. He reached up to lift her down, and as he was swinging her about he caught sight of a boy and girl racing around the side of the house. They pulled up at the sight of him and for a moment there was complete silence.

"Oh, my God," he whispered. "Jed? Jessie?" Billy started across the yard and they met him halfway, filling his arms the instant he bent down. For the first time he could remember, they smelled good—fresh, clean, and outdoorsy, the way kids were supposed to, instead of like a stale saloon. He was so happy to see them, he was crying and he didn't even care. "What are you kids doing here?"

"Uncle Billy, there's a big ole barn cat out back. I want to call it Patches," Jessie gushed. "If I clean it up real good, can I take it in the house and make it my pet? Jed says I'm being silly, that we're not staying. If we're not staying, how come we brought all our things? Are we staying here with you, Uncle Billy?"

He couldn't utter a word to save his life.

"Hello, Billy."

He looked up from his crouch to see his sister standing on the porch—his sister the way he'd always imagined she could look without all the paint, teased hair, and vulgar clothes. She looked surprisingly pretty.

When he didn't say anything, she rushed on nervously. "Your wife wrote and invited us out. You got a real nice place here. The kids, they really love it, the space and all. It's a good place for kids. I thought we might try a visit and see how it goes. I been kinda sick and the fresh air'd do me good. Give me a chance to rest up . . . and Chonita, she's a fine cook. Fattening up them two like they was stray pups. We won't take no charity from you. Jed, he can almost do a man's work, and Jessie, she can be a big help around the place, too. And they'll mind you real good. Can't say how long I'll stay. Maybe you'd rather it be just the kids, but your missus said for me to come on out, too. You sure that's all right with you?"

He tried a swallow and it wedged like a hot brick in his throat. Finally, feeling like a fool kneeling in the front yard, crying like a baby, Billy stood up and took her in his arms, squeezing her hard. When he could force the words, they were raw-sounding.

"You stay, Julie. You stay as long as you like." When he was able to step back, he was grinning wide. He turned. "Julie, I want you to meet my wife, Sarah. Baby, c'mon over here . . . and meet my family."

They sat down to one of Chonita's fine meals and the Mexican woman looked surprised when Sarah set a place for her to join them. The kids chattered excitedly about the day they'd spent exploring and ate like young coyotes who couldn't get their fill. Julie watched them, looking worn and weary and waxing sentimental for the things she'd never had. Billy said little but his eyes were dark and shiny, on the constant verge of spilling over. And Sarah soaked it all up, that feeling of family filling her home again.

Later, with the youngsters tucked away in the loft and Chonita and Julie settling in to share Will and Rebecca's room, Sarah found her husband standing out on the front porch looking up at the stars. He didn't smile when she came up beside him. His gaze was crowded with a lifetime of ghosts and Sarah wondered, as she'd been doing ever since they'd left for Austin, if she'd made a mistake. Maybe he wasn't ready for it. Maybe she'd assumed that just because she needed the surrounding closeness of loved ones he'd feel the same way. She should have asked him, she realized uneasily. She should have consulted him before giving way to the impulses of her heart. But after seeing the simple joy on those children's faces, how could they possibly send them back to the horror of life they'd known?

"I found their address in your sister's letters."

He said nothing. The look behind his eyes just got bigger and bigger.

"Did I go and do it again?" she asked in a constricted little voice. "Did I jump right into the wrong thing by inviting them here?"

"What you did was the rightest thing anyone's ever done for me." He blinked and all the haunting pain washed from his eyes. "C'mere."

She filled his arms and he hugged her tight.

"Are you sure, baby? I mean, you don't have to do this just for me. This is your home and—"

"This is *our* home and home is a place for family."

For her, it was that simple. For him, it was everything. Our home. There, she'd said it. He didn't need an engraved invitation. Her word was good enough for him.

"I love you, Sergeant Cooper. I want this to be your place to belong."

She rode out his deep, accepting sigh with a pleasure that sank clear to the soul.

"And just think," she added, "Chonita can teach me how to cook."

His chuckle rumbled beneath her cheek. "Baby girl, there are things more important than cooking."

"Oh?" Sarah raised her head to give him a devilish look of challenge. "Like what?"

"Like this." He came down for a long, toe-curling kiss, then whispered huskily, "Step inside and I can name a few others that come to mind."

And the list of things he came up with as they lay together in their own bed impressed the hell out of Sarah Cooper.

Please turn the page for an exciting
sneak preview of Dana Ransom's
newest Zebra historical romance
Texas Renegade,
to be published in
March 1996.

"Stay put."

Hard words for a boy of ten to obey when anxiety and anxiousness had him fidgeting right down to the soles of his new boots. But the soft, authoritative tones of his stepfather's voice had never been questioned before and wouldn't be now. His features solemn, the half-breed boy nodded up at the man behind the Texas Ranger star. And the man smiled down at him, a reassuring gesture further reinforced by the light knock of his knuckles beneath the boy's determinedly held chin.

Kenitay returned to his impatient vigil, leaning against the peeled bark porch rail. Beneath the shading tip of his Stetson hat, watchful green eyes missed little of what went on in the dusty surround of Arizona's Fort Apache. He wanted to believe his adopted father could make his wish come true. It would be too cruel to come so far and realize only failure. It could well be his last chance to see his true father, and anticipation swelled amid a bittersweet sorrow for the circumstances.

His father was a proud Apache warrior. For Kenitay's first five years, he and his white mother had lived with him, enjoying the nomadic life of the fierce and free people in the savage beauty of the West Texas Bend. Then the rangers had come, and a great price of horses had been paid for his mother to return her to her own kind. He had gone with her, and while he had done his best to learn the ways of the whites, his soul still stirred with the age-old rhythm of his father's clan.

And now those proud people were no more. People who had ruled the plains and recognized no master had been conquered by the sheer number of invading whites who were unwilling to share a harsh land of plenty with those who had been there first. Surrender was the only way to survive, and a people who had lived off an ungiving land for centuries knew all about the price of survival. It was often bitter but it had to be paid. And pay they had. The cost was their freedom. The cost was their homeland. In order to satisfy the white government's greed and fear, they would be banished from the mountains and plains they loved to return in two years from some foreign place called Florida. A place of hills and water and timber and grass, they'd been told. A place where they could all live together in safety, not as prisoners. Perhaps it would not be so bad, this place Florida.

Then why had his adopted uncle's gaze gone so dark with shadows when they talked of it?

Kenitay hadn't seen his father since he'd taken a Chiricahua wife and followed her people to Arizona, as was the Apache custom. It was distance, not his new family's dictates, that kept them apart. And now, in this final hour of the Apache people, he'd been brought across those arid miles to say goodbye. And his heart was breaking.

It was big enough news to reach them in the sleepy town of Terlingua, Texas. After another year of leading the U.S. Army on a futile chase, Geronimo, their last great leader, was making his terms of surrender. Kodene, Kenitay's father, was one of those last fearless holdouts shunning U.S. government rule even though his Chiricahua wife and remaining family were residing peacefully on the Arizona reservation. Kodene's spirit had been too restless to confine amid the stale smells of camp life and reluctant charity. But now that the time of fighting was at an end, this once legendary warrior was ready to lay down his arms in hopes of finding peace amongst his family. When news had come that these last brave rebels would come through Fort Apache before following the rest of the renegades to Florida, Kenitay had begged an opportunity to see him, to speak with him. Because his own young spirit was troubled. He had to hear with his own ears that his father forgave him for remaining behind in their homeland while the rest of his people were sent away.

It wasn't that he didn't care for his adopted family. He did. He'd found a place amongst them, close to their hearts. His stepfather was a deep-souled man with a quiet strength, an unshakable sense of honor, and a love great enough to accept a half-caste child along with the two he'd fathered. And though Kenitay dressed like a white man in stiff-soled boots and cotton cloth, he'd never lost touch with his Apache roots—his uncle had seen to that—nor had he ever been made to feel ashamed of them. That respect his new family held for the part of his past they didn't share caused his stepfather to bring him all the way from Texas in the brief hopes that a few words could ease a burdened mind.

Kenitay leaned on his elbows and studied the dusty blue-coated soldiers with interest. There was a time in his not-so-distant past when such a sight would have filled him with hatred. They had been his enemy, a threat to his people. Now they were just men, like his stepfather and the rangers he commanded. And he hoped these men would listen to the request of a Texas Ranger captain, the plea of a son to say farewell to his father.

Something was happening outside the gates of the fort. From where he stood on the porch outside the Army commander's office he couldn't quite see what it was. Kenitay glanced over his shoulder at the forbidding door that was firmly closed to him. Behind it, Ranger Jack would be arguing his case. His stepfather had said to trust him and he did . . . implicitly. He'd also said to stay put, but that became more difficult once a ten-year old's curiosity was aroused. He could see the soldiers gathering outside the gates and he could see the reservation Apache gathering—men, women, and children. And there were guns. A furrow of concern lined his brow. Why would the soldiers bring guns to bear upon a peaceful people?

He was off the porch before a conscious decision was made to disobey, and once he started toward the commotion, his own circumstances were easily forgotten. His step quickened and soon he was running, caught up in the confusion and chaos of the moment.

It was the fear he saw on the faces of the Apache people that woke a panic in his own heart. It was a timeless response to yet another betrayal, and though Kenitay was too young to remember such things, still he was shaken to the core. The Chiricahua and Warm Springs people living on the reservation had taken no part in the recent uprisings. They had been living content with their lot, causing no trouble, believing themselves wards of a benevolent government. So why were guns being pointed at them? Why were they being separated, the women and children from the men? The wariness inbred in them bespoke a treachery they were helpless to protest. And then the word they feared was finally spoken: Florida. An exile not only for the rebellious but for the obedient populace as well. Kenitay watched it all, not understanding the connotations.

A sudden shove sent him stumbling forward, out from under his new Stetson hat and in the way of a stern-featured sergeant. Before he could scuttle to his feet, the soldier had him by the shirt collar and was slinging him toward the weeping group of Apache women.

"Git on over there with the rest of yer kind, ya sneakin' little savage."

"But I'm not—"

A sharp kick to the ribs knocked the rest of his objection from his lungs.

"Hey, Sarge. Go easy. He's just a kid."

"Kid, nothing. Nits make lice. You ain't never seen what their kind does when a decent white man turns his back on 'em. Go on, boy. Quit dragging yer feet. The train ain't gonna wait on ya." That was followed by gritty laughter, as Kenitay was hurled to his hands and knees amongst the huddled gathering. In an instant of stark clarity, Kenitay realized the man's mistake. Without a hat to cover his straight black hair, he didn't look like the son of a Texas Ranger captain. He looked like an Apache.

His fright was overwhelming and the distance to that safe porch seemed miles away. Kenitay regained his feet and started to walk back toward the fort. He tried to make his steps sure and unafraid, but one glimpse to the side told his progress was noticed.

"Hey, you!"

And he began to run.

Before he'd gone ten feet, rough hands got a hold of him and wrestled him around, away from where he never should have strayed. His heart was pumping wildly and his thoughts were frozen to all but one, which he screamed aloud in terror as they pushed him back toward where the others cowered.

"I'm not a reservation Indian! I'm not an Apache!"

The words denying his heritage were out of his mouth before he could stop them, words borne of fear and desperation. His wide eyes were fastened on that far building that held his stepfather as he struggled wildly to get free.

"Ranger Ja—!"

His cry was halted by the smashing force of a rifle stock against his jaw. His world went black, and the taste of his own blood was as thick as his terror as he pitched face first onto the hard Arizona ground, sinking into nothingness.

"Kenitay?"

Jack Bass searched the abandoned porch with his gaze, concern mounting to overtake the disappointment of the words he carried. His familiarity with the U.S. Army hadn't inspired much hope in him, but he'd been willing to try just to ease to the desolation in his son's eyes. And now he had nothing good to tell him.

But where had he gone?

"Kenny?"

Surely he wouldn't have wandered off, not after the danger had been impressed upon him. The men in this fort were not the rangers who had accepted him amongst them. These men were hardened Indian fighters, frustrated by long patrols chasing a ghostlike enemy. They wouldn't much care that the soft-spoken boy was half white and lived tame with his mother's family. The Army commander hadn't. There was little sympathy for the Apache here in Arizona, not on this triumphant eve of their destruction. There would be no visit with one of their renegade leaders. There was nothing left to do but go home and try as best he could to comfort the boy he thought of as his own.

But where was he?

" 'Scuse me, Private. Have you seen a boy hanging around where he doesn't belong? He was here waiting for me just a minute ago."

"Sorry, Ranger. Ain't seen one."

"What's going on?" He nodded toward the congestion of soldiers and Indians on the other side of the gate.

"Order just come down that all of 'em was to go to Florida."

Jack frowned. He had no great love for the Apache, but they had earned his respect as an enemy of unequaled ferocity, daring, and endurance. He wasn't ashamed to claim a trace of their proud blood in his own veins. And he wasn't ashamed to raise one of their kin under his own roof.

"I thought these folks were under your protection. I hadn't heard they'd been giving you any trouble."

"An Injun's an Injun. Good riddance to all of 'em, I say. Then maybe a man can rest easy in his hair at night."

A particularly bad feeling came over Jack just then. He stepped down off the porch and started toward the front gates. The private was quick to put himself in front of him.

"Sorry, Ranger. Yer gonna have to steer clear of that. Army business."

"But my son might have wandered down there."

"Don't you worry. The men will shoo him away. Probably jus' prowlin' around like young boys are wont to. Be back as soon as he figures he's been missed."

Then Jack spoke it plain. "He's part Apache." And the

glaze that came over the private's eyes instilled a terror deep down in his heart. "I'd better go look for him."

"No. Can't let you do that. I'll pass the word around for you. What's the kid's name?"

"Kenitay."

That sheen of hostility grew more intense.

"He's not part of this," Jack was pressed to explain. "His people are Mescalero. I want him brought back to me unharmed."

The private's hard gaze said clearly that the loss of one half-breed boy was not a big priority to him. "I'll do what I can, Ranger."

And Jack was still waiting for him to do it as the day stretched into heavy evening shadow. The fort was alive with activity. It was hard to gain a second of anyone's time, but all made it known that his interference would be unappreciated. He was a Texan and a ranger, not of the Arizona military. He had no pull here, just whatever courtesy they thought to extend. And none of them were feeling very courteous. Finally, he breached professional protocol to push his way back into the colonel's office and ask, in a tightly controlled voice, what they were doing about finding his son.

"Cap'n," the officer said with a clinical cool, "has it occurred to you that the boy might not want to be found? That just maybe he wants to go with his own people?"

"I'm his people! Me and his mama and his brother and sister! He didn't come here to run away. He came to say goodbye to his father."

"And perhaps that's what he's decided to do. Cap'n Bass, I wouldn't presume to tell you what to do, but were I you, I'd just head back for Texas. The boy knows where you live and he'll find his way back there if he's a mind to."

"We're not talking about a lost dog here. That boy is only ten years old," Jack ground out.

"He's an Apache, isn't he?"

"And that's that?"

"Yessir, I'm afraid it is."

Seething with frustration, Jack growled, "Guess I'll just have to go look for myself."

"I wouldn't advise that, Ranger. You go stirring things up and I'll have you clapped in irons until the lot of them are moved out tomorrow."

They were at a momentary impasse, intense stares locked, wills grappling, when there was a tap at the door.

"In!"

"You wanted to see me, sir?"

"Yes, Sergeant, step in. Cap'n Bass here says his boy, a ten-year-old half-breed, might have got mixed up by mistake with our reservation Apaches. Do you know anything about that?"

"No sir." The sergeant's features never so much as flickered as he spoke that bold lie. He was seeing the fall of his career along with that of his rifle butt. "Ain't nobody under guard that don't belong there, sir."

The colonel made a self-absolving gesture. "There you go, Cap'n Bass. He's not with them. I suggest you check around to see if any horses have come up missing. Your boy could well have lit out to meet up with his daddy."

Jack clapped on his hat and set it square. "Not without telling me, he wouldn't."

"Be glad to put you up for the night, Ranger Bass. If the sentries get wind of the boy, I'll see you're sent for."

"I'd appreciate it," came his dry-as-Texas dust drawl.

Out in the lonesome darkness of the porch, Jack's steely bravado gave way to a parent's anxiety and pain. His unsteady hands rubbed across the taut angles of his face. What could have happened to the boy? Dear God, there was no way he was going back to his wife to tell her he'd lost another one of her children.

"Ranger!"

The call hissed from the concealing passageway between board and batten buildings. Jack approached with caution, his palm nestling against the stock of his .45 until he could make out the shape of a slight figure hanging back in the shadows.

"Who's there?"

"I have news of the boy."

At that point, Jack abandoned care. He hopped off the porch and strode back into the deeper hues of the night. "What do you know?"

The man came forward, not much more than a boy himself. Jack could tell by his manner of dress that he was one of the Army scouts, an Apache used to tracking down his own kind. He wore the four-button blue tunic over white army issue underwear, a Hardie hat, and a red headband to identify him as a "friendly." Furtive eyes flashed about, then he extended a small garment. Jack took it and his whole world fell away in an instant.

It was Kenitay's jacket. It was black with crusted blood.

Awareness came and went in feverish waves. At first he thought the rocking motion was part of that delirious dream. It went on and on without ceasing, that side-to-side shift awakening pain with every jostle. He was lying down but the position was cramped, forcing his knees up at an odd uncomfortable angle. His head was cradled in softness to cushion the movement that brought such agony to bear. Over the pounding of his misery, he heard gently uttered words phrased in his father's tongue. And that's when it came to him.

He was amongst the Apache.

He was on a train.

The train bound for Florida.

Sitting up nearly cost him his fragile consciousness. His first glimpse out cloudy windows confronted him with a strange lush landscape as foreign and frightening as the pain in his face. He tried to cry out, but his protests were sealed behind massive swelling to his cheek and jaw. A tiny bleating sound of panic was all he could manage.

The woman who held him began a flow of soothing sentiments to persuade him to lie back down and rest. Fretfully, he obeyed, blinking back his distraught tears. He would be brave. Surely, Ranger Jack would come for him. How far

away could Florida be? On the other side of Texas, closer to
home than even Arizona.

Ranger Jack would come.

All he had to do was wait. . . .